The whole world
is watching.
But no one will
see the truth...

W9-CCK-158

"Let me explain," Akhnetzov said, freshening Scorpion's drink.

"If Cherkesov is killed, Russia will invade. Ukraine will call upon NATO."

"You want me to stop this supposed plot to assassinate Cherkesov?"

"I want you to stop a war."

"Over killing a single person?"

"World War One began with the assassination of a single person," Akhnetzov said. Neither man spoke. There was a throb as the boat's engine slowed.

"Seven figures," Akhnetzov said finally, turning the piece of paper so Scorpion could see. It was a big number. "So, Mister Whatever-your-new-name-is . . . We got a deal?"

Forget the money, Scorpion thought. *That isn't what this is about.* Akhnetzov's contact in Washington, the smartest guy in the American intelligence community, wanted this to happen. The only way he would have involved Scorpion was because something absolutely vital to American security was about to go down.

"When's the election?" Scorpion asked, folding the paper and putting it in his pocket.

"In eight days. The assassination could happen any time."

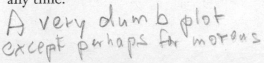
A very dumb plot except perhaps for morons

By Andrew Kaplan

ANDREW KAPLAN

SCORPION WINTER

HARPER

An Imprint of HarperCollinsPublishers

This book is a work of fiction. References to real people, events, establishments, organizations, or locales are intended only to provide a sense of authenticity, and are used fictitiously. All other characters, and all incidents and dialogue, are drawn from the author's imagination and are not to be construed as real.

HARPER

An Imprint of HarperCollins*Publishers*
10 East 53rd Street
New York, New York 10022-5299

Copyright © 2012 by Andrew Kaplan
ISBN 978-0-06-206378-6

First Harper premium printing: August 2012

Visit Harper paperbacks on the World Wide Web at
www.harpercollins.com

10 9 8 7 6 5 4 3 2 1

*Once again for Anne and Justin,
my North Star and my GPS*

SCORPION WINTER

 **CHAPTER ONE**

Penal Colony 9
Siberia, Russia

The prisoner Pyotr S. lay awake in the darkness, listening to Lev die. The cell was icy cold. Inside Strafnaja Kolonija Dyevyit, Penal Colony 9, a prison so secret its existence was known to only a handful within the FSB's headquarters in Moscow, even hardened prisoners accustomed to some of the coldest temperatures on the planet shivered in their sleep. The temperature outside was –51 Celsius, 60 below zero Fahrenheit. The prison was a solitary island in the vast forests of the Siberian taiga, covered with snow; still more snow fell silently through the floodlights on the outer fence.

Pyotr listened to the desperate gasps from the bunk above him as Lev struggled for every breath. Once, after midnight, it got so bad that he thought of killing Lev to get it over with. But if one of the *suki* bitches told on him, it would mean the beating cells. Pyotr waited.

He heard a harsh grating sound as if Lev were trying to say something, and waited for Lev to exhale, only it never came. Pyotr raised his head and listened intently, ears straining for every sound. Inside the crowded cell with eight men crammed into a space designed for two, there were only the usual snores and muffled coughs. Even Fyedka the Belly—who it was said would eat excrement if you put it in a bowl—and his usual racking cough, was finally still.

Carefully, so as not to wake the others, Pyotr slid out of his bunk. He felt his way to the middle bunk above his and put his hand on Lev's chest. There was no rising of the chest, no heartbeat, nothing. It was like touching stone.

Finally, he thought. He himself had been a prisoner for twelve years now, and Lev had been there longer than anyone. Some said Lev was a prisoner going back to the old Gulag. Once, he'd heard that Lev had been a big shot, a real *nachalstvo*. But of this, Pyotr knew nothing. Lev had been imprisoned for "activities against the state," but who hadn't? What was it Gruishin, his first cell-block leader, a true *vor v zakone*—thief-in-law—used to say? "Brothers, sometimes even breathing is an activity against the state."

Pyotr heard someone stir. It sent a ripple of fear through him. *Idiot*, he told himself. He had waited all night for a chance at Lev's boots, and now he was frittering his opportunity away. Lev's boots were made of real felt and still good, while his own were worn through. Gruishin used to tell new prisoners: "You need three things here: food, good boots, and to keep your mouth shut. Anything else and you're free soon enough." That's what the old-timers called dying: going free.

It wasn't easy pulling on Lev's boots. Pyotr's feet had gone numb with the cold. He knew he should stamp his feet, but he couldn't risk it. Once they were on, he began to feel a stinging in his feet. A good sign, but he would have to be careful. He would have to switch Lev's boots for his own. Every boot had to be accounted for. He scratched his head. Was there anything else of Lev's he could use?

The crucifix.

God only knew how Lev had managed to hang onto it all these years. "For my son," Lev had told him once. That day in the factory when little Sasha had gone after the Musselman with his knife. Crazy little *zek*. The guards had been furious. After they shot Sasha, they waded into the prisoners, beating them with iron bars, then left them chained outside in the snow. That was the night Big Pavlo, who had taken Sasha for a wife, couldn't stop his tears and in the morning his eyes had been welded shut forever by the ice. Lev thought he was going to die that night. They all did. He and Pyotr had been chained together. "If I should die, get the crucifix to my son," Lev had begged him, his teeth chattering like castanets. "Give it to the Armenian doctor, Ghazarian. When he comes on his monthly visit. Promise me."

Pyotr had promised.

Pyotr reached for where he knew Lev kept the crucifix hidden in a chink in the wall near his bunk. At first he couldn't find it, but then he felt it with his fingertips. It was a little silver thing, bent and tarnished, that could be cupped in the palm of your hand. He slipped it inside a pocket he had sewn in his underwear. For a moment he considered swapping it to the Adventist for a pack of cigarettes. It ought to be worth at least that, he thought. But then he felt ashamed. Lev had been a good fellow. One who would share part of his meal or a cup of tea with you if you needed it. And if he wanted it to go to his son, well that's where it should go, Pyotr thought, stepping on one of the *suki* bitches sleeping on the concrete floor as he headed for the piss bucket.

He watched the steam rising from the stream of urine that began to freeze the instant it hit the piss ice. He would slip the crucifix to the Armenian doctor the next time he came, he decided, touching the fabric over it for luck.

A simple sort, this Pyotr, the CIA's Office of Collection Strategies and Analysis would later conclude in an emergency PDB report to the President. What the Russians, after a few vodkas, like to call a "Russian soul." He had no way of knowing that the decision he had just made would launch a crisis that within the CIA would be called the Agency's "moment of truth" and would force the President of the United States to an action he would think about every day for the rest of his life.

CHAPTER TWO

Ma'rib
Yemen

From the moment they came into Ma'rib, the American agent code named Scorpion knew they were in trouble. There were tribesmen—Abidah, judging by the way they tied their *shaal* turbans and wore their curved *jambiya* knives—armed with AK-47s all along the main road. Men from AQAP—Al Qaeda in the Arabian Peninsula—had intermarried with women of the Abidah and the two groups were now allied. The double was playing them, Scorpion thought. They were driving into a trap.

His driver, Jabir, felt it too.

"Fe Ma'rib kul agila wa kalabahu yahmeelu kalashnikov," Jabir muttered. In Ma'rib every man and his dog carries a Kalashnikov.

Once, Ma'rib had been a tourist town where visitors came to see the ancient ruins in the sands. Thousands of years ago it had been the fabled city from which Balqis, Queen of Sheba, set forth with gold and frankincense to visit King Solomon. But now the only foreigners were oilmen, come to pay baksheesh to al Qaeda, Scorpion thought as they turned into the narrow streets off the main road under the wary eyes of tribesmen on the rooftops. He hadn't liked the mission when Peterman first told him about it, and he liked it even less now.

Scorpion had met Hollis Peterman in the back room of a restaurant on Hadda Street in Sana'a, Yemen's capital. The restaurant was easy to spot, with its outer door painted blue to ward off the evil eye. Nearby, a dozen or so Yemeni men squatted in a patch of sidewalk shade chewing *qat*, the amphetamine-like green leaves that were the Yemeni national habit. Heading inside, Scorpion spotted one of the Yemenis wearing Oakley sunglasses under a *shaal* and tapping on an iPhone. The idiot should take out an ad, he thought, checking the walls and ceiling for cameras through the smoke from the *shisha* hubble-bubbles as he made his way to the back of the restaurant.

As soon as he entered the room, he began looking for bugs using a handheld electronic sweep unit. When he was sure it was clean, he sat down and waited while Peterman continued to text, as if to underscore to Scorpion how important he was. They were all like that at the CIA now, he thought. Supergeeks who thought they were smarter than anyone else.

When Peterman finally finished, he clapped his hands. A *naadil* padded in on bare feet, and Peterman told him in English to bring them *saltah*, a Yemeni stew, before turning to Scorpion.

"How was your flight?" he asked, putting on a

professional smile. Peterman was a big man, fair-haired and solid-looking, but starting to go to fat.

It had been a while since Scorpion had been called upon to deal with the basic field ops level of the CIA. He didn't have the patience for what CIA old hands liked to call the "usual kiss-kiss before you screw the poor bastard in the ass."

"What's on Rabinowich's mind?" he bluntly asked Peterman.

Dave Rabinowich was a world-class musician, mathematician, and hands-down the best intelligence analyst in the CIA's Directorate of Intelligence. He was one of only two people in the entire U.S. intelligence community who could have gotten Scorpion to come to Yemen on such short notice.

The *naadil* knocked and came in with bowls of *saltah* and glasses of *nabidh* date juice. Neither man spoke until the *naadil* left and Scorpion had checked outside the door to make sure no one was listening.

"This isn't Rabinowich's deal," Peterman said, shoveling in the stew with a scoop of *malooga* bread. "Try the *saltah*. It's pretty good here."

"Are you insane?!" Scorpion snapped, getting up and heading for the door. "The only reason I'm here is Rabinowich—and he's not part of it? And tell that idiot outside pretending he's one of the *qat* crowd not to follow me or I'll send him back with his Oakleys shoved so far down his throat he'll be shitting glass for a week. Enjoy your meal."

"Wait!" Peterman gasped. "We need your help."

"Is this one of Harris's deals? Tell Harris to go

f— Never mind, I don't care what you tell him," Scorpion said. Bob Harris was deputy director of the CIA's National Clandestine Service, and he and Scorpion had had their run-ins. The last time, in Saint Petersburg, had been the worst. Now, Scorpion wanted no part of Harris's operations.

As he opened the door to leave, Peterman said, "We have a double who says he can deliver Qasim bin Jameel."

Scorpion hesitated. Bin Jameel was not only the leader of AQAP in Yemen, but at the moment the operational head of al Qaeda worldwide.

"No good," he said, closing the door, coming over and taking his seat again. "You need someone local."

"We had someone local. McElroy. One of our best. He'd been in-country three years."

"What happened?"

"We don't know," Peterman said.

"What do you mean you don't know?"

"He's gone. Missing."

"Missing, or you just haven't found the body?" Scorpion asked.

Peterman's face reddened. He didn't answer. The two men looked at each other. From outside, Scorpion heard the loudspeaker call of the muezzin for the midday Dhuhr prayer. *Don't do it*, something told him. *There's something wrong here.*

"We can't use local," Peterman muttered.

Worse and worse, Scorpion thought. It meant the local CIA station might have been compromised. No wonder Rabinowich had sent him a message that included the emergency code: Biloxi. To some of the better brains in the CIA, Yemen was a bigger threat to the U.S. than Afghanistan, and it sounded like Alex Station—CIA-speak for the task force assigned to al Qaeda—was falling apart. He watched Peterman take a sip of *nabidh* juice. One of the CIA's agents was missing—possibly being tortured at that second, Scorpion thought—and if someone didn't fix it, they'd lose a dozen more. If he was any judge, this guy Peterman was in way over his head.

"What about an SAS?" Scorpion asked. Special Activities Staff teams were the CIA's paramilitary units specifically designed to perform deep-penetration rescues, extractions, and other high-risk operations. Scorpion's own first CIA assignment had been in SAS, whose teams were comprised of ex-Delta, Navy SEAL, or USMC Reconnaissance types who then underwent advanced training that made even those formidable special units look like choirboys.

"We don't have the intel," Peterman said bleakly, meaning they couldn't use SAS because they had no idea where McElroy was or what had happened.

Neither man spoke then. It was salvage; the worst, highest risk type of mission.

Whatever you do, don't do it for McElroy, Scorpion told himself. Even if he was alive, whatever was left of him wouldn't be worth saving. Plus, AQAP would be sitting there, waiting for whoever came over the fence after him. The prize was bin Jameel. It was a little like buying a lottery ticket. You didn't expect to win, but the payoff was so big, you didn't want to kick yourself for not taking that one-in-a-hundred-million chance.

"What was McElroy's op?" Scorpion said finally.

"Predators," Peterman said.

The Predator drone, an Unmanned Aerial Vehicle, was the Pentagon's primary antiterrorist weapon. It could hover over a target for forty hours and fire Hellfire missiles from 25,000 to 35,000 feet high, too high to be seen or heard from the ground.

"The Hellfire is keyed to the cell phone's GPS," Peterman said, taking a cell phone out of his pocket and handing it to Scorpion. "Just have the guy press Send and leave it somewhere. They'll have sixty seconds to get out."

"And if the Predator has engine trouble or there's a screwup somewhere?" Scorpion said, hesitating to use the word "leak." At this point he had no way of knowing who or what was the problem. For all he knew, he was looking across the table at the problem.

"We'll have two Predators on station; one for backup."

"Did McElroy also have a cell for the Predator?"

Peterman reddened. The implication was obvious. It was his op and he had screwed it up. He nodded.

"Perfect," Scorpion said.

But nothing about the RDV had gone down the way Peterman was supposed to have set it up. Jabir parked the Land Rover near the Ma'rib gun market, its canvas stalls filled with M-4s, AK-47s, and small

pyramids of M67 hand grenades piled on old rugs.
The safe house was a brick building a block from the
market, its arched windows outlined, Yemeni style,
in white. A half-dozen heavily armed tribesmen—
Bani Khum, by the look of them—squatted near
the building's front door, their cheeks bulging like
chipmunks with *qat*.

Scorpion studied the building. Next to the safe
house was another brick apartment building, its roof
about ten feet below the roof of the safe house. If
he had to, he figured that would be the way out. He
told Jabir to wait till he went in, then move the Land
Rover across from the second building and keep the
weapons ready and the engine running.

Ahmad al-Baiwani was waiting for Scorpion on
the roof of the safe house with ginger coffee and *bint
al sahn* honey cakes spread under a tarpaulin shade.
A bearded, heavyset man, he wore an American suit
jacket over a traditional *futa*-style skirt and trousers,
and the *shaal* turban of a *qadi* of the Bani Khum.
As a *qadi*, or tribal leader, al-Baiwani was of the
second highest social class, lower only than a *sayyid*,
a descendent of the Prophet. Scorpion himself was
disguised as a *qabili*, or ordinary tribesman, of the
Murad. Speaking in *fusha* standard Arabic, after the
usual elaborate pleasantries, Scorpion asked about
"the American," McElroy.

Al-Baiwani said he had never seen McElroy. No
one had.

"You know of the *hadith* of Bukhari when the
Prophet of Allah, *rasul sallahu alayhi wassalam*,"
peace be upon him, Scorpion said, "spoke of the

greatest of great sins and said, 'I warn you against giving false witness,' and kept repeating it over and over till his companions thought he would never stop."

"What are you accusing me of?" al-Baiwani asked, glancing at his guards to make sure they were watching.

Before Scorpion could respond, he heard the sound of car doors slamming. He got up and looked over the side of the roof. Below he saw three black SUVs that hadn't been there before. A number of armed AQAP tribesmen got out and headed toward the building door.

"Who's coming?" he asked, putting his hand on the Glock 9mm hidden in his robe. Al-Baiwani's guards tensed, not sure what to do.

"Your *asayid* Peterman said you wanted bin Jameel." Al-Baiwani gestured as if to say, *I gave you what you asked*.

The al Qaeda leader himself, along with a bunch of his men, were on their way up. Scorpion took the cell phone out of his pocket, pressed the Send key, then slipped it under his cushion. He had sixty seconds before the Hellfire hit. He grabbed al-Baiwani, jamming the Glock against his side and whispered into his ear, "*Ta'ala ma'ee.*" Come with me. "We have forty-five seconds to get out or we'll be dead."

Al-Baiwani stared horrorstruck at Scorpion, his face showing that he understood about the Predator. The CIA had used them so often in Yemen that in AQAP camps and villages, anyone found carrying a cell phone could be summarily executed.

"*Yalla*," al-Baiwani said hurriedly. Let's go. He got up and motioned for his guards to follow.

There was a ladder from their roof down to the roof of the next building. As al-Baiwani put his foot on it, Scorpion shoved him, leaping down at the same time. Al-Baiwani cried out in pain. The two of them landed on the lower roof just as bin Jamccl's al Qaeda men swarmed out onto the other roof. Someone shouted, and the al Qaeda men began shooting at al-Baiwani's Bani Khum guards, who fired back. Scorpion prodded a limping al-Baiwani ahead of him as they scrambled down the interior stairs of the building while the shooting went on outside. They could hear children shouting and women screaming.

A little boy, who couldn't have been more than three, stood on a landing, staring at Scorpion and al-Baiwani as they ran down the stairs. A woman, presumably the boy's mother, came out of the apartment and stared at them in terror. When the two fleeing men reached the boy, Scorpion scooped him up and handed him to the mother, yelling at her to lock the door and lay on the floor.

Reaching the ground floor, Scorpion checked his watch. The Hellfire would hit any second. He yanked at al-Baiwani, pulling him down to the floor, where they put their arms over their heads.

They waited, every nerve screaming.

Nothing happened.

Scorpion checked his watch again. The Hellfire should have hit. He waited another fifteen seconds, counting every second. There was no Hellfire. From above, he heard men clattering down the stairs. That son of a bitch Peterman, he thought. It would take a miracle to get out of Ma'rib alive now.

Cautiously, Scorpion peered out from the front doorway, looking for Jabir. The Land Rover was parked across the street, not far from the three black SUVs. Jabir was there, scanning the buildings, an M-4 with a mounted M203 grenade launcher in his hands.

Time to go. Scorpion nudged al-Baiwani, then sprinted across the street to the Land Rover.

An Abidah tribesman from one of the SUVs spotted them and started to aim his AK-47. Scorpion shot him in the neck with the Glock. A moment later, a half-dozen Abidah tribesmen heading toward the safe house turned to fire at Scorpion and al-Baiwani, and Jabir opened up with his M-4 on full automatic. Two of the Abidah went down. Just before Scorpion reached the Land Rover, Jabir was shot in the face and collapsed to the dusty street. Scorpion grabbed the M-4 from his lifeless hands, whirled and cut down two more of the Abidah. The remaining tribesmen turned and fled to the safe house.

Al-Baiwani started to get into the Land Rover when Scorpion grabbed him and instead pulled him toward the front SUV. There was an Abidah driver still in it, and Scorpion fired the M-4 as he ran, bullets spiderwebbing the windshield. Shots from the other SUVs and the buildings kicked up on the street around his feet.

Scorpion fired through the SUV window at the

driver, killing him. Taking an Abidah *shaal* from a dead tribesman, he tossed it to al-Baiwani, who was climbing into the SUV's passenger seat. Scorpion grabbed the dead driver's *shaal* for himself, letting the driver's body tumble into the street, then climbed in. They drove off in a hail of bullets coming from the other SUVs and the roof of the safe house.

"Use this," Scorpion said, handing the M-4 to al-Baiwani as he swerved around a man with a donkey. Looking in the rearview mirror, he saw that the other two SUVs, filled with Abidah tribesmen, were in pursuit.

"What should I do?" al-Baiwani asked.

"Shoot through the rear window!" Scorpion shouted, making a sudden turn around a corner, then careened down the street toward the main road. Al-Baiwani fired on automatic, shattering the rear window.

The first SUV made the turn and sped after them as Scorpion, tires squealing, pulled around another corner and slammed on the brakes. He jumped out, rummaged for a moment in the backseat, then grabbed the M-4 from al-Baiwani and readied the M203 launcher and loaded a grenade as the first SUV came swerving around the corner. He aimed the laser at the SUV's windshield and fired, ducking behind his SUV and pulling al-Baiwani down beside him as the grenade exploded, the hot air ripping past them.

The blast killed everyone inside the other SUV.

What was left of the chassis continued rolling till it bumped against a cart by the side of the road. Scorpion reloaded the launcher with another grenade and peeked around the corner of the building. The second SUV was no longer following them. It was stopped in the middle of the street, guns bristling.

He motioned al-Baiwani back to the SUV and got back in himself. Tucking the M-4 beside him, he headed toward the main road. On the outskirts of the city they saw a roadblock ahead. It was manned by AQAP fighters, their guns aimed at them as they approached.

"What do we do?" al-Baiwani asked.

"We're Abidah, remember?" Scorpion said, touching his *shaal* and slowing as they approached the roadblock.

Scorpion and, after a moment, al-Baiwani raised their fists and shouted, *"Alahu akbar!"* The AQAP fighters shouted back, *"Alahu akbar!"* several firing their guns in the air for effect as one of them waved them through.

They drove carefully through the gap in the roadblock, Scorpion waiting until he was at least a hundred meters away before he gunned the SUV. The roadblock receded in the rearview mirror, then the last mud-brick buildings gave way to desert. Al-Baiwani looked at Scorpion but didn't say anything.

Ten kilometers on, Scorpion pulled to the side of the road and stopped. They were in a sandy desert plain, the road an empty blacktop for as far as they could see in either direction.

"Why are we stopping?" al-Baiwani asked.

Scorpion pulled out the Glock. "Where's McElroy, the American?" he said, pointing the gun at al-Baiwani's groin.

CHAPTER THREE

Jebel Nuqum
Sana'a, Yemen

As the SUV approached Sana'a, the road began to fill with battered cars and trucks laden with produce. In the distance, the silhouette of Jebel Nuqum, the mountain that loomed over the city, could be seen on the horizon. Scorpion was still shaken by what he had found in the farmhouse. His cell phone call to Peterman from the road hadn't helped.

"What happened?" Scorpion had demanded.

"What do you mean? The Predator?" Peterman said, his voice somehow both distant and on edge. Scorpion wondered where he was or what drug he was on.

"This is an open line, dammit! You really want to talk in clear?"

"Right, sorry," Peterman apologized. He was always apologizing, Scorpion thought. He was the type who had a lot to apologize for. He could almost see the sweat on Peterman's face. "Did you find you know who?" Peterman asked, meaning McElroy.

"Yes."

"Was he . . . you know?"

"Fortunately."

"Fortunately?"

"What do you want, a diagram?" Scorpion snapped. There were no words for what had been waiting for him and al-Baiwani at that farmhouse. Even Scorpion, who thought he had seen the worst that human beings could do to each other, had bent over the primitive iron sink heaving at what they found.

"Allahu akbar," God is great, a stunned al-Baiwani had muttered over and over to himself, staring blankly at the wall to avoid looking at what was left of McElroy.

Al Qaeda in the Arabian Peninsula had brought a lot back from Afghanistan, including something the Taliban called "undressing," which involved making incisions in the skin around the waist and up both sides, then down to the ankles on both legs before flaying and rolling up the skin to the neck and down to the ankles. It must have taken a week for McElroy, screaming in agony and covered in blood and flies, to die. Scorpion was glad McElroy was already dead, because otherwise he would have had to kill him.

Going through the farmhouse looking for clues was creepy. The rooms smelled of death, and in one of them, there were chains embedded in a stone wall and evidence indicating that McElroy hadn't been the first person AQAP had brought there. Scorpion knew that if AQAP ever got their hands on him, they would take great pleasure in doing to him what they had done to McElroy.

"Sorry," Peterman said again. Tell that to McElroy, you son of a bitch, Scorpion thought savagely. "We should debrief. Meet me—"

"Shut up!" Scorpion shouted into the phone, to keep Peterman from saying the address on an open line. "I know where you live. Be there," he said, ending the call. This guy was a disaster, he thought as he drove into Sana'a traffic from the roundabout on the Khawlan. At least Rabinowich had done his prep.

Scorpion knew that Peterman had an apartment on Wadi Zahr Road, about half a mile from the American embassy. Except Peterman wasn't in his apartment. Scorpion didn't get that far. Even before he pulled up, he saw the small crowd in the street. He got out of the SUV and pushed his way through the onlookers. Peterman was lying in the gutter, blood seeping from the back of his head. Scorpion looked up at the building. Either Peterman had jumped or been pushed from his fifth-story apartment balcony. Scorpion knelt beside him, and Peterman looked up at him, his eyes wide as if with wonder.

"Hollis . . ." Scorpion began. He wasn't sure Peterman even saw him, or if he did, whether in his fake beard and the Abidah turban from Ma'rib, he recognized him. Then a flicker of something.

"Run," Peterman said, and Scorpion saw the light go out of his eyes.

"When you're blown," goes CIA doctrine, "it's time to perform the classic military maneuver known as getting the hell out of there." By rights, Scorpion knew he should have been on the next plane out of Sana'a. With Peterman's death, he had to assume Alex Station was blown. That could mean AQAP knew about him too.

He eased back out of the crowd gathered around Peterman. NCS protocol was to clean the dead agent's site to make sure nothing fell into the opposition's hands. Except with the body of a Westerner in the middle of the street, the Yemeni CSO security forces were sure to be on their way already. Bad as things were, if Peterman had left anything incriminating behind, it was going to get a lot worse. He looked around. Attention in the street was still on the body. He decided to chance it, but knew he would have to move fast.

He slipped into the building and went up the stairs to Peterman's floor. The hallway smelled of something burnt. The door to Peterman's apartment was closed. Scorpion tried the handle; it wasn't locked. He took out the Glock and studied the walls and door. There was every chance the door was rigged with explosives. He needed to take the time to check it thoroughly and defuse, only there was no time. The police or the CSO would be there any second. The only thing he had going for him was that whoever killed Peterman might have been in a hurry too. His fingers touched the door handle as though expecting an electric shock. He took a deep breath. They had just shoved him off the balcony, he told himself. They needed to get out of there. He grabbed the handle and opened the door.

He went in fast, ready to fire around every corner.

The apartment was empty, the door to the balcony still half open. Scorpion peeked out, then closed the balcony door. The smell of smoke was strong, and he spotted the cause: an empty can of SpaghettiOs and a blackened pot on the stove. Someone had turned the gas off, but the pot was still warm. The apartment hadn't been ransacked. Whoever had pushed Peterman off the balcony must've taken off immediately.

Scorpion moved quickly, going through drawers and shelves looking for anything incriminating. Peterman's laptop was still on the bed. Why hadn't they removed it? He thought for a second and it hit him. He removed the hard drive from the laptop and dropped it into his pocket. Odds were, it had Trojan horse software on it, in which case AQAP knew everything Peterman knew.

From outside, he could hear the klaxons of approaching police vans. They would be coming up the stairs any minute. He grabbed a towel from the bathroom and did a fast wipe-down of everything he'd touched, then made his way down the stairs and out the back of the building.

The clock had started ticking the instant Peterman hit the pavement, Scorpion thought, making his way around the crowd in the street. In theory, he should've been able to make a call to Rabinowich on the way to the airport and let the Company handle it. Unfortunately, with all the ELINT in Sana'a, that could be a death warrant for everyone in Alex Station. What happened to McElroy could happen to them. He couldn't wait for Langley; he would have to warn them himself.

The CIA CP for Alex Station was a brick building on Al Quds Street in the Nuqum district. Because of Peterman, he had to assume that AQAP knew about the location too. It was now a red zone.

He caught a taxi at the corner. The driver made a face when he said "Nuqum." Scorpion understood why. Nuqum was a *mahwa*, or slum, on the eastern side of the city, a dense maze of crumbling houses sprawling in the shadow of the mountain from which the neighborhood took its name. It was an odd location for a Company CP. The narrow streets and trash-strewn alleyways were crowded with carts and aimless young men chewing *qat* and looking for day work.

The people of the district were mostly dark-skinned Akhdam, the despised Yemeni lower class. The Yemeni proverb went: "Clean your plate if it is licked by a dog, but if it is touched by an Akhdam, break it." As the taxi drove into the *mahwa*, prostitutes in *abayas* on street corners beckoned at passing cars, their hands fluttering like dark birds. Every car was a contest, the Akhdam women competing with the more recently arrived Somali women in their brightly colored *hijabs* who could be had for the price of a pack of cigarettes.

He told the driver to stop at a souk a few blocks from the CP building. He had to assume AQAP was watching the CP. The problem was how to get in or out without being seen or killed. He asked around the souk until he found a *qat* merchant with a truck. It took nearly an hour of haggling and making sure the merchant knew what he wanted, an hour Scorpion knew he really couldn't afford, but there wasn't much choice, not unless he wanted to end up like Peterman or McElroy.

"*Ma'a salaama*," he said to the merchant, touching his hand to his chest as he left.

"*Alla ysalmak*," the merchant said, smiling politely, but he looked at Scorpion as if he were crazy because of what they had agreed to.

Scorpion positioned himself outside a small rug store across from the CP building. He waited, putting a bulge in his cheek as though he were chewing *qat*. It's taking too long, he thought, anticipating a bullet coming his way any second. He was wondering if the merchant was going to cheat him when he saw it.

The truck loaded with thick bundles of *qat* turned the corner and rumbled down the street toward the building. When he saw the driver's face he nodded, and the driver nodded back. As the truck rumbled past, someone pushed a heavy bale of *qat* leaves out of the back, then the truck sped up, turned a corner and was gone.

Along the street, a group of young men stopped what they were doing and for a second everything was still, then the street erupted. The young men rushed the bale of *qat*, everyone grabbing handfuls of leaves and stuffing them into their clothes and the bags they made out of their *shaals*. People began to pour into the street. It was like an instant holiday, everyone grabbing *qat* and shouting for his friends to come, women screaming and ululating, children running between adults' legs to grab loose leaves and twigs. In all the commotion, Scorpion was able to slip unnoticed into the building.

A burly American with a military haircut sat at a desk near the front door, a pistol pointed at him. The man wasn't in uniform, but he had U.S. Marines or Special Forces painted all over him. Standing next to the desk, a Latino man leveled the business end of an M-16 at him as well.

"What do you want, Mohammed?" the American demanded.

"Have you ever been to Biloxi?" Scorpion said.

"No, but I've been to Gulfport twice," the man replied, completing the sequence. "Who are you?" he asked then, not putting the gun down.

"Where's Ramis?" According to Rabinowich, someone new, Donald Ramis, was the CIA's Alex Station Chief for Sana'a.

"He's out. Talking with Ali Baba and the Forty Thieves." The American made a face.

"Who the hell are they?"

"Sorry. It's our little nickname for Ali Abdullah and his council," meaning the President of Yemen.

"Take this," Scorpion said, handing him the hard drive.

"What is it?"

"From Peterman's laptop. He's dead," Scorpion said.

"Jesus," the American said, the light beginning to dawn. "Are we blown?"

"What do you think?"

"Shit," the American said. "Time to get out of this shithole."

"Tell Langley be careful with the hard drive. Probably got malware on it," Scorpion said, peeking out the front door. There were men loading donkeys with sacks of *qat* from the fallen bale. Squinting against the sunlight, Scorpion scanned the street and the rooflines. It looked all right, but odds were better than even somebody was watching.

"Hey, amigo! Thanks," the American called out, already talking on the phone, but by then Scorpion was gone.

Back in Western clothes and minus the beard, on the way to the airport, he thought that however it turned out, his part in this was over. As his taxi turned onto Airport Road, he spotted a white Toyota Camry two cars behind them, switching lanes when his driver did.

"Make a U-turn," Scorpion told the driver in Arabic.

"But the airport is this way," the driver said.

"I'll give you a hundred rials. Make the turn now!" Scorpion said, taking out the money.

After a moment's hesitation, the taxi veered suddenly into the opposite lane. An oncoming car jammed on its brakes, the driver's eyes wide, cars and trucks honking from both directions as the taxi sped back toward the center of the city. Looking back, Scorpion saw the Camry make the same turn, drivers cursing and shaking their fists. Although at this angle he couldn't be sure, he thought that the two men in the Camry tied their *shaals* like Abidah.

He couldn't help it. He thought about McElroy

in the farmhouse. He told the driver there was an-other two hundred in it for him if he lost the Camry. The man weaved through the streets, turning corners and darting through gaps as they neared the old city. Scorpion looked back. For the moment the Camry was out of sight. He spotted a taxi parked by a small hotel, facing the opposite direction. But he needed to change the image.

"*U'af!*" Stop! "Give me your *shaal*," Scorpion demanded, shoving rials at the driver.

They screeched to a stop. The man took off his turban and Scorpion put it on, grabbed his carry-on and jumped out of the taxi. He ran across to the other taxi, jumped in, and in seconds they were off.

As his driver made the turn toward the airport, Scorpion saw the Camry come barreling down the other way, the two Abidah men inside scanning the street like crazy, a farmhouse no doubt on their mind.

 **CHAPTER FOUR**

Porto Cervo
Sardinia, Italy

A heavy rain lashed the *piazzetta*, the little piazza near the marina in Porto Cervo. Standing in the shelter of an arcade, Scorpion, known to the locals as *il francese*, the Frenchman, looked for anything that shouldn't be there. Normally, in Sardinia he shouldn't have had to do that, but after Yemen there was no "normally."

He waited until a layover in Dubai before he risked contacting Rabinowich through an iPad at the Apple store at the Deira City mall. They texted using a teenage chat site so heavily trafficked it was virtually impossible to monitor. Rabinowich was presumably a thirteen-year-old girl from Omaha named Madison, Scorpion was a fourteen-year-old boy named Josh from nearby Bellevue.

u clear? Rabinowich texted.

4 the moment, Scorpion texted back.

what about alby? whos she seeing? Rabinowich asked, referring to al-Baiwani.

she broke up with ay kyoo and a-pee—AQAP—now

all shes got is us, Scorpion typed. After Ma'rib, al-Baiwani had no choice. He had burned his bridges with al Qaeda. So long as the CIA fed him arms and money, they would own the Bani Khum.

shes so 2-faced, Rabinowich texted, meaning he assumed that al-Baiwani was a double agent. Running al-Baiwani would be a sword that cut both ways.

considering guys she dates, wouldnt you? Scorpion texted back, saying that after what had happened in Ma'rib and the way things were going in Yemen, it didn't leave al-Baiwani with a lot of choices. He had to play both sides.

2 bad about pete. Peterman.

u loco? he was like so nfg, Valley-speak plus CIA slang for no fucking good.

I miss u, qt. r u ok?

u tell me, Scorpion typed, ending the call. Because it wasn't just the mission failure in Yemen that no doubt had Langley scrambling like crazy. They'd made him run. No one had ever made him run before. It was a bad omen. Winter had come, he thought, looking out at the rain-swept *piazzetta*. And not just for the CIA. Something was wrong.

Shaking off the rain, he stepped into the small realty office nested among the luxury-designer-label shops around the *piazzetta*. Although it was after New Year's, the office was still decorated with Christmas lights. They provided the only color in the gloomy day. He glanced out of the window to see if anyone had seen him go in.

Abrielle, the owner's daughter, was alone in the office. Lithe, with long dark hair, she handed him his mail, and as he glanced at it, they chatted half in Italian, half in English, about his farmhouse in the mountains, an updated *casa colonica* that she looked after when he was away, which was much of the time. Then he saw the envelope.

She had picked it up from the harbormaster's office. A simple request on a white card engraved with a yacht insignia to meet to "discuss matters of mutual interest" and a phone number. He would need to Google it, but Scorpion thought that the area code was Luxembourg, most likely meaning it was a holding company protected by that country's secrecy laws.

"Where'd this come from?" he asked, going deadly still.

"Some sailors in a tender from a yacht brought it. I think they were Russi," Abrielle said. "Is for a Signor Collins. He is a friend?"

"Is the yacht still there?" Scorpion asked, not answering her. He edged closer to the window and looked out. The *piazzetta* was empty in the rain. Beyond the buildings and the harbor, there was only the dark sea. Maybe it wasn't just Alex Station in Yemen that was blown. He had to face the possibility that because of what might have been on Peterman's laptop, he was blown as well. Christ, had they tracked him to Sardinia?

Abrielle shook her head. "They said they were heading for Monte Carlo."

"Big yacht?" he asked.

"*Molto grande.* Sixty meters, maybe more," she said. Scorpion trusted her judgment about the yacht.

The Sardinians were used to big expensive boats. Porto Cervo, with its picturesque harbor and multi-million dollar villas with red-tiled roofs on the hills above the town, was the scene of the annual September regatta, when some of the biggest mega yachts and richest people in the world came to party on the Costa Smeralda. There weren't that many yachts in the world over sixty meters. It meant the note came from someone extremely rich and powerful.

"What makes you think they were Russians?"

She shrugged. "I asked. They said they were Ukraini. It's a kind of Russi, yes?"

He told her he was leaving the island. As usual, while he was gone she was to take care of the *casa* and the two Doberman watchdogs, Hector and Achille. Her face fell when he said he was leaving.

"Quando tornorai?" she asked, a touch wistfully. When will you be back? She had always thought *il francese*, with his gray eyes, like those of a wolf and that scar over his eye, attractive enough that if he wanted, she would have locked the office door and let him have her right there and then. But he was always leaving.

"A few weeks. I'll be back soon," he said, not knowing if he would ever return to Sardinia again.

Driving back in the rain to his *casa colonica* away from the coast, Scorpion kept glancing in the rear-view mirror. The road wound up into the mountains. He pulled over at a turnout at the edge of a cliff. Grabbing binoculars from the glove compartment, he got out of his Porsche and scanned the hills and the road all the way back to Porto Cervo. It appeared no one was following him. With any luck, he still had time; unless they were waiting for him at the *casa*. He wondered if he was being paranoid. In his business, the line between paranoia and spycraft was razor thin. He remembered Rabinowich joking once, saying, "Remember, just because you're paranoid doesn't mean someone isn't out to get you."

He looked down again at the card. Just two hand-written lines under a logo from a yacht, the *Milena II*, getting wet in the rain. For Scorpion, it had red flags all over it.

First, it had been delivered to the harbormaster in Porto Cervo. That was a backdoor emergency network known only to Rabinowich, and even he didn't know at any given moment which of several dozen ports in the world, if any, Scorpion might be at. The envelope had been addressed to "Arthur Collins," a pseudonym for a supposed sailing friend of the Frenchman. Scorpion only used the Collins alias at various marinas and sailors' pubs around the Mediterranean where they held mail.

What made it more ominous was that it had come, according to Abrielle, from a "Russian" yacht. That made no sense. If Ivanov, aka Checkmate, head of Russia's FSB Counterintelligence Directorate, was after him, there would be no note. It would be Spetsnaz-trained operatives in the night, and Scorpion knew he would never see them coming. The only thing he could think of was that either the SVR—the Russian equivalent of the CIA—was after him, or some private Russian outfit had been contracted by someone else he had pissed off, like al Qaeda or Hezbollah.

The worst of it was, they had managed to find him in the one place in the world he thought was safe.

No one in the world knew he lived in Sardinia, not even Rabinowich.

For Scorpion, Sardinia was the answer to a unique business problem. As an independent intelligence agent, a freelancer, he sometimes made very dangerous enemies. His only protection was to be able to make himself invisible. After the realtor, Salvatore, Abrielle's father, had shown him the escape tunnel hidden underneath the old farmhouse in the hills, no doubt used by bandits years ago, he'd decided to make Sardinia his base. The locals had a history of banditry and isolation and tended to mistrust outsiders. They even had their own language, Limba Sarda, in addition to mainland Italian. Sardinia was convenient to Europe and the Middle East, where he did much of his business.

That still left one problem. Anyone who came after him would be looking for an American. He had taken great pains—hacking into databases both outside and within the Swimming Pool, as the French foreign intelligence service, the DGSE, was known because their headquarters in Paris was located next to the French Swimming Federation—to ensure that his French cover identity was bulletproof.

Now all of that might have been blown, and he had no idea how—or who was after him. Unless, and this was worse, he had gone over the edge.

* * *

On the flight to Nice, deliberately booked with the Collins ID—he could either find them or make it easy for them to find him—he went back over what he'd learned about the yacht. Using a computer at Fiumicino Airport, he discovered that the *Milena II* was convenience-flagged in Malta, and as he suspected from the telephone area code, it was registered to a privately held company in Luxembourg. Landing in Nice, he used the Arthur Collins British passport for the rental car, spotting two burly-looking men in leather jackets near the car rental counter.

Using a disposable cell phone, he called the phone number on the card from the yacht. He left a message in response to a recorded voice, telling it in English that he would be waiting at Le Carpaccio, a waterside restaurant in Villefranche, a resort town on the coast east of Nice, not far from Monaco. He picked a public place to try to minimize the damage if they were going to come right at him.

A few minutes out from the airport, Scorpion spotted the gray Mercedes sedan following him. The men in leather jackets he had seen near the car rental were in it. Just to be sure, he pulled into an Agip station and knelt down to check the air in his tires, watching the Mercedes drive by. The two men barely glanced at him. He waited five minutes, then drove the Basse Corniche road between the hills and the sea toward Monaco, and a few minutes later saw the Mercedes waiting at a turnout. As he drove past, they started up and followed. A blue BMW pulled in front of him, with two men in that car as well. He was boxed in.

He had an armed escort to Villefranche.

CHAPTER FIVE

Milena II
French Riviera

The main salon of the mega yacht, *Milena II*, was furnished in white Italian leather, soft and buttery to the touch, and looked out to the aft pool deck. The designer had gone for Metro modern, and what looked like a genuine Rothko painting hung on an interior wall. They were cruising eastward along the French coast. Through the salon windows, Scorpion could see seaside villas and the villages in the mountains. The sun broke through the clouds and sparkled on the sea.

The yacht's tender had come into the harbor at Villefranche and picked Scorpion up on the stone quay just steps from the restaurant. When he boarded the ship, the two shaven-headed men from the Mercedes asked him in accented English for his gun. He handed them the Glock 9mm from the holster at the small of his back.

Vadim Akhnetzov came into the salon with a rush of energy. He was a medium-sized man, trim, with blond hair cropped almost to the skull. He wore a striped Armani suit and under it a blue and red T-shirt from Arsenal Kyiv, a Ukrainian soccer team. An attractive blond woman in a Chanel suit followed him in.

"Mr. Collins—or are you going to throw that name away—what you are drinking?" Akhnetzov asked in serviceable English as he sat down opposite Scorpion.

"Bloody Mary with Belvedere," Scorpion said. The blond woman tapped on her BlackBerry as if taking notes.

"Not Russian?" meaning the vodka. "Would you like some Beluga caviar? Dimitri?" Akhnetzov said, glancing at the white-jacked bartender behind the mahogany bar, who began preparing dishes.

Scorpion shook his head.

"Of course, business first. Perhaps later. Evgeniya?" he said to the blond woman.

"Goodbye, Meester Collyins," she said in a thick accent, and left. She had a lovely body in the well-fitted skirt, and for a moment the two men watched her leave.

The bartender brought Scorpion's Bloody Mary and an iced bottle of Iverskaya water for Akhnetzov, who gestured, and both the bartender and one of the leather-jacketed men standing by the door left.

"Better?" Akhnetzov asked.

"Do you mind?" Scorpion said, pulling an electronic sweep unit out of his pocket and showing it to Akhnetzov, who gestured that he could use it. Scorpion stood up and began walking around the salon, checking for eavesdropping bugs and hidden cameras.

"Maybe we should both take off our shirts?" Akhnetzov said, starting to take his jacket off.

"Maybe we should," Scorpion said, unbuttoning his shirt as well, then gesturing it was okay.

"We are on our way to Monte Carlo," Akhnetzov said. "Is the only local port big enough for the *Milena*. When we finish talking, you may make business there. Your rental car is being brought from Villefranche."

"You're assuming a hell of a lot. Such as that I'm interested in whatever it is that made you want to get me here," Scorpion said, sitting down.

"No, not assuming. Talking," Akhnetzov said, studying the man in front of him. There was something about him: his strange gray eyes and the scar over his eye, his stillness, as if he could erupt into action in an instant. Akhnetzov lived in a world with many powerful and dangerous men, and he knew when he was in the presence of one. Indeed, he himself was one.

"Out of curiosity, why do you use the Collins identity, which I assume you will get rid of?"

"Either I found you or I let you find me. The latter was simpler, faster. Who'd you bribe, the man at the car rental in Nice?"

"Something like that." Akhnetzov smiled.

"How'd you find me? Who told you to leave a card for Collins in Porto Cervo?" Scorpion said casually, masking his tension. His identity and base in Sardinia was on the line.

"We had a list of some dozen Mediterranean ports. We left notes at all of them. We assume you have a boat and would pick up the note at one of them."

"Who told you how to contact me?"

"Friends of friends. As you know, one cannot do business in our part of the world without certain . . ." Akhnetzov paused, groping for the word in English. " . . . understandings."

"With the SVR and a back channel to the CIA?"

"I have many friends," Akhnetzov said. "Everyone, it seems, likes money."

Scorpion sipped his drink. Whoever Akhnetzov had bribed, it wasn't Rabinowich. If Dave had given Akhnetzov a list of ports, it was because the CIA wanted him to talk to Akhnetzov.

"So now that you've impressed me with how rich you are," Scorpion said, gesturing vaguely at the salon. "What do you want?"

"I want you to stop something bad from happening."

"Bad for whom?"

"For me," he replied, tapping his chest. "Bad for my business. For my country, Ukraina. Bad for America too."

"What makes you think I'm American? Or that I give a damn about you or your country?"

"I think you are American. You are CIA, but not CIA. My sources say you kill 'the Palestinian,' terrorist impossible to find, but you do in only two weeks. They say you are the best."

"What else do you know?" Scorpion said quietly.

The question of how much Akhnetzov knew about him was still very open and very dangerous.

"Listen, *drooh*. This is maybe your first Ukrainian word. It means 'friend.' I am billionaire from a part of the world that is not so simple. I don't get this way by being stupid. I own Ukengaz Company. We do maybe eighty percent of *gaz* pipeline, natural *gaz* from Russia for Europe. Also chemicals, steel, television, real estate. This team, Arsenal," tugging at his football T-shirt, "I own. I begin with nothing. My *maty*, my mother, clean toilets in Metro so I can be student at Shevchenko Kyiv University. One night I take money from nightclub where I am working as dishwasher. The *shef*, the boss, send *krutoy paren* gangsters to get money back. They beat me with iron bar so bad I am in hospital. But I do not tell them where is money. I keep. Later, I use this money for my first *gaz* trade. You and I, Scorpion, my *drooh*, we are both wolves. We must understand each other or we must kill each other, yes?"

The two men looked at each other. Akhnetzov leaned forward, his muscled forearms on his thighs. Scorpion sat casually, but he was ready to move. The code name Scorpion lay between them like a ticking bomb.

"What do you know about Scorpion?"

"Less than I want," Akhnetzov said. "I know you were CIA then not CIA. Independent. It says you know Arabic from when you are child," glancing at a tablet PC. "Real name unknown. Raised by Bedouin in Arabian desert." He looked at Scorpion. "What is American kid doing in Arabia?"

"My father was an oilman. He was killed. The Bedouin saved me."

"Is true? You're unusual guy. Also tough guy. What were you? Navy SEAL? Delta? Marines?"

"Girl Scouts. I sold cookies."

"Okay, you don't talk. Like I said, tough guy. Only one thing important . . ."

"What's that?"

"I know your enemies respect you. There are worse ways to judge a man than by how his enemies fear or respect him. For you, both I think."

"So this is a job interview?" Scorpion asked, taking a sip of his drink.

"In a way. One thing I must know," Akhnetzov said, tapping a cigarette on a gold case and lighting it. "Why did you leave CIA? For money?"

Scorpion smiled. "To tell you the truth, it never entered my mind. At the time, I hadn't thought about making a living that way. I just quit."

"What happened?"

"I don't talk about that."

"Listen, *drooh* . . ." Akhnetzov looked at Scorpion, his eyes ice cold, and Scorpion had a sense he was seeing the real man. "For what I am about to tell you, this is important. I don't ask for nothing."

"I don't talk about missions."

"I don't care mission. I care why you leave, okay?"

Neither man spoke. The only sounds were the ship's engines and the slap of the waves on the hull.

"It was a termination. A street outside the target's location. He was supposed to be just with body-guards, but his little boy was with him. They told me to go ahead anyway."

"Did you?"

Scorpion shook his head. "No. At that moment, I realized I was through. *Tvajo zdorovy*," Scorpion toasted in Russian, and drank.

Akhnetzov got up and poured himself a glass of Ukrainian Nemiroff vodka from a bottle on the bar. "*Za vas!*" he toasted back. He brought the vodka bottle over and put it on the table between them. "Listen, maybe you see on CNN. There is election for president in Ukraine."

"What of it?" Scorpion said. From Akhnetzov's posture, he could tell Akhnetzov was at the moment, in CIA-speak, when the Joe drops his pants.

"One of the candidates will be assassinated."

"I see," Scorpion said, putting his drink down.

"No, you don't. It will mean war. Also end of Ukengaz. We must stop this. This is why I seek you out."

"We . . . ?" Scorpion raised his eyebrows.

"Let me explain," Akhnetzov said, freshening Scorpion's drink with a splash of Nemiroff. "There are two candidates: Kozhanovskiy, a good man, a man of the West, favored by Europe and the Americans, darling of the students and the Kyiv *intelli-hensia*. He wants Ukraine to be partner in EU and NATO. The other is Cherkesov. A strong man, tough like bull. He is supported by ethnic Russians and people in eastern Ukraine. He is for close ties with Russia. Like this," smacking his fist into his open hand and holding it.

"Which one do you support?"

"Me, I do business with the devil so long we make money. Russia fears if Kozhanovskiy wins, Ukraine joins NATO, and worse, terminates lease of Sevastopol as base for Russia's Black Sea navy fleet. For Russia, this is casus belli. My sources tell me there is a plot to assassinate Cherkesov."

"Sources . . . ?"

"The same sources that led me to you."

"SVR?" Scorpion asked.

"I will tell you once we agree. These same sources assure me that if Cherkesov is killed, Russia will invade. Ukraine will call upon NATO. This will be most dangerous world crisis since Cuba."

"You want me to stop this supposed plot to assassinate Cherkesov?"

"I want you to stop a war."

"Over killing a single person?"

"Why not? World War One began with the assassination of a single person," Akhnetzov said. Neither man spoke. There was a throb as the engines slowed. Through the salon windows, Scorpion could see the harbor and buildings of Monte Carlo piled against the backdrop of the Alpes Maritimes.

"You've got the wrong guy," Scorpion said, putting down his drink. "This is not my type of assignment. Besides, I'm not a bodyguard."

Akhnetzov shrugged. "Cherkesov has dozens of bodyguards. This is not what is needed. What I need is an operative, the right operative."

"It's no good. What makes me effective is a certain unique combination of skills," Scorpion said,
leaning forward. "Languages, for one. I don't speak
Ukrainian and my Russian is pretty limited."

"But you speak some Russian, yes? Nearly all
Ukrainians speak Rossiyu."

"Just basic Russian plus some of the dirty words."

"The best part of any language." Akhnetzov
smiled, but his eyes weren't smiling. "But you are
wrong. What makes you effective is your knowledge
and ruthlessness. Like wolf, like me."

Akhnetzov leaned forward and wrote something
on a piece of paper.

"What's that?" Scorpion asked.

"A number," still writing.

"Six figures?"

"Seven," Akhnetzov said, turning the paper so
Scorpion could see. It was a big number, enough for
him to live comfortably for the rest of his life.

"That's a lot of money," Scorpion said carefully.

"BNP Paribas is private bank near the casino in
Monte Carlo. Monaco has the same bank secrecy
laws and discretion as Switzerland. You can have
half this money in your own account within thirty
minutes. So, Mister Whatever-your-new name and
nationality is," Akhnetzov said. "As the Americans
say, we got a deal?"

Forget the money, Scorpion told himself. *That isn't
what this is about.* Rabinowich wanted this to happen
or he never would've told anyone about the back
channel. And the only reason he would've done it
was because something absolutely vital to American

security was about to go down. Rabinowich was the smartest guy in the American intelligence community. There was more to this than just some Eastern European politician. A lot more. And it was a lot of money.

"When's the election?" he asked, folding the paper and putting it in his pocket.

"In eight days. The assassination could happen any time."

 **CHAPTER SIX**

Bucharest
Romania

The two men sat in the back of a café in Lipscani, Bucharest's Old Town district. It was late and the café was almost empty. Through the window, Scorpion could see the wind blowing the falling snow, the occasional pedestrian holding onto his hat as he headed for home.

"Akhnetzov. Who's he fronting for?" Scorpion asked.

"You mean is he a shill for the SBU?" Shaefer said, referring to the Ukrainian secret intelligence service. A big lanky man, African-American, with a clipped mustache and a fullback's shoulders, Shaefer was the CIA core collector in Bucharest, a backwater to which he had been posted for being too outspoken inside Langley. He was also Scorpion's best friend. Sometimes, Scorpion thought, his only friend. They had been in the Joint Special Operations Command's Delta Force together; the only two survivors of an ambush by the Taliban at Forward Operating Base Echo in the Chaprai Valley in North Waziristan—where, officially, American troops didn't exist. FOBE had forged a bond between them; in Scorpion's mind, a blood bond. It was Shaefer who had originally recruited him for the CIA.

"Or the SVR?" he asked, meaning the Russians.

"Or the SVR," Shaefer agreed.

"Is he?"

Shaefer nodded. "He swims in pretty oily waters. He's bound to get dirty."

"He left messages for me at various marinas in Europe. Rabinowich was the only one who knew about that channel."

"What you're really asking is, are you blown?"

"Am I?" Scorpion said, his mouth suddenly too dry to swallow.

Shaefer shook his head. "Dave provided a list of marinas to Akhnetzov."

Scorpion felt a flood of relief. "So I'm not blown?"

"Not even your hair mussed. No one even knows which marina you picked the note up from, including me," wiping beer foam from his mustache. "You have a boat?"

"A sailing ketch. You get out at sea, it clears your mind."

"Bullshit. In this business, if you think you understand something, you probably got it wrong," Shaefer said, and they both laughed. He motioned Scorpion closer, holding the bottle in front of his mouth to cover what he was saying. "This thing with Akhnetzov—the Company can't go near it, but Langley's desperate to see you in Kiev."

"Why? What's going on?"

"Above my pay grade, but—" Shaefer hesitated. "It's hot."

"You wouldn't be holding out on me, Top?"

Shaefer looked at him sharply. "I haven't forgotten," he said, and Scorpion knew he was talking about FOBE. His friend studied his long fingers, which Scorpion had seen him bend coins with without even trying. "All I know is that Dave Rabinowich wanted you on it because somebody way high up is scared shitless." He looked up. "That good enough for you, bro?"

Scorpion took a deep breath. Now he understood why Rabinowich had pointed Akhnetzov toward the marinas—his emergency back channel—instead of just giving Akhnetzov one of the dummy Gmail addresses that were his normal contact points. Rabinowich had done it to get his attention. Something was up all right. But why? Ukraine seemed out of the way, a minor regional dispute. Why would someone high up be so anxious for him to go in?

"I could use a few things," he said.

Shaefer nodded. Scorpion told him what he wanted, and Shaefer nodded again.

"One thing still bothers me. Why me?"

"You have to remember, they're Eastern Europeans."

"Meaning paranoid?"

"Wait till you have to live here like I do. If they were a whole lot more trusting, they'd be paranoid."

"Sounds like they wanted someone independent," Scorpion said. "Someone who could play both sides.

Especially if the CIA is involved." After a moment he added, "So are we?"

"What a dirty little mind you have." Shaefer grinned.

"It's a dirty little world."

A young Romanian couple got up and walked past their table. For a moment the two men fell silent. They waited till the couple went out into the night.

"Akhnetzov says Russia will invade if anything happens to this politician, Cherkesov," Scorpion said.

"Does he?" Shaefer said. "Who's feeding him this stuff?"

"He says SVR."

"Did he tell you who his contact is?"

"Somebody named Gabrilov, Oleg Gabrilov. Cultural attaché at—"

"I know who he is." Shaefer made a face. "Gabrilov is SVR, all right; Directorate S for Kiev."

"Akhnetzov says it could mean war. Lot of saber rattling going on."

"Rabinowich thinks so too."

"Christ. You really see us going in?"

"Who the hell knows?" Shaefer shrugged. "Technically, Ukraine is a member of the NATO Membership Action Plan. They sent troops to support us in Afghanistan. If Russia were to invade, in theory we'd have to do something." He hesitated, as if he knew what he was about to say wasn't something he should ask as a friend. "When you get to Kiev, my bosses would appreciate anything you could toss our way."

"I can't go near Kiev Station. Besides, there's ELINT all over the place," meaning heavy Russian and Ukrainian surveillance on electronic communications, and that he wouldn't go near any CIA operatives or locations in Ukraine.

"We'll stay clear," Shaefer agreed. "Have to. If anything goes south, they'll blame the CIA bogeyman. Suppose you need to get hold of Rabinowich or me?"

"Give me a dead-drop."

"Old school." Shaefer nodded approvingly and gave him the details and how they would handle Scorpion's cover.

Scorpion glanced at the café window. It was still snowing; the street was empty. He wasn't anxious to get back out in it and to the airport. They were the last ones in the café, and the waiter had glanced over at them more than once.

"We should get going," he said.

Shaefer touched Scorpion's forearm. "About Ukraine. How much time have you got? Did Akhnetzov say?"

"The election's in a week. Whatever is going on, it's already running."

Shaefer whistled silently to himself. "You'll have to force the issue. You watch your ass, bub. The difference between the SVR, the SBU, and the Ukrainian mafia, that's a pretty thin line. Those are some very badass Mike Foxtrots," Army slang for motherfuckers. "Makes Waziristan look like apple pie and motherhood. You Romeo that?"

"Happy days," Scorpion said, finishing his beer.

CHAPTER SEVEN

Maidan Nezalezhnosti
Kyiv, Ukraine

The giant television screen blasted the Plach Yer-
emiyahi rock band to tens of thousands of demon-
strators clapping and moving to the beat in Kyiv's
Independence Square. The night was frigid and the
crowd was dressed in heavy coats, wool caps, and
Russian fur hats. Many were in their twenties, there
more for the music and the noisy crowds than the
politics. But scattered among them were older faces,
some with orange scarves and flags. They looked
around uncertainly, as though they had gotten lost
on their way to a college rally. A giant banner on a
Soviet-style building lit with floodlights proclaimed
VSEUKRAYINSKE OBYEDNANNYA BATKIVSHCHYNA, the
All-Ukrainian Union Fatherland Party, and signs
in the crowd read KOZHANOVSKIY FOR THE PEOPLE.
On the towering white column in the center of the
square, someone had taped a poster with a squint-
eyed photo of Kozhanovskiy's opponent, Cherkesov,
that read: HET ZLODIY. Down with the Thief.

"Podyvit'sya na nykh." Look at them, a long-

haired young man in a jacket standing in front of Scorpion said to his blond girlfriend, indicating a middle-aged couple waving orange T-shirts in time to the music. "You'd think it was the Orange Revolution all over," he added, his breath like puffs of smoke in the cold. For Scorpion, trying to acclimatize to the winter here, it was so cold it hurt to breathe.

"Well, I think they're *klevyy*," cool, his girlfriend said.

Scorpion continued to move through the crowd. It had been a busy day for him. He had never been in Kyiv before, and flying into Boryspil Airport, looked out over the city dusted with snow. The gray Dnieper River divided Kyiv in two, the east or Left Bank an endless spread of apartment buildings and factories, the Right Bank a jumble of Soviet-style buildings, gold-domed churches, and, beside the river, a statue the size of the Statue of Liberty of a woman with a raised sword.

He rented a fourth-floor apartment on Pushkinskaya on the Right Bank near *vulytsya* Khreshchatyk, Kyiv's main street. His cover was as a Canadian journalist named Michael Kilbane working out of London, in Kiev to cover the election for Reuters.

Being a journalist was standard cover, good enough to explain why he'd be poking around and asking questions. Shaefer had provided him with authentic-looking press credentials and promised to have MI-6 backstop his cover with the Reuters office on Canary Wharf in London. It was good enough for a standard police check. If he needed deeper cover, he would already be in bigger trouble than any story or identity could protect him.

The music in the square stopped to cheers and shouts for *"Bolshe!"* more, and *"Prodolzhaite igrat' muzyku!"*—Keep on playing! A man on the giant TV screen announced something to more cheers and good-natured catcalls, and then a woman in a black leather overcoat and Russian fur hat suddenly appeared and began speaking. The crowd quieted down, not because of what she was saying— Scorpion caught only that she was apparently introducing a speaker—but because, even bundled up as she was and distorted on the large TV screen, her looks were extraordinary.

"Kto ona?" Scorpion asked a man in a heavy jacket and wool cap standing next to him. Who is she?

"You don't know Iryna?" the man answered in Russian, pronouncing her name *Ee-ree-na*, his eyebrows raised in surprise. Scorpion shook his head. "Iryna Mikhailivna Shevchenko. Her father was the founder of the Rukh, the Independence movement."

"Spasiba," Scorpion said, nodding thanks and moving on around the edge of the crowd as the woman began leading them in a chant.

"Kozhanovskiy! . . . Kozhanovskiy! . . . Kozhanovskiy!" the crowd shouted in response, erupting into a roar of approval as the candidate himself replaced the woman at the podium.

"Ukraintsi!" the older, barrel-chested man shouted, grinning widely. "The time has come to choose your future!" The crowd roared again. There were ripples of applause as Kozhanovskiy went on,

and then, from the edge of the square, a jumble of shouting and women screaming.

"Dopomozhit!" a woman screamed. Help! *"Prypyny!"* others shrieked. Stop it! *"Militsiyu!"* Security Police! And at the edge of the crowd, *"Bandity!"* as people began to surge away, shouting and running.

Scorpion couldn't see what was causing it. Someone banged into him and without looking, continued running. A gap opened in the melee and he finally saw what was happening.

A mob of perhaps a hundred men, many armed with clubs, had waded into the crowd. They were swinging wildly, smashing heads, shouting *"Het Kozhanovskiy!"* Down with Kozhanovskiy! As people trampled each other to get out of the way, Scorpion waited. The front wave of the attackers came toward him. They looked like thugs, and he saw what seemed to be criminal tattoos on many of their necks.

Two burly men were coming at him, clubs upraised. One had a spiderweb tattoo on the side of his neck, a Russian prison tattoo signifying that he was a drug dealer. He swung his club, and Scorpion sidestepped him with a leg sweep, taking him down as he blocked a punch from the other thug, using an aikido *ikkyo* wrist lock to bring him to the ground. As the mob surged past them, Scorpion lay on top of the second, pressing hard on his elbow and wrist, causing him to cry out in pain. The drug dealer started to get up. Scorpion kicked him in the face and he collapsed, his nose spurting blood. Someone else kicked at Scorpion then, who kicked back and caught a knee, this third thug grunting and stumbling on.

"*Kto vas poslal?*" Scorpion demanded of the man he still held to the ground. Who sent you? He could see a crucifix tattoo on the back of the man's neck. Another *blatnoi* thug, he thought, applying sharp pressure to the man's wrist and elbow.

"*Poshol na khui!*" the man cursed at him, his breath smelling of onions. He managed to grab Scorpion's neck with his free hand and try to choke him. Scorpion applied more pressure to the wrist, pried one of the man's fingers from his neck and bent it back suddenly, breaking the finger. The man screamed.

"*Kto vas poslal?*"

"*Yob tvoiyu mat'!*" the man shouted, telling him to do something obscene with his mother.

Scorpion grabbed another finger and bent it back till he felt the finger crack like a twig. The man screamed again. "*Yesche vosem raz?*" he shouted. Should I do this eight more times? *Kto vas poslal?*"

"*Yob!* You are making a mistake— *Aieee!*" he screamed as Scorpion started bending the next finger. "Syndikat says do this, I do."

"*Kto avtoritet?*" Scorpion asked. Who's the boss? Around him, he could hear the klaxons of *militsiyu* police vans approaching.

"Everybody knows. Mogilenko is the *pakhan*, the boss. *Sukin sin*, you broke my fingers," the man said.

"Good. Where do I find Mogilenko?"

"Dynamo Club. Mogilenko fix you good, *upiz-*

dysh," the man cursed, suggesting Scorpion had sex with his mother.

But Scorpion had already gotten up. He moved fast, working his way through the crowd. People were lying on the ground or stood around holding handkerchiefs to bloody heads. By the time *militsiyu* police in riot gear moved in, he had already left the square.

The Dynamo Club was a multistory building, bright with neon and electric lights, near the end of Khreshchatyk Street by the Bessarabsky Market. A half-dozen unsmiling men, all over six feet and bulky in down jackets, acted as security at the door as a line of people waited to get in. Scorpion got out of the taxi, showed three one-hundred *hryvnia* bills, pronounced "grivna" and worth about forty dollars, to a doorman with longish hair, and then he was inside, raising his hand to his face so the security camera wouldn't catch his image.

Strobe lights flashed in the otherwise dark club, and speakers blasted Eurotrash rock so loud the room shook. It was packed with good-looking women and older men who looked like they could afford them. On red-lit platforms, naked young women swirled on poles, gyrating to the beat. His hand still covering his face, Scorpion made his way through the crowd to the bar.

He handed another three hundred *hryvnia* to one of the bartenders, a sexy blonde in a low-cut top that left little doubt about her assets.

"What you want, *golubchik*, my darling?" the blonde asked in fractured English.

"I'm looking for Mogilenko."

The blonde recoiled. "You nice-looking guy. Why you want trouble?" she asked, tucking the money in her cleavage.

"How do I find him?"

"Listen, my darling, stay here. Plenty beautiful girls. Have good time. Don't do this," she said, her eyes wide, watching him.

"I just need to talk to him," Scorpion said, handing her one of a number of different business cards he had had made up in Bucharest; this one said his name was Luc Briand from an offshore services company headquartered in Marseilles.

She motioned him to the side of the bar. "Go away. Now," she whispered.

"What's the problem?" he said.

"Listen. A year ago, young man come. Same thing. Nice, clean-cut, like you. Ask for Mogilenko. They take to see him. Only Mogilenko thinks this man looks at girlfriend, Valentina. They cut out his eyes, then his *khui*," referring to the male organ. "Valentina try to look away. He shoot Valentina in head. Bang! Young guy, bang! Bury them together, man's *khui* in her mouth. This is Mogilenko."

"Why do you work here?"

She looked at him. Around them the music and lights pulsed, making patterns of light and shadows on their faces.

"You new in Ukraine, *golubchik*. Is not so easy," she said.

Scorpion touched her arm. "Just tell me."

"You sure you want?"

Scorpion felt a pang. Forcing the issue with a psycho Ukrainian mafia chief wasn't the smartest way to go about this. But the clock was ticking. If the assassination was real—and it had to be or Rabinowich wouldn't have been so desperate—whoever ordered it had two choices: use one of his own or contract the hit with the mafia. He needed to find out which.

He nodded. said, "Yes, it's what I want."

"You don't need look," she said, tucking his card into her cleavage. "He find you."

He watched her make a call on a phone by the bar, glancing at his card as she talked. As the strippers wrapped themselves around their poles, he thought about what he was getting into. What was it Shaefer had said? *The difference between the SVR, the SBU, and the Ukrainian mafia, that's a pretty thin line.*

He didn't have time to finish his drink before two men—one small, one very large, at least six-foot-six, both in unzipped military-style parkas—came up on either side of him. The smaller one showed him a Makarov 9mm pistol tucked in his belt.

"You come," he said.

"We're going to see Mogilenko?" Scorpion asked.

"You come," resting his hand on the gun.

"*Buvay, rodimy,*" Scorpion said to the blonde. So long. He smiled at her, but she looked straight through him as though he were already dead.

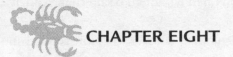

CHAPTER EIGHT

Patona Bridge
Kyiv, Ukraine

"He's *un con*, an asshole, Cherkesov, but he will win," Mogilenko said in French. They were in his office on the top floor of the Dynamo Club. The room was ultra modern. Mogilenko wore Prada tortoise-frame glasses, jeans, and a Ralph Lauren blazer, his long graying hair tied back in a ponytail. He looked more like a fashion designer than the head of Syndikat, Ukraine's most powerful mafia gang. He sat on a sofa, a bottle of Khortytsya *horilka* between him and Scorpion. In the plate-glass wall behind Mogilenko, Scorpion could see the lights of the city. Through the thick carpet beneath their feet, he could feel the floor vibrate to the beat of the music below.

They were not alone. A tall man with prison crosses tattooed on both sides of his neck lounged against the wall. His eyes, along with a Russian SR-1 Gyurza pistol with a silencer, were fixed on Scorpion. Mogilenko introduced him as *Andriy la machine.* "Because when he eliminates problems, it's like a machine." When Mogilenko said that, Andriy didn't smile.

"What makes you so sure?" Scorpion replied in French.

"Les Russes want it," Mogilenko said. "In this country, when the Russians want something, that's how it works."

"Where'd you learn French?" Scorpion asked.

"I did my MBA at INSEAD near Paris."

"Is that a job requirement for a Syndikat *pakhan*?"

"You'd be surprised. Business, as the Americans say, is business. *Budmo*," Mogilenko said, pouring Khortytsya for both of them and then drinking. Scorpion took a sip.

"I was at the Kozhanovskiy rally," Scorpion said. "Any idea why a bunch of *patsani* leg-breakers might bring iron bars to a political rally?"

Mogilenko shrugged. "Maybe someone paid them. I heard one of the Kemo got his fingers broken," he added, looking straight at Scorpion.

"Maybe he stuck it where it didn't belong."

"Very likely," Mogilenko said, nodding.

"So the Syndikat supports Cherkesov? Is that why somebody sent *patsani* thugs to the rally?"

Mogilenko laughed. "Last week we broke up Cherkesov rallies in Kharkov and Donetsk. This week, a Kozhanovskiy rally. We support whoever pays." He shrugged. "And don't get taken in by Iryna Shevchenko because of her pretty face. She's a *douleur cuisante*," meaning sharp as a whip.

"So it's strictly business. You don't give a damn who wins?"

"Whoever wins, we do business." Mogilenko put his glass down. "And now, monsieur, we've had our *horilka* and our little conversation. So before you go *baise-toi*, why don't you tell me what the fuck you really want, *upizdysh*?" His eyes glittered behind his glasses. The blonde was right, Scorpion thought. He was a psychopath.

"I've been approached for a job," he said, leaning forward. "Kyiv is Syndikat *territoire*. I figured I better check with you first."

"What job?"

Scorpion took a deep breath. He was about to cross a red line.

"Maybe not everyone likes Cherkesov," he said.

"Who sent you?" Mogilenko asked, looking at Scorpion as though he were an insect in a science experiment.

"Sorry. I don't talk about clients."

"I won't ask twice." Mogilenko looked at Andriy.

"You think I'm a *mouchard*?" Scorpion snapped, using the French slang for stool pigeon.

"I think, you miserable *fils de pute*, you made a big mistake. *Sortez!*" Mogilenko snarled, gesturing for Scorpion to get out. To Andriy, he said in Russian, "Get rid of him."

They went out the back door to an alley that led to the street. There were four of them: Scorpion, Andriy, and the two men in the bulky parkas who had brought Scorpion up to see Mogilenko. The wind had come up. It was very cold. As they walked to a black Mercedes sedan waiting down the block, its engine idling, Scorpion knew that he had made a terrible mistake. It was like that infinitesimal moment when you step on a land mine just before it explodes. If Mogilenko and the Syndikat were involved in the assassination plot, Mogilenko would have tried to get information out of him. If the assassination was news to Mogilenko, he would have tried to coopt him, or tried to use the information to his advantage. But he had done neither.

Mogilenko was going to get rid of him. Probably to score points with whichever side won, Scorpion thought as he got in the back of the Mercedes, sandwiched between Andriy and the big man. Andriy pressed the muzzle of his silencer against Scorpion's side.

The small man got into the front passenger seat next to the driver. He turned around, a gun in his hand. Scorpion's heart was pounding.

"What is your name?" the small man said in Russian.

"Briand. Lucien Briand. In Russian, Lukyan," Scorpion said.

"You worried, Lukyan?" indicating the gun.

"I don't know. Where are we going?"

"Make no difference to you pretty *yob* fucking soon," the small man said, and the big man next to Scorpion snickered.

They drove up Khreshchatyk toward the Maidan.

The street was lined with Soviet-style buildings, glossy billboards, and shops whose windows reflected the streetlights and the bare winter trees. It was getting late; there were only a few pedestrians. It started to snow.

"What you want from Mogilenko?" the small man asked.

"Maybe I wanted to fuck his girlfriend," Scorpion said.

The small man grinned widely.

"You heard that story?"

"Seems everybody has."

"That's no story, *upizdysh*. Me and my *drooh* had to bury those *govniuks*," he said, racking the slide on his gun. "You made a big mistake, Lukyan. He's a crazy guy, that Mogilenko."

"Don't be stupid," Scorpion said, measuring angles and distances with his eyes, barely able to breathe. "I'll pay you a hundred thousand *hryvnia*. Each."

"No good, Lukyan," the small man said. "You know what Mogilenko would do to us?"

"You don't want to do this. I know people. I've got *blat*," Scorpion said, meaning influence. He suddenly had a terrible urge to urinate. He was running out of time.

"You don't got *blat*, *drooh*. Mogilenko, he got the *politsiy* and half the Verkhovna Rada on his payroll. He got the real *blat*," the small man said, rubbing his thumb on his fingers in the universal sign for money.

They drove onto the entryway to a bridge over the Dnieper River, ice floes floating on the dark water. The roadway was coated with snow, and at that late hour there was almost no traffic. The driver stopped the car midway on the bridge.

"Get out," the small man said.

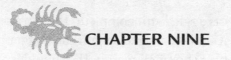 **CHAPTER NINE**

Pechersk
Kyiv, Ukraine

Koichi, his instructor at the Point in North Carolina, used to say there were two key elements to surviving deadly violence: surprise and distance. Scorpion knew he had a better chance inside the Mercedes than outside, where they could shoot him down at a distance of their choosing. The guns were the problem, the big man was just a brute. Makarov pistols had a clumsy grip that made the recoil sloppy. It wouldn't take much to make the small man miss. The biggest danger was Andriy's Gyurza pistol with the silencer pressed against his side. The fraction of a second would be critical, he thought as he shouted at the top of his lungs.

"*Pazhalusta!* Don't kill me! I don't want to die!" he screamed, already moving his right palm as Andriy hesitated, the Krav Maga move causing him to reflexively fire. The bullet tore through the front seat, barely missing the driver. At the same time, Scorpion kicked the front seat hard where the small man was sitting facing to the rear. The shot from Andriy's Makarov echoed loudly inside the car.

As Scorpion struggled to complete the Krav Maga sequence, Andriy managed to pull the trigger again. The bullet hit the small man in the shoulder, and he cried out in surprise and pain as Scorpion managed to twist the pistol away from Andriy, then turned the gun and fired. The bullet ripped through Andriy's hand and into the bridge of his nose, blowing off the back of his head. Before the small man could move, Scorpion fired again, hitting him in the neck. The man stared at him wide-eyed, blood gurgling out of his throat.

The big man then grabbed Scorpion's throat in a massive grip, choking him, while reaching with his other hand to grapple for the pistol. He was immensely strong. Scorpion couldn't move his head. His arm felt like it was caught in a vise. He smashed upward at the man's chin with his left elbow, and the man merely grunted. Scorpion hit him again, this time in the throat, loosening his grip for a fraction of a second, then he fired, almost blindly. The bullet hit the big man in the eye, killing him instantly. He slumped back, his hand still around Scorpion's neck.

The driver had disappeared. The entire fight had taken perhaps five seconds.

Scorpion pried the big man's fingers from his neck. The interior of the car smelled of blood and sweat. He shoved Andriy's body aside and staggered out. He gulped the cold night air in great heaves, his breath coming out in plumes of clouds, staggering to the side of the car and leaning on it to remain standing. He could see the driver near the end of the bridge running back toward the Right Bank of the river, too far away to shoot even if he'd had strength enough to try.

Opening the driver's door, he looked in. The small man was sprawled against the passenger door, bubbles forming in the blood from his neck. He was still alive, his eyes on Scorpion as he raised the gun. Scorpion saw the eyes go dead as he put a bullet into the center of the small man's forehead.

The engine was still running. He got in, put the car in gear, made a slippery U-turn in the snow and drove back across the bridge. Coming off the roadway, he scanned the streets for the driver, but he had gotten away. He knew he should track him down, but there wasn't time. He had to get rid of the Lucien Briand ID and the Mercedes with the bodies, and find a place to dump the car. He wiped prints off anything he had touched in the Mercedes and left it on a residential street off Moskovska Avenue, ripped up the Briand ID and dropped the car keys into a trashcan by an apartment building and the pieces of ID into a curb flood drain.

He'd screwed it up, he thought. Less than one day in the country and he'd made an enemy of the Syndikat. The only good thing was that they thought he was a Frenchman named Briand, who no longer existed. He considered aborting the mission and getting out while he still could. It was just Ukraine. Then he reminded himself that Rabinowich, whom he respected, had gone to a great deal of trouble to get him involved. There was a whole hell of a lot more to this.

The funny part—and he had to suppress an almost hysterical laugh—was that what he'd initially thought of as the most dangerous part of the night was still ahead.

The signal was a ribbon tied on a lamppost near the steps, indicating a pickup. Good old Shaefer, he thought. The dead drop was under a bench in the amphitheatre in Pechersk Landscape Park near the river. It was after eleven and the paths were deserted, although *fartsovchiki* drug dealers were known to do business in the park at night. Scorpion waited in the shadows. It was snowing heavily. At the top of the snow-covered slope, the gold-domed Pecherska Lavra Monastery, a Kyiv landmark, was illuminated by floodlights. He untied the ribbon and let the night breeze carry it away.

From where he stood he could see the giant Rodina Mat statue of the Motherland, defending her country with a sword. Facing east, his apartment concierge had joked—the joke being that although built by the Soviets, she was looking east as if to defend Ukraine against Russia instead of against the Nazis. He studied the footprints in the snow by the bench. The falling snow would fill them in. That was good. It would fill in his footprints as well.

He watched the shadows around the amphitheatre area. It looked clear to approach, but still he waited, shivering inside his overcoat. His meeting with Mogilenko had accomplished one thing.

It confirmed that the assassination plot was real. Mogilenko hadn't been surprised. That meant he already knew about it, probably either from Cherkesov's people or the SVR.

Assumption: Cherkesov had probably hired Syndikat and Kemo goons to break up the Kozhanovskiy rally. Second assumption: Mogilenko knew about the plot but had questions. That's why he had agreed to meet with him. If that was true, it meant Mogilenko and the Ukrainian mafia knew about it, but they hadn't been contracted to do it themselves or they would have wanted to keep him alive, to either find out what he knew or use him to play one side against the other. Although, Scorpion had to admit, it was all speculation; there were a hell of a lot of ifs.

Checking the shadows one last time, he walked to the first bench near the steps and felt underneath for something buried in the ground. He had to pull off his gloves to feel through the snow and the frozen ground. The cold was intense; the snow burned his fingers. Maybe it wasn't there, he thought as he dug for it. Then his fingers touched something: a metal ring. He pulled hard, yanking out a wedge-shaped box—called a "spike"—buried in the snow-covered ground.

He rubbed his frozen hands to warm them, then opened the spike. Inside was a Glock 9 x 19mm pistol, four standard seventeen-round magazines and four thirty-two-round extended clips, cell phones, SIM cards, bugs, a button spy video camcorder, NSA software on a flash drive, and other equipment. It was good to have a decent weapon again, he thought, loading and checking the Glock. When he was done, he put his gloves back on, forced the spike back into the ground under the bench, spread snow over it and left.

He headed up the hill past the church. It was too late for the Metro to be running, so he walked until he caught a late night *mashrutka* minibus on Povstannya. It was nearly empty and smelled of cigarettes and wet clothes. As the minibus moved through the snowy street, he thought about his next move. The obvious candidate for someone with a motive to get rid of Cherkesov was his opponent, Kozhanovskiy, but all the information about a plot had come to the billionaire, Akhnetzov, from the SVR; and if his assumption was right, had been transmitted to Mogilenko from the same source.

Scorpion's eyes began to close. He was tired and jet-lagged, but soon the SVR and the SBU would find out he was in the game. The best time to hit the SVR was now, before they were aware of him. The problem was, how to do it without getting killed?

CHAPTER TEN

Shevchenkivskyi
Kyiv, Ukraine

The apartment was on the fourth floor of a Soviet-style building near the Golden Gate, the thousand-year-old stone gateway of ancient Kyiv. Scorpion studied the facade from a doorway across the street. There were no exterior security cameras or alarms. The street was empty and white with snow. He could hear it crunch underfoot as he crossed to the building. Using a Peterson universal key with a tap from the Glock, he opened the outer door lock and stepped inside.

The hallway was dark. It smelled of cigarette smoke and fried onions. Somebody had made *varenyky*—dumplings—he thought, taking out a pocket LED flashlight. As he made his way up the stairs to the fourth floor, the building was silent, and in the light of the flashlight cold enough to see his breath. He paused on the fourth floor landing and peered into the hallway.

A security camera was hidden in a wall lamp mounted near Gabrilov's apartment, positioned to cover the area in front of the door. It looked like a simple single-channel model. Standard SVR off-site, he thought, then approached from the side away from where the camera was aimed. He used the screwdriver of his Swiss Army knife to disable the channel so it wouldn't record or set off an alarm.

That done, he checked the door for alarms, but couldn't see any. He didn't expect Gabrilov to be home. He had called the Russian embassy earlier in the day to confirm that there was a reception that evening to promote a new Russian film. There would be bigwigs and the Russian stars of the movie, and as a cultural attaché, Gabrilov would have to be there as well. Just to make sure, Scorpion knocked, waited, then put his ear to the door. There was no sound, only a midnight silence. It only took a few seconds with the Peterson key to open it.

The living room was sparsely finished. Just a sofa, a table with a half-empty bottle of *horilka*, and a TV. The apartment smelled of pipe tobacco. He tiptoed to the bedroom door and opened it. The bed was unmade and empty. Using the flashlight, he checked the tiny kitchen and bathroom and a second bedroom. There was nothing of interest except for a laptop computer and a telephone on a table against the wall.

Scorpion turned the computer on, went back to the living room, took off the wall outlet cover and put in an electronic bug. Then he went back to the laptop and, using a flash drive, installed untraceable NSA software that would forward everything on Gabrilov's computer to NSA receivers in Fort

Meade, Maryland, and from there to a server he could access with his laptop. He heard a dog bark and froze. The sound came from somewhere outside. Another building, he thought. He turned the computer off and, using the knife screwdriver, unscrewed the base of the phone and put in another bug.

Just then he heard voices and the sound of a key in the lock. He had only seconds. A man was talking to a woman, and as the door opened, he just managed to duck behind the door in the tiny bathroom. He waited there in the darkness, smelling the bad plumbing, the Glock in his hand. He was hoping neither of them came into the bathroom, but if one of them did, he'd have no choice but to confront Gabrilov right then. They were talking. The woman said something about *horilka* and money. He's got a whore, Scorpion thought, listening to the clink of glass and a bottle and Gabrilov toasting, *"Budmo!"*

Through a crack between the door and the jamb, he saw the woman in the dim light on her knees in front of Gabrilov, his pants around his ankles. She was a buxom blonde, and after a minute she stood up and they went into the bedroom. Scorpion waited till he heard the bed creaking and the sound of heavy breathing.

Gabrilov had left his pants on the living room floor. He fished in the pockets and found the man's cell phone. He input the number into his own cell phone, then replaced Gabrilov's SIM card with a NSA-modified SIM. Waiting for a moment when he could hear the blonde moaning like it was worth extra, he opened the door carefully and left the apartment. In the hallway, he reconnected the security camera, and in less than a minute was down the stairs and outside the building.

By the time he walked back through the snow to Khreshchatyk, it was two in the morning. The boulevard was empty and it was too late for a taxi. He saw a lone car coming and flagged it down. The driver was a young bureaucrat on his way home. He said something in Ukrainian to Scorpion, who just handed him a hundred *hryven* bill and told him the address of his apartment. That was the thing about Ukraine. You could buy anything; they all needed money.

Scorpion closed his eyes and let the young man talk and drive. He was exhausted and jet-lagged, and everything that had happened that day finally hit him. Gabrilov would lead him to where information on the assassination was coming from, without ever knowing that he was doing it . . . in the morning.

 **CHAPTER ELEVEN**

Povitroflotskyi Prospekt
Kyiv, Ukraine

The Russian embassy was a concrete structure on Povitroflotskyi Prospekt, an area of government buildings and wide boulevards covered with snow. By morning it had stopped snowing. Scorpion crunched through the snow into the embassy and went up to a man at a desk in the marble lobby, done in a style Bob Harris had once facetiously called "dictatorship *moderne*." Framed pictures of the Russian president and prime minister were on the wall behind the man and a bored-looking Russian soldier sat in a nearby chair beside a metal detector.

"I would like—" Scorpion began.

"No visas here. Go to Consular Division on *vulytsya* Kutuzova, Pecherska Metro," the man said in English.

"I'm here to see Oleg Gabrilov."

"You have appointment?"

"Tell Gospodin Gabrilov I'm about to publish a story that names him, but prefer to give him a chance to talk to me first," Scorpion said, handing the man his Reuters business card.

The man looked at the card.

"You wait," he said, and picked up the phone. He dialed an extension and spoke in rapid Russian. It sounded like he was arguing with someone. That didn't surprise Scorpion. Unlike the CIA, senior SVR officials often held low-level positions in Russian embassies. "With the Russkies, don't look at the guy being chauffeured around, look at the driver," Rabinowich used to say.

The Mercedes killings had been on TV and were the second lead on the front page of the *Kyiv Post* that morning, the top story being accusations of corruption and bribery alleged against presidential candidate Viktor Kozhanovskiy by a newspaper associated with the Cherkesov campaign. Scorpion had read the story over breakfast at a local Dva Gusya fast-food restaurant.

The *politsiy* believed the Kutuzova Street killings, named for the street where he had left the Mercedes, were a mafia hit. They were questioning Syndikat informants but so far had no leads. The Syndikat boss, the notorious Genadiy Viktorovych Mogilenko, was "unavailable" for comment.

The man at the lobby desk hung up the phone and motioned to Scorpion.

"Gabrilov upstairs. You go through," he said, motioning him to the metal detector. "He take you," indicating the soldier.

Scorpion went through the metal detector and followed the soldier to a second floor office. The soldier knocked and gestured for him to go inside.

Gabrilov was a medium-sized man in a sagging gray suit. His face sagged too, like a basset hound, and his office reeked of the same pipe tobacco Scorpion had smelled in his apartment just a few hours earlier.

"*Govorite li vy Rossiyu?*" Gabrilov asked him if he spoke Russian.

"*Ochen malo,*" very little, Scorpion said.

"What wants Reuters agency with me?" Gabrilov said in an odd English-Russian hybrid, a hodge-podge Harris, referring to someone else, had once called "Bering Strait English."

"I'm an investigative reporter on a story about a possible assassination attempt on one of the Ukrainian candidates," Scorpion said. "Your name came up."

"Which candidate?"

"Cherkesov."

"This *sumashedshy*! You understand, crazy!" tapping his head with his fingers. "Cherkesov is good *droog* friend of Russiya. Who tells you this?"

"*Izvinitye.*" Sorry. "I don't name my sources."

"You sure? They say my name?"

"My sources say the assassination story comes from you."

"Is mistake. I know nothing of this! You must not spread such lies!" wagging his finger at Scorpion.

"Of course, it could be disinformation. Just to throw suspicion on Kozhanovskiy to hurt him in the election. There's been a suggestion you might

be SVR. They've been known to do such things."
Scorpion smiled.

"This is big lie! I am *kulturnye* officer. *Vydi von!*"
he shouted. "Get out!" gesturing for him to leave.

"That's too bad," Scorpion said, starting to rise
out of his chair. "We could have cleared this up and
no one would know. I could keep you as an unnamed
source. Now, you'll be famous. Probably not what
the SVR had in mind."

"Wait! *Pazhalusta!*" Please! Gabrilov held up his
hand. He looked shrewdly at Scorpion. "Who are
you? CIA?"

"I'm not even American," Scorpion said.

"*Nichivo.*" Never mind. Gabrilov shrugged.
"What your nationality?"

"Canadian; working out of London. Who's your
source on the assassination plot?"

"I know nothing."

"Yeah, I know. You're just a *kulturnye* officer. *Da
svidaniya, miy drooh,*" Scorpion said, getting up. He
had almost reached the door when Gabrilov called
after him.

"Wait! Was someone from Kozhanovskiy campaign. Secret. I cannot say name."

"You have someone embedded in the Kozhanovskiy campaign?"

"This election important to Russiya. We have informants in both sides. No doubt your CIA is doing
same."

"I told you, I'm not American. It's not my anything."

"Of course not! You Canada-man, not Amerikanyets. I am *kulturnye* officer, not SVR. We understand each other perfect," Gabrilov said, and lit his pipe, wreathing himself in a cloud of smoke.

"You're saying someone in the Kozhanovskiy campaign is planning to assassinate Cherkesov?"

"This is bad thing, understand? This not good for Russiya, not good Ukraina. Will be very bad. Someone must to do something, *da*?"

"*Da*," Scorpion said. "Someone must to do something."

CHAPTER TWELVE

Lypky
Kyiv, Ukraine

She blew into the room telling him he had three minutes. Her armament included a gray Prada suit, pearls, and a Ferragamo purse. Her hair was black and pageboy straight, and her eyes were like no one else's, a disturbing lapis lazuli blue. Iryna Shevchenko was stunningly beautiful and knew it. Even more, Scorpion thought later, there was something about her. A presence. Even in a room full of people, you wouldn't be able to take your eyes off her.

She waved away a male aide who had followed her in and sat on a desk.

They were on the top floor of a building on Instytutska in the Lypky district that served as a campaign office. Through the window behind her Scorpion could see buildings, and beyond them the snowy expanse of Pecherska Park and the Dnieper River glazed with ice.

"Mr. Kilbane," she said, peering at his Reuters badge after they said hello. "They said you were an investigative reporter, Reuters, London. You don't sound British."

"Canadian. Where'd you learn your English?" Scorpion asked.

"Benenden and Oxford. Plus some time in Washington," she said, lighting a cigarette. "What's this about?"

"There's a story going around that someone in your campaign is planning to bump off your opponent, Cherkesov. Care to comment?"

"Good God! Where'd you get such a story?" she said, color draining from her face. Her fist clenched and unclenched in her lap.

"Let's just say a source."

"What source?"

"Sorry." He shook his head. "Do you have any comment?"

"It's a lie. You can't print that. Barely a week before the election. It would destroy us."

"It would help," he said, "if you told me what you knew."

"Is this coming from the Cherkesov campaign? It's a plant. Surely you can see that?"

"It's not coming from your opponents. Is it true?" She got up from the desk.

"Who's saying this? Tell me."

It's you, he thought. Because eight minutes after he had left the Russian embassy, Gabrilov had made a call on his cell phone that, thanks to the SIM he had replaced in Gabrilov's cell phone and the software on his laptop, had enabled the NSA to track it to a cell phone registered in her name.

"Suppose I said it was another country that was the source?"

"Who, the Russians? It's the SVR, isn't it? Only a fool would believe anything from them," she said, exhaling a stream of cigarette smoke. "The Russians want Cherkesov to win. They'll say or do anything."

"Normally I would agree. Except, one," he held up a finger, "it's my job to check it out, and two," holding up a second finger, "turns out they got it from you."

"From me? What are you talking about?"

"From a cell phone that belongs to you."

"That's impossible! Besides, there are at least a hundred cell phones registered in my name. I bought them for the campaign."

"What about this one?" Scorpion said, holding up his cell with the number Gabrilov had called displayed on the screen.

Iryna peered intently at it.

"It can't be," she said, brushing her hair away from her face. "It's Alyona, one of my aides." She looked at him curiously. "How did you get this?"

"How I got it is my business. Is it true?"

"You can't print this. It'll kill us," she said, coming closer. He could smell her perfume. Hermès 24 Faubourg, he thought; hints of orange and jasmine, vanilla and sex.

"It's my job; providing I can confirm it," he said.

"You don't get it, do you?" She shook her head. "If Cherkesov takes power, you think it'll be like Democrats and Republicans in America? We'll just call each other nasty names and try to screw each other? If Cherkesov wins, you think he'll leave us around to oppose him?"

"Sounds like a pretty good motive for murder to me," Scorpion said, watching her closely.

She stubbed her cigarette out in an ashtray on the desk and looked out the window. "All right, how much?" she said.

"Don't," he said sharply, getting up. "I'm not a whore. Don't play me like one."

"I'm sorry," looking straight at him. "Neither am I—despite being a politician," she said with a wry smile. "What can I do?"

"Tell the truth. Help me get to the bottom of this. For instance, this Alyona. Did you know she was in contact with the SVR?"

Iryna shook her head. "I've known her since she was a girl in senior school. She came to work for me as an intern. What you say she's doing; it's not possible."

"You'd be surprised what people will do," Scorpion said. "I've seen them betray their country, husbands, wives, everything they believe in. They do it for love, money, sex, revenge, sometimes out of sheer boredom."

"Not Alyona," Iryna said, getting her cell phone out of her handbag. "She's a serious girl, an artist. She believes in what we're doing."

Scorpion grimaced. "So you say. Look, I need to talk to her. Where is she?"

Iryna dialed her cell phone and after a moment said something rapidly in Ukrainian. She listened, then clicked off and looked at Scorpion.

"That's odd. She was supposed to be in our Saksaganskogo office today. No one seems to know where she is. I should call her fiancé. She's engaged," she said, a flicker of a smile lighting her face.

Her male aide walked in then and they spoke in Ukrainian. He handed her a sheaf of papers, pointing at something. She looked at Scorpion.

"We have new numbers," she explained. "Thirty-four percent for Kozhanovskiy in Kharkov."

"Doesn't sound so good."

"It's not bad," she said. "Kharkov is a Cherkesov stronghold. Another minute, Slavo," she told the aide in English. He glanced curiously at Scorpion as he left.

"Alyona. I need to talk to her. Now," Scorpion said.

Iryna looked at him as though trying to decide something.

"So how do we do this?" she asked.

"For the moment, I'll hold off. There's no story till I find out what's going on. I'll keep you as background. An unnamed source. But from now on we stay in touch," he said, pulling on his jacket.

The male aide, Slavo, had come back. He stood in the door and pointed to his watch. "Iryna, *bud'laska*," he said, in accented English. "Viktor Ivanovych is waiting. We must go." Scorpion assumed he was referring to Kozhanovskiy. She nodded and waited. After a moment, he left.

"All right," she said. "Meet me tonight. Call me," writing her cell number on a slip of paper and giving it to him. She started to go, leaving behind a lingering scent of Hermès, then stopped at the door. She had an odd look on her face. "Cherkesov has a big rally in Dnipropetrovsk tomorrow night," she said. "It would be the perfect place."

"You mean for the assassination?"

"Yes," she said, and was gone.

CHAPTER THIRTEEN

Andriyivsky Uzviz
Kyiv, Ukraine

A sign with the silhouette of a black cat hung above the door of the Chorna Kishka Theatre Café on Andriyivsky Uzviz, a cobblestone pedestrian street winding steeply up the hill from Kontraktova Square. A poster in the café window advertised a play with a cubistlike drawing of a clown's face dripping blood, as if it had been drawn by an untalented Picasso. There were few people out. It was very cold; the wind blowing traces of snow across the cobblestones, the sky steel-gray and promising more snow. Scorpion hunched inside his overcoat and went inside.

The café was nearly empty. Half the space was taken up by rows of folding chairs fronting a small stage. There were photos with the names of the actors in the play on the wall next to the bar. On one side of the stage hung an odd-looking puppet. It looked like a fairy-tale woodsman holding an ax. A young man sat at the bar, reading a paperback and nursing a beer, ignoring the nearly silent TV on the wall. A waitress in jeans came over. She was young, thin, her short reddish hair streaked with blue, metal studs in her nose and upper lip. Her photo was one of those hung by the bar.

"*Yestli u vas menyu?*" Scorpion said, asking in Russian for a menu.

"We got borscht," she said in a thickly accented English.

"What else?"

"Borscht is good," she said.

"I'll have the borscht and an Obolon," Scorpion said.

A few minutes later she brought him a steaming bowl of soup with a dollop of sour cream, some garlicky *pampushkamy* rolls, and a bottle of Obolon beer.

"*Kak vas zavut?*" he asked her in Russian as he started to eat. What's your name?

"Ekaterina," she said, turning back toward him, one hand on a bony hip.

"Are you an actress?" indicating the photos on the wall.

"Why? You want to put me on the *televidenie?*" she smirked. "I've heard this story before, *krasivyi.*"

"I'm looking for Alyona Kushnir," he said. "I'm told she's an actress in the play."

The young man sitting at the bar stopped reading his paperback and turned to look at him. "What you want with Alyona?" he asked in clumsy English, putting down the book.

"She's missing. I'm working with Iryna Mikhailivna Shevchenko. She asked me to help," Scorpion said, watching them.

"That *sooka suna*! I knew something would happen!" the woman said, looking at the young man.

"*Zatknysya!*" Don't say anything, the young man said, coming over. "*Kto vy?*" he asked Scorpion. Who are you? "Are you *politsiy?*"

"I'm a journalist. I was doing a story on the election. I need to talk to Alyona, only she didn't show up at work and no one's seen her. Iryna is worried. Do you know anything?" Scorpion said in English.

"Me? I not know nothing," the young man said.

"She didn't come for play last night," the waitress said.

"Are you her *drooha?*" Scorpion asked, meaning her friend.

Ekaterina shrugged. "We are actresses both. Last night she is supposed to come for play. He call her cell, her flat," jerking her head toward the young man. "No answer. *Nichego.*" Nothing.

"You didn't seem surprised when I told you she hasn't come in," Scorpion said, gesturing for her to sit. "Why not?"

She hesitated a moment, then glancing at the young man, sat down at the table. Scorpion watched both of them. He could see something in the young man's eyes warning her not to say anything.

"*Nichego.* It is nothing. Sometimes I exaggerate. I am actress," she said, trying a smile, but her eyes weren't smiling. She looked scared, Scorpion thought.

"When you said *sooka suna*—son of a bitch—who were you talking about?"

"Why you want to speak with Alyona?" the young man asked.

"She's missing," Scorpion said. "She may be in danger. That's all I can tell you."

"This is *politika*? Is this *opasno* . . . you understand, dangerous?" the young man said.

"*Ochen opasno*," Scorpion said. "It is very dangerous. Who is the *sooka suna*?"

"I knew this would happen!" Ekaterina said. "I warn her, but she is afraid!"

"Be quiet! Say nothing!" the young man hissed. "We don't know him," indicating Scorpion.

The waitress said something fast in Russian that Scorpion didn't catch, though he thought he heard the word *pamagat*, help. He held up his cell phone.

"*Zdyes*, here. Talk to Iryna Shevchenko yourself. I think Alyona is in danger. I think you already know that. Who's the *sooka suna*?"

The young man looked at the phone. "Is her *droog*, her boyfriend," he said finally, coming over and joining them. He lit a cigarette, his fingers yellowed by nicotine. The girl nodded.

"Is this her fiancé?"

Ekaterina nodded again. "His name is Sirhiy. Sirhiy Pyatov. He is electrician. At first when she knows him, she is happy. But he gets drunk, beats her. She tries to leave, he puts knife to her throat, here," touching her neck, "telling her if she leaves he will kill her. I tell her you should not stay, but she says afterward, he is so sweet, like little boy. He kisses her, tells her he didn't mean it. One day she comes to do play, her face is like balloon, blue, here," touching the left side of her face. "I put heavy makeup on so everyone doesn't see. She wants to do play, she says."

"He is Syndikat guy," the young man said. "Mafia, you understand? He tells me like is good thing, thing to be proud of. Three weeks ago he comes to café, buys Nemiroff *horilka* for everyone. Happy, yes? He tells me he has big deal going, but is secret. *Shhhh!* He does not come back after that."

"And Alyona, she says nothing," Ekaterina added. "But she is worried."

"Scared?"

She nodded. "Yes. Sirhiy is big guy. Scary guy."

"Is *politika*. Is Syndikat. Is best to be scared," the young man said, glancing over his shoulder at the TV, which was showing a riot in the streets. There were scenes of Cherkesov supporters with signs reading НЕТ ZLODIY KOZHANOVSKIY!, Down with the Thief Kozhanovskiy, attacking students with clubs. The bloody face of an unconscious young man filled the screen. The camera pulled back to show his lifeless body, head dangling as he was carried away by friends.

"Turn up the TV," Scorpion said.

The young man went over and turned it up. The announcer rattled in rapid Ukrainian over images of riots and groups of men, workers and students on both sides shouting and waving banners and clubs.

"What's he saying?" Scorpion asked.

"He say Cherkesov is making groups to ensure voting is fair," Ekaterina said, her eyes wide. "He say they will be at every voting place. Kozhanovskiy say

Cherkesov is try to intimidate voters. Students is also forming groups for Kozhanovskiy. There is fighting in Kyiv, in Kharkov, Donetsk, Odessa, all over."

"It's bad," Scorpion said.

She and the young man nodded. "I never see this," she said, and shivered. The announcer's voice stopped and the TV went to a commercial. The young man took the remote and turned the volume down.

"When was the last time you saw Alyona?" Scorpion asked.

"This morning, about eleven," Ekaterina said. "She came to the café. She says she cannot be in play anymore. She is crying, shaking like a leaf. I ask her, is it Sirhiy?" She looked at Scorpion. "But she says, is more than Sirhiy. 'He has put me in the middle,' she says. I ask her what is happening, but she says not tell to anyone. She must run, hide. I ask where she will go. She does not answer. I ask if she has place to go. She says something I do not forget. She says, 'I try, but I think is too late.' I try to stop her, but she run away."

Eleven o'clock, Scorpion thought with a pang. Less than an hour after he had spoken with Gabrilov at the Russian embassy and Gabrilov had called Alyona's cell. While he was talking with Iryna, Alyona was making a run for it.

"Do you have her address?" he asked.

She nodded, then wrote it down on a piece of paper and gave it to him.

"Do either of you want to come with me? It would help," he said.

She started to say yes, standing up, then looked at the young man.

"We should stay out of this," he said. She looked down at her feet and nodded.

"Is her picture up there?" Scorpion asked, pointing at the photos on the wall.

Ekaterina went over to the wall and pointed.

"This is Alyona," indicating a pouty blonde, a Slavic Marilyn Monroe type.

"Can I have it?" Scorpion asked.

She took the frame down and handed it to the young man, who took the photo out of the frame and handed it to Scorpion.

"What you do?" the young man asked.

"Try to find her. See if I can help," Scorpion said, taking a last taste of the borscht and a swig of beer. He tossed some money on the table, pulled his overcoat on and got up.

"Alyona is good girl," the young man said, reaching for the half-finished beer. "Don't take too long."

Alyona's apartment building was in a working-class neighborhood on a hill near the Central Station. Boots and galoshes had tracked a path through the snow by the entrance. Trash lay half buried in piles of snow on the curb, and as Scorpion got closer, he spotted what could have been droplets of blood. Although it was early afternoon, it was already growing dark. The wind had come up. Except for the occasional passing car, the street was deserted, locked in winter. He studied the building. Its windows were frosted over, the shades drawn, silent. He wasn't looking forward to what he might find.

It only took a second with a credit card to open the building's front door lock. The door was frozen shut and he had to lean his shoulder into it to crack the ice and open it. The hallway was dim, with fading floral wallpaper that looked like it had come from another era. From one of the ground floor apartments came the indistinct sounds of what could have been a TV game show. He checked the names on the mailboxes. Alyona's last name was Kushnir. He saw it with a hand-lettered *Пьятов* for Pyatov scrawled over it, nearly obliterating KUSHNIR. It was like a metaphor for how Pyatov had taken over her life, Scorpion thought, heading up the stairs.

He waited, listening at the apartment door. No sound came from inside. Just to be sure, he listened at the doors of the apartments on either side. In one of them he could hear a television and smelled borscht cooking. He would have to be quiet. He studied the lock for a second, then took out the Glock and the Peterson key. He unlocked the door and opened it, snapping into the apartment in shooting position.

The studio apartment was empty. Whoever had left was in a hurry. There were drawers open and clothes on the floor. He searched the lone closet. If there had been any luggage, it was gone. The bed hadn't been made. Scorpion examined the bed, the frayed sheet and blanket, and under the thin mattress. There were rust-colored stains on the sheet and mattress. It looked like dried blood, not very long ago. The hairs stood up at the back of his neck.

The girl was doomed and she knew it, he thought. But it didn't fit. If Pyatov had done something to Alyona, there were two problems. The walls were thin. He could hear the television from the next apartment. How come no one heard anything? And if Pyatov had killed her, how could he have disposed of the body in broad daylight?

Scorpion got his answer to the second question in the bathroom. The tiny curtainless shower stall had dark stains around the drain. He studied them, ran the water and using a folded piece of rough toilet paper rubbed at one of the stains. It ran red on the paper and down the drain. At the moment, he would have given a lot for access to a police lab, but he had no lab and not a lot of time either. Assumption: Pyatov killed the girl silently, perhaps by cutting her throat in the bed, then cut her up in the shower and carried the pieces out in a suitcase. Tough but possible. The alternative was that she wasn't dead. But if not, where was she and why the bloodstains in the shower?

What would he have used to cut her up? he wondered, looking in the small cupboard over the kitchen sink. In the counter under the sink he found a stained butcher knife and a rusted hacksaw frame minus the blade. It also had traces of blood. A torn sticker on the frame indicated it belonged to Filostro Elektrychni, Ltd. on Dymytrova Street. After taking one last look around and making sure to wipe off anything he might've touched, he left the apartment, locking the door behind him with the Peterson key.

He knocked on the door of the apartment next

door; the one with the television on. A jowly middle-aged woman in a housedress opened the door.

"*Dobry dyen*. I am friend of Pani Kushnir," Scorpion said in his best Russian.

"*Shcho vy khochete?*" What do you want? she said in Ukrainian, peering nearsightedly at him.

"*Pazhalusta*, your neighbor, Pani Kushnir, is missing," indicating next door, "*Vy videli yee?*" he asked in Russian. Have you seen her?

"*Kto vy?*" Who are you? she answered in Russian, her face hardening. "You're a foreigner."

"*Ya zhurnalist*," I'm a journalist, "*iz Kanady*," from Canada. "It is very important."

"*Slushaite*, you make them stop making so much noise with the television next door. Around noon there is shouting and screams and suddenly the *televidenie* is so loud I cannot hear my own," she said, shaking her finger in Scorpion's face.

"Have you seen her today?" he asked.

The woman shook her head.

"What about her *drooh*?" Her boyfriend.

"That *batjar*," she said, her eyes hardening. "A few weeks ago I thought he was going to hit me! I knocked on the door. It sounded like he was going to kill her in there."

"What about today?"

"I heard him leave a couple of hours ago, the pig," her mouth wrinkling like she wanted to spit. "They finally turned the *televidenie* off. You find her, you tell her I am calling the *pomishchyk*." The landlord. "All this business—and now you, a foreigner! *Plah!* Where does it end?"

"Was she with him?" Scorpion asked.

"*Ni.*" She shook her head. "He was leaving. For good I hope."

"How do you know?"

"I saw through the peephole."

At first Scorpion didn't understand. He shrugged, holding his hands up. She pointed at the door peephole. "*Glazok,*" she said, repeating the word, annoyed. "He had a big suitcase on wheels. It looked heavy."

Jesus, Scorpion thought. Just like that. "And you haven't seen her?"

"*Ni*—I don't want to be involved and I don't talk to foreigners," she said, closing the door firmly in Scorpion's face.

That left him on the Metro to Respublikansky, the station near the football stadium. According to the Kyiv map, it was the closest station to Dymytrova Street, the address on the hacksaw frame where Pyatov, an electrician, presumably worked. He had thought of calling, then decided it was best if he just showed up in case Pyatov was there.

The subway car was crowded with people. It had that Eastern European winter smell of sour bodies, wet wool, and cigarettes. A train headed in the opposite direction passed theirs with a roar, lighted windows speeding by. One of the passengers in the other train, a shaved-headed type in a cheap leather jacket who had *blatnoi* thug written all over him, happened to look up at Scorpion. He was gone in an instant, but it hit Scorpion like an electric shock. It was a reminder. Mogilenko undoubtedly had informants scouring the city looking for him.

He also realized he'd been avoiding thinking about Alyona, the pouty blonde, so young and wannabe sexy in the photo and yet who already knew she was doomed. He hadn't wanted to think about it, but after being in the apartment and hearing what the neighbor woman had said, there was no escaping it.

The probability was that his visit to Gabrilov had triggered her death.

He was getting in very deep, very fast, feeling the drag as the train slowed, pulling into the Metro station, all modern lighting and arched white ceilings.

He came up the long escalator to street level. The Kyiv Metro was one of the deepest subways in the world. The sky outside had turned dark and threatening. Billboards and shop windows were already lit and power lines over the street swayed in the wind. Scorpion walked on a sidewalk trail in the snow, his collar pulled up against the wind. He spelled out the Cyrillic letters of FILOSTRO ELEKTRYCHNI, LTD. in the electric sign on top of a long brick building and went inside.

A young blond woman in a thick sweater looked up from behind a glass window.

"*Dobry den*," she said, opening a small window in the glass.

"*Zdrastvuitye*. I'm looking for the *shef*," he said in Russian. The manager.

She picked up the phone, and a few minutes a paunchy balding man in a sagging shirt and tie came to the front and said something in Ukrainian that Scorpion didn't understand.

"*Ya ishchu kogo-to*," Scorpion said in Russian. I'm looking for someone. "An employee. Sirhiy Pyatov."

"What you want with Pyatov?" the manager said in a broken English Scorpion was becoming accustomed to.

"He works here?"

"Not no more. I fire three weeks ago. I not see him in month, the *sooka suna*. You friend of him?"

Scorpion shook his head.

"*Kharasho*. Otherwise get out or I call *militsiyu* police," the manager said.

"Do you have an address for him?"

"What? He owe you money? *Na vse dobre!*" Good luck. The manager smirked.

"Can I get his address?"

The manager said something to the girl. She looked it up on her computer, scribbled something on a piece of paper and handed it to Scorpion.

"*Spasiba*," Scorpion said. Thanks.

"You see Pyatov, you tell him no come back. He don't work here no more," the manager said.

No, Scorpion thought. When I see him, I'll kill him.

His latest prepaid cell phone vibrated in his pocket. It was a text from Iryna. *Urgent we meet. Hurry!* she wrote, and specified an address in the Podil district.

When he stepped outside, it was snowing.

CHAPTER FOURTEEN

Podil
Kyiv, Ukraine

The night was very cold; the snow had stopped
falling. Scorpion huddled in the shadows near a
kiosk across from the building. He watched a red
and yellow tram go by, the light from its windows
reflected on the snow. He was supposed to meet
Iryna in an apartment above a pub in Podil, the old
river port and former Jewish district, on a street off
Kontraktova Ploscha, Contracts Square, but he was
about to call it off. He had spotted at least three
men in thick jackets covering the front entrance,
and there were probably more covering the back and
inside. He called her cell phone.

"*Pryvit*," she said, and at the sound of her voice he
imagined her tilting her head to the side to hold the
phone to her ear under a black curtain of hair.

"Get rid of your muscle with the guns. It's like a
mafia meeting in Vegas," he said.

"Someone wants to meet you. He needs protection. Besides, what if you're the—" She stopped

abruptly. He waited for her to say, *what if he was the assassin*, but she didn't.

"We both know that's not true," he said. "Besides, if I was the one . . ." He left the threat unfinished.

"Give me a minute," she said, and must have covered the phone because he heard only muffled sounds. "All right. Come up when it's clear," she said, coming back on the line.

He saw one of the men near the pub open his cell phone to answer a call. He hung up, then made more calls. Scorpion watched as two of the three men left their posts and went inside the pub. He waited another minute, then crossed to the front door.

"*U vas yest pistolet?*" the man with the cell phone said, asking in Russian if he had a gun.

"*Da,*" Scorpion said, handing him the Glock from the holster at the small of his back. "I want it back."

"*Bez bazaar,*" the man said, then thoroughly frisked him. When he was done, the man indicated that he should go up to the second floor.

Scorpion stepped into the lobby and took a narrow elevator to a single apartment that occupied the entire second floor. Slavo, the aide he had seen with Iryna, was waiting with a pair of *tapochki* house slippers. After Scorpion stepped across the threshold, Slavo handed him the *tapochki*, and Scorpion took off his street shoes and put them on. As was the custom, he left his shoes by the door and went in.

They were waiting for him in the dining room. Iryna was sitting at the table with a stocky middle-aged man with a shock of graying hair and a cleft chin. Scorpion immediately recognized him as

Viktor Kozhanovskiy from his posters and images on television. Kozhanovskiy got up to shake his hand. He did it like a politician, clasping Scorpion's hand with both of his as if to convey his deep friendship and sincerity. On the wall behind him a silent TV showed the lead news of the day: a fistfight in the Verkhovna Rada—the parliament—between members of Kozhanovskiy's party and supporters of Cherkesov, who were accusing Kozhanovskiy of corruption.

"Welcome, Mr. Kilbane. Will you have some tea?" Kozhanovskiy said in good English as Scorpion sat down.

"Why not?" Scorpion said. "But first . . ." He took out the handheld electronic sweep unit. "Do you mind?"

"We should do the same to you," Kozhanovskiy said. "Go ahead."

As Scorpion scanned for bugs, Iryna poured the tea into a *stekans*—a glass with a metal base and handle. When he completed the scan, he sat down. Iryna gestured that he should help himself to sugar, jam, or honey, and passed him a plate with *horishke* pastries and *bublyky*, almond cookies.

"Of course, we called Reuters in London," Kozhanovskiy said, pouring himself more tea and mixing in a teaspoon of jam. "It seems you are who you say you are."

"Nice to know," Scorpion said, thinking it was a good thing Shaefer had followed up. But the cover was thin, very thin.

"Iryna has briefed me. Firstly, has anyone seen

Alyona? None of our people seems to know anything."

"She was at the Black Cat, the café on Andriyivsky Uzviz, this morning. She was supposed to be in a play but hadn't shown for last night's performance. She told her fellow actors she couldn't be in the play anymore."

"They were concerned?" Kozhanovskiy asked.

"With good reason. Apparently, her boyfriend—this Sirhiy Pyatov—is abusive. She was afraid of him. She told them they were mixed up in something."

"Isn't he with the campaign?" Kozhanovskiy turned to Iryna.

She nodded. "Dirty tricks."

"Like what?" Scorpion asked.

"You have to understand, this is self-defense," Kozhanovskiy said, lighting a Marlboro Menthol. "The Cherkesov campaign paid someone to publish a story in *Sevodnya* that claimed I looted the treasury when I was Minister of Finance. Among other things, they've accused us of running a heroin ring out of our campaign headquarters, that I'm a puppet for the Americans, and even that I've fathered a secret love child with Iryna!"

"That's a better story than the assassination. Is it true?" Scorpion said.

Iryna looked directly at Scorpion. "I work with Viktor Ivanovych. I don't do it with my legs spread. *Gospadi!* To be taken seriously as a woman in this country isn't so simple."

"Iryna is a public figure in our country." Kozhanovskiy said. "And because she's beautiful, she gets more than her share of media attention, which is helpful to us. But trust me, her brain is more valuable to us than her looks."

"So what kind of dirty tricks did Pyatov do?" Scorpion asked Iryna.

"He created a false Facebook page supposedly of one of Cherkesov's officials named Makuch," she said. "It implied that Makuch is a pedophile. Pyatov also put out leaflets in Donetsk claiming Cherkesov is a homosexual. They put Photoshopped pictures of him in a woman's pink panties and bra on the Internet," a ghost of a smile on her lips. "He sent out notices in Kharkov oblast, an area we expect to go overwhelmingly for Cherkesov. They were supposedly from the Central Election Commission, telling people they hadn't registered properly and were not eligible to vote." She shrugged. "Things like that. They do the same to us."

"What else can you tell me about Pyatov?"

"In the beginning, he was useful, as I said. Then he stopped showing up. No one's seen him in two or three weeks."

"And neither of you has heard anything about an assassination plot?"

"Not till you showed up," Iryna said. She looked hard at Scorpion. "What's happened to Alyona? She's only been missing for a few hours. What aren't you telling me?"

She was good, Scorpion thought. Whoever judged her just on her looks underestimated her. She had that extraordinary combination of being cool, smart, and sharp that the Russians call *krutoy.*

"She's probably dead," he said, watching them. Kozhanovskiy stared at him, stunned. Iryna had to stifle a gasp. Either they were both great actors or he had caught them by surprise.

"What do you mean 'probably'?" Iryna said, taking a deep breath.

"There's no body. I entered her apartment. There were traces of blood in the bed and in the shower. I found a hacksaw from Pyatov's work hidden under the sink, its blade missing. The hacksaw frame had traces of blood. Her neighbor told me sometime around noon there were screams and sounds of a quarrel and the *televidenie* got very loud. Later, she saw Pyatov leave alone with a big suitcase on wheels."

"*Gospadi*," Iryna said softly, almost to herself. My God.

"What about Pyatov?" Kozhanovskiy asked. "Does anyone know where he is now?"

"I checked at his work," Scorpion said. "They haven't seen him in three weeks."

"You've been busy," Iryna said, looking at him with those intense blue eyes with a tinge, he could swear, of real interest, as if seeing him for the first time.

"If Pyatov killed Alyona, it means . . ." Kozhanovskiy began.

"*Tak*, yes—it means he couldn't trust her," she said. "The assassination plot could be real."

"Pyatov worked for us!" Kozhanovskiy said. "The media will crucify us! It's a disaster."

"It's worse than that," Iryna replied, her fist

clenched on the table. "If the Russians think we killed Cherkesov, they'll invade. It's the end of Ukraine!"

"NATO will have to do some—" he started to say.

"Nichivo!" she snapped. Nothing! "NATO will make noise and the UN will tsk-tsk; the Europeans will cluck and the Americans will shake their fingers and say, 'Shame on Russia,' and they—will—do—nothing," she concluded, enunciating each word.

Kozhanovskiy looked at her. "We should call the *politsiy*."

"Before we find out who else might be implicated?" she said. "And what if they arrest us? On the eve of the election! Half the *politsiy* are crooks and the other half are working for Cherkesov!"

"What can we do?" he asked.

"We have to stop Pyatov," she said.

"How do we even know he's the assassin?" Kozhanovskiy growled. "All we know is what this *journalist*," indicating Scorpion and using the word like a curse, "is telling us. We have no idea who he is."

"Alyona's friends, the actors at the Black Cat," Scorpion said, "told me that three weeks ago Pyatov came into money. They said he had a big deal going. The same time he stopped showing up for work."

"The same time he stopped working for us," Iryna murmured.

"They said he was Syndikat," Scorpion added. "They were afraid of him."

"Sooka suna, it fits," Kozhanovskiy cursed. He looked at Iryna. "Now what?"

She took a sip of tea, eyeing Scorpion.

"Mr. Kilbane, you mean to track Pyatov down, don't you? We couldn't stop you if we wanted to, could we?"

"Wherever the story takes me," he said.

"Yes," Kozhanovskiy put in. "Where exactly do you fit in all of this, Mr. Kilbane? This doesn't seem to be normal journalism."

Scorpion shrugged. "My definition of 'normal' is pretty elastic. I promised Iryna I wouldn't print the story till I had the facts."

"Your word!" Kozhanovskiy said, stubbing his cigarette out in the ashtray. "Can we trust him?" he asked Iryna.

"Of course not!" she snapped. "If he's going after Pyatov, one of us has to go too. And it can't be you, so it has to be me."

"I haven't agreed to any of this," Scorpion said.

"Just tell me. Do you really think Pyatov will be at Cherkesov's rally in Dnipropetrovsk?" she asked.

"It was your idea," Scorpion said. "Nighttime, a big stadium with a clear shot and multiple exits, crowds, chaos. Like you said, it's perfect."

"I don't like this," Kozhanovskiy said to her.

"We can't let Kilbane go off on his own. It's too important," she said.

Scorpion started to get up. "You two will want to talk this over," he said.

"Kilbane, stay. Please," Kozhanovskiy said, holding his hand up. "I know this isn't your country, but there are millions of lives at stake." He turned to Iryna. "What about one of the others? Slavo? Misha?"

"We don't know how far this goes. No one else must know," she said.

"Forget it. I work alone," Scorpion said.

"You think I'm not tough enough," Iryna said, fishing in her handbag. She pulled out a small Beretta Storm 9mm pistol and showed it to them.

Scorpion smiled. "You know how to use that?"

"My father took me hunting in the Carpathian Mountains from the time I was a little girl," she said, putting the gun back. "I'm a pretty good shot."

"Yes, but are you willing to use it?" he asked quietly.

"You really don't understand, Mr. Kilbane." She smiled oddly. "We members of the upper class like to kill things. It's our way of proving we're tough enough to deserve our privileges."

"What about the campaign?" Kozhanovskiy said. "You don't have the time. We need you." He looked at her. "I need you."

"What choice do we have? Besides," she grimaced, "Slavo is dying to take my place. You won't be sorry. He's very good."

"Not like you," Kozhanovskiy said.

"People look at me, they see my father. To be the child of a great man is to be an afterthought." She looked down at her plate.

Kozhanovskiy glanced at his watch, then stood up. "I have an interview on Inter TV," he said. "What about Pyatov? And him?" indicating Scorpion.

Iryna got up as well. "I'll handle it," she said, air-kissing Kozhanovskiy once on each cheek.

"Are you sure?"

"No. But I have to try," she said, brushing off his suit jacket with her hand.

"All right," he said, going to the closet. "From now on this is your only assignment. Slavo!" he called out as he pulled on his fur hat and overcoat, then said to Iryna, "Keep me posted," and to Scorpion, whose hand he shook before he left the room, "*Buvay*, Mr. Kilbane. You are quite a reporter. Only two days in Ukraina," shaking his head. "I've never met one like you."

Scorpion watched him talking in rapid-fire Ukrainian to Slavo and two of his bodyguards who stood outside the apartment door. They all left together. When he looked back, Iryna was watching him.

"Just so you know," she said, holding her cell phone in her hand. "I don't give a tinker's damn what Reuters says. I don't trust you even one centimeter. You don't act like a journalist. You have no interest in politics or in interviewing me or Viktor Kozhanovskiy. A real reporter would've jumped at the chance. Who the bloody hell are you?"

 **CHAPTER FIFTEEN**

Centralny Vokzal
Kyiv, Ukraine

They spent the night in a first-class sleeper compartment on the overnight train to Dnipropetrovsk. Two beds narrow as coffins and facing benches so close, if they both sat at the same time, their knees were touching. The curtains were drawn over a window caked with ice as the train rocked across the countryside in the darkness.

Iryna had changed into wool clothes, a synthetic down overcoat, and a woolen hat pulled down over a curly blond wig. When she met him on the freezing platform of the Central Station, he had barely recognized her. She gave him a start because in the blond wig, she looked like Alyona in the pouty photo. She could have been any pretty Ukrainian blonde. Scorpion had changed his image too. Instead of a suit and overcoat, he wore a heavy sweater, jeans, ski jacket, and a wool cap. Designed so no one would give him a second glance.

Back at the apartment over the pub she had asked him: "Who the bloody hell are you?"

"I'm exactly who you think I am," he'd told her.

"Are you CIA?"

He shook his head.

"How do I know you're not working for the other side?"

"Anyone who speaks Russian as badly as I do couldn't possibly be working for the other side." He paused. "Why didn't you tell Kozhanovskiy?"

"You know why."

"To protect the campaign? Is that what this is?" he asked. "Trying to live up to Daddy?"

"Self-preservation," she replied, shaking her head. "You said it yourself when you first came to see me. The trail leads back to me."

Now, settled in the compartment, they didn't talk about what happened on the train platform.

A crowd of about twenty tough-looking men wearing black armbands began grabbing people. They let some alone and shouted at others. Then all at once fighting broke out. A group of the men with armbands surrounded a man with his wife. They manhandled the woman aside and began beating the man with their fists. He fell to the platform. One of the men took out a workman's hammer, and the man screamed as his hands and knees were smashed with the hammer. The assailant continued to hit him in the face with the hammer, while the other men crowded around and kicked him as he lay on the platform.

Three of the men with armbands had come up to Scorpion and Iryna.

"*Cherkesov abo Kozhanovskiy?*" one of them asked.

Scorpion grabbed Iryna's arm.

"*My z Kanady*," Scorpion had said—We're from Canada—meanwhile staring at the men savagely kicking the fallen man on the platform whose face was bleeding and who could no longer protect himself.

The man questioning Scorpion had followed his glance.

"*Ne khvylyuy tesya*," he said. "*Vin prosto Zhid.*" Don't concern yourself, he's just a Jew, waving it off. Scorpion felt Iryna start to move forward and tightened his grip on her arm.

"Remember why we're here," he whispered to her, turning them away from the beating.

In the train, the female *suputnikh* brought them tea and biscuits. Iryna lit a Dunhill cigarette, her fingers trembling. For a long time neither of them spoke. It was warm inside the car, and Scorpion took off his heavy sweater.

"Maybe we're on a fool's errand. We should let him kill Cherkesov," Iryna said finally, meaning Pyatov.

"Is war better?"

"I don't know," she said, looking away. "He hasn't been elected yet and look what he's doing. I'm watching my country commit suicide."

"It isn't pretty," he said.

They sipped tea and listened to the rhythm of the wheels on the track.

"What will you do when we get to Dnipropetrovsk?" she asked.

"I assume you have someone undercover with the Cherkesov campaign?"

She nodded. "You won't tell me anything about yourself?"

"What about you? Are you married?"

She shook her head. "Not anymore. He was older. Like my father."

"What happened?"

"He wanted a pretty ornament. I outgrew it—him. I'm nobody's anything," she said, tossing her hair. "Your father? What was he like?" she asked.

"I hardly knew him," Scorpion said. "We'd only been together about a week, then he died. I was four." He was surprised to find himself telling her the truth. She had that effect on him, or perhaps it was the compartment, the intimacy of it: the one overhead light, the darkness outside, the rocking of the train detached from the rest of the world.

"What about your mother?" she asked.

"She was already dead. They'd been separated."

"So who raised you?"

He thought about Arabia. The hot days and starry nights and Sheikh Zaid, the closest thing to a father he'd ever had. He thought about the Mutayr, the Bedouin tribe that saved him from the Saar and took him in, and his strange Arabian Huck Finn childhood and the paths it had taken had somehow brought him to Ukraine in the dead of winter.

"It's a long story," he said.

"It's four hundred kilometers to Dnipropetrovsk," Iryna replied, folding her arms.

He looked at his watch. It was past one in the morning. The train would be arriving in five hours.

"We should sleep," he said, pulling off his T-shirt.

Her eyes widened at the sight of his lean, muscled torso. The scars on his arms and ribs.

"How'd you get those?" she asked.

"I tripped," he said. He got into the narrow bunk and put his forearm over his eyes to block the overhead light. He heard the swish of her clothes as she undressed. He couldn't help thinking about that. She shut the light and he heard her get into her bunk. All he could see in the darkness was the glowing tip of her cigarette. For a time neither of them spoke.

"Whoever you are, I'm glad you're on our side," she said. It sounded like she had rolled on her side toward him. It was strange, talking like this in the darkness. He could almost feel the warmth of her body pulling at him from across the narrow space between them, and more viscerally, the tingle in his groin.

"I'm on no one's side," he said. "Our interests coincide, that's all."

"*Gospadi*, you're cold."

"No," he said after a moment.

"What then?"

"Honest. Or as honest as someone who lies for a living can be."

"What's going to happen when we get to Dnipropetrovsk?"

"Someone's going to die."

A few minutes later, "You're not what I expected. Michael . . . ?" she whispered.

There was no answer.

Scorpion was asleep.

 **CHAPTER SIXTEEN**

Dnipropetrovsk
Ukraine

Dnipropetrovsk was hidden when they pulled in. A thick frost covered the window, and when they stepped off the train, a yellowish smog obscured the skyline. The platform was icy cold after the warmth of the train.

"It's from the smokestacks," Iryna explained as they pulled their luggage toward the station building, their breaths visible puffs in the icy air. "Dnipropetrovsk is a big industrial city."

Scorpion's stomach tightened at the sight of three *militsiyu* police standing by the entrance to the station. Nearby, he saw a half-dozen men wearing the black armbands they had seen at the station in Kyiv. These armbands had a yellow Ukrainian cross: a double crossbar on top and a slanted crossbar near the bottom, where Christ's feet would have been nailed. It gave them the appearance of a religious order. They were passing out leaflets, shoving anyone who didn't take one. The police did not appear concerned about the men with the armbands.

As they passed, Scorpion took one of the hand-outs, a crude leaflet that Iryna translated for him. It accused Kozhanovskiy of theft of the national treasury and of being a tool of the United States and the Zionists. The other side was an invitation to the Cherkesov rally that night at Stadion Dnipro, the soccer stadium. The eyes of the man who handed him the leaflet lingered on Iryna, and Scorpion felt a chill at the thought that he might have recognized her. He watched them as Scorpion hustled her through the station hall and into a taxi outside.

"Grand Hotel Ukraina," she told the driver, and in response to Scorpion's look, whispered to him in English, "I know. That Black Armband recognized me."

The taxi made a turn into a broad avenue lined with trees, their limbs bare. The street snow had turned to slush from the traffic; the sidewalks were still under snow.

"Pyatov has only two choices," Scorpion whispered back, his lips brushing her ear. "Either he'll try to work his way into the campaign to get close, or use a Syndikat contact. Also, how is he going to kill him? Using a gun at close range is the equivalent of committing suicide. He doesn't strike me as the type."

"Me either."

"So it's either a long range rifle, which requires a certain preparation and expertise, or explosives, or something else. I'm betting something else."

"What do we do?" she asked.

"You contact your campaign mole. I'll work other

angles. Here," he said, handing her one of their new prepaid cell phones and turning his on. He had gotten rid of their previous phones and SIM cards on the train by flushing them down the filthy toilet at the end of the sleeping car, and put in contact numbers so they could call each other. "Only use once and then discard," he cautioned.

"Look," she whispered. They were passing an office building with a giant banner sign that announced: ЧЕРКЕСОВ ДЛЯ ПРЕЗИДЕНТА КАМПАНІЇ ОФІСУ. Scorpion laboriously spelled out the Cyrillic lettering: Cherkesov for President Campaign Office. Two men in the black armbands with the yellow crosses were passing out leaflets in the street.

"*Chort bandytiv!*" the taxi driver said, meaning the Black Armbands.

"What did he say?" Scorpion asked her.

"He called them filthy thugs! This has to stop," she said, half to herself.

"*Astanavityes,*" he told the taxi driver in Russian. Stop here. The cab pulled over, double parking. Horns immediately started honking behind them.

"Where are you going?" she asked.

"To find Pyatov," he whispered.

"We'll meet later?"

Scorpion nodded. "Don't do anything stupid— that means heroic. I'll call," he told her as he got out.

"*Yid' te dali,*" she said to the driver, motioning him to go on.

Scorpion watched the taxi pull away, the wheels skidding in the slush. He climbed over snow, its surface black with soot between parked cars, and walked through the snow to the campaign office. One of the Black Armbands in front of the office handed him a leaflet, but then blocked his way as he tried to go in.

The Black Armband said something to him in Ukrainian. Scorpion showed him his Reuters ID.

"*Ya zhurnalist iz Anglii,*" he explained in Russian. I'm a journalist from England. "I must to speak to the *nachalnik,*" the boss.

The Black Armband squinted at his ID, clearly unable to read the Latin lettering. He jerked his head for Scorpion to go inside.

The office was crowded with people talking, working at computers, on the phones. It could have been a campaign office anywhere. Scorpion spoke to four people before someone handed him off to a young woman who took him up the stairs to a tiny second-floor office.

"You are from England! *Laskavo prosymo!*" Welcome, a burly man in a shirt and tie called out. A cardboard sign in Cyrillic lettering on his desk spelled out his name: IHOR OLIYNYK. Although it was only eight-thirty in the morning, the man put a bottle of Khortytsya *horilka* and two glasses on the desk. He too wore one of the black armbands. He poured the vodka and they raised their glasses.

"*Za zdorowya!*" Oliynyk toasted.

"*Bod'mo!*" Scorpion toasted back, and they drank.

As Oliynyk refilled their glasses, Scorpion handed him his business card.

"What can I do for a friend from the Reuters

agency of England?" Oliynyk asked, glancing at the card and putting it in his pocket.

"I'm looking for someone," Scorpion said, fishing out a photo of Pyatov that Iryna had had Photoshopped from a group picture. He handed it to Oliynyk.

"I never see him before." Oliynyk shrugged, tossing the photo on the desk.

"I need to talk to Pan Cherkesov."

"This close to the election. Impossible!"

"I need to speak to him now, today. Can you arrange it?"

"What is this about?"

"I'm a reporter. I have a story that could change the election. Before I print it, I need to talk to Cherkesov."

"Talk to me," Oliynyk said. "I'll pass it on to him."

Scorpion shook his head. "There isn't time. Come with me if you like, but I have to see him at once."

"What is this?" Oliynyk stared at Scorpion. "You want money? Is that what this is?"

Scorpion stood. "I'm obviously wasting your time. This is how elections are lost," he said, taking back the photo and starting to leave.

"Wait!" Oliynyk called. "What is this story?"

"Come with me and find out," Scorpion said, stopping at the door.

"Let me see the photograph again," Oliynyk said, motioning. Scorpion handed it back. "This man?" He looked at Scorpion. "Is he dangerous?"

"What do you think?"

"*Hivno*," Oliynyk cursed. He got up and grabbed his scarf, hat, and overcoat. "Come with me," he said, taking Scorpion's arm. "But if this is not legitimate, believe me, I would not want to be you if Gorobets gets his hands on you."

"Who's Gorobets?" Scorpion asked as they pulled on their outerwear. Oliynyk nodded to two Black Armbands who came with them, both obviously armed, their hands in their overcoat pockets. They waited in the street in front of the office, the wind whipping at their clothes. A red and white tram whirred by, its roof covered with snow.

"He's a power in the party," Oliynyk said. "Close to Cherkesov. Among other things, he's the father of the Chorni Povyazky." The Black Armbands.

A black Audi A8 pulled over. Scorpion took a deep breath before he got in. For the second time in barely thirty hours he was getting into a car with men who might try to kill him.

"So who is this man?" Oliynyk asked in the car, handing the photo back to Scorpion.

"His name is Sirhiy Pyatov."

"And why should he concern us?"

"Not here," Scorpion said, indicating the other men. They drove in silence. There was a sense of menace in the car. These were violent men, Scorpion thought. They longed for violence the way other men longed for a woman.

"You want see Gorobets?" The Black Armband in the front passenger seat asked him in English.

"*Da*," Scorpion said.

The Black Armband who was driving said something in Ukrainian, and the one next to him in the passenger seat laughed.

"What did he say?" Scorpion asked Oliynyk.

Oliynyk smirked. "He say Gorobets don't like what you say, you dancing with Shelayev."

"Who's he?" Scorpion asked.

"He is Gorobets's protector man. How you say in Angliskiy?"

"Bodyguard."

"*Da*," Oliynyk nodded. "One time man with cane attack Gorobets in Verkhovna Rada. Shelayev could stop easy, but *nyet*. He take man's skull one hand and squeeze," making a squeezing motion with his fingers. "Break skull like egg."

"*Kak khorosho*," Scorpion murmured. How nice. He looked out the window. The day was dark, the sky slate gray, and even though it was morning, shop and office windows were already lit. He wondered what in hell he was doing, trying to save this Cherkesov son of a bitch. *Rabinowich and Shaefer. They want me here*, he told himself. There was more to this than a Ukrainian election.

They pulled up in front of a modern-style hotel just off Karl Marx Prospekt, the city's main street, got out and went inside in a group. There were at least a dozen Black Armbands armed to the teeth in the lobby. They took an elevator to the top floor, where a group of Black Armbands stood guard outside a suite. The guards started to frisk everyone, and Scorpion took out his Glock. He removed the ammunition clip and handed the gun to Oliynyk.

"What's this for?" Oliynyk asked him.

"Protection. Even in England, we've heard of the Cassette Scandal," Scorpion said, referring to a notorious case from 2000 when the then Ukrainian president, Kuchma, was accused of arranging the kidnapping of a journalist whose body was later found beheaded. "I'll want it back when we leave."

A Black Armband frisked Scorpion, and Oliynyk knocked at the door. When it opened, they went inside.

The hotel suite had been turned into an office, with desks, telephones, and computers jammed in. There were more than a dozen men and women working. A bank of TVs mounted on the wall showed every Ukrainian channel plus Russian ORT and CNN.

A heavyset bald man in shirtsleeves and wearing horn-rim glasses stood in the center of the room talking to a young woman, who nodded and went to her desk. He looked like the uncle who tells a dirty joke at a family gathering, Scorpion thought, and could see that the way the others treated him, he was clearly the *nachalnik*—the boss.

"This is Gorobets," Oliynyk said to Scorpion, and began talking rapid-fire in Ukrainian to the heavyset man, who didn't respond. Oliynyk paused, began again, and Gorobets made a slight gesture, waving him away.

"You are from England?" Gorobets said in English to Scorpion. Although accented, his voice was soft and very clear. A whisperer's voice, Scorpion thought.

"Canadian," Scorpion said. "I work out of the Reuters office in London."

"You have ID?" Gorobets asked.

Scorpion showed him his press pass. Gorobets peered nearsightedly at it. His eyes, magnified behind the glasses, were strange, like blue glacier ice.

"What is this about?"

"I need to talk to Cherkesov. It's urgent."

"It always is." Gorobets allowed himself a thin smile. "Yuriy Dmytrovych is not available. You will have to talk to me or—" He hesitated.

"Or?"

"Nothing. You will have to talk to me."

Scorpion glanced around. "Not in all this crowd," he said.

Gorobets glanced at one of his aides, a tall man with thick sandy hair, who shouted something. Within seconds the room was cleared of everyone except two Black Armbands. One of them was a heavily muscled type over six-three, with long blond rocker hair. By the way he held himself, Scorpion would've bet that he was Spetsnaz-trained. Shelayev. The guy who crushed heads like eggshells.

More impressive than that was the way everyone had obeyed, without Gorobets having to say a word. It was unmistakable, Scorpion thought. Gorobets was feared.

"You have thirty seconds," Gorobets said, looking at his watch. "After that, you can talk to Shelayev," indicating the Spetsnaz type.

"May I?" Scorpion said. He reached into his pocket and pulled out Pyatov's photo. "I've been tracking this story since I got to Ukraine. This man," tapping the photo, "plans to kill Cherkesov."

"So?" Gorobets shrugged.

"You're not impressed? Suit yourself," he said, starting to turn away.

"We get one or two of these threats a week, Mr. Kilbane. Why should I take this one more seriously than the others?"

"Because it is. This man," indicating the photograph, "his name is Sirhiy Pyatov, may have already killed his girlfriend to cover it up. He worked for the Kozhanovskiy campaign."

"So!" Gorobets's eyebrows went up a notch. "That's more interesting."

"Not really. You'd blame anything on Kozhanovskiy. If something happens, you need me, a Reuters independent, to make it credible."

"Perhaps." Gorobets shrugged. "When is this 'assassination' supposed to take place?"

"Tonight."

"At the rally?"

Scorpion nodded. "Have any of your people seen this man?"

"And you are helping us because . . . you have sympathy for our cause or some great love for the Ukrainian people?"

"You know perfectly well I don't give a *govno* shit about your cause or the Ukrainian people. Whether Pyatov kills Cherkesov or you kill Pyatov, I just want the story," Scorpion said.

"Or perhaps this is a plot to infiltrate us. Anyone can have an ID," Gorobets said. "How do I know you are not working for Kozhanovskiy or one of the Western powers? CIA? MI-6? Why not let you discuss it with Mr. Shelayev," indicating the big blond skull-crusher staring at him coldly, "and see if he can convince you to be more forthcoming?"

"Because it won't solve your problem. I gave my Glock to Pan Oliynyk. Here's the magazine," he said, taking out the clip to show him. He sensed Shelayev tensing, ready to move. "If I were the danger, I wouldn't have given it to him, I would've used it. You'd be dead now. Go on, check."

Gorobets looked at Scorpion in a way that made him understand why people were so afraid of him. Gorobets tapped his cell phone and spoke into it briefly. Suddenly, he was all smiles, the friendly uncle. Now he's really dangerous, Scorpion thought.

"I'm very grateful, Mr. Kilbane. You've done us a great service. I apologize for my suspicions," he said, putting a friendly hand on Scorpion's shoulder. "May I keep this photograph?" not handing it back. Fortunately, Iryna had made copies for him.

"Yes."

"We will check to see if anyone from the campaign has seen this Pyatov. Of course, we'll check you out too," Gorobets said, handing the photograph to Shelayev. "If I learn anything, I'll call you. Give me your cell number," still smiling.

"Give me yours. I'll call you."

"Afraid we'll track you? Not very trusting, are you?" Gorobets said, still smiling.

"Something we have in common," Scorpion said. He turned to go.

"A moment," Gorobets called after him. "Kilbane, that's a British name?"

"Irish," Scorpion said, turning back.

"Catholic?"

"Not in a long time."

"But you believe in sin, original sin?" watching Scorpion closely.

"There's plenty of it around. Everywhere you look," staring directly back at Gorobets, who smiled again, looking at him the way a scientist might look at an interesting laboratory specimen.

"I'm sure we'll see each other again, Mr. Kilbane. You'll come to the rally? I'll arrange a pass."

"Wouldn't miss it," Scorpion said.

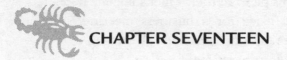

CHAPTER SEVENTEEN

Kharkovskaya
Dnipropetrovsk, Ukraine

"Why are we meeting here?" Iryna asked. They were in a booth at the Paradise, a strip club on Kharkovskaya near the Dnieper River. By her tone, Scorpion could tell she was annoyed. On the street outside, it was growing dark, the wind whipping snow and grit from factory smokestacks into the faces of passersby. Inside the club, except for the spotlights on two completely nude women onstage, it was so dark it was almost impossible to see.

"No one would look for you here," he said. "Besides, this is a Syndikat club. I had to be here to meet somebody."

"Why?"

"Assume we're right; Pyatov is the assassin. If you were him, how would you go about it? We agreed he's not the suicide type, so no bomber vests or close-up shooting, where he gets gunned down by Black Armbands. There's nothing in his background to suggest sniper expertise, and explosives are tricky and unreliable. Even if they work, you don't always get the right person. But I had to make sure that wasn't his plan. Earlier, I met someone here."

"Odd place for a business meeting," she said, checking out the dancers on the stage.

"Not for these types."

"What types?"

"He's called 'Bohdan.' "

"Bohdan what?"

"Just 'Bohdan.' These types don't have last names. He's what the *blatnoi* call a *makler*—a fixer."

"I've heard the term," she said. "Why do you need him?"

"If anyone was going to be getting a high-powered rifle or explosives through the Syndikat here in Dnipropetrovsk, he would know."

"And?"

"Nothing." Scorpion shook his head.

"Do you believe him?"

"Hard to say, but I offered him enough money and came well-recommended enough, which means dangerous enough, that he had every reason to tell me."

"Did he believe you?"

"He believed my money," he replied, not telling her how it had actually gone down.

He had met Bohdan at the same table two hours earlier, and assumed the man was known here. Bohdan was short, with ferretlike features and dark little eyes that darted about constantly, never still. He had a nervous tic of rubbing his fingers together as if continually signaling money. Scorpion had used Mogilenko's name, implying to Bohdan that he was an out-of-town hit man brought in by the Syndikat's Mogilenko, and that Bohdan better tell him the truth or he would be the target instead of Pyatov.

"They say Mogilenko looks for a foreigner, a Frenchie," Bohdan had told Scorpion, counting the money he'd given him faster than a bank machine. "He's *ochen serdit*." Really angry. "Says he will chop pieces from this Frenchie and feed it to his cat every day for a year. They look everywhere."

"That so?"

"Foreigner like you," Bohdan said, counting the money a second time.

"Good thing I'm not French," Scorpion said, reaching for his pocketknife.

"For you, very good," Bohdan agreed, his fingers making the sign for money again, Scorpion putting another thousand *hryvnia* on the table. When Bohdan reached for it, Scorpion pierced the back of his hand with his pocketknife, trapping it on the table.

"I'm a Kiwi," Scorpion said.

"What's that?" Bohdan asked, wincing.

"From New Zealand. Good to remember."

"Sure," Bohdan said, wincing again. "Wherever the *yob* that is."

"Far away."

"I understand. *Vy ne frantsuzy*," you are not French, Bohdan said in Russian.

Scorpion pulled the knife out and put it away. He called one of the girls over and asked for a handkerchief. If Bohdan holding his hand bleeding was an unusual sight here, she didn't say anything about it.

"So did he tell you anything, this *makler*?" Iryna

asked now, raising her voice. The music was blaring so loud it was hard for them to hear each other.

"Not much," Scorpion said. "No one's bought a high-powered rifle or explosives in the past week. What about your mole?"

"She saw Pyatov yesterday."

"Where?"

"Cherkesov's hotel. The lobby."

"The one on Voroghilov Street?" Cherkesov's Dnipropetrovsk headquarters; where Scorpion had met with Gorobets.

"Mmm," she nodded, lighting a cigarette, the match flaring in the darkness.

"What else?"

"She doesn't know. If he's not going to use a rifle or explosives, how's he going to do it?"

"With this," Scorpion said, taking one of the black armbands with the yellow Ukrainian cross out of his pocket.

Iryna looked at him, her eyes reflecting the light from the stage in the darkness.

"Where'd you get that?" she asked.

"From Oliynyk, one of their campaign leaders here. I'm their pal, their *drooh*."

"Are you?" she said, and he could hear the fear in her voice.

"Don't be stupid."

According to the TV and Internet, there had been street fighting all over Ukraine between supporters of Kozhanovskiy and the Black Armbands. In Kyiv and Dnipropetrovsk, Black Armbands had smashed Jewish shop windows. In Kharkov, three

students and one Black Armband had been killed in
a riot near the National University. Scorpion had
seen it on TV that afternoon at the car rental shop
where he'd rented a BMW 328i all-wheel-drive in
case he needed a getaway through the snow from
the stadium.

"They should shoot them all," the car rental
manager had said, referring to the TV.

"Who?" Scorpion had asked.

"Those *studentov*," meaning the students sup-
porting Kozhanovskiy. "All they do is make trouble.
They should get a job, have to work like every Vasja
Pupkin, instead of all the time marching, making
trouble. Am I right, *bratan*?" meaning bro, clapping
Scorpion on the shoulder.

Later, trying out the BMW's AWD on the slushy
streets on the way to his RDV at the Paradise Club,
he had seen groups of Black Armbands brandish-
ing clubs and spoiling for a fight heading toward
Maidan Zhovtneva, October Square, the main
square in Dnipropetrovsk.

"We have to fight them," Iryna said, sitting next
to him in the club. "If we let the Chorni Povyazky
go unopposed, people will be afraid to even show up
to vote."

"I don't think you should come to the stadium,"
Scorpion said.

"Now who's being stupid?" Iryna said. "All you've
got is a photo and a hunch. I've seen Pyatov. Hell, I
was the one who hired him! You need me. Anyway,
it's settled. I'm coming."

"You're too well known. How long do you think

it'll be before someone in the crowd recognizes you?"

"I brought these," she said, taking black plastic-rimmed glasses out of her handbag and putting them on. "What do you think?"

With her blond wig and bright red lipstick, he thought it made her look like a schoolteacher moonlighting as a hooker.

"Perfect if you want to give blowjobs to professors," he said. "Go back to the campaign, Iryna. Now, while you still can."

"No," she said softly. He had to strain over the loudspeaker music to hear her. "This is my fight, my country. If you don't let me come, I'll take off the disguise and walk in there openly."

In spite of the glasses, Scorpion could see the bravery shining in her eyes. She's bluffing, he thought. Or crazy. Either way, she was a hell of a woman. He couldn't just leave her as a loose end. He waved at one of the dancers with a surgically enhanced chest, wearing nothing but a G-string the size of dental floss. When she came over, he ordered Nemiroff for both of them.

"What's this?" Iryna asked when the dancer brought the drinks.

"Might as well, because the odds are we're both going to die tonight. You, almost certainly."

"In that case, *za zdorowya ta scasty vam!*" she toasted. Health and good luck.

"We'll need it," Scorpion said.

 **CHAPTER EIGHTEEN**

Stadion Dnipro
Dnipropetrovsk, Ukraine

It was dark when they arrived at Dnipro Stadium. Scorpion parked the BMW on a side street. If they needed to get away, he didn't want to be tied up in a parking lot. If anything went wrong, they'd meet at the car, he explained. They walked on icy sidewalks toward the stadium. Iryna was bundled up in a heavy outer coat and hood. Only a few yellow curls of her wig were visible under the hood, and with her glasses and lipstick, she'd be hard to recognize, Scorpion thought. But it was still iffy.

The street became crowded as they approached the Khersonska Street entrance. They were joined by more and more people heading to the stadium. *Militsiyu* police outside the stadium entrance watched the crowd pouring in. Vendors sold hand-held blue and yellow Ukrainian flags and small black flags with the yellow Ukrainian cross, while Black Armbands near the gate handed out signs for people to carry. The signs read: HET KOZHANOVSKIY, Down with Kozhanovskiy; CHERKESOV MAYBUTN

OMU, Cherkesov is the future; and CHERKESOV DLYA PREZYDENTA, Cherkesov for President.

Scorpion bought one of the Ukrainian flags and handed it to Iryna. A Black Armband tried to hand him a sign. Scorpion shook him off.

"*Zhurnalist*," he said, pointing to his Reuters badge that he wore on the lanyard outside his coat. They joined the crowd pressing through the gate.

"*Khay zhyve Cherkesov!*" Long live Cherkesov! one of them shouted, and people around them cheered and clapped. Scorpion and Iryna made their way up a staircase and along a ramp. They came through an opening and into the oval stadium filling with people and more pouring in.

The snow on the playing field had been cleared away. Thousands of people were sitting on chairs on the field and microphones and lights had been set up on a stage in the middle. A giant TV screen showed patriotic images: the gold-domed churches of Kyiv, the Carpathian mountains in spring, peasant girls in costume, the Ukrainian flag, Ukrainian soldiers goose-stepping to the sounds of military music. Around the field, Black Armbands guided people to their seats or scanned the stands for trouble.

"Not here," Scorpion said to Iryna, pulling her toward an exit. Pyatov wasn't going to take a pot-shot from the stands, and trying to pick him out of tens of thousands of people was next to impossible. Pyatov would try to get close to Cherkesov, Scorpion thought, but in a place where he had a chance to get away. He and Iryna made their way back down the stairs against the flow of people still coming in and toward one of the entrances to the field. A half-dozen Black Armbands blocked the way.

"Ask him where Oleksandr Gorobets is," he whispered to Iryna. "We're supposed to be his guests. You're my translator." A Black Armband who was missing several teeth stood in front of them.

She told the Black Armband. He peered at Scorpion.

"*Khto vy?*" he asked. Who are you?

"*Zhurnalist* Reuters," Scorpion said, holding up his ID and pointing to it.

The Black Armband said something.

"He says Gorobets will be on the platform, but we are not allowed," Iryna translated.

"Ask him which entrance Cherkesov will be coming in," Scorpion said.

Iryna translated. The Black Armband responded and pointed to an entrance to the field to the right of where they were.

"*Spasiba*," Scorpion said and tugged Iryna away. They made their way around the ground level under the stands toward the tunnel entrance. As they walked, they heard an immense cheer from the crowd.

"Cherkesov! Cherkesov! Cherkesov!" the crowd shouted. They began to stamp their feet in unison, shaking the stands like a storm. The roar continued for at least five minutes.

Suddenly, a voice rang out over the loudspeaker: "*Ukraintsi!*"

The crowd exploded in cheers and applause. Scorpion and Iryna approached the tunnel entrance. In a small parking area outside the entrance, he spotted a number of Mercedes sedans and Mercedes GL SUVs.

"Why here?" Iryna asked. They could hear Cherkesov on the loudspeaker now.

"Pyatov will have to get reasonably close to Cherkesov," Scorpion explained. "He's not going to do it from the stands. He might miss and anyone around him could mess it up. The stage is too well guarded, and even if he succeeded, he'd never get away. His best bet is an entryway or exit, like with the Bobby Kennedy assassination."

"So how does he get away?"

"He'll be a Black Armband. He's banking on the confusion. Everyone'll be shooting."

The gate was closed, and a dozen armed Black Armbands stood guard at the tunnel entrance. As they approached, they peered past the guards into the tunnel.

"Oh my God," Iryna gasped. "I see him."

Scorpion spotted Pyatov in the tunnel. He was wearing a hooded jacket with the hood up and a black armband. But it was Pyatov, all right.

"Get out of here. Wait by the car," Scorpion said, pushing her away.

"I'm not going. If you make a scene, they'll stop you," meaning the Black Armbands.

"Last chance," Scorpion said as they approached the tunnel gate.

"For you too," she said, taking his arm.

"Give them the same story. Reuters, we're guests of Gorobets," Scorpion said.

As they approached the gate, one of the Black Armbands called out something.

"He says this entrance is not for the public," Iryna whispered, putting on a broad smile and answering in Ukrainian. A Black Armband the size of an offensive lineman stepped forward to stop them.

"*Vy zhurnalist?*" he asked, peering at Scorpion.

"*Da, s Reuters v Anglii,*" Scorpion said in Russian, holding out his press ID.

"*Khto vy?*" a second Black Armband asked Iryna. Who are you? He peered at her oddly, and Scorpion got a queasy feeling. Clearly, he saw something familiar about her.

Iryna rattled off something quickly. Probably the same story, that she was his translator. The second Black Armband checked his laptop and said something to the others.

"You're on the list," she whispered to Scorpion as two of the Black Armbands opened the gate and let them enter the tunnel, where a dozen or so people, most with press credentials and cameras, waited.

Scorpion moved ahead of Iryna. He didn't want Pyatov, who wasn't looking at them, to see her. Like the others, he was staring out to the brightly lit stage in the middle of the field and the giant TV screen. The crowd was cheering something Cherkesov had just said. Pyatov was bigger and blonder than Scorpion had imagined, his hand in his jacket pocket. It looked like he was holding a gun.

Scorpion glanced around. The tunnel was no place for a conversation. He spotted a sign over a door that said: TUALETY. The WC. It would have to do, he thought. There wouldn't be much time. Pyatov started to turn just as Scorpion followed by Iryna came up. At first Pyatov looked confused, then his eyes widened as he recognized Iryna. Before he could move, Scorpion grabbed his wrist in a one-handed *ikkyo* wristlock. With his other hand, he jammed the muzzle of the Glock hard into Pyatov's ribs.

"Tell him we're going to the *tualet* to talk."

"*Vali otsjuda!*" Pyatov cursed, telling Scorpion to piss off.

"Tell him I'll kill him right here. They'll think I'm a hero," Scorpion said.

Iryna told him.

"*Payuhali!*" Let's go, Scorpion said in Russian, tightening his grip on Pyatov's wrist and shoving him toward the toilet door. Pyatov started to make a move, and Scorpion said, "*Ya strelyat!*" I'll shoot. "Stay outside. Don't let anyone in," he told Iryna, and shoved Pyatov inside.

The WC wasn't much bigger than a stall, with a single lidless toilet. The walls were covered with dirty tiles that looked like they'd never been washed, and the smell was appalling. Scorpion shoved Pyatov forward and smashed his head against the wall, cracking the tiles. Pyatov bounced back from the wall, his head bleeding, and pulled his gun from his pocket. Scorpion grappled with him for the gun with one hand as he kicked at the inside of Pyatov's knee. Pyatov tried to smash his face with his elbow as Scorpion blocked with his forearm, still holding the Glock that he now smashed into Pyatov's nose, breaking it. Dropping the Glock, he used both hands to take the gun away from Pyatov, who put him into a bear hug. Pyatov was immensely strong. He tried to lift Scorpion up and smash him to the floor. Scorpion kneed him in the groin and jammed the gun into his bleeding mouth.

"*Ya strelyat!*" he shouted.

Pyatov stopped. Scorpion stepped back, picked up the Glock and put Pyatov's Makarov pistol in his pocket.

"Who paid you?" Scorpion said in Russian, pressing the Glock against Pyatov's face.

"*Yob tvoiyu mat,*" Pyatov said, blood spraying from his mouth as he snarled the usual obscenity about Scorpion's mother.

"I pay you more than they do," Scorpion said. "You do not have to die."

"If I tell you, they'll kill me anyway."

"Why did you kill Alyona?"

"What are you talking about? *Ya—*" Pyatov started.

The door smashed open. Two men in *militsiyu* uniforms filled the doorway firing AK-47s. Scorpion dived to the floor. They riddled Pyatov with dozens of bullets, killing him instantly, the bullets ripping apart the water tank and sending chips of tiles flying like shrapnel. Water poured down from the shattered tank, mingling with Pyatov's blood on the floor. Scorpion fired the Glock twice, killing both *militsiyu* with shots to the head before they could turn their guns on him. Wet and dripping red-stained water, he jumped over their bodies and raced out the door, thinking what an idiot he'd been. It was a setup! He was the fall guy! And what had they done to Iryna?

Everyone had heard the shooting. People on the field and in the stands were screaming and rushing for the exits. The speeches had stopped. Men were running in the tunnel. Iryna was struggling with the two Black Armbands who had stopped them at the gate. For a fraction of a second Scorpion hesitated. To take Iryna with him would be like walking around with a big neon sign. It would make escape impossible. CIA protocol was to limit the damage by leaving her behind. The rule was that it was better to lose the Joe than have the operations officer fall into enemy hands. Especially in this case, where there was a good chance they were setting him up.

One of the Black Armbands had lifted Iryna off the ground, a meaty hand around her throat. The second Armband had grabbed her kicking legs and was spreading them apart. Her hat, wig, and glasses had fallen off in the struggle and it was glaringly obvious who she was. Her head was twisted as she fought to breathe. Four or five more Black Armbands were running toward them from the outside gate, automatic weapons ready to fire.

Scorpion fired once, hitting the Black Armband holding Iryna's legs in the back of the head, dropping him. He charged the bigger man, who let go of Iryna's throat to swing an elbow at Scorpion, who blocked with his forearm, then fired the Glock almost point-blank into the man's face.

The Black Armband clutched his face, letting Iryna go. Scorpion fired again, shooting him through the hand, killing him. Then he whirled and fired at the Black Armbands running toward them from the gate, bringing two of them down. As the others stopped to take firing positions, he fired again and again, glad he had used the extended clip, remembering Delta training—that in the middle of a firefight, you don't just shoot, but take the extra fraction of a second to be deliberate. He hit three of them, one after the other, grabbing Iryna's hand as they went down. Together, they raced out into the turmoil on the field. Three more Black Armbands ran after them.

People in the stands were screaming and trying to get out. On the field, they were crashing into chairs and each other as they swarmed toward the exits. Someone was shouting something on the loudspeaker, saying that everyone had to leave.

"Pyatov?" Iryna asked as they ran. Scorpion shook his head.

A phalanx of *militsiyu* followed by dozens of Black Armbands shepherded Cherkesov and others from the stage toward the tunnel. Scorpion headed for a side exit, away from the tunnel, trying to lose himself and Iryna in the crowd. He risked a glance behind. The Black Armbands who had been chasing them were looking everywhere in the crowd. He and Iryna were caught in the middle of a dense wedge of people shouting and pushing toward one of the exits.

"You're covered in blood," Iryna said to him.

"We've got to change our look," he said, snatching

an oversized rabbit fur Ushanka hat, long earflaps and a wide front brim, from a woman's head and planting it on Iryna. The woman started to scream, and a man with her shouted at Scorpion, who peeled out some money and shoved it in the man's mouth before shoving people aside to put distance between them.

"You're a crazy man, you know that?" Iryna snapped. "You can't just take things from people."

"Pull it down. Make sure it covers your hair," he said.

The crowd pressed in on them. They let the force of it sweep them toward the exit. Scorpion glanced back at the tunnel. The officials with Cherkesov disappeared into it, surrounded by Black Armbands.

"What happened? I heard shooting," a man wedged next to Scorpion asked him in Russian.

"*Ya ne znayu.*" I don't know, Scorpion said. "You want *babki*?" Slang for money.

"You kidding me?"

"I like your *shlyapa* hat." The man wore a rounded trapper-style sheepskin hat.

"What about me?" the man asked.

"Here's five hundred *hryvnia* to keep you warm," Scorpion said, managing to pull more money out of his pocket despite the press of the crowd.

They were moving off the field with the crowd, heading through the gate under the stands, the sound of talking and shouting echoing in the crowded space.

"It's yours," the man said, grabbing the money. He ripped off his hat and handed it to Scorpion.

"What do you think?" he asked Iryna.

"Your jacket's still bloody."

"I'll deal with it. Sometimes it only takes a little change to throw people off," he said.

They poured out with the crowd into the icy street. Facing them was a line of Black Armbands with AK-47s scanning the crowd. Scorpion moved to try to shield himself behind a tall man.

"Don't look at the Armbands," he cautioned Iryna. "Talk to me in Ukrainian. Tell me this is an outrage."

Iryna began talking, raising her voice even as she looked away from the Black Armbands. They followed the crowd funneling through a gap in the line of Black Armbands, one of whom was waving people through. It's no good, Scorpion thought. They were looking closely at everyone squeezing through the gap. He scanned the scene to see if there was another gate, but the crowd pressed in behind them, pushing them toward the gap. They were almost there.

Iryna's eyes searched his. He put one hand on the Glock and the other on the SR-1 Gyurza pistol he had taken from Andriy in the Mercedes. It was bad and it was stupid, but he knew there wasn't another way as they came up to the gap.

The eyes of one of the men watching them suddenly grew wide. Whether he had spotted Iryna or his bloody jacket didn't matter, Scorpion thought, starting to pull the pistols out of his pockets. He saw the man take a breath to shout.

Suddenly, a car exploded in the parking area near

the tunnel entrance. A ball of flame soared into the darkness, throwing a red glare over the scene. People were screaming and running in every direction in a panic. Scorpion dropped the Glock back into his pocket. No one was looking at them. The Black Armbands, everyone, were staring at the fire from the explosion.

He grabbed Iryna's hand and ran with a mass of others through the gap and out toward the street. As they ran, Scorpion looked back at the burning car. It was one of the big Mercedes sedans. His knees sagged. The realization of what had to have happened hit him as though he'd run smack into a brick wall. Cherkesov was dead. Pyatov had been a red herring, a decoy. He and Iryna had been set up. If Akhnetzov and Gabrilov were telling the truth, Europe was on the brink of war.

Heads down, he and Iryna began to edge away from the crowd, then kept walking away from the stadium. She almost slipped on the ice and he had to grab her arm to keep her from falling. It was worse than mission failure, he thought, a sickening feeling in the pit of his stomach. He looked at her, that beautiful face wrapped in the fur Ushanka hat, and couldn't tell whether she had realized it yet. They were the fall guys. Within the hour they would be the most hunted criminals in the country.

Just then something touched his eye. He looked up.

It had started snowing again.

 **CHAPTER NINETEEN**

Zaporozhye
Ukraine

The checkpoint was at the Zaporizka Shosye highway fork on the outskirts of Dnipropetrovsk, just past Babuskinskyi. They were in a district of factories, apartment buildings, and fields covered with snow. Scorpion had hoped to get out of the city before roadblocks were set up, but the *politsiy* had moved too quickly.

He moved the BMW into a waiting line of trucks, mostly Russian Kamazes and Czech Tatras. The checkpoint blazed in the darkness with light from the *politsiy* police vans' headlights shining through the falling snow.

"Do you have a false ID?" he asked Iryna. It was the first time they had spoken since the Stadium. She shook her head no. He looked behind them in the rearview mirror. A big Tatra truck had come up behind, boxing them in. The truck cab was too high for its driver to see into the BMW through the back window.

"There's a blanket in back. Hide under it on the floor and keep still," he said.

"What about you?" she asked, still not taking it in. The news they had been listening to on the car radio since leaving the stadium area had stunned her into silence. Cherkesov and three of his aides were dead, including Ihor Oliynyk, the man who brought Scorpion to Gorobets. The bodies of eight more men had been recovered from the tunnel shootout. The election was in chaos. According to Radio Europa News, Kozhanovskiy campaign advisor Iryna Mikhailivna Shevchenko had been seen in the stadium. She, along with a foreign journalist named Mikhail Kilbane, were wanted for questioning.

"I have another ID," Scorpion said.

"What about Michael Kilbane?"

"He no longer exists. I'm a South African businessman named Peter Reinert."

"You can do that? Change your identity like that?" snapping her fingers. "*Gospadi!*"

"You'd better hurry," he said, checking the mirrors to make sure no one could see. "We're going to have to move any second."

"I'm scared," she said, her eyes wide.

"I know," he replied, motioning for her to get in back.

She opened the passenger door and got out. A moment later he heard the rear passenger door open and close. There was the sound of rustling as she got under the blanket, then nothing. He glanced back. She was hidden. The truck in front of him began to move, and he eased the BMW forward. His pulse began to race. In his left hand he had his South African passport, in his right, close to his body so it couldn't be seen by someone looking in, the Glock and five hundred *hryvnia*, about sixty dollars. Not too much, not too little, for a highway bribe.

He thought about his cover. Downside, he couldn't disguise that he was a foreigner. Upside, he'd come up with a cover reason to be going to Zaporozhye. The *politsiy* were looking for two people, not one, so if they didn't inspect the car, he was okay. Also, they would be looking for them to be heading north, to Kyiv, not south, to Zaporozhye. He didn't want to think about what would happen if it didn't work. If they decided to inspect the car and found Iryna, they were as good as dead.

A *politseysky* policeman bundled against the cold motioned him forward. A second *politseysky* came around to the passenger side window and peered in. Scorpion rolled down his window. A blast of frigid wind blew snow into the car.

The *politseysky* said something in Ukrainian. Scorpion smiled and shrugged as if to say he didn't understand.

"*Ya iz Yuzhnoi Afriki,*" I am from South Africa, he said in Russian, handing *politseysky* the passport.

"Why are you going to Zaporozhye?" the man replied in Russian.

"I go see women," Scorpion said. In his searches on the Internet, he had found it was almost impossible to look up anything on Ukraine without being hit with ads from Ukrainian dating sites for women seeking foreign men. It seemed plausible, he thought. Only a fool hot for finding women would drive at night through the snow to an industrial city like Zaporozhye.

The *politseysky* smirked and said something to his partner about Scorpion being a *bolvan*, a dumb jerk. The partner laughed. The *politseysky* looked at Scorpion's photo on the passport, comparing it to his face, then said something in Russian too fast for Scorpion to catch.

"*Chto? Ya ne ponimayu,*" Scorpion said. What? I don't understand.

"*Vyidite iz avtomobilya,*" the *politseysky* said, motioning for him to get out of the car.

Scorpion's hand passed the money to his left hand and tightened on the Glock. Although it was dark, if he got out they might spot the blood on his jacket. They might inspect the car. He wasn't going to get out.

"*Vyidite iz avtomobilya!*" the *politseysky* repeated. His partner rapped on the window with a 9mm pistol, indicating that Scorpion should get out.

"Listen, *drooh,*" Scorpion said in English. "I got a date. Beautiful girl, *krasivaya devushka,*" making a motion for sex with his left hand, the one with the money. "*Pazhalusta,*" he said, Please, and passed the money to the *politseysky*. The *politseysky* looked at it, then slid it into his coat pocket. He looked at Scorpion, didn't say anything, then motioned for him to get out of the car.

Scorpion took a deep breath and stayed seated, his hand tightening on the Glock. *He doesn't want to shoot you*, he told himself. *Yeah, tell that to him.*

He knew a shoot-out would be a disaster. He let go of the Glock. Instead, he took out his money and handed the *politseysky* another five hundred *hryvnia*.

"Make sexy with Ukraine girls," the *politseysky* said, grinning all at once and making a vulgar gesture for intercourse as he took the money. His partner laughed. The *politseysky* made the gesture again and waved him on. Scorpion put the BMW into gear and drove, forcing himself to breathe normally.

He drove for ten minutes, checking the rearview mirror every few seconds to make sure they weren't being followed. The highway had been cleared by snowplows, two lanes in each direction, but the snow was making it harder and cutting down the visibility. Because of the roadblock and the weather, there was hardly any traffic.

He pulled off to the side of the road at a spot where the snow didn't appear too deep and looked around. Except for the highway in his headlights, it was almost impossible to see anything. The land was flat and empty, covered with drifts of snow, the occasional light from a farmhouse gleaming in the darkness like a star. He opened the back door and told Iryna to come back up front. She threw off the blanket and climbed back into the passenger seat. It only took a few seconds, and then they were driving again, the BMW fishtailing till Scorpion got it under control as he pulled back onto the icy highway.

They listened to the news on the car radio. Gorobets, speaking for the Cherkesov campaign, accused the Kozhanovskiy campaign of assassinating Cherkesov and of the massacre at the stadium. Kozhanovskiy denied the charges, but Russian president Evgeni Brabov called the assassination an outrage and threatened that Russia would not stand idly by while innocent Russian-speaking civilians were threatened by a "Kozhanovskiy coup" and "genocide."

Ukrainian interim President Lavro Davydenko, called for calm and ordered *militsiyu* police to patrol the streets. The foreigner wanted by the police—a Canadian journalist named Michael Kilbane—and Kozhanovskiy aide Iryna Mikhailivna Shevchenko were considered fugitives. The authorities were moving to charge them in the stadium murders. The *politsiy* announced they were to be considered armed and dangerous.

Scorpion turned off the radio. The only sound was of the snow tires on the highway.

"I should have listened to you," Iryna said. "I shouldn't have come."

"We got lucky just now," meaning at the checkpoint. "The good thing about a corrupt country is you can buy anything, even the cops. Especially the cops."

"Now what?" she asked.

"We have to get back to Kyiv."

"So why are we going south, to Zaporozhye? Kyiv's the other way."

"It's four hundred kilometers to Kyiv. We'd never make it by road, even if it doesn't get shut down by the snow. The airports, trains, all public transport will be watched. By this time the *militsiyu* has locked Dnipropetrovsk down tight as a drum. They're probably going through every hotel room and apartment rental in the city right now. Not to mention we've got the *politsiy*, the SBU, the Syndikat, probably the SVR and God knows who the hell else after us. Oh, and did I forget to mention I'm with the most recognizable woman in the country?"

"I'll turn myself in. I'll tell them you were just trying to save me. Oddly enough, that's the truth, isn't it?" she said, looking at him.

"Too late. They'd never let you talk to the press. They'd torture you till you swore you and Kozhanovskiy were behind every assassination in history including Kennedy."

"So we go south to Zaporozhye because they won't expect it," she said, taking a deep breath.

"Plus it's got an airport. It's only seventy kilometers. We'll be there in about forty minutes to an hour, even in this weather. I thought I could get through before they put up roadblocks, but now that we're through, it's even better. They won't be looking for us there."

"So we get to Zaporozhye. Then what?"

"We go to Kyiv and find out who was really behind Cherkesov's killing," he said. "It's our only chance."

"What about the election? The Russians?"

"Same thing. The only way Kozhanovskiy has a chance, and to try to stop the war, is to solve this thing."

The snow made driving treacherous, even with all-wheel-drive. He peered through the arcs of the windshield wipers and tried to stay in the tire tracks made by trucks far ahead. There was almost no traffic except for the headlights of an occasional truck coming the other way. She lit a cigarette.

"The Chorni Povyazky killed Pyatov?" Iryna asked.

"It was the *militsiyu*."

"Did Pyatov say anything about who is behind this?"

"We only had a few seconds before they came in."

"And Alyona? What did he do with her?" she asked, not looking at him.

"He seemed confused. Almost as if he didn't know what I was talking about."

"Did you believe him?"

"No," he said, and shook his head. He didn't want to tell her what Pyatov had actually said. It was bothering him. A loose end that didn't fit. "He was just starting to talk when they killed him."

"Christ, what a mess." She looked at him. "I don't even know what to call you now."

"Peter."

"You saved my life. I'm grateful, but I don't know who you are. You're like a ghost. I don't know how to do this."

"If we get captured," he said, "the less you know about me the better."

"We were set up, weren't we?"

He nodded, then checked the rearview mirror. There were headlights behind them in the distance. He'd have to keep an eye on it.

"Who did it?" she asked.

"When we find that out, we'll have our assassin," he said.

Following the GPS, he drove across a steel bridge over the river and down Lenina Prospekt, the main avenue of Zaporozhye. The street was wide and gleamed with electric lights from advertising signs and buildings. As with Kyiv and Dnipropetrovsk, the sidewalks were lined with winter-bare trees and crowded with cars, yellow trolley buses, and *mashrutkas*, despite the falling snow.

"What do we do first?" she asked.

"Change the image. Get rid of the car," he said, making a turn to go around the block to make sure they weren't being followed. After several more turns, the GPS squawking, and he was sure there were no trailing headlights, he drove to a big Trade Ukraina shopping center and pulled into the parking garage.

"Take everything," he told her, getting out and grabbing his backpack from the trunk. "We're leaving the car here. Use your hat to wipe everything down."

They went over everything they had touched, stopping when anyone was near to make sure they weren't seen doing it. He had Iryna put her Ushanka hat back on with a scarf over the lower part of her face so no one would recognize her. When they were finished, he locked the car and they walked into the mall.

Most of the stores and cafés were still open. On the second floor, they found a beauty supply and wig store. They went in and bought some things, then went shopping for clothes. When they were finished, they stopped in a café where Scorpion checked for rental apartments on his laptop. They found one not far from the mall and Iryna called. By the time they left the mall pulling new carry-ons, she was wearing a curly-haired redheaded wig and steel-rim glasses under her Ushanka hat. Scorpion wore a suit under a new overcoat and a peaked Cossack-style fur hat. He carried his old clothes, including the bloody jacket, in a plastic bag.

The snow was still falling.

"You think there'll be a flight tonight?" she asked.

"Not in this," he said, indicating the snow.

They walked on side streets near the mall. Scorpion left the bag of old clothes in a trash bin behind an apartment house. He dropped the BMW keys along with his Michael Kilbane passport and press pass torn into pieces in a sewer opening. They walked to the rental apartment in the snow.

The rental was in a Soviet-style brick apartment building on Stalevarov Street, just a block from Lenina Prospekt. The apartment concierge met them at the front door. He was a fat balding man in a Metalist Kharkov soccer sweatshirt. He showed them an apartment on the fifth floor, the living room window looking down at a lone street lamp in the snow-empty street. It was four hundred *hryvnia* a night. Scorpion told him they'd take it for a week for 2,500 *hryvnia*.

The concierge asked for their identity cards.

"No identity cards, no questions, no *militsiyu*," Scorpion said. He added an additional two thousand *hryvnia* to the money he held out.

Iryna said something to the man in Ukrainian and he nodded, a smirk on his face as he took the money. After he left, she told Scorpion, "I told him we were both married to other people. I don't think we're the first to use this place for sex. That—and the money."

"He didn't seem to recognize you," Scorpion said.

"The wig," she said, taking it off along with the glasses. "But I still need something in case I have to get rid of the wig," she added, sitting in front of a mirror, a towel wrapped around her neck. She took out a scissors she'd bought in the beauty supply store and began cutting her hair. Scorpion watched her, then checked for cargo flights to Kyiv on his laptop. There was an old-fashioned TV in the living room. He turned it on.

They found a news channel. Kozhanovskiy and Gorobets had accused each other of staging the assassination to win the election. Gorobets demanded a postponement so the Svoboda party could select another candidate. Open fighting had broken out between the Chorni Povyazky and Kozhanovskiy supporters in every major city in Ukraine. A female reporter interviewed a Black Armband who stared menacingly into the camera and said that if they found Iryna Shevchenko or the foreigner before the *militsiyu* did, they'd know what to do to them. For a moment Iryna stopped working. She and Scorpion looked at each other in the mirror.

Scorpion helped cut her hair in the back. When she was done, the change was incredible. She had a short pixie cut and bangs slanting sideways across her forehead, which made her look almost completely different and yet unbelievably sexy.

"I feel naked. It's not too awful, is it?" she asked.

He had never seen anyone so beautiful. The world had shrunk to just two of them. Everything that had happened, the stadium, the shootings in the tunnel, their desperate escape, seemed to come together like a thunderclap. He couldn't stop himself, was no longer in control. He grabbed her and kissed her hard. She kissed him back hungrily and they staggered toward the bed. They pulled at each other's clothes and bodies. It was as if they couldn't get enough of each other. It was like madness. They tumbled onto the bed naked and she grabbed at his hips, pulling him into her. Even inside her, he couldn't get enough of her. When they finished, they lay there, gasping.

"*Gospadi*, what was that?" she said.

"I don't know."

"What do we do?" she asked, her eyes reflecting the light from the living room.

"I don't know that either," unable to take his eyes off her. In the middle of this mission with the whole world against them, this was crazy, he told himself.

"You have to tell me something," she said. "Anything. I can't keep going with somebody whose name changes by the minute, who might disappear forever any second. Do you have a code name or something?"

He hesitated. "Scorpion," he said finally.

"It's horrible," she said, making a face.

"I chose it."

"Why?" She lit a cigarette and lay on one elbow, watching him.

"When I was a boy, the man who became the closest thing I ever had to a father used to call me 'Little Scorpion,'" he said.

"I don't understand. Why would he say such a thing?"

Scorpion thought about his real father lying face-down in the sand, of the Saar raiders, the "wolves" of the Arabian desert, who had killed his father and tried to kill him too, and how Sheikh Zaid had saved him and, when the sheikh tried to touch his dead father, he had stabbed the sheikh with his Boy Scout knife. That's when Sheikh Zaid had called him Little Scorpion for the first time.

"Long story," Scorpion said now. He became aware of the news announcer's voice from the TV in the living room. "What's he saying?" he asked.

"The Russians are moving large numbers of troops and tanks to the Ukrainian border. I can't believe this," she said, stubbing out her cigarette. "Maybe the snow will slow them down."

"Maybe," he said.

That night he dreamt about Arabia. He was in Sheikh Zaid's tent, sitting by the fire at night, the way it was when he was a child. He was telling Sheikh Zaid he had found a woman. The sheikh told him that before he could marry he first had to find out who he was, the same question Iryna kept asking. He couldn't tell her, he told the sheikh. Someone, some thing, had been pursuing him since Yemen. The tent grew dark. He could no longer see Sheikh

Zaid. His enemies were getting closer; he could feel them right behind him in the darkness. He started to turn around . . .

He awoke suddenly in the middle of the night reaching for the Glock under his pillow. The apartment was freezing cold. Iryna lay next to him. Even asleep she was unbelievably beautiful. She looked like she was dreaming; perhaps of snow slowing the Russian troops. He got out of bed and went to the bathroom. After washing his hands in ice-cold water, he went to the window. It was covered over with frost. He rubbed a circle on the window with his hand and peered out.

The street was white with snow and empty under the streetlight.

It had stopped snowing.

 **CHAPTER TWENTY**

Metrograd
Kyiv, Ukraine

They flew to Kyiv from Zaporozhye on a cargo flight, no questions asked, thanks to bribes all around. While they waited in a shedlike area to board, they watched a female news commentator on a TV behind a counter. Iryna translated in a whisper.

The United States and Britain had called for a special meeting of the UN Security Council to deal with the crisis. In Brussels, the foreign ministers of the NATO countries were meeting in emergency session. Satellite reports indicated that Russia had moved four tank divisions of the Second Guards Tank Army plus three infantry divisions to the border area near Kharkov. Kozhanovskiy had called on the United States and the Western powers to honor their NATO treaty obligations to Ukraine. Oleksandr Gorobets, speaking for the Svoboda party, declared that the election must be delayed for a month to allow Svoboda to choose another candidate.

There had been more street fighting in Kyiv. The

streets close to Khreshchatyk Avenue and around the Pechersk district were filled with roaming packs of Black Armbands. Kozhanovskiy's supporters had begun to form what they called "Citizens Militsiyu" to defend themselves. Someone had bombed the Central Synagogue of Kyiv on Shchekovitzkaya Street. Two people, a woman and a nine-year-old boy, were killed. In Dnipropetrovsk, police were conducting a house-to-house search for Iryna Shevchenko and the foreigner, Michael Kilbane, wanted for questioning in the killing of presidential candidate Yuriy Cherkesov.

Iryna was translating it for Scorpion when the flight company manager they had bribed signaled for them to board the plane. They sat behind the crew in the cockpit, facing each other on fold-down jump seats. She was in her blond wig, glasses, and Ushanka hat; he, with a two-day stubble, in his overcoat and peaked Cossack hat.

The aging Antonov turboprop shuddered as it climbed into the frigid air. It dipped and rattled over the snow-covered landscape. The noise of the engines was so loud, Scorpion thought they could risk talking.

Iryna leaned toward him and whispered in his ear. "It's happening. Everything we feared," her breath visible in the cold air.

He nodded.

"How can I stop it? How can anyone?" she said, biting her lip.

"Somebody went to a hell of a lot of trouble to frame us. We need to find them."

"Any idea who?"

"Yes," Scorpion said grimly.

The flight got them back to Kyiv in an hour. They passed through the Boryspil Airport cargo area the same way they had gotten through the Zaporozhye terminal—with bribes passed in handshakes. Once inside the terminal building, they separated, staying in contact by cell phone as they stayed alert for anyone who might be watching them. Scorpion used his hand to shield part of his face from security cameras while walking toward the street, saying, "*Tak, tak*"—Yes, yes—in Ukrainian into the cell phone, because he knew they were looking for a foreigner. He spotted two men, both in overcoats, by the exit doors.

"*Ni*, Dmitri," he said to his cell phone as he walked by them. Outside on the street, he waited in the queue for a taxi, pretending to talk and meanwhile watching for Iryna. The two men in overcoats watched her walk by, their eyes following her. One of them said something and they started after her.

Scorpion called Iryna on his cell phone as he got into a taxicab. Calling her "Nadia," the cover name they'd agreed on for her, he told her to take a different taxi and tell the driver to follow his cab, then told his driver to take him into Kyiv. Through the rear window he saw Iryna get into the next taxi and spotted the two men who followed her running toward a sedan parked behind the taxi queue.

Scorpion's taxi headed to the Boryspilske Shosye Highway to Kyiv, Iryna's taxi four cars behind his. Looking through the rear window again, he saw the sedan following in traffic. His taxi got on a highway heading west, four lanes in each direction, cleared of snow.

Why didn't they try to take them at the airport? he wondered. Maybe they weren't sure it was Iryna, or wanted to see if they could tie them to Kozhanovskiy and destroy the opposition altogether. Either way, he knew they had to lose the tails. He told the driver to take him to the Metrograd, the big shopping mall downtown in Lva Tolstoho Square.

They drove past block after block of apartment houses on Kyiv's Left Bank. Scorpion's cell phone rang. It was "Nadia." He told her he had to do some shopping at the Metrograd, and she said she would meet him in the tennis store in the sports section of the mall and hung up. The taxi drove across the bridge to the Right Bank, then turned up along the river before cutting over toward downtown. He was thinking what a beautiful city Kyiv was, in spite of everything, with its gold-domed churches and parks covered in snow, when he saw a man's body sprawled on the sidewalk. No one stopped. People scurried past, giving a wide berth to the body.

Scorpion checked the rear window again. The sedan had moved right behind Iryna's taxi. His taxi stopped at the entrance to the mall. He went inside and down the escalator to the lower underground floor. The mall was modern, bright with goods and shiny windows, and filled with people shopping in spite of the crisis. But there was an air of unease; people were looking around suspiciously, not talking much or in whispers.

He went into a department store, and after checking to make sure no one was watching, went out another door and through the mall, crossing from one underground hallway to another. He stopped in an electronics store to buy four new disposable cell phones and an iPod Nano with a radio, then went to the tennis store in a section of the mall devoted to exclusively to sports and called Iryna's cell phone.

"Are you clear of them?" he said in English. "Pretend you're talking to a boyfriend."

"*Nyet, glupyi chelovek*," she said in Russian. No, you silly man.

"Go into a store with multiple exits. Duck behind something so they lose sight of you. Go out one of the exits. I'll wait," he said, pretending to inspect tennis racquets while he activated and programmed the new cell phones.

A few minutes later she walked into the tennis store. He pretended not to know her and checked the mall to make sure she hadn't been followed. It looked like she'd lost them. Motioning her to follow, they went out of that store and into a ski store.

"What are we doing?" she whispered, checking ski jumpers in a rack.

"We've got to get you a new ID," he said.

He told her to go into a dressing room, and a moment later followed. Once inside, he took her photo with his cell phone camera, first with the blond wig on, then in her new pixie cut. They took the escalator down to the Metro station under Tolstoho Square and switched subway trains twice to make sure they weren't followed.

"Who were they?" she asked, watching the doors as they pulled into a station.

"SBU, *militsiyu*, *politsii*, Syndikat *blatnoi*, the Chorni Povyazky, take your pick. The only one not after us is the Salvation Army."

"Is this how it's going to be?"

"If we're lucky."

"*Gospadi*," she said, half to herself. "What next?"

"I need an Internet café. Also a place to stay. Someplace where they won't ask questions."

"I can do that," she said.

He nodded. "If they think we're in Kyiv, they'll probably be looking on the Right Bank, so make it someplace on the Left Bank. Here." He handed her one of the new cell phones. "Use this. We'll dump the ones we're using."

"Get off at the next stop, Vokzalna," she said.

"Why?"

"There's a twenty-four-hour Internet café on Chokolovsky Avenue."

The café was full despite the cold weather and dangerous streets. Many were young people tweeting about demonstrations and what was happening. Scorpion paid a young man who looked like a student a hundred *hryvnia* for his seat at a desktop computer facing the wall. A few minutes later Iryna got a computer too.

Glancing around to make sure no one was looking, he inserted the flash drive and loaded the NSA software onto the computer. He logged onto the NSA server and began reading the translated transcripts of the calls made by Oleg Gabrilov since he had last checked. Thanks to his bugs, the NSA had all of Gabrilov's calls, from the embassy, from his apartment, and from his cell phone. There was a single phone number that Gabrilov had called once a day; the first time, after he'd made his call to Alyona's cell phone following Scorpion's visit. A transcript of another call caught his attention. Gabrilov had said: "They've taken the bait."

The SVR was running something, probably the frame for the Cherkesov killing, Scorpion thought. But why would the SVR want to assassinate Cherkesov, Russia's biggest ally in Ukraine? And how would Gabrilov know that he and Iryna had taken the bait about Pyatov? What was happening at the time? Scorpion checked the date and time of the call. And then it hit him.

Gabrilov had made the call yesterday, before the assassination, right after he told Gorobets about Pyatov. That meant Gabrilov knew Michael Kilbane was in Dnipropetrovsk, and the only reason for him to be there was because he knew about Pyatov. Scorpion checked the phone number on the NSA database. When he read it, it made no sense. The number was registered to a Chinese trading company, Lianhuay China Trading, Ltd., on Vorovskogo Street in western Kyiv. The SVR and the Chinese intelligence service, the Guoanbu, were deadly enemies. Why would Gabrilov be contacting the Chinese?

Things were spiraling out of control. And what the hell did the Chinese have to do with it? He needed to get to Shaefer. He plugged earphones and a minimicrophone into the computer and Skype'd

Shaefer's BlackBerry. It was a private BlackBerry, not in Shaefer's name, and that the Company didn't know about. On the third ring, someone picked up.

"*Cine este?*" Shaefer said in Romanian over sounds of a conversation in the background.

"It's FOBE. Can you talk?" Scorpion said in English.

"*Un moment,*" Shaefer said, and Scorpion heard him say something to someone in Romanian. When he came back on the line, the background sounds were quiet. "Are you out of your mind!? I shouldn't talk to you! I shouldn't know you!"

"We were set up," Scorpion whispered.

"Who gives a crap? Have you any idea how hot you are? You are so PNG you don't exist!" CIA-speak for persona non grata.

"I need a drop."

"Don't you get it? If I wanted to—which I don't—I can't come near you with a ten-foot pole."

"What about FOBE?" Scorpion said. What he and Shaefer had been through together in Forward Operating Base Echo had to trump anything coming down the Company's chain of command. They were foxhole buddies. Shaefer was one of the good guys.

"You're out past Pluto, amigo. This is a bridge too far."

"I just need—" Scorpion started.

"I'm burning this number. Don't call again," Shaefer said, and hung up.

Scorpion sat there for a moment, stunned, staring blankly at the computer screen. Not Shaefer, he thought. It couldn't be. In Chaprai in Pakistan, bad intel had turned FOBE into a death trap. Their Delta Team had come under an intense Taliban attack that lasted three days and nights, at the end of which he and Shaefer were the only ones left alive. When they finally got evac'd out, they'd decided to join the CIA so no other American grunt would get killed because of lousy intel.

Only now, even Shaefer had cut ties with him. It meant this was so hot the CIA didn't want to be associated with this thing. It also meant the Company—and the NSC—had concluded that unless the U.S. walked away now, they were headed for war. It was too big. He had to get to Rabinowich.

He checked his watch. It was almost 11:00 A.M., four in the morning in Virginia. He Skype'd Rabinowich's home number. The phone rang three times, then clicked over. A recorded telephone company voice came on the line. It said the number he was calling was no longer in service and there was no new number. Christ, they'd gotten to Rabinowich too. The CIA's best brain and ultimate in-house rebel! Apart from Shaefer, the only person he had always counted on.

The only connection he had left was the teenage chat room where Rabinowich, posing as a teenage girl from Omaha named Madison, chatted with him as her online boyfriend, Josh. Scorpion unplugged the earphones and mike and went to the online chat room. When he tried to log in, however, he was blocked. Instead of a login, he got a message telling him he had been permanently removed. Only the chat operator using a kill command for him specifically could've done that, he thought, feeling like he'd been kicked in the stomach. Even Rabinowich wanted no part of him. He was alone; completely cut off.

"Everything all right?" Iryna asked him.

"Fine," Scorpion said, entering the Alt key sequence that would cause the NSA software to completely scrub any trace of his activity or that he had ever been on the computer, even resetting the computer's clock and clearing his transactions from its local Internet server. When it finished, the software would delete itself. He tried to think of what to do next.

"I found a flat," Iryna whispered. "In Desnianskyi *raion*. It's on the Left Bank, near Volhogradska Square."

Scorpion looked toward the door as a pair of Black Armbands walked in and began shoving people out of the way. They grabbed one young man at a computer—he looked like a student—and threw him to the floor. They started kicking him. No one interfered.

"Let's get the hell out of here," Scorpion said.

 **CHAPTER TWENTY-ONE**

Desnianskyi
Kyiv, Ukraine

That afternoon, they watched television and made love. The apartment was on the tenth floor. It was small, with only a few pieces of furniture, and had a view of the street below. Their next door neighbor, Pani Pugach, a short, round woman in a housedress, came over to introduce herself. She chatted with Iryna about the building, gossiping about the other tenants as Scorpion sat at the kitchen table with his laptop computer. He let Iryna do the talking, saying only, *"Dobry den,"* Good day, when Pani Pugach came in and *"Buvay,"* So long, when she left.

"She told me where the local Furshet supermarket is," Iryna told him. "I can go shop, and when I come back, I'll make us borscht."

The male announcer on TV started talking very loudly. The screen showed Russian troops marching, followed by a man in a suit speaking at a press conference. Scorpion recognized him immediately. Brabov, the Russian president.

"What's he saying?" he asked Iryna.

"He's demanding an end to the crisis. He says Russian lives are being threatened. He says that Russia will take over as much of Ukraine as necessary in order to ensure the safety of ethnic Russians." She looked at Scorpion. "It's what we feared."

"Wait," he said, indicating the TV. It had switched to a conference going on in Brussels. Scorpion couldn't understand the commentary and could only catch a word or two of the news ticker on the bottom of the screen: NATO V STANI KRYZY. KOZHANOVSKIY: "VIYNA YDE." "What's it say?" he asked.

"NATO in crisis," she read. "It quotes Kozhanovskiy: 'War is imminent.' I've got to talk to Viktor."

"Wait till I get you a new identity," Scorpion said.

"I can't. Things are moving too fast."

"Listen, they're not kidding around. The ones who set us up are safer if you're dead. Then the only one putting out a story is them."

"I know," she said, "pulling on her coat, wig, and Ushanka fur hat. "I'll call Viktor from the Furshet store. I'll be back."

"Be careful," he said when she headed out.

While she was gone, he tried to think it through. The only way for him and Iryna was to find who killed Cherkesov and why. The key was that so far everything had come from or through the SVR agent, Gabrilov. Even though Scorpion didn't think Gabrilov knew about his taps, somehow Gabrilov had set up Pyatov as a red herring and he and Iryna as the fall guys. The whole thing had SVR fingerprints all over it, he thought grimly.

Assumption: the Russians wanted to invade and were using Cherkesov's assassination as an excuse. But why? What were they after? Somehow the answer involved the Chinese. The Lianhuay China Trading Company could be a front for the Guoanbu Second Bureau, the Chinese CIA. But what the hell did they have to do with this? What did China want in Ukraine?

He shaved, trimming his stubble to form a mustache—another little something to change the image—and got dressed. He was getting antsy. What was taking Iryna so long?

He took out the Glock, took it apart, cleaned and loaded it and did the same with the SR-1 Gyurza. He was just finishing up when Iryna came back from shopping. She looked frightened.

"I think I was followed," she said.

Scorpion went to the door, Glock in hand.

"Who was it?"

"A man. He wore a black parka and a wool cap. I had a sense someone was following me when I left the building, but I didn't see anyone. But when I left the supermarket, he was behind me. I went up a side street and came back on the other side just to make sure. He stayed with me. This stupid wig isn't working!" she said, pulling off her blond curls and throwing it on the table.

"It's not the wig," Scorpion said. "Did he follow you into the building?" he asked, pressing his ear against the apartment door.

"I don't think so. He was across the street when I came in."

Scorpion stood beside the window.

"Come here," he said. "Peek out just for a second, then duck back. Tell me if you see him or anybody in the street watching the building."

She came over beside him, peeked out and ducked back.

"No. No one," she said. He could feel her body trembling against his. He wished he could tell her it was going to be all right, but it wasn't.

He got his minibinoculars. Checking the angle of the light coming from outside to make sure they wouldn't reflect, he peeked out from behind the curtain. The sky was leaden gray. There were no reflections and he didn't see anything in the street or in the windows of buildings. Then he spotted it. A break in the roofline of the building across the street. The silhouette of something, someone.

"Shit," he said, pulling back and closing the curtain. "They know we're here. We've got to get out now. Pull your things together."

"It's my fault," she said, getting her carry-on. "I'm no good at this."

"It's not the wig and it's not your fault," Scorpion said, throwing his things into a backpack. "Until a few hours ago even we didn't know we were going to be in this building in this *raion*. They were already on to us."

"How could they be?"

"Only two ways. You used your cell phone to call Viktor. It was the first time you used it, so they weren't tracking you, but ten-to-one they were tapping his phone. Once you called, they could've

GPS-tracked your cell. That's not Syndikat *blatnoi*. Those are pros. The second explanation is even simpler."

She stopped for a moment.

"The building manager," she said, talking about the fat man with a wheeze who couldn't take his eyes off her chest when they rented the apartment. "He seemed shifty to me. I don't think he believed our story."

"Not for a minute," Scorpion said, grabbing his pack and jacket. "My screwup. Between your chest and the money, I thought it would hold him. Either that or everybody's favorite busybody, dear old Pani Pugach. Too bad I don't have time to deal with either of them."

Iryna packed her carry-on and zipped it up. She put on her outerwear, wig, and Ushanka hat.

"Give me the cell phone you used to call Kozhanovskiy," he said, holding out his hand.

She gave it to him, and making sure it was on, he put it in a kitchen drawer.

"Now what?" she asked, watching him go to the door, the Gyurza with its silencer in his hand.

"We leave. How do you say 'Come here' in Ukrainian?"

"Idy syudy."

"I'll go first. You stay back but follow close enough to hear me. If I shout, 'Nadia,' come fast. If I shout, *'Idy syudy!'* do the exact opposite. Run back to the apartment, lock yourself in, call Kozhanovskiy to come with his bodyguards and get you."

"You're scaring me," she said.

"Good. It's about time you understood what game you're in. Ready?"

She took a breath.

"What about the TV?" The TV was still on. It was a soap opera about an upper-middle-class Kyiv family. The wife had been kidnapped by her evil identical twin sister.

"Leave it on." He put his finger to his lips, cracked the door open and stepped into the hallway, looking both ways, ready to fire. The hallway was empty. He listened at the door to Pani Pugach's apartment and moved on. He checked the stairway in both directions, up and down. It looked clear.

He went back to the elevator, pushed the button, took Iryna's hand and led her to the staircase. He told her to wait on the landing till he called her with one of the signals, then walked down slowly, pivoting at each landing, Gyurza ready to fire.

Just as Scorpion approached the landing of the fourth floor, two men came up the stairs from below, one of them in the black jacket and wool cap described by Iryna. They all saw each other at the same time. As they started to point their guns at him, he fired twice, hitting the first man in the head, the second—the one in the wool cap—in the shoulder. The man in the wool cap managed to fire twice as Scorpion leaped down to the landing, the bullets just missing, ricocheting off the metal stairs. He tripped as he landed, dropping the Gyurza. The man in the wool cap kicked the Gyurza away and aimed his own pistol. He smiled, showing broken teeth.

He was still smiling as Scorpion ripped his Glock from its holster at the small of his back and fired into the center of his forehead. The door to the landing opened then, and another man was on him, using a Russian Sambo kick to his middle along with a forearm that knocked the Glock from Scorpion's hand. He was a big man, broad as he was high, and looked as strong as an ox.

Scorpion bounced off the wall to close in, using a CQC strike and parry combination with a leg sweep that took the big man down. He broke the man's nose with an upward palm smash and put a guillotine choke hold around his massive neck, using the crook of his elbow and forearm to cut off the flow of blood through the carotid artery to the brain. The big man struggled violently, repeatedly slamming Scorpion back against the wall. He groped for Scorpion's eyes with his sausagelike fingers. Scorpion barely held on, his ribs and back feeling like he'd been hit with a sledgehammer. He grabbed his wrist to tighten his grip around the man's neck and pulled up with all his strength.

The man slammed him again, knocking the wind out of him. All Scorpion could do was hang on, desperately squeezing his neck. Then all at once his efforts succeeded. The man went limp, falling back, a dead weight on top of him. Scorpion kept the choke hold tight another thirty seconds till he was sure the man was dead.

He squeezed out from under the massive body and, staggering, retrieved the Glock and the Gyurza pistols from the stairs. A woman with a little boy, who had no doubt heard the shots, peeked at him from the landing above.

"*Ischezni!*" he snapped at her in Russian. Beat it. She and the boy disappeared.

"Nadia! Nadia!" he called up to the landing above, and after a moment he heard Iryna's footsteps on the stairs. He went through the dead men's pockets. They carried cell phones and ammo clips, but none of them had ID of any kind. Even the labels from their shirts and jackets had been removed.

"Christ," he said to himself as Iryna knelt beside him.

"What is it?" she asked.

"They have no ID," he said as they went quickly down the stairs toward the back exit he had checked out when they first moved in.

"So they're not *politsiy* or *militsiyu*."

"Or Syndikat *blatnoi*. The thugs have to carry ID in case they get stopped by the cops."

"So who are they?"

"Can't you guess?" he said, pausing at the back door. He cracked it open and peered out at an alleyway piled with snow and trash. He scanned the roofline for snipers. It looked clear. They probably figured three men inside plus the front covered and the element of surprise was more than enough to arrest a man and a woman.

"SBU," she said.

"Probably," he nodded. "Let's go!"

They ran out the door into the alley, slipping in the snow, its surface black with dirt. Scorpion went ahead toward the corner. Iryna followed, her carry-on balanced on her head like an African woman. Scorpion stopped at the corner and, motioning her to keep back, lay down in the snow. With Iryna behind him, breathing hard, he edged forward, peeked around the corner and ducked back.

He stood up and brushed the snow off. "It looks clear, but they'll be waiting to hear from their men inside. We won't have much time."

"What are you going to do?"

"Wait here. Keep out of sight. When you hear a car horn, run toward it and get in. If you hear shooting, go out in the street and run the other way."

"How will you get a car?" she asked, but Scorpion was already walking quickly down the street path in the snow, his backpack over his shoulder. As soon as he was sure no one was watching, he slipped the Glock into his overcoat pocket.

He spotted a Lada sedan parked by the curb. After trying the driver's door and finding it locked, he knelt in the street. He didn't want to smash the car window. There was always the chance of an alarm, and driving in this cold with an open window was not only uncomfortable, it would attract attention. He fished in his backpack for his lock kit, pulled out the Peterson universal key and within seconds opened the car door and got in. Using the kit's cylinder extractor, he pulled the cylinder from the car's ignition switch and started the engine with a jiggle of the Peterson key, then unlocked the doors and honked the horn for Iryna.

As he turned the wheel, ready to pull out, he

saw her in the rearview mirror, pulling her carry-on toward him through the snow. She was bending over to see which car he was in and he honked again. He felt for the Glock as the seconds ticked by. The rear door opened and she tossed her carry-on in back. As she got in beside him, he spotted two men in the side mirror coming out of the alley.

They saw Iryna get into the car and started running toward them. Before she even closed the door, Scorpion pulled away, the tires slipping on snow and ice. He swerved the Lada into the street and heard shots behind them as he accelerated, skidding, toward the corner. He made a sharp turn, cutting off a snow-covered van, and cut into the lane of cars moving on a wide street thick with slush churned by the traffic.

"Now what?" she breathed.

"Where's the nearest Metro?"

"I'm not sure. I'm a Right Bank girl. Probably Lisova," she said, looking back. To their left was a lake or inlet of the Dnieper, the ice frozen solid, and in the distance tall apartment blocks. "I've never even been in this part of Kyiv before."

"We have to get rid of the car," he said. "They're probably already calling in a description to the *politsiy*. We don't have much time. What did Kozhanovskiy say?"

"I didn't want to risk his cell. I spoke to Slavo. He says they are all stunned."

"I'll bet."

"Gorobets called Viktor and told him he should

agree to a three-week delay in the election for the Svoboda party to pick another candidate."

"Svoboda meaning Gorobets."

"Yes."

"What's Viktor going to do?"

"Slavo doesn't know. No one knows what to do. There's going to be a vote tomorrow in the Verkhovna Rada." She turned to Scorpion. "I have to go back."

"They'll arrest you."

"No, I'll get away. I'll see you later."

"It's better if we're not together," Scorpion agreed. "Together we're like a neon sign."

"Is that what you want?" turning to him.

"What I want is irrelevant."

"Not to me," she said, then exclaimed, "Look!"

"What is it?"

"That *mashrutka*!" she said, pointing at a minibus they were passing, with a hand-lettered sign on its window. "It's going to the Chernihivska Metro."

"Okay," he said, accelerating. He looked for a place to lose the Lada. If he pulled ahead about two blocks, that should give them enough time. He scanned the street ahead. There was a parking space in front of a shoe store. He cut over and swung into the space at an angle.

The two of them jumped out of the car. They grabbed their things from the back of the Lada and ran to the corner, just getting there in time to wave the *mashrutka* down. It stopped and they squeezed in, breathing hard.

They didn't speak inside the minibus; anyone could have heard them. A man next to Scorpion was reading a *Kyivsky Telegraf*, and though he couldn't read the Ukrainian headlines, he was stunned by the prominently displayed photos of Iryna and him, side by side. His photo was taken from the Canadian passport, which had been scanned at the airport when he first entered the country. He coughed and used his gloved hand to cover his mouth and nose. The noose around them was being drawn tighter and tighter.

The *mashrutka* stopped by the entrance to the Metro. They got off along with the other passengers, taking the escalator down to the station platform. It was the first chance they had to talk.

Before Scorpion could speak, Iryna said, "I know. I saw the photos in the paper. Now what?"

"After tonight, you'll have a different identity and it'll be harder to track us."

"How?"

"I'll take care of it. You stay out of it."

"Because it's dangerous?"

He didn't answer.

"Those men, three of them. You killed them," she said, taking his arm and leaning close so he could hear her as the train approached.

"Yes," he said.

"It was the way you did it. Just like that," snapping her fingers.

"What about it?"

"Good," she said.

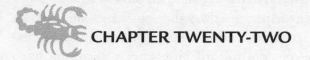

CHAPTER TWENTY-TWO

Nyvky
Kyiv, Ukraine

It took Scorpion less than an hour to find the *podlog*. He'd simply hailed a taxi and told the driver to take him to a late night club that was *"pryvatnyy,"* private, and *"ne dlya turistov,"* not for tourists.

"This is not club for you, *pane*. No *turistiv*. Bad people," the taxi driver said.

"That's the kind I'm looking for. *Peryeiti*," Scorpion had told him. Go.

The taxi took him to a hole-in-the-wall club called the Crocodile. It was in a square building on a hill in the Verkhny Gorod, near the Golden Gate museum. Once inside, Scorpion told the first prostitute who approached him what he wanted. In exchange for a thousand *hryvnia* slipped into her cleavage, she came back with a slip of paper with the address of a counterfeiter, a *podlog*, that she said was named Matviy, who did fake identity cards. He left the club and took the Metro to the Tarasa Shevchenka station in the Podil district, then walked down to a warehouse area near the river.

The street was dark, icy, traffic lights swaying in the wind. He passed an open lot where a shadowy red-lit shape moved on the snow; a group of street boys huddled around a trashcan fire. They spotted Scorpion, ran toward him, knives glittering from the streetlights, and surrounded him. Their clothes were ragged, their dirty faces looking hungry, almost feral, but they scattered like wolves when he showed them the Glock. He waited till they were gone before finding the address of a small storefront with apartments above.

The shop was locked, dark, but there were lights in the frost-covered windows of the apartment above. Scorpion pounded on the shop door until a voice from upstairs finally yelled out, *"Khto tse?"*

"Ya ishchu Matviy," Scorpion shouted up in Russian. I'm looking for Matviy. He pounded on the door again. "It is cold. Open up!"

"Ischezni!" the voice said. Go away.

He pounded even harder then, and began kicking the door. A minute later a light came on in the shop.

"Dosyt!" he heard someone grumble. Enough.

The door opened, and without waiting, Scorpion shoved his way inside.

Matviy was a small, stoop-shouldered man in an old sweater. He looked at Scorpion and motioned him to follow. They went into a small workshop at the back lit by a single hanging lightbulb. Scorpion showed the *podlog* what he wanted.

He watched Matviy download the two photos of Iryna, one in the blond wig, one in the pixie cut, from his cell phone camera to Matviy's computer. Although the stoop-shouldered man didn't say anything, Scorpion was certain that despite the change in appearance in the photos, he recognized Iryna. Just to be safe, while he worked, Scorpion planted a bug near the back of the computer. Twenty minutes later Matviy handed over two new Ukrainian *posidchenaya osoby* identity cards for Iryna: as a blonde, she was Valentyna Khodyneva; as a dark-haired pixie, she was Nadiya Zhdanova. Scorpion watched as Matviy deleted the images from his computer.

"These don't exist," he said in Russian as he paid Matviy. "She does not exist. I do not exist."

"*Pazhalusta*, this is my business. No one will ever know," Matviy replied.

"You do not want me to come back," Scorpion said, then left.

He walked around the corner of the building and waited, putting an earplugged Bluetooth to his cell phone set to the bug he had planted at the back of Matviy's computer. A moment later he heard Matviy make a phone call. Although Scorpion couldn't understand the Ukrainian, it was enough. Dammit! he thought. He went back to the shop, opened the door with his Peterson key and burst in on Matviy, who turned toward him, cell phone in hand.

Matviy's eyes opened wide. He dropped the phone and tried to run, but Scorpion tripped him, then went back and hung up the phone. He took out the Glock and Matviy stared at it.

"*Ya govoryu, prezhde*, I said before you don't want

to see me again," Scorpion said, motioning Matviy to sit with his hands on the worktable. Matviy came and sat hesitantly down. Holding the Glock to his head with his left hand, Scorpion picked up a microscope he had spotted earlier, probably used for fine detail work, and smashed the base of the microscope down on Matviy's index finger, breaking it. Matviy cried out.

"*Zatknis!*" Scorpion hissed. Shut up. He jammed the muzzle of the Glock hard against Matviy's head, then smashed the microscope down twice more till the index finger was a bloody pulp. Matviy moaned but didn't cry out.

"If I have to come back again . . ." Scorpion said in Russian as he headed for the door, not finishing the sentence. The look in Matviy's eyes made clear he didn't have to.

Scorpion wasn't sure what to do next. He needed more information on the Lianhuay company, but didn't want to risk using WiFi for the Internet. There was always a chance someone was scanning, and there were too many people chasing him. He walked toward the Metro and took it back to the Internet café on Prospekt Chokolovsky. Finding an open computer, he looked up the Lianhuay Trading Company. There wasn't much.

The company, headquartered in Shanghai, produced light and heavy machinery. Lianhuay's local Kyiv office was headed by Li Qiang, a graduate of Tsinghua University in Beijing with a Masters in Economics from USC. There was a photograph of Li Qiang, a thin Chinese man with glasses. There was something about him that, as Rabinowich would have said, wasn't kosher. What was it? He was looking at the entry, knowing it had to be there, but didn't see it. Then he read the brief description on the company's web page again and had it.

Tsinghua was one of the best universities in China, equivalent to a top Ivy like Harvard or Princeton. So why would the Lianhuay company's managers post an up-and-comer like Li Qiang to such a minor market for China as Ukraine? Not to mention his masters from USC, which meant Li spoke English. He was someone the Chinese would want to post to San Francisco or New York or London. Having Li Qiang in Kyiv was like having Einstein work as a high school teacher. Unless he was Guoanbu, the Chinese CIA, in which case the Lianhuay company was a front. But Gabrilov was SVR. The Guoanbu and the SVR were mortal enemies. So if Gabrilov regularly called Li Qiang, the real question was, who was running whom?

Were the Chinese running Gabrilov or the other way around? And what the hell did this have to do with assassinations and a crisis in Europe?

At that moment he looked up and saw Iryna. She was on the Internet café TV, wearing a black wig cut the way she had worn her hair before, the way people were used to seeing her. Scorpion clicked a few times on his computer to bring the TV image up on his computer screen. She was saying something vehemently, those incredible lapis eyes flashing, and he felt a twinge in his groin at the thought that he'd been in bed with her only hours before.

She was pointing to their photos in the newspaper and obviously denying that they'd had anything to do with Cherkesov's assassination. The camera pulled back to show Kozhanovskiy standing next to her. He was speaking now. Scorpion recognized where they were: the dining room of the apartment above the pub near Kontraktova Ploscha.

He wished he could understand what they were saying. The screen switched to show a stormy meeting in the Verkhovna Rada, members screaming and shoving each other, then cut back to Kozhanovskiy. So it was something to do with the election, he thought. For now, he had to decide who to go after: Gabrilov or the Chinese?

He needed intel. Badly. He thought about Vadim Akhnetzov. Lianhuay did heavy machinery business in Ukraine. Akhnetzov had to have heard of them, he thought. It was long past time he connected with the man who was paying him anyway. He sent an emergency e-mail to a cover Gmail account Akhnetzov had given him and logged off after deleting any record that he had been on that computer.

One overarching question nagged at him: Why would the Chinese want Cherkesov dead?

The short man wore a Swiss hat and a red plaid scarf draped over one shoulder. Hardly a typical Ukrainian male outfit, and Scorpion thought he might be gay. The man was standing on the Nyvky Metro platform, looking around every few minutes.

"*Ne oborachivaisya*," Scorpion said, coming up behind him. Don't turn around. They were near the edge of the platform.

"*Ya rodom iz Finlyandii*," the man said. I come from Finland.

"I used to like the jazz in Esplanade Park," Scorpion said in English, completing the sequence. The man started to turn around, and Scorpion stopped him. "I said, *ne oborachivaisya*."

"I'm Boyko," the man said in excellent English. "You Collins?" he asked, using Scorpion's cover name from when he had first met Akhnetzov.

"Never mind who I am," Scorpion growled. "Tell me about the Lianhuay Trading Company."

"What about them? They're a Chinese company. Officially, they sell machinery and do construction projects."

"And unofficially?"

"We've heard stories about illegal arms and trade intelligence. They're said to pay well."

"Are they Guoanbu?"

"Well . . ." Boyko shrugged. "They're Chinese."

"Why would the Chinese want Cherkesov dead?"

Boyko started to turn around. Scorpion stopped him.

"You think they were involved?" Boyko asked.

"You tell me," Scorpion said. "What did they have against Cherkesov?"

"Haven't the foggiest. Could be the new gas pipeline."

"What pipeline?"

"There's a proposed new pipeline from Kazakhstan through Ukraine to supply natural gas to additional countries in Europe. The Chinese and the Russians are both bidding for the contract."

"How was Cherkesov involved?"

"At Ukengaz, it was our understanding that if Cherkesov had been elected, he'd have gone with the Russians."

"Sounds like a motive to me," Scorpion said. "Why didn't Akhnetzov tell me about this?"

"Don't use his name. Just Vadik. I have to tell you, he's not happy."

"Neither am I."

"Not at all. May I smoke?"

"Set yourself on fire for all I care. Let's talk about Vadik and the Chinese."

"He wasn't sure it was relevant," Boyko replied, lighting a cigarette.

"Excuse me? The Russians and the Chinese are in competition for a pipeline worth billions. Cherkesov and Ukengaz are poised to give it to the Russians and you don't think that gives the Chinese a motive? What planet are you from?"

"The SVR never mentioned the Chinese," Boyko said. "This is awkward talking this way. Can I turn around?"

"No," Scorpion said, putting his hand on Boyko's back and moving a half step behind him. "Pyatov was a decoy to pull me off the scent. It also made me the fall guy. Everyone's looking for me."

"Makes you less effective. You failed. Vadik's ready to call this whole adventure off."

"No deal," Scorpion said. "Our agreement was no

Russian invasion. If I can stop it, he still owes me the rest of the money."

"I'll tell him. Anything else?"

"Who set me up? The SVR? Tell Vadik if it's him, his money won't save him."

"It wasn't him. He said even now he wants to believe in you."

"So who was it? Gabrilov or the Chinese?"

"Gabrilov's no genius. Maybe the Chinese?" Boyko shrugged.

"Tell me about Li Qiang."

"You've made progress," Boyko said, starting to turn his head, then stopped. "You're right. He's head of the Guoanbu in Kyiv."

"I know that. Tell me what I don't know."

"He has a male friend."

"How thrilling."

"No. A *special* male friend," Boyko said, emphasizing the word.

"And who's this special friend?"

"His name is Ruslan. Ruslan Ardiev."

"Where can I find him?"

"He performs at the Androgyne Club. Frankly, his body's better than his voice. If not there, there's a massage place, the Congo, on Berezhanskaya; *goluboi*, of course," he added, using the Russian slang word for gay. "And watch out for Li Qiang's bodyguard, Yang Hao. Never leaves his side."

"Dangerous?"

"We've heard stories," Boyko said.

They heard a train coming and felt a rush of cold air ahead of it as it approached the station.

"Are we boarding?" Boyko asked.

"Just wait," Scorpion said.

"I'm not comfortable with the train coming with you behind me."

"Funny, I'd've thought you'd love it," Scorpion said.

Boyko snorted. "Cheeky boy. Not before I see what you look like." The train stopped and opened its doors. "Are we boarding?"

"Tell Vadik what I said."

"I will. Are you coming, Collins?"

"You go," Scorpion said, giving him a nudge forward.

Boyko got on, turned and looked at Scorpion, who had turned and was walking away on the platform.

"Pity," Boyko said.

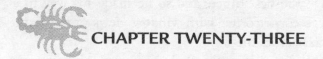

CHAPTER TWENTY-THREE

Expo Plaza
Kyiv, Ukraine

The Lianhuay company office was on the ninth floor of an office building across from the Expo Plaza Exhibition Center. There were two security cameras covering the front entrance, but only one at the back. Scorpion used his Leatherman tool to chip a toehold in the wall at the back of the building, then climbed up and disabled the camera. A tap on his Peterson universal key and he was inside.

The building was dark and empty. His footsteps echoed as he climbed the stairs to the Lianhuay office. There was an alarm on the office door, but it was only single channel. It took him less than a minute to disarm it. The door lock was a card reader. He used an NSA card and waited while the software read the magnetic reader setting and opened the lock.

Before entering, he used his flashlight to check for motion detectors. He didn't see any and went inside. It was hard to tell whose office was whose; the name plaques were in Mandarin, which he couldn't read. But hierarchy was the same no matter what language it was in, he thought. Li Qiang would have the best office, and so he made his way to a large corner office with window views of the Expo Plaza across the way.

He turned on the desk computer, plugging his NSA drive into a USB port. The NSA software automatically figured out how to log itself into any computer with administrator privileges. It also scanned the password files for account passwords and provided English translation on the fly for all major languages, including Mandarin. While the software was running, he checked the desk drawers. In one of them he found a Chinese M-77B 9mm pistol, checked to see if it was loaded and put it back. He went through the rest of the drawers but found nothing of interest.

He hit the Start and the All Programs arrow and pressed the NSA Ctrl key combination for translation to English. Then he saw it. A client software program on the PC for the CCB Bank. Based in Beijing, CCB was one of the largest banks in the world.

Scorpion accessed the bank's website with the software client, letting the NSA software provide the user ID and password. There were multiple accounts. This was going to take a while, he thought, settling down to open them one by one. Then he got lucky. In the second account he opened, he spotted an electronic bank transfer of $2,500 in U.S. dollars to an account in Pravex Bank, Kyiv. He didn't bother with the NSA software, but letter by letter translated the Cyrillic account name. It belonged to Oleg Nikolayevich Gabrilov. He did a Find all search and saw repeated transfers to Gabrilov's account in amounts ranging from $1,000 to $6,500 over the past two years.

Well well. Scorpion smiled to himself. The only thing better than having a potential Joe's balls in a vise, he thought, was getting proof he was being paid by the wrong people.

After copying the files to the plug-in drive, he shut down the computer. Before leaving, he used an antiseptic wipe to clean everything he had touched and then rearmed the security camera. Ten minutes later he was out on the snowy street on his way to the Nyvky Metro station.

So it looked like Gabrilov was Li Qiang's double agent in the SVR. It wasn't about politics. It was about money. Natural gas. Maybe if he could produce the real assassin, he and Iryna would be off the hook. Maybe.

The street was cold and empty and he shivered inside his coat. Not far from the Metro station he saw an open café, stepped inside and ordered *chorna kava*, black coffee, piping hot, and gulped it down. The TV on the wall behind the counter showed a press conference going on in Washington. The President of the United States was speaking. He was warning Russia not to invade Ukraine. As a precautionary measure, he announced that he had ordered the Joint Chiefs of Staff to raise the level of American military readiness to DEFCON 2, the second highest level before war.

Scorpion put down his coffee and went back outside, walking as fast as he could to the Metro.

He was running out of time.

CHAPTER TWENTY-FOUR

Shulyavska
Kyiv, Ukraine

She was beautiful, blond, and sexy in a tight red dress cut low to reveal perfect cleavage. She was singing Madonna's "Take a Bow" in a throaty contralto, stage lights gliding across her body, and she almost had you going, except that she was a man.

"*Razve chto Ruslan?*" Scorpion asked the waiter in Russian. Is that Ruslan?

"*On nazyvaet sebya Svetlana,*" the waiter said. He calls himself Svetlana.

"Can you bring her over?" Scorpion asked, holding out two one-hundred *hryven* bills.

"*Konechno.*" Sure. "You got good taste," the waiter said, taking the money.

Scorpion was sitting in the shadows, in an alcove with a plush sofa and a view of the stage. The club was chrome and black, cigarette smoke spiraling in colored lights, and filled with gay men and a few lesbian couples. A few minutes after her set, the waiter, smirking, brought Svetlana over to his table.

She looked at Scorpion, smiled, and sat next to him, motioning for the waiter to stay.

"*Kupitmne champanskogo, dorogoi,*" she said, squeezing Scorpion's thigh. Buy me champagne, darling.

"*Skolka?*" Scorpion asked. How much?

"Twelve hundred," the waiter said. About $150.

Scorpion nodded. Svetlana looked triumphantly at the waiter, who grinned and left.

"Do you speak English?" Scorpion asked.

"Little only, *dorogoi,*" Svetlana said, groping up Scorpion's thigh toward his groin till he stopped her.

"Let's talk first," he said.

"*Konechno, dorogoi.* After *champanskogo,* we go VIP room," Svetlana said, indicating a room with вип in red neon over the door. "You will like me, I promise," she whispered in his ear.

"You will like me better," Scorpion said, showing her a stack of large *hryven* notes.

Svetlana took his hand and started to pull him up.

"Forget *champanskogo* and fuck me now," she said.

Scorpion pulled her back down.

"What about your *droog?*" Your boyfriend.

"What boyfriend?" looking at him suspiciously.

"Your Chinese *droog,* Li Qiang."

"What is this?" she said, exhaling smoke.

"I need to talk to Li Qiang. No trouble, just business."

"So go his office. Don't come sex me. Make trouble," she said, staring glumly at the stage, where a drag queen pulled up her plaid schoolgirl-style skirt and wiggled her behind at the audience to laughs and scattered applause.

"I need to see him alone. Without his body-guard," Scorpion said.

"Why?"

"You don't understand. He doesn't have to be afraid of me. I am afraid of his bodyguard, Yang."

"Ne svisti." Don't lie. "You not type guy who is afraid," she said, putting the cigarettes back in her purse and starting to get up. "I not like."

Scorpion grabbed her wrist and pulled her back. He put a stack of money on the sofa and held her hand on top so she could feel it.

"You really like him that much?" he asked.

"He okay," she shrugged. "To tell truth," looking at Scorpion, "he kind of *lokh*, understand?" Russian slang for a mark, a sucker. She wrinkled her nose as if smelling something bad. "I get bored. China men not so big where is important, understand?"

"Help me tonight, I'll give you ten thousand. Half now," Scorpion said, removing her hand and counting it out. "No trouble, I promise."

She took the money and smiled.

"You look big enough," she said, exhaling a thin stream of smoke at him.

"Not for you," he said, putting the rest of the money away. "Like I said, this is business, *rodimy*."

He waited while Ruslan went back and changed. When Ruslan came out looking like a man, they took a taxi to the massage parlor on Berezhanskaya. Without the makeup and the wig, Ruslan was a young man, handsome enough to be a model, and it was easy to see how he made such a good-looking woman.

They drove down the hill toward the Shulyavska neighborhood, the streets wet with slush, overhead power lines sagging with snow. On the way, Ruslan called Li Qiang on his cell phone. Following Scorpion's instructions, Ruslan insisted they have one night that was just the two of them, without having Yang Hao waiting outside the door.

"*Ya hochu tebya, moi dorogoi,*" Ruslan told him. I want you, my darling. "For once, the whole night, just the two of us."

After hanging up, he said, "He's coming."

"What about the bodyguard?"

"Yang is staying in car. He promise not come inside." Ruslan held out his hand. "You give rest of money, *kharasho?*"

"Inside," Scorpion said.

The taxi pulled up to the massage parlor with its blue neon sign that read CONGO MASSAGE SPA in the curtained window. Scorpion paid the driver and he and Ruslan went in separately, acting as if they didn't know each other. Ruslan got the deluxe room, number 4. He slipped the man behind the counter fifty *hryvnia* to let Li Qiang know where he was.

Scorpion got the key to Room 16 and went through the main lounge, where a dozen or so naked men lounging on benches and in the steaming Jacuzzi pool checked him out. He found his way to Room 4, knocked and went in. Ruslan was lounging on a waterbed. He jumped up when Scorpion came in.

"You want I wait?" he asked.

Scorpion shook his head and gave him the rest of the money. Ruslan started for the door, then stopped.

"No trouble, *da*?"

"No trouble," Scorpion said.

"You want, I wait in other room. After, we make sex. No money. Best *zhopa* in world," Ruslan said, slapping his ass and wiggling it suggestively.

"I like women," Scorpion said.

"I am better. The woman always she make trouble."

"Well, we're no bargain either," Scorpion said. "Go out the back way and don't let anyone see you,"

"*Buvay, rodimy*," Ruslan said—So long, sweetheart—and left.

Scorpion waited behind the door. It was after midnight when he heard a knock. A moment later the Chinese man from the photo walked in.

Stepping out, Scorpion motioned with the SR-1 Gyurza for Li Qiang to sit on the waterbed.

"*De Ruslan?*" Li Qiang asked in Ukrainian.

"He's not here. Speak English," Scorpion said.

"*Na zhal, ya ne hovoryu po angliyski.*" Sorry, I don't speak English.

"You went to USC, you son of a bitch. Don't bullshit me," Scorpion said, sitting on the only chair in the room, just out of range if Li Qiang made a move.

"What's your problem? You go to UCLA?" Li Qiang said in perfect English, studying the man in front of him.

He's good, Scorpion thought. Li Qiang was sizing him up so he could provide a description in case he survived. He approved, one professional to another.

Li Qiang looked at the gun pointed at him. "Are you going to kill me?"

"That depends on our conversation."

"I have a man outside."

"Yang Hao. In the car. For the time being, he lives. Like you," Scorpion said.

"Who are you? CIA? MI-6?"

"The goddamn Boy Scouts! What difference does it make? You're running the Russian, Oleg Gabrilov."

"Am I? And how did you come across that particular piece of disinformation?" Li Qiang said, sliding back on the waterbed so he could rest his back against the wall. He folded his arms across his chest and bobbed up and down on the bed, sitting perfectly straight, like a yogi riding the waves into nirvana. He's good, Scorpion thought again. The fact that his most important Joe was blown should've rocked Li Qiang down to his socks, but he looked unfazed.

"Bank transfers from CCB to Gabrilov's Pravex account," he replied.

Li Qiang shrugged. "Second-rate hacker stuff. You'll have to do better."

"Not sure the folks in Yasenevo will see it that way. Or Zhongnanhai, come to that," Scorpion said, referring to the Moscow suburb where the SVR was headquartered and the Beijing headquarters of the

Guoanbu. It effectively told Li that he knew Gabrilov was SVR and that he headed Guoanbu operations in Kyiv.

"That is better. Much better," Li agreed. "So is this about money, Mister . . . ?"

"Vasja Pupkin." Russian slang for John Doe.

"Cute," Li smirked. "What do you want Pane Pupkin?"

"Who killed Cherkesov?"

"Don't you watch TV? The authorities suspect Iryna Shevchenko and a foreign journalist, name of . . . I forget."

"Kilbane," Scorpion said.

"That's it. I believe they're after you, Pane Pupkin—or is it Kilbane?" looking directly at Scorpion. So the son of a bitch recognized him, Scorpion thought.

"Now who's being cute?" he replied. "Especially since we both know Iryna and I didn't do it."

"No, but that won't stop them from executing you. Bullet in the back of the head seems to be their style. Do you like *travka*?" Li asked, using the Russian slang word for marijuana.

Scorpion shook his head. "Not while I'm working."

"Of course. Mind if I light up?"

"*Mne po figu*," meaning he didn't give a damn. "And you didn't answer me. Who killed Cherkesov?"

"What makes you think I would know?" Li had pulled a joint out of his pocket and was now lighting it, filling the air with the scent of marijuana.

"You and Gabrilov hired Sirhiy Pyatov as a decoy

to lure someone from the Kozhanovskiy campaign as the fall guy. Plus you had a motive to get rid of Cherkesov."

"Which is?" Li said in a choked voice from holding the smoke in, then exhaling.

"The new gas pipeline from Kazakhstan. Cherkesov was going to throw the deal to the Russians."

"*Nanyi zhi xin!*" Li exclaimed in Chinese, shaking his head. "This is a CIA fantasy! You can't seriously believe that we're stupid enough to jeopardize everything we're trying to do in Europe over a Ukrainian gas pipeline?"

"Why not? It's billions of dollars," Scorpion said, having expected Li Qiang to deny involvement, but this was something else.

"First of all," Li said, "it isn't the pipeline we care about; it's the gas. And we want it to go the other way, to China. Killing a hundred Cherkesovs wouldn't make that happen. Second, to get to Ukraine the pipeline has to go through southern Russia near Astrakhan anyway, so the Russians were always going to be part of the deal."

"You bid on it."

"Of course we bid on it. Better that than to have them focus on something important. You should learn from Sun Tzu."

" 'All war is deception,' " Scorpion quoted.

"So . . ." Li Qiang looked at Scorpion speculatively. "Not entirely stupid." He shrugged. "In the end, we'll do business with Kozhanovskiy or whoever Svoboda gets to replace Cherkesov—or Vasja Pupkin, for all we give a damn." He coolly exhaled a long stream of marijuana smoke. "This is good shit. Sure you don't want some?" holding the joint out to Scorpion, who shook his head.

"Let's assume for a second I believe you," Scorpion said. "If you didn't kill Cherkesov and no one in the Kozhanovskiy campaign did, who did? It couldn't be the SVR. The Russians wanted him to win."

"Can't you guess, *bratan*?" Li said, grinning like the Cheshire cat, his eyes glassy with the marijuana. Now they were brothers, Scorpion thought. A little more grass and maybe he'd get some truth out of the son of a bitch. "Think. Who stood to gain from Cherkesov's death? Who did he threaten?" All at once, Scorpion realized what Li Qiang was trying to tell him.

"You're saying it's a CIA operation?"

"They have the most to gain." Li shrugged. "You know you're an attractive man. Not so handsome as that lying *bljad* whore Ruslan, but not bad."

"It's not a CIA op," Scorpion said. But was it? he wondered, then thought about some of the ops-within-ops Bob Harris, the Deputy DCIA, had pulled. But why would they want him and Iryna as the fall guys? It would ensure that Kozhanovskiy would lose. It didn't add up.

"Then it's a mystery," Li said. "You're not going to kill me for that, are you?"

"I'm going to give you one chance to live," Scorpion said. No matter how you turned this thing, he thought, Gabrilov was the key. He had set up Pyatov as a decoy to cover the real assassination. If he didn't do it for the Guoanbu, he sure as hell did it for someone. "Set up a meeting. Private. Just you and Gabrilov. Only I'll be there instead of you. I'll call and tell you where and when."

"Suppose I don't cooperate? Or suppose I decide to send my bodyguard, Yang Hao, instead, or maybe just turn you in to the *politsiy* or the SBU?"

"You know, I thought we were getting along. Now I'm beginning to think you don't understand me, *bratan*," Scorpion said quietly. For a moment the only sounds were the rhythmic sexual groans coming from the room next door. Li looked at him with glassy eyes, then shook his head as if to clear it. "You think I haven't arranged backup? If anything happens to me, you and Gabrilov will be blown all over the Internet. Even if I'm dead, Yasenevo and Zhongnanhai will know exactly who to blame."

"And if I agree to make the call?" Li said. "Consider it professional courtesy. I'm curious myself, especially since I pay the son of a bitch."

"Then have a nice day," Scorpion replied, getting up.

"You'll call me?" Li said.

"If anyone shows up except Gabrilov, Yang Hao won't protect you."

"He always has," Li said.

"Wait ten minutes, then leave," Scorpion said, and left.

Li's last remark had forced his hand. He went out to the Jacuzzi area and found his way to the rear exit, first checking Room 16 to make sure Ruslan had gone. It was empty.

He stepped outside into an alley, heaped with snow, crunched through it and peeked around the corner, looking for Li Qiang's car. He spotted an Audi parked down the street, smoke coming from its tailpipe. It had to be Yang Hao, he thought, with the engine running to keep himself from freezing in the bitter cold.

He figured Yang Hao would be watching the spa's front door and, if he was good, the side mirror as well for anyone coming up behind the car. He wouldn't be looking for anyone coming on the passenger side from across the street. Scorpion stepped out of the alley, pulled up his overcoat collar and adjusted a scarf across the lower part of his face. Keeping to the shadows, he walked in the opposite direction, away from the Audi, till he was out of sight. Then he crossed the icy street and headed back. This late, after midnight on a weeknight in the dead of winter, there was no traffic.

He checked the Gyurza pistol with the silencer, to make sure the safety was off and ready to fire, and approached the Audi from behind on the opposite side of the street, keeping the gun shielded by his body from anyone in the car. When he was almost parallel with the car, he cut across the icy street. He saw the silhouette of a man sitting behind the wheel. The man was watching the Congo spa's front door, the sound of the radio playing Russian hip hop coming from inside the car.

Stepping up to the passenger side, Scorpion fired three times through the window.

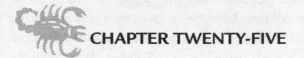

CHAPTER TWENTY-FIVE

Babi Yar
Kyiv, Ukraine

The hotel was out from the center of the city, near the Dorohozhichi Metro station. It was across the street from a wooded park, covered with bare trees and snow and dominated by a giant TV tower as tall as the Empire State Building. Coming out of the Metro, Scorpion saw a strange bronze statue at the edge of the park. It was of a child standing beside a seated child with the head of a bird. Another statue, a massive sculpture of twisted figures, stood farther back in the snow closer to the woods. The park was dark, silent in the night, and looming above it was the TV tower. When Scorpion checked in, he asked the hotel clerk about it.

"Is Babi Yar," said the clerk, who acted like he had been asked about it many times and was in any case more interested in the two hundred *hryvnia* Scorpion gave him to not ask for ID.

"What's Babi Yar?"

"Place where Germans kill Jews in Great Patriotic War."

"Were many killed?"

"I don't know." The clerk shrugged. "Many thousands. All Jews in Kyiv," drawing a finger across his throat. "Nazis kill Ukraintsi too, but all anyone care about is Jews," slapping the room key on the counter and turning away.

Scorpion went up to the seventh floor in the elevator, then walked down the stairs to the sixth, where his room was. He peered out at the empty hallway and went quickly to his room. He had booked adjacent rooms in case Gabrilov didn't come alone. Always a possibility with the SVR, especially after what he had done to Yang Hao. He'd had no choice, he thought. It was essential that he, not Li Qiang, was driving things, and that Li Qiang understood that.

Walking by the park on the way to the hotel he had heard from Iryna. A text message on the cell phone he had in sync with hers telling him it was urgent she see him. It was followed by a second text indicating an address, with, as he had instructed her, the numbers transposed by one, so 2 became 3, 3 became 4, and so on. Things were coming to a head. He had texted back: *c u. late.*

He checked that both hotel rooms were empty. In the room he'd had Li Qiang arrange for the RDV, he unlocked the window, checking the distance to the window of the room next door. There was no ledge, but it was only about a meter away. He looked around to get the lay of the room, knocking on the wall for the best spot to listen. He left, then, locking the door behind him, and went into the room next door.

He opened his pack and got ready. He readied plastic ties that he kept coiled inside a Band-Aid kit and a roll of duct tape he never went anywhere without. He got a glass out of the bathroom and put it next to the wall, then took out his Glock, attached the sound suppresser and snapped off the safety. He had already gotten rid of the Gyurza pistol after terminating Yang Hao, taking it apart and wiping each part clean of fingerprints before dropping pieces of it in various sewer openings on the way to the Metro. Having used the Gyurza in the Mercedes in Kyiv and on Yang Hao; it was past time to get rid of it. The Glock tied him to the shoot-out at Stadion Dnipro, but once he found the real assassin, he would get rid of that too. He got ready by the door, peering through the peephole.

Then, before he saw them, he heard them coming, men speaking Russian. Gabrilov appeared with two men in black jackets, both carrying guns. Even though Li Qiang was supposed to have told him to come alone, the meeting was enough out of the ordinary that Gabrilov was afraid to take chances. Unless they were there because Gabrilov had found out about Yang Hao.

Gabrilov knocked on the door of the room where the RDV with Li Qiang was supposed to take place, then flattened himself out of the way against the wall, while his SVR bodyguards aimed at the door. When there was no response, he handed them the key and they went inside with a show of force, aiming their guns. A minute later, having found it empty, the two men came out of the room. One positioned himself in the hallway by the elevator; the other peered out from behind the staircase door.

Scorpion put the glass to the wall and listened. There was nothing, only the sounds of Gabrilov moving around, sitting down. Time to go, he thought, slinging his pack over one shoulder, going to the window and opening it. Icy air instantly poured into the room.

He stepped out, squatting onto the windowsill, fingers gripping the lintel. He tried not to look down at the street, six stories below. Pressing against the side of the building, he reached the toes of his left foot to the next door windowsill. It was longer than he had thought. He was about three inches short, would have to push off with a small leap and grab onto the next window's lintel, hoping he didn't make any noise. It was freezing cold. The alternative, he thought, was to have a shoot-out with the SVR guns in the hallway. Not for the first time, he thought about getting into a different line of work. Then he thought about what might happen if he didn't stop the Russian invasion.

He took a breath and half swung, half leaped, across to the other window. The front of his foot landed on the sill as he grabbed for the lintel. For an instant his fingers slipped and he felt himself falling, but managed to grab and hold on by his fingertips. Squatting, he looked into the room. Gabrilov was looking at the door. Scorpion raised the window up in a sudden move and aimed the Glock at Gabrilov who, hearing the sound, had turned around, his eyes wide.

"*Zatknis!*" Scorpion hissed in Russian. Shut up! He motioned with the Glock for Gabrilov to raise his hands. Gabrilov started to say something. Scorpion shook his head no. He pulled the window the rest of the way up and stepped into the room.

"Close the window," Scorpion told him in English, frisking him as he went by. Gabrilov closed the window and turned around.

"You!" Gabrilov said, his eyes narrowing.

"Call your man by the elevator with your cell phone. Tell him to come in. You need help with something. Remember, *Ya govoryu na russkom.*" I speak Russian.

"You speak *govno* shit Russian."

"True, but if you say the wrong thing, I'll kill you."

Scorpion could see Gabrilov calculating, his eyes darting. He was putting it together, realizing that he had gotten to Li Qiang.

"What is it you want?" Gabrilov said.

"Call your man," Scorpion said, coming close and touching the silencer muzzle to his head. Gabrilov took out his cell phone and called him.

A moment later there were two knocks on the door, followed by two more knocks. Scorpion moved beside the door and nodded to Gabrilov, who came and opened the door.

"*Ostorozhna!*" Gabrilov cried out. Look out! But it was too late. Scorpion had put the Glock to the SVR man's head while grabbing the man's pistol with his other hand and twisting it out of his grip. He kicked the door closed and pushed his knees against the back of the knees of the SVR man in front of him, forcing his legs to buckle. He pushed the man face-down to the floor.

"*Ne dvigat'sya.*" Don't move, he told the SVR man, glancing at Gabrilov, who started to back away. The look in Scorpion's eyes stopped him. Covering both of them with the Glock, Scorpion grabbed his pack, took out the plastic ties and, using one hand, tied the SVR man's feet together and his hands behind him. Then he got up, Gabrilov's eyes never leaving him.

"You shouldn't have done that," Scorpion said, twisting Gabrilov's wrist while keeping the gun to his head to force him to sit on the floor. He kicked Gabrilov's legs apart. "Remember. *Zatknis,*" he said. Shut up. Then he kicked Gabrilov between his legs as hard as he could.

"*Oyyyy! Sukin-sin!*" Gabrilov moaned. You son of a bitch!

"You have no idea," Scorpion said. He crossed back to the SVR man and duct-taped his mouth, eyes, and ears. "Call the other one," he said.

Holding his groin with one hand, Gabrilov did as he was told. In a few minutes Scorpion had both SVR men bound, taped, and tied together, facing each other so one couldn't use his hands to try to help the other. He took Gabrilov by the arm, and after checking the hallway, walked him to the room next door, Gabrilov gasping in pain at every step. Once inside, Scorpion used another plastic cuff to tie Gabrilov's hands behind him and then propped him to sit on the floor against the bed. He sat down in a chair facing Gabrilov.

"Now we can talk," he said.

"What you want, *zhurnalist*?" Gabrilov said, spitting out the word like an epithet.

"Who killed Cherkesov?"

Gabrilov shrugged. "How I should know?"

"Pyatov was the *bolvan*—the idiot, the decoy. You used him to set up Iryna Shevchenko and me so Kozhanovskiy would lose the election. Except it wasn't you. Russia wanted Cherkesov to be president."

"Is maybe Kitaiskim." Chinese.

"Get a new song. That one's getting old," Scorpion said. "The Chinese aren't going to risk a war. Not over a pipeline that's got to go through Russia anyway. So who did it? Who had something to gain by killing Cherkesov?"

"CIA." Gabrilov smirked. "You want assassin, look in mirror."

Scorpion shook his head. "The Americans don't want a war in Europe any more than the Chinese." He aimed the Glock at Gabrilov. "No more twenty questions, you *mudak* son of a bitch. Tell me or I'll kill you."

"Even you kill, I not telling," Gabrilov said, folding his arms over his chest.

"Not even when I tell Yasenevo about the money the Guoanbu's been depositing in your Pravex account?"

Gabrilov stared at him. Scorpion could see his hands tremble.

"It's no longer a matter of the SVR and maybe just a bullet in the back of the head, is it? It's the FSB, you fool," Scorpion said. He waited. *You can't just lead the Joe all the way to the Promised Land*, Koenig used to say. *When it comes time for him to drop his pants, you have to let him come to it himself. People would rather die than face who they really are.*

"I not know," Gabrilov said.

Scorpion shook his head. "No good. Everything about the assassination came from you. No matter which way I turn, the compass needle points to you." He stood up. Time to play his hole card. "I have to end this. Do I contact Checkmate?" he asked, referring to Ivanov, the legendary spymaster of the FSB.

Scorpion waited for Gabrilov to get the picture. The FSB hated the SVR even more than they hated the CIA. He wanted Cherkesov to picture himself being questioned in Lubyanka. Especially about the money from the Chinese. From somewhere in the hotel, he heard the sound of a TV commercial, something about Obolon beer.

"What you want, mister?" Gabrilov said at last.

"No more lies. Who killed Cherkesov?"

Gabrilov licked his lips. He looked lost. "His own peoples," he said.

"Who? What are you talking about?"

"I not sure. You will find."

Jesus, it made sense, Scorpion thought. A power struggle within Svoboda. He was about to question Gabrilov about what the Russians really wanted when his cell phone vibrated. It was another message from Iryna.

She texted: *come now. urgent.*

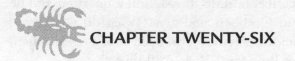

CHAPTER TWENTY-SIX

Darnytskyi
Kyiv, Ukraine

"Who's the ski jacket in the van across the street?" Scorpion asked.

"Danylo. Viktor sent him to—" Iryna started, but couldn't finish because they were kissing, tongues searching, exploring, tearing off their clothes as if it were the first time; if anything, more intense. Bittersweet too, as if they sensed their time together was coming to an end. Afterward, in bed, she lit a cigarette and told him more.

"You heard there was a riot in the Verkhovna Rada? Anyway, it's settled. The elections will be postponed for three weeks. It hasn't been made public yet, but Svoboda is going to announce that Lavro Davydenko will be the party's new candidate for President."

"Who's Davydenko?"

"A nobody. A nonentity. He's the kind of man that when he enters the room, you get the feeling someone just left," she said, exhaling smoke angrily.

"Why'd they pick him?"

"He's Gorobets's man. If Gorobets sent him to fetch coffee, he'd do it. Ask him a question and he turns to Gorobets and says 'What do you think, Oleksandr Maxymovych?' Such a man—not a man, a thing! President! Now of all times!"

"What happened?"

"Didn't you see the news? As prime minister, Viktor sent a request to NATO to stop the Russian invasion. NATO is meeting in emergency session. Viktor spoke on the phone with the American president. The Americans say they will issue a stern warning to the Russians. A stern warning!" She turned to him "The Americans. Can we trust them?"

"I wouldn't know. I don't do politics," he hesitated. "Then too . . ."

"Then too what?"

"America has its own interests to look out for."

She stubbed out her cigarette in a jar top she was using as an ashtray.

"I smoke too much."

"You do," he said.

She turned to him on her side, her naked breast nudging his arm.

"Did you find out anything?"

"It's not the Guoanbu. The Chinese made a show of interest in the new gas pipeline to distract the Russians from what they really want: new markets and gas for China."

"So who killed Cherkesov? The CIA?"

"That's what the SVR is trying to sell. Except you and I both know it's not true."

She traced her finger down his face from his forehead down his nose and lips to his chin.

"How do I know?"

"You were with me," he said. "It was an inside job. A power play inside Svoboda. So we just need to figure who stood to gain from Cherkesov's death."

"Gorobets! He's the big winner, especially if that clown, Davydenko, wins! He'll be running the country. We'll denounce him!" She sat up excitedly.

"Right now everyone, including the *politsiy*, thinks we're the killers. We need proof. We need the bomber." He looked at her. "What was so urgent that you texted me?"

"I heard from Oksana."

"Your mole in Gorobets's office?"

Iryna nodded. "She said something. Gorobets has a bodyguard. Big guy with scruffy blond hair in his eyes."

"Shelayev." Scorpion nodded. The guy who crushed heads like eggshells. "What about him?"

"She said she hasn't seen him since the assassination. No one seems to know where he is, or if they do, they're not saying." She looked at Scorpion, her face with its pixie haircut barely visible in the darkness. "Could he be the assassin?"

"He's Gorobets's man. And he's Spetsnaz-trained. Possible, very possible."

"She said something else. It bothered me. That's why I had to see you."

"What?"

"She said that two days before the rally in Dnipropetrovsk she went to a café near the university here in Kyiv. She saw Shelayev having coffee with Alyona."

Scorpion sat up suddenly and slapped his forehead. "What an idiot! How stupid of me not to have seen it!" He looked at Iryna. "Did they see her?"

"She didn't think so. She hasn't told anyone."

Scorpion gripped her shoulder. "You have to get hold of her! Tell her not to say a word to anyone. If she says anything, she'll be killed. And especially nothing about Shelayev."

Iryna nodded. Scorpion got up and walked naked to the window. They were on the twelfth floor of a Left Bank apartment building that overlooked a bridge over the Dnieper, the lights from the bridge reflected on the ice in the river. The van with Danylo was still parked on the street below. Something about it bothered him, but he wasn't sure what. He turned and looked at her.

"Where did she live, Alyona?"

"You know. The apartment near the Central Station."

"No, before then. Maybe with her parents or something. If she were in trouble, where would she go?"

"Her father died. Her mother came from Bila Tserkva, I think. *Gospadi*, you don't think she's alive?"

"Very unlikely. But whatever happened, she's at the center of this thing," Scorpion said, grabbing his clothes and starting to dress.

"What are we going to do?"

"When we get there, we'll figure it out," he said, turning on his laptop computer.

He gave her the new identity cards he'd had Matviy make for her, one with the blond wig photo, the second with her pixie haircut.

"How'd you get these?" she asked, studying the names she would be using.

"Santa Claus. Shit!" he said, looking at the laptop screen after he had clicked onto the BBC's news.bbc.co.uk website.

"What is it?" she said.

"Have a look." He turned the screen for her to see. There had been a shooting incident involving Russian troops at a border village called Vovchansk, near the city of Kharkov in eastern Ukraine. The headline was that Viktor Kozhanovskiy, acting as prime minister, was expected to announce a full mobilization of the Ukrainian Armed Forces at 0600 hours local time.

"*Gospadi*," she whispered. "It's really happening. What will NATO and the Americans do?"

Scorpion didn't answer. He went back to the window and peered down from behind the curtain. The van was still there, no smoke coming from its exhaust. If Danylo had been sitting in it through the night, he would have frozen to death. An SUV was double-parked behind the van. As he watched, he saw five men crossing the street toward their building. He began grabbing things and shoving them into his backpack.

"We have to go," he said.

This time she didn't say a word. She immediately began cramming things into her carry-on. He went into the kitchen and rummaged like a madman through the pantry and under the sink, throwing contents and cans onto the floor. He found a bag of flour and two aerosol cans of cleaning spray. He came back to the main room, dumped the flour out of the bag onto the sagging sofa and tossed the cans on top.

"Do you have any fluids? Perfume, nail polish, hair spray, anything?" he asked her.

"Here. Why?" she said, digging in her handbag. She handed him a bottle of eau de cologne and another of nail polish remover. He poured them both over the sofa, the cans and the flour. He went back to the kitchen, turned on the gas in the oven but didn't light it, and left the oven door open.

"Give me your lighter," he said, shoving her toward the door. She handed it to him, her hand shaking.

"Do you ever leave an apartment normally?" she asked.

"Apparently not in Ukraine," he said, flicking the lighter and holding the flame to the drapes. When they started burning, he put the lighter flame to the spilled perfume and nail polish remover on the sofa. An acrid cloud of flame and smoke mushroomed up.

"How do you say 'fire' in Ukrainian?" he asked as they headed out of the apartment.

"*Pozhezha.*"

"Come on," he said, heading to the next apartment. He started pounding on the door and yelling, *"Pozhezha! Pozhezha!"* then ran to the next apartment and shouted and pounded again.

Iryna ran the other way to another apartment, shouting, *"Pozhezha! Dopomozhit!"* Fire! Help!

They ran past the elevator. It was coming up. As it did they shouted and pounded on other apartment doors on the floor. People, most in pajamas or half dressed, were coming out of their doors. They could smell smoke in the hallway. Scorpion spotted tendrils of smoke coming from the bottom and sides of their apartment door. Men, women, children, everyone began shouting, screaming, and rushing out of their apartments and into the halls.

Scorpion grabbed Iryna's hand and led her toward the staircase. Suddenly, a massive explosion rocked the hallway. It blasted the door off their apartment, lifting them off their feet and knocking them to the floor. A whoosh of flame shot out of the blasted doorway into the hall. People screamed in panic. Everyone began running.

"Zabyraysya!" Get out! "Down the stairs! Hurry!" Iryna screamed in Ukrainian as she and Scorpion joined a cluster of people pounding down the staircase. On the floor below, she and Scorpion ran out to the hallway. They pounded on doors and shouted again, and when they got back to the staircase, a river of people were scrambling down.

Scorpion spotted two men, one with a prison cross tattoo on the side of his neck, trying to come up the stairs. The two men were swamped by the people swarming down, and after a moment of trying to go against the tide hearing the cries of *"Pozhezha!"* they gave up and joined the flood of people running down the stairs. Scorpion and Iryna were swept with the crowd out into the frozen street.

Iryna spotted the van. She started toward it, but Scorpion grabbed her arm and pulled her away. She struggled, trying to go back.

"I have to see Danylo. Make sure he's all right."

"He's dead. Come on," he said, pulling her with him.

"How do you know?"

"Because he's dead," Scorpion snapped. They walked quickly away from the van toward the street corner. She started to look back.

"Don't," he said, pulling on her arm to keep her walking with him. The prison tattoo was a dead giveaway, he thought. The men after them were Syndikat *blatnoi*. Mogilenko's thugs. He should have taken care of Mogilenko before. The question was, how did they find them? How did they know about the apartment? And how did they know about Danylo? As they turned the corner, Scorpion spotted a man getting into a small Skoda sedan.

"Call him. Tell him we need a lift. We'll pay him," he told Iryna.

"Probachte! Pryvit!" Excuse me! Hello! she called out, waving to the man, who just looked at her.

"Anything else, your highness?" she whispered to Scorpion.

"Smile," he said.

For a hundred *hryvnia* the man agreed to take

them to Tolstoho Square. Within minutes they were driving across the bridge Scorpion had looked down on from the apartment window. A pale sun, pale as the moon, cast a cold light on the frozen river. The man tried to talk to Iryna, but she answered in monosyllables. They drove through traffic. The man dropped them off near the Metro entrance on the museum side of the square. They waited till he drove off, then began walking.

"Where are we going?" she asked.

"We need a car. I looked it up before. There's a car rental agency on *vulytsya* Pushkinska."

"I can't keep doing this," she said. For a moment she stood there, trembling.

"No," he said.

They spotted the car agency on the ground floor of an office building. Scorpion used his South African passport and driver's license in the name Peter Reinert to rent a four-wheel-drive Volkswagen Touareg SUV.

While they waited for the car, Iryna took off her Ushanka hat and he saw she was in her pixie cut; she hadn't had time to put on the blond wig. Scorpion was instantly on guard, but no one seemed to recognize her. After the rental agent programmed the GPS, they drove the Volkswagen into traffic.

"What's the best way to Bila Tserkva?" he asked.

"Go left, there," she said, pointing. "We need to get to the M5 going south."

"How far?"

"Eighty kilometers, give or take," she said.

A few minutes later she had input the town into the GPS and they were getting directions from it in Russian. Scorpion turned onto a wide street that had been cleared of snow.

"Feel better?" he asked.

She didn't answer. She stared straight ahead. They were driving on a boulevard with a broad divider lined with bare trees and with trees along both sides. Not for the first time, it occurred to Scorpion that in summer, Ukraine would be beautiful. He glanced at the rearview mirror. So far there was no sign of a tail.

"Are you sure Danylo's dead?" she asked.

"Pretty sure," he nodded. It was next to impossible that the Syndikat *blatnoi* knew about the apartment and not about the van. He hadn't wanted to go near it not only because they needed to get away, but also because he didn't want Iryna to see would likely be left of Danylo inside the van.

"I don't understand," she said, looking at him. "Who were they?"

"Mogilenko is a sociopath," he said.

"Mogilenko?"

"Head of the Syndikat, the mafia. His *shpana* did it. They were the ones after us."

"Tell me, do you always make everyone so angry with you?"

"It's a gift," he said, and in spite of herself, she almost laughed.

"Impossible man," she muttered.

"Besides Danylo, who else knew about us and that apartment?" he asked.

"Viktor, of course." She turned to him. "You don't think . . . ?"

"What does Viktor gain if you die?"

"Nothing. He loses the support of women—and also those who remember my father. Without my father and the Rukh, this country would have never achieved independence. Not Viktor," she said.

"Well, I'm not buying two landlords in a row. Who else?"

"My aide, Slavo. You don't think . . . ?"

He didn't answer.

"It can't be! Not Slavo!"

"Why not? You have a mole in Svoboda. Why shouldn't they?"

"You said this was mafia, not politics," she said, glaring at him.

"Didn't you say Cherkesov and Gorobets were corrupt? With ties to the mafia?"

"You mean use them as hatchetmen? No dirt on them or their Chorni Povyazky? It almost makes sense. But Slavo?"

"You better call Kozhanovskiy. Let him know. He needs to get rid of Slavo. After you call, get rid of your cell phone. Wipe off your fingerprints and toss the phone and the SIM card out the window separately, about a minute apart."

Iryna called and spoke rapidly, intensely, in Ukrainian. Afterward she threw the cell phone away and took out another of the prepaid cells Scorpion had given her. As they drove out of the city, they began to see trees and fields of snow. She started to light a cigarette, then stopped and instead tried to find news on the radio. A commentator was arguing with someone on a Russian language talk show. She translated for Scorpion. One man said that if Ukraine was invaded, Ukrainians would have to fight. Not to fight would mean the end of Ukraine as an independent country. The other man wondered if the country was ready for war. They agreed that everything depended upon what NATO and the Americans decided. After a while she shut the radio off and they rode in silence through farmlands on the outskirts of the city.

They passed a long convoy of Ukraine Army trucks filled with soldiers, coming in the opposite direction. Many of the trucks were flying the blue and yellow Ukrainian flag.

They passed truck after truck, all heading toward Kyiv.

CHAPTER TWENTY-SEVEN

Bila Tserkva
Ukraine

The coffin lay in front of the altar. There were candles and the smell of incense, but no other mourners except for a middle-aged woman with a plain face and a withered leg, limping up the aisle toward them. The church was near a park, its gold-painted spires covered with snow. During the warmer months the park would be green, but now there were only naked trees, the branches heavy with ice and snow, creaking in the cold wind. They had found the church by a note taped to the front door of Alyona's mother's apartment.

"*Laskavo prosymo.*" Welcome. "Are you members of the family?" the woman asked in Ukrainian. Her name was Pani Shulhaska, and Iryna translated for Scorpion.

"We're friends of her daughter, Alyona," Iryna said.

"Is she coming, *slava Bohu*?" Glory to God.

"We don't know," Iryna said, glancing at Scorpion. "I don't think so."

"Would you like to look at her?"

Iryna translated, and Scorpion nodded, then walked up to the open coffin. It was the face of an older woman, white as plaster and made gaunt by disease. If Alyona had gotten any of her prettiness from this woman, he couldn't see it. He returned to the pew, where Iryna sat with Pani Shulhaska.

"It's sad no one came," the woman said. "Most of her friends had already passed or moved away."

"What did she die of?" Iryna asked.

"The breast cancer. It was terrible. I'm her neighbor. I did what I could to help," she said, clasping and unclasping her hands in her lap. "I don't understand. It's so strange about Alyona. The son, we understood, of course."

"She had a son?" Iryna asked.

"Her boy, Stepan. He was a few years older than Alyona," Pani Shulhaska said, glancing at the coffin. "So sad."

"I didn't know Alyona had a brother," Iryna said.

"They didn't talk about him. He is in *likarni*." She lowered her voice. "Ivan Pavlov Hospital."

"Pavlovka, the mental hospital in Kyiv. The worst cases," Iryna explained to Scorpion.

"What was the strange thing about Alyona?" Scorpion asked, Iryna translating.

"Four nights ago she called me. I told her she should come. The doctor said her *maty*," her mama, "did not have long. She had to come home at once."

"What did she say?" Iryna asked.

"She said a strange thing. She said she wasn't sure she could come. She begged me to stay with her *maty* and not let her die alone. She said she would send money."

"What happened?" Iryna said.

"I told her she should come say *do pobachennya*." Goodbye. "It is your *maty*. We were both crying. That's when she said something even more strange."

"What was it?"

"She said she couldn't come. She was doing it for Stepan. That's all she would say. She had to do it for Stepan. It made no sense." She looked at Iryna and Scorpion. "Stepan is in Pavlovka."

Scorpion was doing the arithmetic. Four nights ago was the night before Alyona disappeared. The night before Pyatov left for Dnipropetrovsk. What about her brother was so important that it forced Alyona not to come see her dying mother?

"You knew Stepan?" Scorpion asked through Iryna.

"*Tak*, God help us!" Pani Shulhaska crossed herself. "A strange boy. So strange."

"In what way?" he asked.

"The way he looks at you. Even when he was little. His eyes, like dead eyes. Like he is dead or you are dead."

"What else?"

"He would kill things. Then he would burn them. He liked to play with fire. One day I came home from work and there were the burned remains of a cat in the snow in front of the building. I was afraid he would burn down the building. The other children were afraid of him. People used to turn away and spit when they saw him. They called him, '*Syn Dyyavola*,' the Son of the Devil." She crossed herself again. "Then one day I came home early, *slava Bohu!*" Thanks to God. "I smelled smoke coming from their apartment. I ran in. He had tied Alyona to the bed and set it on fire. His own sister!"

"What happened then?"

"The *politsiy* came. Olga Vladimyrivna, Alyona's *maty*, had no choice. They sent Stepan to Pavlovka. That's what is so strange."

"What is?" Iryna asked.

"Alyona hated her brother. She hated and feared him. She wanted nothing to do with him. So why, when her *maty* is dying and trying to stay alive just to see her, would she not come because she has to do something to help Stepan? It makes no sense."

Scorpion's mind raced. The *pani* was right. It didn't add up. And why, when Alyona was in the middle of a political assassination plot involving both of her lovers and needed a place to hide, didn't she come home to her dying mother?

"And now this," Pani Shulhaska said, opening a straw basket and taking out an envelope. "This comes in the mail today." The envelope had money in it, about five hundred *hryvnia*. "With a note from Alyona," showing it to Iryna, who translated it out loud.

Dearest Lyubochka Vasylivna,

Please take this money and look after my maty. *I will come as soon as I can. I pray God she will still*

be with us. When I see you I will explain why and
you will understand. Bud'te zdorovi, *God bless*
you, and in Jesus' name please forgive me.

Alyshka

She had mailed it the morning she disappeared
or was murdered, Scorpion thought. Whatever plot
she was involved in with Shelayev, she still thought
she'd be able to come, until Pyatov or someone else
stopped her. But it wasn't of her own free will. The
note made clear she didn't want to let her mother
die without seeing her, that if she could come, she
would. That little triangle—she and Shelayev and
Pyatov—was the key to everything. "We have to
go," he told Iryna. They stood up.

"You're not staying for the service? He's good,
this priest," Pani Shulhaska said.

"*Pereproshuyu,*" Scorpion said, I'm sorry, and he
pressed a hundred *hryven* bill into her hand.

"*Slava Bohu,*" Iryna said. God bless. She kissed
Pani Shulhaska on the forehead and held her hand
for a moment. Afterward, she joined Scorpion outside the church. Although it was early afternoon, the
winter sky was already growing dark. It was very cold.

"Now what?" she asked.

"If we find out what happened to Alyona, we'll
find Shelayev," Scorpion said.

"It's getting late," Iryna said, looking at the sky.

"I know," he said, shivering inside his overcoat.

The wind blew snow from the trees in the park
across the way.

CHAPTER TWENTY-EIGHT

Kreshchatytsky Park
Kyiv, Ukraine

All the approaches were bad ones. The Puppet Theatre, looking like a miniature castle with spires, stood alone on a hill in the middle of a park, a large public space near the river. The steps and walkways leading up to the theatre were covered with snow. Footprints showed that people had come this way even though the theatre was closed mid-week. On a wooded slope away from the steps, Scorpion spotted two pairs of footprints in the snow; two people, one close behind the other. An unusual way of walking, he thought, unless someone was walking behind a captive.

The park was deserted. As the crisis escalated, people were leaving the city. Coming into Kyiv, Scorpion and Iryna had passed cars going the other way. A long line of army tanks and trucks were parked single file on Prospekt Akademika Glushkova. On the main street, Khreshchatyk, soldiers and Black Armbands patrolled silently as nearly empty *mashrutkas* went by. The shoppers were gone, the stores shuttered. Scorpion could feel the city's fear, as real as the icy wind.

At a traffic light, a uniformed *politseysky* stared curiously at their SUV, reminding Scorpion that in spite of the crisis, the police were still hunting them. To be stopped now would be a disaster. The man studied them, while Scorpion kept his hand on the Glock in his holster. All they had going for them, he thought, was his mustache and her stupid blond wig. Iryna saw the *politseysky* watching them and quickly turned away. Scorpion could see the man shifting his weight, trying to make up his mind. He had just started toward them when the light changed and Scorpion drove on. When they were a block away, he and Iryna looked at each other, neither of them saying a word.

They left the SUV on a side street near the top of the hill and walked down Andriyivsky Uzviz to the Black Cat theatre café. The café was open, light from the window spilling out in the early darkness. Inside, there was only one customer, an old man smoking his pipe and reading a book by the window. A bald man Scorpion had never seen before was behind the counter. The woodsman puppet he remembered from his last visit still hung beside the stage, only now it was in shadow, making it look odd, more sinister.

"*De Ekaterina?*" Scorpion asked the bald man behind the counter. Where is Ekaterina?

"*Ya ne znayu,*" I don't know, the man said, eyeing them suspiciously. "Who are you?"

"We're friends of Alyona and Ekaterina," Iryna explained. "We were wondering if you had seen them."

The man wiped his hands on his apron.

"Are you ordering?" he asked, glancing over at the old man by the window.

"We'll have the borscht," Scorpion said, following his look.

"And *chay*," Iryna said, ordering tea as they sat at a table away from the old man.

A few minutes later the bald man brought them two steaming bowls of borscht. He came back with their tea and black bread and butter, sat down at their table and motioned them close.

"Be careful what you say," he whispered in passable English. "I don't know this guy," indicating the old man. "He is just coming the past three nights." He looked at Iryna, obviously recognizing her. "I knew your *batco*," your papa. "He was a good man, a patriot."

She looked around as if ready to flee.

"It's okay," the bald man said, edging even closer. "I tell no one."

"What about Ekaterina or the young man who was here a few days ago?" Scorpion asked while eating.

"Ah, her *drooh*, Fedir." The man nodded. "I haven't heard from either of them. Not in two days. I was hoping you knew something. We had to close the show." He shrugged. "As if with the crisis, anybody was coming anyway."

"So all three of them have disappeared?" Iryna

whispered to him. "What about Ekaterina's apartment?"

The man shook his head.

"Do you have any idea where they could have gone?" Scorpion asked.

The old man by the window tapped his pipe on the side of the table. He closed his book, and leaving a few coins in a saucer on the table, stood up. He put on his overcoat, scarf, and hat. Before he left, he looked at each of them in turn, as if memorizing their features.

"I don't like that guy," the bald man said.

"No," Scorpion agreed, making a mental note to make doubly sure there were no tails when they left. "What about Ekaterina?"

The bald man motioned them closer.

"I remembered something Fedir said about a year ago. He had no place to stay and he told me he'd found a way into the Lyalkovy Teatr." The Puppet Theatre.

"The one in Kreshchatytsky Park?" Iryna asked.

The man nodded. "He said he stayed in the basement under the stage. A big storage space where they keep the puppets. He said it was very private there."

"Did you check it out?" Scorpion asked.

"Too dangerous. This city is crazy now," looking out at the dark street. "Soldiers. Black Armbands. *Politsiy.* I got a wife, kids. I can't go," he said, not looking at them.

"We understand," Iryna said, touching his hand.

"*Ni.*" No. "I should have looked. There's something wrong. They're good kids," he said, looking away; in that moment his face seemed older.

When they left the café, they were followed by two men who stayed well back so their faces could not be seen. They walked quickly down the street's steep slope to Kontraktova Square, where they waved down a *mashrutka* that took them to the Metrograd mall in Lva Tolstoho Square. Scorpion wasn't sure if a dark Lada was following them. Once inside the mall, they started to run, going from one level to another, through stores and out another entrance, then took two taxis, one after another, going in opposite directions before they were sure they had lost whoever had been tailing them.

It took them more than an hour to get back to where they had parked the Volkswagen SUV. But they had wasted their time, Scorpion thought. Because all the approaches to the Puppet Theatre were across open ground. He crouched behind a tree, Iryna next to him, and looked up the snow-covered slope at the shadowy outline of the theatre at the top of the rise. It was completely dark; the only light came from a streetlight that cast the shadows of the building's spires across the snow.

"What do we do?" Iryna asked.

"You go to Viktor. They need you," Scorpion said, taking out the Glock and fitting the silencer on it.

"*Gospadi*, you don't know a damn thing about women, do you?" Iryna said through clenched teeth. "I'm not some delicate flower and this matters to me more than you, so I'm coming. Got it?"

"In that case, make yourself useful. Where's your Beretta?"

"In my purse," she said, fishing it out.

"Wait three minutes, then follow. Watch where I go in. Don't make a sound. If anybody gets in your way, don't hesitate for a second. Kill him. Are we clear?"

They looked at each other. Her face, hard to see in the shadows, was beyond beautiful, he thought. Without a word, he began to move up the open slope. The snow was frozen hard under his boots, and he leaned forward, almost on all fours, to keep his silhouette low. His eyes scanned the castle—that was what it looked like and that was how he had come to think of it—for any light or sign of movement. There were only shadows, the cold wind trailing plumes of snow from the castle spires.

He reached the flat area at the side of the building. Keeping low, he went around to the back, looking for an entryway that Ekaterina's boyfriend, Fedir, might have used. At the back of the building he saw a basement window, low to the ground. It was locked but it had a top latch that could have been left open at some time. He put his backpack on the ground and felt inside the pack till he found his Leatherman tool, the night vision goggles, and the duct tape.

Using the Leatherman's awl with the hardened tip as a glass cutter, he cut a circle on the glass and pulled it away from the window with a small wad of duct tape. Reaching through the circular opening, he opened the latch and pushed the window open.

When he had the goggles and the Glock in his hand, the safety off, he crawled inside.

He had come in on a worktable in a dark basement room, which was a workshop for building sets. He put on the night vision goggles. Strange cutout shapes stood against the wall, eerie in the green light of the goggles. The room smelled of sawdust and glue.

Scorpion eased down from the table onto his tiptoes, then moved quietly toward a door and pressed his ear against it. He could hear the sound of something, but it made no sense. It sounded like the squeak of a pulley and splashing water. Whatever it was, someone was on the other side of the door. He held the Glock ready.

He turned the handle and inched the door open. The light was bright, blinding his night goggles. He pulled them off, catching a brief glimpse of a room filled with hanging objects; dozens of medieval-looking puppets, witches and ogres, princesses and humanlike animals resembling something out of Grimms' fairy tales.

There were two hanging objects too big to be puppets. He started toward them when a shadow next to him moved and an iron bar smashed down on his hand, stunning him and causing him to drop the gun. Almost before he could react, a second blow from the iron bar wielded by a big man came down at his head and he barely got his injured hand up in time to block the blow with a forearm. The pain was instantaneous; his entire arm felt numb and useless.

Almost without thinking, Scorpion twisted

toward the attacker, closing with him. With a leg sweep, he used his uninjured left elbow to smash into the side of the big man's neck. The man grunted but didn't go down. As they fought, they banged against the dangling puppets, which swung and slammed into each other; a forest of grotesque swinging shapes.

"When attacked by surprise, go inside," his CQC instructor, Koichi, used to say. The big man swung the bar again. Scorpion stepped inside the arc of the swing and kicked at the inside of the man's knee while grabbing the arm holding the bar. Using the man's own momentum, Scorpion hurled him with an arm bar twist down to the ground. Before the big man could react, Scorpion kicked him savagely in the side of the head, and using both hands like pointed claws, stabbed down at the big man's eyes, deep into the sockets, blinding him. The man screamed with pain and rage. He swung the iron bar blindly at Scorpion, who just managed to dodge out of the way.

A second man, who seemed to come out of nowhere, launched a Russian Sambo-style kick at Scorpion's midsection. With only an instant to counter, he grabbed the man's foot mid-kick and twisted it violently with both hands, forcing him to the ground. Meanwhile, the big man had gotten to his feet. He couldn't see and was swinging the iron bar blindly. Scorpion timed his swing, grabbed the man's arm in mid swing and turned it into a shoulder lock, dislocating the man's shoulder. He screamed in intense pain as the other man got up.

Scorpion twisted the iron bar out of the big man's hands and smashed it into the side of his head by the temple as the second man came at him again. Scorpion feinted a high swing then jabbed the iron bar like a fencer's thrust at his knee, hearing it crack as he sent him down. Incredibly, the big man staggered up again. His good hand grabbed blindly at Scorpion, getting hold of his neck and choking him with crushing strength. Scorpion swung the iron bar with all his might at his temple, landing a blow that sent him crashing to the floor, lifeless. Scorpion whirled with the iron bar to deal with the second man, who was backing away now, getting tangled in the hanging puppets. Scorpion started to look for the Glock, but it was too late.

A third, tall man with thick sandy hair and wearing a black armband had retrieved the Glock. He stood in a shooting stance, the Glock aimed at Scorpion's chest. A powerful lamp beside him cast the shadows of the swinging puppets, dislodged by the fight, dancing across the room.

Scorpion recognized the sandy-haired man. He had been Gorobets's aide in the hotel suite in Dnipropetrovsk. For the first time, Scorpion was able to look around. In addition to the puppets, there were two bodies hanging from a ceiling pipe by their necks, the large shapes he had seen earlier. They were clearly dead.

The bodies were those of a young man and woman, both naked, their hands tied and both covered with welts and dark bruises. It took Scorpion a second before, with a shock, he recognized their bloated faces. The young people from the Black Cat café: Ekaterina and Fedir.

He had no time to pay attention to them, because there was another woman, also naked. She hung upside down, tied by her feet from a pulley, her long blond hair trailing down into a tub of water filled with chunks of ice. Her body was bruised and cut like the others and her mouth had been taped so no one could hear her scream. The pulley he'd heard earlier had been used to raise or lower her head into the ice water. There were wet rubber gloves lying next to the tub. The sandy-haired man had been holding her head under the water. She was still breathing, her eyes dazed, wild almost to the point of insanity. It took a few seconds till Scorpion recognized her from the photo. It was Alyona.

"Pane Kilbane, we saw you coming," the sandy-haired man said in English. The damned approaches, Scorpion thought. There was bound to be someone watching.

"Remind me again. What's your name?" he asked.

"Why?"

"I plan to remember you," Scorpion said. He sensed the second man coming up behind him.

"I'm Kulyakov," the sandy-haired man said. "I want you to remember me. Do you know Alyona?"

"Only by her photo in the Chorna Kishka café," he said, so if she were listening she would know he knew who she was and that he was there to help. Unless her mind, after what they had done to her, was too far gone.

"She's being very stubborn," Kulyakov said. "All I want is some information."

Then a heavily muscled arm put Scorpion in a choke hold from behind. The second man, he thought. His wrist was grabbed and twisted behind him in a painful hammer lock.

"Call off your *sobaka*," Scorpion gasped. Your dog. "I can help. We want the same thing."

"What thing is that?" Kulyakov said, motioning to the second man to hold still for a moment.

"Shelayev. We're both looking for him."

"Are we?"

"Gorobets needs to make sure Shelayev doesn't talk. Only he's disappeared."

Kulyakov shrugged. "So?"

"So you need to find him. Otherwise you'd have no interest in Alyona or her friends, except for your perverted little fantasies."

"What is this, a Glock?" Kulyakov said, looking at the pistol in his hand. He smiled, showing bad teeth. "It's light. I like this *pistolet*. You shouldn't tempt someone holding such a light *pistolet*; so easy to shoot," and he aimed it at Scorpion.

"Don't be stupid. Killing me will make an assassination that everyone assumes I did into an assassination that everyone will assume Gorobets did," Scorpion said, wondering where the hell Iryna was.

"No," Kulyakov said. "Killing Cherkesov's assassin will make me a hero."

Then Scorpion heard a sound from somewhere behind him. Damn, he thought. She needed to be quiet.

Kulyakov said something in Ukrainian that sounded like an order. Scorpion felt the second man let him go and head back toward the other room.

"Don't move," Kulyakov said, aiming the Glock at Scorpion. "I'm dying to try out this *pistolet*."

Two shots rang out. At the first shot, knowing the sound would distract Kulyakov for an instant, Scorpion moved. He stepped forward, parrying the Glock aside, the first move in the Krav Maga sequence, followed by taking the gun away from Kulyakov in a twisting wrist move. Scorpion debated killing him as he reversed the gun and pointed it in a shooting stance at Kulyakov. No, he needed to question him. He motioned Kulyakov to his knees. After a moment's hesitation, Kulyakov glaring at him, knelt on his knees.

From the next room, Iryna screamed. Scorpion kicked Kulyakov in the face, whirled and ran back toward the other room, where he saw Iryna struggling with the second man. Sensing Scorpion behind him, the man turned and jumped at him. There was no time to think. Scorpion shot him in the head. The man fell facedown at Scorpion's feet.

"What happened?" he asked Iryna, stepping over the body.

"I shot him in the shoulder," she said. "He came too fast."

"Come," Scorpion grabbed her hand. "Hurry!"

They went into the puppet room.

"*Gospadi.*" Iryna gasped at the sight of Alyona and the hanging bodies. Kulyakov was gone. Alyona's naked body was jerking like a fish on the line, her head underwater in the tub again. Before he had fled, Kulyakov lowered her back into the ice water.

Scorpion grabbed Alyona and lifted her up so her head was out of the water. She was coughing, squirming as she fought him. Holding her slippery body up, he tried to kick the tub of water over, but it was too heavy. He moved her body so it hung beside the tub and let her dangle head down while he ran to the other room to grab his backpack. She was still jerking on the line when he came back and used his Leatherman pliers' blades to cut the cable holding her. He cut her bonds and freed her, pulling the tape from her mouth.

When Alyona saw Iryna, she screamed, clutched at her and began to sob. Iryna held her in her arms. The room was in a shambles, the puppets swaying in the shadows. Scorpion looked around. Kulyakov had to have used the metal stairs to the stage to get away.

He ran up the stairs and onto the stage. A door banged in the lobby. He leapt from the stage to the aisle and ran out to the lobby and the theatre doors, scanning the snow-covered walkways and steps. There was no sign of Kulyakov.

He went around to the side of the building, but it was too dark to see. He should've brought his night-vision goggles, he thought as he scanned the slope. There were what looked like fresh footsteps and a bloodstain on the snow. It could have come from Kulyakov's nose when he kicked him. But there was nothing moving on the slope. He realized that Kulyakov must have made it to the trees, his eyes searching the mass of branches in the darkness. He was about to start down the slope when he spotted a *militsiyu* van, moving slowly on the road along the periphery of the park. The van stopped.

Scorpion stepped back into the shadows of the theatre entrance. From inside the van, a powerful flashlight was pointed at the theatre. The light moved toward him and he froze against the wall, holding his breath. If they found him, he would be in prison and the war would start. The beam of light almost touched him, then moved past. After what seemed like an hour but was probably less than fifteen seconds, he heard the van move on. He peeked out and saw it was gone, then went back down the stairs to the puppet room.

Iryna had found a canvas tarp to wrap around Alyona. She lit a cigarette and held it for Alyona, whose hand was shaking too much to hold it herself.

"She saw them killed," Iryna said, indicating the hanging bodies. "She needs to go to a hospital."

"What about Shelayev?" Scorpion asked.

"Can't it wait?" Iryna said sharply. She put her arms around Alyona. "She's shaking like a leaf."

"No, it can't," Scorpion said.

Iryna used her sweater to dry Alyona's wet hair. "We need a doctor. Now."

"Get someone private. Someone who won't talk. Is there anyone you know?"

"I don't know. My gynecologist. What good is that?" Iryna said. "Look at her!" Alyona was slumped over, her head down, the cuts raw and bleeding, her body still shaking.

"Why the hell do you think they were torturing her? Why do you think they killed the other two?" he asked, grabbing his backpack. He hooked it over his shoulder and went looking for Alyona's clothes.

"I don't know. Shelayev?" Iryna said.

Scorpion nodded grimly. "Whatever help we get her has to be safe or they'll grab her again. Where are her clothes?"

Iryna asked Alyona in Ukrainian and she pointed with a trembling hand at a corner. Scorpion went over and found a pile of clothes. Some were from the dead couple, Ekaterina and Fedir. A pair of jeans, a top, and a jacket looked like they would fit Alyona. They used the dead couple's clothes to dry Alyona off. Iryna helped her dress, while Scorpion went back upstairs to see if anyone was coming.

The park was deserted, the snow pale under the lone streetlight.

"We have to go. They'll be back any second," he said, coming back down to the puppet room. Iryna had succeeded in getting Alyona dressed. She sat on a bench, her head slumped.

"Can you stand?" Scorpion asked Alyona.

She didn't move. Iryna looked at him.

"Take this," he said, handing her his backpack. He stood Alyona up and threw her over his shoulder, switching the Glock back to his other hand. He climbed the metal stairs, Alyona a dead weight over his shoulder, and carried her outside, the going difficult on the frozen snow. She was shivering violently, making it hard to carry her. He kept looking around for any sign of Kulyakov as he went forward.

For the moment they were hidden from the street. Luckily, they were going downhill, with nothing around but snow and bare trees.

Alyona had protected Shelayev despite the torture, Scorpion thought, and had seen Kulyakov kill her friends. She would protect Shelayev from him as well. He had to figure a way to get her to tell him where Shelayev was hiding. He sensed Iryna just behind him. It was hard going and they had to hurry. Gorobets's men might be back any second.

Scorpion pushed on harder through the snow.

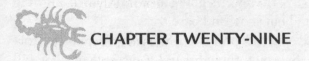

CHAPTER TWENTY-NINE

Vyshhorod
Kyiv, Ukraine

Scorpion drove out of the park past a large public building, checking his mirrors. Iryna was in the backseat with Alyona.

"Where are we going?" Iryna asked.

"We need someplace safe."

"There is no safe. We need a doctor." She thought for a moment. "There's a Medikom out by Vyshhorod."

"What's that?"

"A twenty-four-hour private clinic. I took a girlfriend there once. I don't know how safe it would be."

"Call them," Scorpion said. "Tell them it's an emergency, but it needs discretion. Tell them you'll give them money."

Iryna called on her cell phone. He heard her talking softly, urgently. When she finished, she said, "They're waiting. I told them I'd give them each a hundred *hryvnia* extra. They said to come around to the back door." She gave him directions and soon they were driving on Kostyantynivska past the university. Iryna put her arm around Alyona, who was barely able to sit upright.

"How is she?" Scorpion asked, trying to avoid skidding, the streets icy with frozen slush.

"I don't know. *Pereproshuyu,*" she said to Alyona. I'm sorry. "We thought you were dead."

Alyona looked at her as though from far away. "It was Dimitri's idea. Dimitri Shelayev," she clarified, her voice shaking. "He thought it would protect me."

"You and Shelayev were lovers?" Scorpion asked, glancing at her in the rearview mirror.

Alyona nodded. She began to cry and pressed her face to Iryna's shoulder.

"*Bud'laska, vybachte mene,*" she sobbed. "Forgive me! I did not want to lie to you. I had no choice."

"What about Pyatov?" Scorpion asked.

"Can't you let her alone?" Iryna said sharply.

"No. Where does Pyatov fit in all this?"

"We told him about us," Alyona said, her voice shaky, almost dreamy. "Dimitri and me. Pyatov was like crazy man."

"He was jealous?" Iryna asked.

"He was crazy jealous. I was afraid. I knew he was secretly working with the Cherkesov campaign. At first I thought Dimitri was his contact. But Dimitri told me no."

"You spied on us," Iryna said. "You gave information to the SVR."

"No, not SVR. I wouldn't give to Russians. It was for the SBU," Alyona said, looking up.

"They false-flagged her," Scorpion said. "She thought she was spying for the SBU, but it was Gabrilov, the SVR."

"Why?" Iryna said to her. "Didn't we treat you like one of our own?"

"I loved you," Alyona said, grabbing Iryna's hand. "You are the hope of our country, especially for women. I didn't want to do it. Please believe me." She kissed Iryna's hand.

"Why did you do it?" Scorpion asked. He had spotted a *militsiyu* van behind him in the rearview mirror. He drove carefully, keeping them in sight. They couldn't afford to be stopped. Not now! He breathed a sigh of relief when the van turned off toward the university.

"My brother, Stepan," Alyona said, looking down.

"The one in Pavlovka, the mental hospital?" Iryna said.

"You know?!" Alyona said, her eyes wide.

Iryna nodded. "You were afraid?"

"They said they would release him. My *maty* cannot take care of him. He is very bad. I was afraid . . . And now there is no Dimitri! He is gone." She looked at them, her eyes wet.

"So we had two assassins: Pyatov and Shelayev," Scorpion said. "Who was Pyatov supposed to kill?"

"It was a secret," Alyona said. "Pyatov would kill Davydenko, and Cherkesov would blame it on the Kozhanovskiy campaign."

"Sure," Scorpion said. "Cherkesov puts it out that he was the target. He gets a sympathy vote boost, destroys Kozhanovskiy, and he gets rid of a rival, all at the same time. Meanwhile Gorobets schemes to get rid of Cherkesov first. Quite a nest of vipers, Svoboda."

"Sirhiy was a fool. I tried to tell him. He wouldn't listen."

"The blood in your apartment. Where did it come from?" Scorpion asked.

"It was Dimitri's idea. I used my own blood. It was my time of the month. It had my DNA. Dimitri said if people thought I was dead it would protect me."

She was breathing heavily, speaking in spurts. Scorpion knew she could go into shock any second. He had to get her medical help soon. He sped up, despite the chance it might attract the *politsiy*.

"Did Shelayev put the bomb in Cherkesov's car?" he asked. "It would have been easier for him than anyone. He was Gorobets's security man."

"I didn't know. He told me Cherkesov had to be stopped. He had learned something."

"What was it?"

"He didn't tell," Alyona cried, burying her face on Iryna's shoulder.

"Where's Dimitri now?" Scorpion asked. Shelayev had the answer to the riddle. He was also the only evidence, Scorpion thought that would prove that he and Iryna had nothing to do with Cherkesov's assassination and maybe stop the war. Producing him alive was the only chance they had.

"I don't know," Alyona said. "He wouldn't say. Only that when it was safe, if he was still alive, he would come for me." She grabbed Iryna's hands. "If he did this, he had a reason."

"We need to talk to him," Iryna said. "Everyone thinks we killed Cherkesov," indicating herself and Scorpion.

"I don't know where he is. He was protecting me," Alyona said. She took out a cigarette, but her hands were shaking so much that once again Iryna had to light and hold it for her. Alyona inhaled and spoke with a shaky voice. She was breathing heavily, almost panting. Scorpion thought she might pass out any minute. "He said . . . he going . . . where no one . . . find him. I wanted . . . go . . . but my *maty* . . ."

"Your *maty*," Iryna said. "She's gone. I'm sorry."

Alyona whimpered. Her eyes were shiny, but she didn't cry. Scorpion guessed she had been through so much she was numb. Iryna gave him directions.

They went across a bridge over a frozen inlet of the Dnieper. The clinic was on the northern outskirts of the city; fields of snow stretched into the distance. To the right, he saw the clinic standing by itself, a yellow ambulance parked by the entrance. He drove into the parking lot and parked at the back of the building.

They helped Alyona out of the car. She couldn't walk. Scorpion picked her up and carried her. They knocked at the back door until a nurse let them in. Iryna spoke to her, gave her money, and the nurse led them to a private examining room. Scorpion laid Alyona down on the examining table.

A minute later the nurse came back with a doctor, a middle-aged man with a jowly neck. His badge read: DR. YAKOVENKO. He took one look at Alyona, then at Iryna and Scorpion.

"*Ya znayu, chto vy,*" he said to Iryna in Russian. I know you. "You're wanted by the *militsiyu.*" He started toward the door. Scorpion stood in his way, showed him the Glock.

"You're a doctor. She needs help. I'll give you five hundred if you keep quiet about this," he said in Russian.

"*Otvali,*" Dr. Yakovenko muttered. Go to hell. But he went over to examine Alyona. His expression changed when he saw the cuts and bruises. He turned on Scorpion.

"Did you do this?"

Scorpion shook his head no.

Iryna touched the doctor's arm. "Someone else. He saved her," she said, indicating Scorpion.

Frowning, Dr. Yakovenko went back to examining Alyona. He pressed her abdomen and she cried out in pain. He shook his head and after a moment sent the nurse out, telling her to get the operating room ready and start an antibiotic drip.

"We have to operate," he told them. "She's bleeding internally. If we don't act immediately, she'll go into shock. Who did this to her?" he snapped.

"Black Armbands," Iryna said. "An aide to Oleksandr Gorobets."

"I don't believe you." He looked at Iryna and Scorpion. "By law, I should notify the *politsiy.*"

"If you do, they'll kill her," Scorpion said. "Probably you too. They don't want witnesses."

"So you say," the doctor replied, examining Alyona's external wounds. "These are less serious. If you didn't do anything, why are the *politsiy* after you?"

"If you know who I am," Iryna said, "you know there are people who would do anything to stop me. Anything. Ask her. She knows it wasn't us who killed Cherkesov."

"Is this true?" he asked Alyona.

She looked at him as if from a far distance, but finally nodded.

"Here's a thousand," Scorpion said, handing him money. "Be a doctor. We'll keep you and your staff out of this. If we're in danger, so are you."

"You really think—" Dr. Yakovenko started. "*Hivno*, shit," he said, rushing to Alyona, whose eyes were turning up. "*Medsestra!*" he shouted. Nurse! "She's going into shock."

The first nurse rushed into the room, followed by two more nurses with a gurney. In seconds they had moved Alyona onto the gurney and were rushing her to the operating room.

Scorpion and Iryna settled down to wait in a small waiting room by the nurses' station. The TV was on. It showed movements of soldiers and tanks, then cut to a conference room and a reporter outside a government building. The reporter was talking rapidly and there was a news crawl at the bottom.

"What's it say?" Scorpion asked.

"'NATO warns Russia not to violate Ukrainian sovereignty. Ukraine mobilizes for war. American forces in Europe are on full alert,'" she read. "What are we going to do?"

"We're at a dead end," Scorpion said. "She says

she doesn't know where Shelayev is. If he didn't tell her, he didn't tell anyone. Without him, we have nothing."

"Actually, she did tell us," Iryna said, lighting a cigarette. "I think I know where Shelayev is."

CHAPTER THIRTY

Chernobyl
Chernobylska Exclusion Zone

"*Damy i gospoda takzhe*, ladies and also dear gentlemen, on night of twenty-six April of 1986, at one hour and twenty-three in morning," the Inter-Inform guide, a bulky man with a reddish-brown goatee, Denys—Call me Dennis—said, "under supervise of Alexandr Akimov, chief engineer night shift, is starting safety test of shutting down of reactor *chetyre* number four."

Scorpion was sitting in a classroomlike conference room in the Tourist Office in Chernobyl, a village at the second or inner checkpoint, some ten kilometers out from the nuclear reactor site. With him were three couples—a pair of male backpackers from Munich; two British women, Sarah and Millicent from East Putney; and an American couple, the Dowds, retirees from Maryland—who were set to take the tour.

In the early hours of the morning, while it was still dark, he had left the clinic. Dr. Yakovenko had managed to stop Alyona's abdominal bleeding.

Iryna stayed with her, registering Alyona under a false name. As soon as she knew Alyona was stable, Iryna would be meeting with Viktor Kozhanovskiy. They would try to buy some time for Scorpion to find Shelayev. No more than forty-eight hours, Iryna had insisted. Even trying to negotiate that much time with Gorobets and the Russians was going to be nearly impossible.

Overnight, Russia's president, Evgeni Brabov, had reacted to what he called the "NATO ultimatum and Ukrainian provocations," by declaring Russia would protect Russian "nationals" and Russian borders, even if it meant war. "Russia is not intimidated and will not be intimidated. Russia will defend her people," he had declared in a televised speech to the Duma in a rare night session, a clip of which was being replayed around the world.

The UN Security Council was meeting in emergency session, where Russia had threatened to veto any action that did not support the legitimate right of Russia to defend itself and her people, including ethnic Russians in the former Soviet Union. In reaction to what was happening in Europe, China had raised the readiness level of the People's Army. Other nations were beginning to react as well. Iran sent warships into the Persian Gulf.

Before he left Kyiv, Scorpion decided to try the dead drop in Pechersk Landscape Park one last time. The Company had written him off, but all hell was breaking loose and there was a chance they were trying to reach him.

The park was deserted in the icy darkness. When

he got to the top of the steps down to the amphi-theatre, he saw it: a ribbon tied on the lamppost. He released the ribbon, tossed it away, and dug through the frozen earth under the bench to retrieve a cell phone left in the spike.

Sheltering in the trees from the bone-chilling wind, he called the cell phone's only preset number. Someone picked up on the second ring.

"Are you still GTG?" someone said, meaning good to go, operational. It was Shaefer, and despite the early hour, he didn't sound sleepy. Something was up. The CIA needed him again.

"Didn't know you still cared," Scorpion said, pulling his collar closer around him against the wind. The Company had cut him loose, and he wasn't about to let them forget it.

"Who says I care?" Shaefer said. Then with a different tone: "Mucho has changed, bro. You still dealing with our Asian amigos?"

Akhnetzov must've forwarded his earlier suspicions about Li Qiang and the Guoanbu to Rabino-wich, Scorpion realized. The CIA was a couple of critical steps behind.

"It was a *surkh* fish. You five by five?" he said, using the Urdu word for *red* that he knew Shaefer would know from their time in Pakistan, meaning the Chinese were a false trail, a "red herring," and asking if Shaefer copied.

"Romeo that," Shaefer said, meaning he got it. "So who killed JR? Do you know?" asking who was really behind the assassination of Cherkesov.

"Yes."

"I'm all ears," Shaefer said. Scorpion pictured him sitting up ramrod straight in bed, fingers hitting his keyboard to connect to Langley.

"It was an inside job."

"Inside as in inside Freedom?" The name in English of the Svoboda party.

"You're getting warmer."

"Can you prove it? Maybe get us off the hook?" Shaefer asked, and Scorpion could hear the tension in his voice. Washington must be going ballistic over the crisis.

"I need forty-eight hours."

"Man, don't you watch TV? We don't have forty-eight hours," Shaefer said.

"Find it," Scorpion said, and hung up. They'd hung him out to dry, and now he was telling them he knew who the real assassin was and there was a chance he could stop the war if they could delay forty-eight hours. They could try, he thought grimly. If there was one thing Washington knew how to do, it was delay.

Leaving the park, he drove north on the P2 highway from Kyiv. Along the way, he got rid of the cell phone and SIM he had used to call Shaefer, tossing them separately in empty fields miles apart. Shaefer had sounded desperate. That could mean only one thing. Washington had decided to call Russia's bluff.

The day broke cold and gray. By the time he reached the small town of Sukachi, some eighty kilometers north of Kyiv, the road was a beat-up two-lane and traffic had disappeared. The landscape was like the Arctic, an endless expanse of white, the road bordered by rusty fences and dead grasses sticking out of the snow.

He stopped for breakfast at a roadside trailer that doubled as the town's only restaurant. Breakfast was *hrechany*, a chicken soup thick with buckwheat, plus tea and black bread. The woman behind the counter told him she had been born in Pripyat, but her family had moved down to Sukachi when she was a teenager because of the radiation. On an impulse, Scorpion bought a bottle of Nemiroff *horilka* to take with him.

He reached the Exclusion Zone border at Dytyatky. Ukrainian *militsiyu* soldiers manned a checkpoint that stretched across the main street of the town. He stepped inside the checkpoint building and showed them his passport and InterInform Chernobyl tour receipt and brochure. They had him sign a release in Ukrainian and English stating that he knew that by entering the Chernobylska Exclusion Zone he might be endangering his health. The soldier behind the counter told him it was another thirty kilometers from Dytyatky to the nuclear power plant. There would be a second checkpoint at the town of Chernobyl, ten kilometers out from the reactor. He would have to leave his vehicle there and join the tour. When he returned to Dytyatky, he would be tested for radiation.

Scorpion drove beyond Dytyatky toward Chernobyl. The landscape was empty; only an occasional abandoned farmhouse and snow. He wondered if the snow was radioactive and decided it was. He had the car radio tuned to news in Russian but could only understand a fraction of what he heard.

He was supposed to get a dosimeter to wear when he got to Chernobyl and wished he had it now. A leaflet from InterInform had stated that normal background radiation around the world averaged twelve to fourteen microroentgens. Inside the Exclusion Zone around Chernobyl, the background radiation had decayed over the years to an average of twenty, exposure equivalent to a transatlantic flight. But this was only an average; actual radiation varied greatly from one place to another. The real danger was in hot spots in various locations.

He turned on his cell phone's iPlayer app to get the news from the BBC. The tinny voice of a British announcer came on.

"The crisis in the Ukraine has grown more serious following Russia's veto in the Security Council of a U.S.-led resolution for a withdrawal of all military units to a distance of twenty kilometers from both sides of the Russian-Ukraine frontier. The Pentagon announced today that the American military has been ordered to a DEFCON-1 level, the highest level indicating war is imminent.

"In London, the prime minister told Parliament that Britain stands with the United States and NATO in this dangerous hour. Within the NATO alliance, member nations are still debating their response. Both France and Germany continue to express reservations about a military response to Russia's actions, citing their concern that Ukraine is not an official member of NATO, but only a participant in the NATO Membership Action Plan, and that since the breakup of the Soviet Union, the status of ethnic Russians and the Russian-speaking minorities in former satellite nations such as Ukraine have been issues of contention. The Italian representative, Mr. Vincenzo Cassiani, told the BBC that we may be seeing the end of the NATO alliance.

"In the meantime in the Ukraine, it has been reported that one of the leading candidates for president in the election that sparked the crisis, Mr. Viktor Kozhanovskiy, has approached his opponent, Mr. Lavro Davydenko, with a suggestion that they meet to try to hammer out a joint statement regarding the steps Ukraine is prepared to take to deal with the crisis. Mr. Davydenko was selected as a replacement candidate by the Svoboda party leadership following the assassination of that party's candidate, Yuriy Cherkesov. So far, there has been no response from Mr. Davydenko's representatives."

Iryna, Scorpion thought, unable to keep an image of her naked in bed, her breast barely touching his arm, out of his mind. She was trying to buy him time.

A shape darted in front of the Volkswagen and he slammed on his brakes, just missing it. The car fishtailed and swerved, coming to a stop in a snow pile on the side of the road. He saw a wild boar crash into the underbrush. The boar disappeared in the woods. Radioactive boars, he thought. What's next?

The four-wheel drive got him out of the snow and moving again to the second military checkpoint at the town of Chernobyl. Many of the streets were overgrown with trees and foliage. It was a small town, easy to find your way around. The Tourist Office was a two-story building just beyond a strange-looking steel monument.

"The test begin normal," Denys—Call me Dennis— said, sitting on a table next to a slide projector showing images from the 1986 disaster. "Steam to turbines is shut down and turbines is begin to slow down. At 1:23:40 Operations Engineer Leonid Top- tunov is starting 'SCRAM'; test emergency shut- down of reactor number 4. Power level is stable at two hundred megawatts. Too low. Also, main com- puter, SKALA, is shut off. Why they go forward with low power and no computer is not clear. What happens now is big controversy, big mystery. We cannot ask either Akimov or Toptunov, because soon both men and everyone in room is being dead from radiation. Toptunov push EPS-5 button; cause insertion of all control rods into core, even manual control rods. Why he do this? Is only for ultimate emergency. We will never know for sure.

"In one second comes giant power surge, more than 530 megawatts. What cause surge? Some say is design of control rods; displace coolant. Less cool- ant is allowing more fission, thus more power. An- other big question: Does power surge come after Toptunov press button or does Toptunov panic at spike in power? Who can say?" Dennis shrugged.

"Now everything happening very fast, maybe one or two seconds. Spike in power make big increase in temperature inside reactor. Make big big steam. Steam pressure is going crazy. Pressure is break- ing fuel channels, causing control rods still going in to getting stuck," punching his palm with his fist to show the control rods getting stopped. "Control rods is breaking. Jammed. Now control rods not moving, stuck partway into core, partway out. No control rods in bottom of core is meaning zero control down there. This make thermal energy in bottom of core go very very high. Steam explode!" splaying his fingers open to convey an explosion. "Explosion so big it ripping two thousand ton steel plate riveted to top of reactor fly like champagne cork. *Bang!*" slapping his hand loudly on the table, startling them.

"Two seconds later comes second explosion. Nuclear excursion in core. Is baby nuclear bomb. *Boom!*" Slapping his hand again on the table and holding up a fist. "Explosion is blowing radioactive dust from core, from pieces of walls and ceilings in building into sky. Is very bad. But," holding up a finger, "now is getting worse.

"Explosion exposes graphite control rods in air; they are catching fire. Now burning pieces of building is flying up in sky. Fire is burning in Reactor 4 building; also burning pieces make fire on roof of Reactor number 3. Both buildings is burning. Fire is sending big smoke of radioactivity fallout in sky. Cloud of smoke and dust equivalent for radioactivity to four hundred Hiroshima bombs. Wind blow on radioactivity in cloud. Is going over all Europe. This is Chernobyl."

Dennis jumped down from the table.

"Come," he said. "We go see reactor."

He handed each of them a dosimeter with an LED screen and helped them pin it on. Another tour guide, Gennadi, came in to join them. He would be taking the others. Scorpion had booked Dennis exclusively for the entire day. Dennis cautioned them about radioactive hot spots. They were not to wander off or go anywhere without his or Gennadi's okay.

"How much radiation was there when it happened?" Mrs. Dowd, the American, asked as they started to leave the room.

"Was 5.6 roentgens per second. Is equivalent twenty thousand roentgens exposure in one hour. These workers stay. Very brave. They trying put water in for cooling core, but is no good."

"How bad is that? That level of radiation," Mr. Dowd asked.

"Fatal is five hundred roentgens in five hours. You get five hundred you die. First five hours they get 100,000. Is plenty bad," Dennis said.

The others got into a minivan with Gennadi by the gray metal monument to the firefighters who had fought the blaze at the reactor buildings and paid for it with their lives. Scorpion got into the passenger seat in Dennis's old Lada. Dennis climbed in and they drove off.

"Why you pay separate tour? Is all same," Dennis said.

"I like privacy," Scorpion replied.

Dennis shrugged. "Here was village," he said, pointing at empty fields and bare trees as he drove.

"Was bulldozed after accident. Put under soil brought in. You want take picture?"

Scorpion shook his head. He wasn't sure when to broach what he really wanted or how to get Dennis to go along. His instinct cautioned him to wait. They drove down the empty road till they saw the smokestacks, construction cranes, and buildings of the reactors looming over the line of trees. Dennis's handheld Geiger counter, which had been beeping regularly, started beeping faster. When they got closer, Scorpion saw the reactor buildings surrounded by electrical towers and power lines. They pulled up in a parking area next to the minivan.

The others were standing by a sculpture of a pair of giant hands holding something in front of the concrete sarcophagus that had been built over the destroyed Reactor 4 building. They were posing for pictures. Dennis's Geiger counter was beeping rapidly. He showed Scorpion. The LED read .883.

"Is okay for picture, but then we going inside the Zhytla," the Shelter, pointing to a nearby building. "You want picture?"

"Let's just go on to Pripyat," Scorpion said.

"The others going," Dennis said, pointing to the people filing into the building. "You get nice picture of reactor building from window inside."

"Let's go," Scorpion said, walking back to the Lada.

"You not care Chernobyl. What you wanting, mister?" Dennis said, getting back behind the wheel.

"I want to see Pripyat," Scorpion said.

"Sure. Is interesting," Dennis said, backing out

and driving down the road. He stopped the car in the middle of the road. "Rush hour in Pripyat," he joked, the road empty for as far as could be seen. He pointed to an empty snow-covered field bordered by stunted trees. "Here is Rudyi Lis, famous Red Forest. Is called because after accident, trees is turning red from radiation. No more green."

"Where are the trees?"

"Bulldozers is burying trees. Is gone. These new trees replanted," indicating the stunted trees. "Don't grow so good."

They started driving again. Soon they were at the entrance to the city of Pripyat. A concrete sign read: ПРИПЯТЬ 1970. Pripyat 1970. Dennis drove onto a bridge over a frozen river, decaying half-sunken boats and rotting piers trapped in the river ice, then stopped.

"On night of accident, stream of colored light is shooting up in sky from reactor. Beautiful colors, millions blue and red sparks spraying up like fountain in sky. Is so beautiful, people in Pripyat is coming out of house to see. Some is coming on this bridge. But beautiful colors is ionized air. Everyone on bridge who is seeing colors is becoming dead," he said, lighting a cigarette.

He drove off the bridge, past an abandoned train station and into the center of the city. The streets were empty except for the occasional rusting car or tree growing up through the asphalt, most of it covered by snow. There were abandoned buildings with their broken windows everywhere. One of the high buildings was topped by the concrete hammer and sickle of the old Soviet Union. Dennis stopped the car in the middle of the street near the central town square and they got out.

It was very cold, the sky leaden. They were in the middle of a city without a single person. Trees and shrubs had grown out of the pavement, their branches growing through broken windows and cracks in building walls. Scraps of old newspapers were blown by the wind through the snow-covered streets. It felt like the end of the world.

A wolf walked out of an apartment building. It showed no alarm at the sight of them. It looked at them for a moment, then walked away. From somewhere came the sound of a shutter banging in the wind. Not far from where they stood, they could see a Ferris wheel above the tree line.

"Children's amusement park," Dennis said. "You want see?"

They walked to the amusement park. Near the entrance, Dennis brushed away snow over a patch of moss on the ground and laid the Geiger counter on it. It nearly went ballistic, beeping furiously. The LED screen showed 2.651.

"Vegetation worse than asphalt. Don't touch," Dennis said. "You sit on ground, you fry balls. No babies. Maybe babies with three heads," he joked.

"What about the animals? How are they doing?"

"Who can say?" Dennis said. "We see many animals, but no one knows nothing. They send robot with camera into reactor. Find walls covered with strange black fungus. Like no fungus on earth. This fungus mutate to exist on radiation only. Imagine."

They walked through the park, filled with broken, rusting rides. The metal chairs from the Ferris wheel swayed and creaked in the wind. "Children park never used. Park is schedule to open two, three days after accident. People had to run, leave city forever. Come," he said.

They walked to the hotel.

"Best hotel in town, but for you is room. Make good price," Dennis joked. "We go top. Best view."

They went inside the lobby. There was broken glass everywhere. Walls were torn open with holes where scavengers had removed pipes. Snow had blown in and branches from vines and trees had threaded their way into the hotel through broken windows. Scorpion followed Dennis up the stairs to the top floor. They went to the penthouse suite. The rooms were bare except for an old armchair, its upholstery torn and rotting, and a cracked and tilted picture of Lenin on the wall. All the windows were broken. Icicles dangled from the windowsills and a drift of snow had blown in onto the floor. They looked out over the city through a broken panoramic window. From where they stood they could see the reactor and smokestack and cranes sticking above the tops of the apartment houses in the distance.

Scorpion started to sit in the armchair.

"Don't!" Dennis said, and put the Geiger counter on the chair. It read 1.397. "We go."

"Wait," Scorpion told him. "Let's stay a while."

"This is not good place to stay. What you want, mister? Is not tour."

"I'm looking for someone."

"Someone here? In Pripyat? Cannot be. Only crazy peoples live in Exclusion Zone."

"Maybe he's crazy."

"Maybe you crazy, mister. We go now," Dennis said, starting for the open doorway.

"How much do you make?" Scorpion called after him.

Dennis stopped and looked at him.

"What you think, mister? I like radioactive? I think *zona* nice place? You think I not know I get cancer someday? I was English teacher. I make fifteen hundred *hryvnia* in one month. Now I am tour guide; with tips I am making more than double; three, four thousand."

"I'll give you five thousand just for today," Scorpion said, taking out a wad of money. Dennis looked suspiciously at the money. "What is this?"

"Five thousand," Scorpion said, holding it out.

After a long moment Dennis came over, took the money and stuck it in his pocket.

"Okay, what you for sure want?" he asked.

"I'm looking for a man. His first name is Dimitri. I won't tell you the rest. He would have come sometime within the last four or five days. I have reason to believe he's somewhere in the Exclusion Zone. Have you heard of anyone coming here recently?"

"No," Dennis said. "But I am guide. I come, go. Best to asking Pani Mazhalska."

"Who's she?"

"Old woman. She is knowing all *samosely*, is what

they call squatters in *zona*. Lives alone in village, Krasnoe, in little hut in forest."

"Like Baba Yaga," Scorpion said, trying a joke, mentioning the old witch in Russian fairy tales.

"Is no joke. People say she has 'the bad eye,'" Dennis said, shifting uncomfortably.

"What about Pripyat? Is it possible he's hiding in an abandoned apartment here?"

Dennis took off his fur cap and scratched his head.

"Is possible. But radioactive in Pripyat not good. Too high."

"We're here."

"Not for days and nights. Also, Pripyat was city of fifty thousand. Many buildings here. How you find someone?"

"I figured we'd wait till dark. See if we could spot any lights. He'd need heat and light," Scorpion said.

"Wait in hotel?" Dennis said.

Scorpion shook his head. "Other tourists might come. This was the first place you took me. Besides, we need to move the car. It's best if he doesn't know we're looking for him."

"He don't want to be found, this guy?"

"He's hiding in the *zona*. What do you think?"

They walked down the stairs. Outside, they saw the other tourists, the Dowds and the Germans following Gennadi into a school. The Dowds and the Germans waved and they waved back. Scorpion and Dennis got into the Lada and started to drive through the empty streets.

"I know place behind Palace of Culture. We put car. No one see."

"What about Gennadi and the others?"

"They think we go back Chernobyl."

They parked next to a shed behind the Palace of Culture, a large building covered with bare trees and shrubs that had sprouted through the concrete. They walked from the car toward an apartment building near the center of the city.

"You don't want this guy see car. Is dangerous?"

"It could be." If Shelayev was Spetsnaz-trained, as Scorpion suspected, he was plenty dangerous. Not to mention the skull-crushing.

Dennis stopped walking.

"Maybe five thousand not enough," he said.

"Maybe it isn't, but it's all you're getting," Scorpion said, and kept walking. He spotted Gennadi's minivan moving through the trees and motioned Dennis to take cover with him behind an abandoned kiosk. They watched the minivan drive away. It was like watching the last vestige of civilization leave, he thought.

They resumed walking toward the tall apartment house. The wind had come up. They could hear the same shutter banging. In another hour or so it would be getting dark. They went into the lobby of the apartment house, the floors as usual covered with snow and broken glass and vegetation growing inside, and climbed the stairs to the top floor.

The door to an apartment overlooking much of the city was missing. It had a balcony with a tree growing in the center of it, its branches extending into the living room. They walked through, stepping carefully on the broken glass. This was no place to get a cut.

There was a broken child's highchair on its side in the kitchen. In another room they found a discarded Misha bear, stuffing coming out of it, lying on the floor. Whoever once lived here had children, Scorpion thought. Dennis put the Geiger counter to the bear. It registered 3.816. No wonder it had been left behind by scavengers. A yellowing magazine on the floor showed a smiling Gorbachev on the cover. Dennis checked the apartment with the Geiger counter. It averaged 1.05 overall; about as good as they were going to get.

After checking an area of the floor with the Geiger counter, they squatted down. Dennis lit a cigarette. Scorpion retrieved the bottle of Nemiroff from his backpack and they each took a swig.

"This guy," Dennis said. "What he do to you?"

"Nothing. It's business."

"Business you risking life for? Is not business," Dennis said. "He take your woman?" he asked.

Scorpion shook his head. No, but he took Pyatov's woman, he thought. That might have been the whole problem right there. He took out the button camcorder—a video camcorder disguised as a coat button—and clipped it to his outer jacket. He set it up to record to a flash drive that he put in an inside pocket. Dennis watched.

"What is this?"

"Video camcorder. I'm a lawyer. I need to take this man's testimony in a case."

Dennis's eyes showed he didn't believe him. Outside, it was getting dark. In winter in this part of the world, night came early. A hawk landed on the tree on the balcony and stared at them. Scorpion stood and it flew away. He walked over to the balcony and looked out at the city. The buildings were becoming dark shapes. He felt Dennis come beside him.

"We need a 360 degree view," Scorpion said. "Let's go up on the roof." They gathered their things and went up. It was colder in the wind. Scorpion stood on the roof slowly rotating to see in every direction. There was nothing. It was a ghost city. Then Dennis nudged him.

"Look," he said, pointing toward the apartment building with the hammer and sickle symbol on the roof, its outline only dimly visible in the darkness. There was a light glimmering. Scorpion took out his binoculars. The light appeared to be coming from a lantern or a candle in an apartment on the top floor. He put the binoculars back in his pack and got out the Glock. Dennis stared at the gun.

"Time to go," Scorpion said.

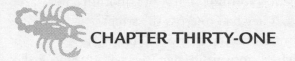 **CHAPTER THIRTY-ONE**

Pripyat,
Chernobylska Exclusion Zone

The danger point would be crossing the empty
street and the area in front of the building in full
view of Shelayev or whoever was in that apartment.
Up till then they kept close, moving in the shadows of the buildings. Scorpion had Dennis shut off
the Geiger counter beeper. It helped that they wore
dark clothes and there were no streetlights of any
kind. To be in this city at night was bizarre; a ghost
world of ice and darkness, Scorpion thought, forcing his mind back to the target. He had to assume
Shelayev was armed. Unless he caught him by surprise, the situation would go out of control as fast as
Chernobyl had.

Scorpion studied the building. There was a drift
of snow by the front entrance. He put his night
vision goggles on and looked for footprints in the
snow. There weren't any. That either meant there
was no one there, which wouldn't explain the light,
or that Shelayev had used another entrance. Scorpion looked up at the apartment on the top floor

where they had seen the light. He could see no movement. Nothing. There was nothing for it, he thought. They had to cross the street.

Dennis looked up at the building.

"Maybe I go wait in *avto*," he said, meaning the Lada.

"Maybe you leave me stranded here with no way to get back," Scorpion said.

"I am not liking."

"Neither do I. You want to give me back the five thousand?"

Dennis didn't say anything. In his mind, Scorpion thought, he'd already spent that money. He nudged Dennis, motioning him to follow. They ran across the street, nearly slipping on the frozen snow.

Dennis followed him to the side of the building. Keeping close to its walls, they went around to the rear entrance. Through the night vision goggles, Scorpion spotted footprints in the snow by the rear entrance. He heard Dennis breathing as he came up behind him. The obvious choice was to go in the back entrance and up the stairs. But Shelayev was Spetsnaz, he thought. He would likely reason that if someone trained was coming after him, they would come in the back way. They had passed a steel fire escape on the side of the building. Scorpion decided to go in that way. He started back toward the fire escape, motioning Dennis to follow.

"Why we going—" Dennis began.

Scorpion clamped his hand over Dennis's mouth.

"*Zatknis!*" he hissed into Dennis's ear. Shut up.

He looked up the ladder at the metal landings

above but saw nothing, then tested his weight on the fire escape. Everything was radioactive and had been rotting for a long time but it seemed solid. He put his finger to his lips, then climbed step by step up the fire escape to the second floor. Dennis followed. Their footsteps grated hollowly on the metal stairs. Too loud, Scorpion thought. If he Shelayev was there, he'd know they were coming. They needed to get off the fire escape. A broken window on the landing was open, and Scorpion stepped through it into an empty apartment and onto a snowdrift. Dennis came in behind him. Scorpion motioned for him to follow.

They tiptoed through the apartment trying to avoid crunching on broken glass and went out to the hallway. Even there they could feel the icy wind. Adjusting his night vision goggles, Scorpion started carefully up the hallway stairs. When he reached the top floor, he paused and peered down the hallway, with its glints of broken glass from a faint glow of light coming from the corner apartment. It appeared empty. No cameras, no surveillance, no wires. He stepped into the hallway but stayed close to the wall, not walking down the middle of the corridor. He sensed Dennis behind him, breathing heavily.

Scorpion stopped at the half-open door of the apartment next to the corner apartment. Shelayev was Spetsnaz, he told himself again. He couldn't go straight in. He turned to Dennis, put his finger to his lips and motioned for him to stay there. Dennis nodded that he understood. Scorpion pressed his ear against the wall but could hear nothing. If someone was in the corner apartment, he wasn't moving around. He stepped through the half-open door into the next-door apartment, the Glock ready, walked into an empty room and checked the door to the balcony. It had no glass. Stepping out on the balcony, he peered around the edge of the wall at the corner apartment balcony. It was close enough to jump over, and he could use the balcony wall to help balance himself.

He just started to put his foot on the balcony ledge when he heard a sound behind him. He looked over his shoulder and saw Dennis starting to walk toward the corner apartment. He must've gotten bored waiting or he had seen or heard something, Scorpion thought.

"Dennis, don't!" he shouted, thinking, You stupid son of a bitch as he climbed back into the room. He ran back through the room toward the hallway, catching a glimpse of Dennis as he passed the open doorway.

The explosion flung Scorpion off his feet, hurling pieces of the wall at him.

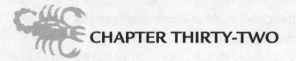

CHAPTER THIRTY-TWO

Krasnoe
Chernobylska Exclusion Zone

The forest was silent except for the sound of the wind. Scorpion shook his head. His ears still rang from the explosion. He had left the Volkswagen on what passed for a road and had come through the woods on foot, stopping at every step to check for trip wires and other booby traps. It was his fault Dennis was dead, he thought. He should've kept him out of it. But he couldn't just leave him, not knowing what Dennis might have done or who he might've talked to.

He had found Dennis's body blown a dozen feet from where the explosion went off. Using his flashlight, he found the trip wire Dennis had set off when he walked into the apartment. From the size of the explosion, it had been hooked to just an ounce or two of C-4, Scorpion calculated. Strictly antipersonnel. The light they saw from the roof of the tall apartment house was lying on the floor. It was an LED that had been on a battered old table until the explosion knocked it over, still connected with a copper wire to a double-A battery. A simple lure, like those used to catch fish at night, and right out of the Spetsnaz manual, he thought.

Except for the light and the booby trap, there was no sign of Shelayev. Scorpion looked around the apartment, checking for more booby traps or surveillance. Shelayev had left the booby trap for whoever came after him. Sending a message: don't come any further.

He went back to Dennis's body and fished around in the pants pockets until he came up with the keys to the Lada. He took back the five thousand *hryvnia* he had given him. Whoever found Dennis would just take it. *Damn you*, he silently cursed the dead body. *Why didn't you just stand there like I told you?*

One thing was clear. Iryna had been right. Shelayev was somewhere in the Exclusion Zone, or he wouldn't be trying to chase pursuers away. When he did find Shelayev, he thought grimly, he would be ringed with defenses out of the Spetsnaz playbook.

Scorpion stepped out onto the balcony. Shelayev wasn't in Pripyat. But he had known that when someone came looking, sooner or later, they'd have to check the city, so he set a trap. Scorpion looked out over the city hidden in the darkness. There were no lights anywhere and only one or two stars in the sky, the rest hidden by cloud cover. He saw no movement except for the wind. If anyone heard the explosion, there was no sign of it. He went back to the body, picked up Dennis's Geiger counter. Heaving his pack over one shoulder, he went back down the stairs and out the back of the building.

Walking down the middle of an empty avenue toward the Palace of Culture, Scorpion heard a sound behind him and whirled into shooting position. At first he saw nothing, and then spotted an odd-looking long-eared owl perched on top of a child's swing near an apartment building. He let the gun hang down at his side and went on. Being alone in this city at night was like a postapocalyptic movie; *Mad Max* without even the crazies, he thought. When he reached the Palace of Culture parking lot, he got into the Lada and drove through the city, the shadowy silhouette of the reactor building and the smokestacks and cranes looming above the trees.

He drove back to Chernobyl, his headlights carving a tunnel of light in the darkness. There were only bare trees and the snowy road. He turned on his cell phone to try to get the news, but this deep into the Exclusion Zone, there was no reception. The phone was useless, which meant there was no WiFi either. No way to know what was happening with the crisis.

When he got to Chernobyl, he'd have to bribe the *militsiyu* at the checkpoint, he thought. But driving up to the checkpoint, he saw it was closed. Evidently no one ever came this way at night. Why should they? It was a dead world.

He parked the Lada not far from the Tourist Office and left the keys in the ignition, taking Dennis's map of the Exclusion Zone from the glove compartment. Since he'd been wearing gloves all along, he didn't need to wipe the Lada down for prints. He went back to the Volkswagen, got in, and turned on the car's inside light to check Dennis's map. Krasnoe was almost exactly due north of the nuclear reactor.

He drove back toward the reactor site. It took a while in the dark, but he found the unmarked road to Krasnoe. Meanwhile, having turned on Dennis's Geiger counter beeper, he listened to it beep. The radiation level was serious, and he knew if he wasn't careful, there was a good chance he'd come out of this with cancer.

The road north from the reactor site led through a wooded area, spindly limbs covered with snow. A single pair of tire ruts and the four-wheel drive kept him moving through the snow. It took a half hour to cover half a dozen kilometers. When he saw a house with no lights covered with vegetation like a house in a fairy tale and trees growing through the roof, he knew it had to be Krasnoe. Stopping in the middle of the road, he got out and checked the Geiger counter. It read: 1.824. It would have to do, he thought, grabbing his gear and the Glock.

He walked into the deserted village. There was an onion-domed wooden church next to what might have once been a village square, now taken over by the woods. The houses were like wooden islands in the forest, every one of them abandoned, covered with moss and trees. He tried to stay in the clear, not touching the trees if possible, turning off the

Geiger counter's clicking sound. Icicles and dead branches hung down from the trees like stalactites. There were no sounds, not even birds.

He walked through the town looking for a hut with a light on the outskirts that might belong to Pani Mazhalska, tramping for what seemed hours through the foliage, though it was only minutes by his watch. Seeing a light glimmering through the trees, he stopped.

When Scorpion got closer he saw that the light was coming from a low hut, almost a shed, hidden in the trees. The window was shuttered, the light leaking from an opening where the shutters didn't fit together. He peered through the opening into the hut, saw a candle on a table and a pot cooking on a burning log in the fireplace. He didn't see anyone. The door to the hut was so low he had to stoop to knock.

"Pani Mazhalska, *dobry vecher*," he called out in Russian. Good evening. There was no answer. He knocked again, harder. "Pani Mazhalska?"

Still no answer. He opened the door and went in, ducking his head to clear the top of the door. The walls were covered with animal skins, vegetation, and a shelf full of bottles with dark colored liquids. There was a wooden bench near the fire. Scorpion checked it with the Geiger counter: 1.271. He sat and waited. About ten minutes later the door opened and a tiny old woman with a round peasant face came in. She was carrying a bundle of wood and a dead squirrel. When she saw Scorpion, she screamed and dropped the wood and the squirrel. She reached into her sack and pulled out a straw doll that she held before her.

"*Ne byyete mene!*" she cried out. Don't hurt me!

"*Ya droohoo.*" I'm a friend. "I won't hurt you," Scorpion said.

"*Ne trogaite moyu belku,*" don't touch—he couldn't catch the rest—she said, putting the dead squirrel on the table. Scorpion guessed *belku* meant squirrel.

He took the bottle of Nemiroff out of his pack and asked if she wanted some.

"*Khto vy? Shcho vy khochete?*" she asked, going to a cupboard. Who are you? What do you want? She took out a mismatched pair of jars that served as glasses and put them on the table. Scorpion poured them both good shots.

"*Ya droohoo. Budmo,*" he toasted, and drank. She watched him, her eyes narrow, then sat down and drained her jar.

'What do you want?" she asked again, in Russian.

"*Informatsiya,*" he said. "I can pay," and he put a few hundred *hryvnia* on the table.

"The tours come in the day. Tourists come. Always the same questions. Why do you live here? Aren't you afraid of the radioactivity? Stupid." She shrugged, holding up her jar for a refill.

"You're not afraid?" Scorpion asked, pouring her another drink.

"*Pah,*" she sneered, and tossed back the *horilka*. "The same tourist people who ask me, you think they'll live forever? What difference?" She wiped her mouth with the back of her hand. "When God wants to crush us, we're done," she said, crossing herself. "An old Jew once told me—you know before the war, there were many Jews in Chernobyl—he told me a saying: 'Men make a plan—and God laughs.' I like this saying. I like it very much," she said, taking the money and sticking it in her pocket. "What do you want to know, *miy drooh*?"

"I'm looking for a man. Big man, long blond hair." Scorpion gestured hair falling over his eyes. "His name is Dimitri Shelayev. He is maybe using a different name. He came here in the past four or five days. Have you seen him?"

Her eyes narrowed.

"I see *nichoho*." Nothing. "No one," she added, and looked away. She stood and got a knife, spit on it, then came over to the table and started skinning the squirrel in front of him. "What makes you think I know?"

"Dennis. The tour guide," Scorpion said. "He says you know everything, everyone in the *zona*."

"I know nothing, *nichoho*," not looking at him.

"I know he's in the *zona*. *Gde on?*" Scorpion asked. Where is he?

She didn't answer. When she finished skinning the squirrel, she wiped her hands on her dress and speared the squirrel on an iron spit, head and all. She went over to the fire and lifted the lid on the pot. The smell of kasha groats filled the hut.

"You've seen him, this Dimitri, haven't you?" Scorpion said. "What did he tell you? That people were coming to kill him?"

She stopped what she was doing and took a crude wooden crucifix on a string, the kind that might be found in any flea market in Ukraine, from around her neck. She slapped it into his palm and closed his hand around it.

"You are a *ubiitsa*," killer. "I see it in your eyes," she said. "Why?"

"Not by choice."

"I see that too," she said, looking up into his eyes. "What do you want with this man?"

"I want him to tell the truth."

"Only that?"

Scorpion nodded.

"Worse and worse. Sometimes the truth is more dangerous than an army," she said, putting the spit over the fire to roast the squirrel. She turned the spit. The hut filled with smoke and the smell of roasting meat.

"True," he said.

"This man," she said. "He is not called Dimitri. He says his name is Yevhen. Most of the *samosely*— the squatters—who live in the *zona* of Exclusion are old, like me. We come to live our last days in a place we know. Here there is no rent, no taxes. Only death. But this Yevhen is new. He lives in a cabin near Zimovishche. It's three kilometers from here, east of Pripyat."

"*Spasiba*," thanks, Scorpion said, getting up. He handed the crucifix back to her. He started to close his jacket and put the bottle of Nemiroff back into his pack.

"You want to stay and eat?" she asked. "Kasha and *belku*. It's good."

"*Nyet, spasiba*," he said, getting ready. As he stooped to go out the door, she called after him.

"This Yevhen. He has eyes like yours. Maybe you kill him," she said. "Maybe he kill you."

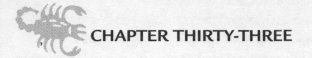 **CHAPTER THIRTY-THREE**

Zimovishche
Chernobylska Exclusion Zone

The farmhouse was in the woods at the edge of an abandoned village. Scorpion had taken a road that led from the river into what must have once been farmland and was now an empty landscape covered with snow. The tree line was beyond the fields. She-layev had chosen well, he thought. The woods could not be approached from the road except across the open snow. It would give Shelayev plenty of warning if anyone tried to approach.

He stopped the car in the middle of the road, got out and studied the open field from behind the car through his night vision goggles. He could see light coming from somewhere in the trees, the only sign of life in the night. The snow in the field had footprints going from the road to the woods, but was otherwise empty. Crossing the field was not only a giveaway, it was possible the field was mined or booby-trapped. Shelayev had already shown he knew how to make a bomb and set a trap.

Scorpion looked to the right, at the abandoned

houses of the village. He could approach the woods from that side, he decided. The houses would give him some cover and possibly had lower radiation levels.

There was an irrigation ditch beside the road, with a glimmer of ice at the bottom. He slid into the ditch and made his way toward the edge of the village. While in the ditch, he was hidden from anyone looking out from the woods. He nearly stumbled over something in the bottom of the ditch. It smelled appalling. As he climbed around it, he saw it was the remains of a wild horse.

When he got near the village, he peeked out over the top of the ditch. An abandoned house, shrubs and bare trees growing on its roof, shielded him from the woods. He scrambled out of the ditch, went around the back of the house and into the woods.

He stepped slowly, using his night vision goggles to scan for trip wires before he took each step. Then he heard something and froze. The cry of a night bird and a sudden flutter of wings. Damn, he thought. If Shelayev was waiting, that would have sounded the alarm. He froze behind a tree, took a deep breath and peered around the trunk. With his night goggles, he could see the house about two hundred meters ahead. It was overgrown with vegetation and snow on the roof, like all the other houses in the zone. As he stepped out from behind the tree, a bullet tore a chip of wood from the trunk a few inches from his head. He dove to the ground behind a fallen log.

He hadn't heard the shot, just a faint chunking

sound, so Shelayev had used a sound suppressor. If he was Spetsnaz-trained and using a rifle at two hundred meters, Scorpion reflected, he shouldn't have missed. Odds were, Shelayev was using a pistol. The question was, what to do about it? He couldn't stay behind the log. He looked around. There was a tree with a thick trunk about ten meters away. He found a pinecone and tossed it at a bush in the opposite direction, then made a dash to the tree as a bullet ricocheted off a tree behind him.

"Dmitri Shelayev, *ne strelyaite*!" Scorpion called out in Russian. Don't shoot! "Alyona's safe. I just want to talk."

Two bullets thunked one after the other into the tree trunk he was standing behind.

He's good, Scorpion thought as he scrambled on all fours, dodging through the trees on a diagonal toward the cabin. He still couldn't tell where Shelayev was firing from, except that it was from somewhere near the house. Through his goggles, he spotted movement from near the house into the shadows of the trees. He crouched beside a bare tree that had grown at a strange angle, realizing he needed a diversion.

Scorpion placed the Geiger counter in the crook of a branch on the angled tree and got ready to move. He turned on the beeper and fired the Glock toward where he'd last seen movement, then ran to a large tree close to the house, the beeper sounding behind him. He could hear shots coming from a stand of trees about forty meters from the angled tree. Holding his breath, he strained to listen. It was very faint, but he heard it. The sound of someone moving through the branches, toward the angled tree. The sounds stopped. Time to move, Scorpion thought.

He ran toward the house and around to the side, crouching low. He was below a small windowsill, and risked raising his head to peer into the house. The light he had seen was from a candle on a table. The house was furnished. It had the feel of someone living there, but he could see no movement. Ducking back down, he moved slowly on all fours to the corner of the house, where he waited and listened. He could hear the Geiger counter beeping faintly. It still seemed to be coming from where he had left it.

Something was wrong, he sensed. Shelayev should have reached the Geiger counter by now. He could hear nothing coming from the direction where Shelayev had been. Deciding it would be safer on the side of the house away from where he'd just come from, Scorpion eased his way around the corner, keeping the Glock ready. On this side the trees were closer to the house. The branches of a large tree had grown through a broken window into the house.

He started to go around the large tree when something hit his wrist hard, followed by a wrist grip that forced him to drop the Glock even as he began to react. He could feel Shelayev reaching around to grab his jacket in back. A pure Sambo move that would be followed by a leg sweep, he thought as he went into a two-hand Krav Maga wrist counter, stepping back to avoid the leg sweep. He was just in time, as a punch hit him in the side of his head and a Sambo sidekick grazed his ribs. It knocked his goggles off. Shelayev was good and strong and fast as hell, he realized as he countered with a grapple throw and leg sweep of his own, which Shelayev countered with a countergrapple. They were throwing elbows and kicks in a rapid sequence, fighting blindly in the dark by feel and with only a sense of each other's shapes.

Scorpion spotted the glint of a knife in the darkness. Knowing he was in a fight for his life, he desperately kicked at Shelayev's knee as a feint to grab the hand holding the knife in order to do a Krav Maga disarm. Although it was almost impossible to tell, he thought the blade had holes in it: Jesus, a Spetsnaz ballistic knife, he thought, blocking a Sambo grapple and attempt to throw, and doing the Krav Maga knife disarm, just managing with all his might to twist the wrist against Shelayev's immense strength. Scorpion followed with a quick front kick, taking the knife away.

He was staggered then by a Sambo sidekick to his thigh, just missing his groin, followed by a lightning-fast second sidekick to his knife hand to try to knock the knife away. He counterblocked as he reversed the knife and, stepping inside—remembering Koichi saying once that Sambo expects the opponent to use an outside leg sweep—hit Shelayev with an elbow smash to the throat. He heard Shelayev grunt, then grabbed him around the back of the neck in a guillotine choke hold combined with a hip throw to take him down. As they struggled on the ground, Scorpion hanging onto the choke hold with one hand while Shelayev hit him with an elbow to the face, Scorpion used his left hand to put the point of the knife to Shelayev's throat, his thumb on the release that would shoot the blade through the other man's throat and windpipe.

"*Ya hochu pogovorit,*" Scorpion gasped. I want to talk. "Dimitri, *Ya drooh* Alyona." I'm a friend of Alyona's.

He felt Shelayev suddenly relax and stop fighting.

"Where's the *pistolet*?" Scorpion asked.

Shelayev indicated his pocket.

With his other hand keeping the knife to Shelayev's neck, Scorpion pulled out the pistol—an SR-1 Gyurza—and put it in his pocket.

"Who are you?" Shelayev asked in Russian.

"We met before. In Dnipropetrovsk. I'm the journalist, remember?"

"Kilbane," Shelayev said, taking off his night vision goggles, which were similar to Scorpion's, and getting to his feet as Scorpion released him. The goggles had gotten wrapped around his neck during their struggle. "You didn't learn to fight like this in journalism school," he said, rubbing his neck.

"You'd be surprised. The girls at Columbia are pretty tough," Scorpion said, picking up his pack and goggles. They spoke in a mixture of Russian and English. Using the goggles, he searched until he found the Glock lying on the ground.

"What do you want?" Shelayev said.

"If it isn't broken, I have a bottle of Nemiroff in my pack. All you have to do is promise not to kill me," Scorpion said, unable to see Shelayev's face, deep in shadow. A few minutes later they were sitting at the table inside the house passing the bottle between them.

The house was cold as ice. Scorpion kept his jacket on, their breath visible in the candlelight. Before coming in, he had gone back to retrieve the Geiger counter, and while in the woods, threw away the ballistic knife and reattached the button video camcorder. When he got inside, he activated it. The only source of light was the candle on the table, casting their shadows on the walls, and Scorpion kept his fingers crossed that the hidden video camcorder would be able to pick up Shelayev's face in the dim light. Scorpion removed the ammunition clip, emptied the chamber from the Gyurza pistol, then put the empty gun on the table between them.

"How did you find me?" Shelayev asked.

"Something Alyona said."

"Alyona told on me?" Shelayev clenched his massive fist, though otherwise his face betrayed nothing.

Scorpion shook his head. "Only that you had gone where no one would find you. Iryna thought—"

"Iryna?"

"Iryna Mikhailivna Shevchenko. We've been working to try to clear our names. We've been accused of killing Cherkesov."

"You and Iryna Shevchenko kill Cherkesov?" Shelayev snorted. "Is *absurdnyi*."

"Tell that to the *politsiy* and everyone else who is after us."

"Why did Alyona say anything about me?" He looked sharply at Scorpion, the candle flame reflected in twin pinpoints of light in his eyes. "How did you find her?"

"The bald man from the Black Cat café where she works. He guessed about the Puppet Theatre. First Alyona disappeared, then her friends, Ekaterina and Fedir. He was worried about them."

"And Alyona told you about me? She said where I'm going? Just like it was nothing, that *kurva* bitch!" he snarled.

"She was tortured," Scorpion said. "She was in shock with internal bleeding when we got to her. Ekaterina and Fedir were already dead."

"*Ahhhhh!*" Shelayev screamed, smashing his fists on the table, nearly knocking over the candle and the *horilka*. He got to his feet and began pacing and smacking his fist into his hand. He turned on Scorpion.

"Who did this?"

"Who do you think?"

"Tell me!" Shelayev demanded, balling his fists.

"Kulyakov. We found them under the stage in the Puppet Theatre. He was holding her head in a tub of ice water."

"You're lying. Prokip wouldn't do that. He is a *drooh*," Shelayev said. A friend.

"Kulyakov is a sick *sukin sin* son of a bitch *i vy khorosho znayu*, and you damn well know it," Scorpion said. "He does what Gorobets tell him to. The enjoyment he gets from torturing people, especially naked women, is just an extra bonus."

"Why should I believe you?"

"Because it's true," Scorpion said, taking a slug of the Nemiroff and passing the bottle over to him.

"Where is she now, Alyona?" Shelayev asked, taking a long swig of the *horilka* and wiping his mouth with the back of his hand.

"We took her to a Medikom in Vyshhorod. Iryna was with her. She was cut all over. Plus internal bleeding, but the doctor said she would live."

Shelayev rubbed his hand over his face, then looked sharply at Scorpion.

"Did you kill Kulyakov?"

Scorpion shook his head. "He got away."

Shelayev smirked. "How did you let that happen?"

"There were two of them. The other was about to kill Iryna. I had to stop him."

For a time neither of them spoke. It was strange sitting there by candlelight in a dark house, just the two of them, in the middle of a radioactive forest. Something told Scorpion he would remember this scene for the rest of his life.

"Why should Prokip torture her?" Shelayev asked.

"To find you. You know it's true, that's why you're hiding from them."

"You're wrong! I expected Kozhanovskiy's people or his SBU *mussory* to be after me. Gorobets has no reason. I followed orders."

"*Ne dorak*," Scorpion said. Don't be stupid. "You're a witness; the only one who can tie Gorobets to Cherkesov's death. He needs you dead."

"But killing Cherkesov was his idea. It had to be done," Shelayev said.

"Why?"

"Cherkesov was a traitor, that filthy *ebanatyi pidaraz* motherfucker!" he shouted, slamming the table with his fist, making the candle and bottle of Nemiroff jump.

"Who told you he was a traitor? Gorobets?"

"*Ladna*, you are not entirely stupid," Shelayev said. "Sure Gorobets. He showed me. A secret text to Cherkesov."

"Who was it from?"

"A man named Gabrilov."

"The one from the Russian embassy?"

"He is head of the SVR in Kyiv."

"I know. Also Alyona's contact," Scorpion said, stopping himself from saying *case officer*.

"So!" Shelayev said, shaking his finger in Scorpion's face. "You didn't learn that either at Columbia, Pane Kilbane. I think you are CIA."

"Also Mossad and MI-6. I'm a triple threat. What did the message say?"

"That *sukin sin!*" Shelayev snarled. "Cherkesov wants good relations with the Russians. *Horosho!* Okay! Extend lease for Russian naval base at Sevastopol. *Horosho!* But that *mudak* bastard wanted to give Crimea back to Russia. For what? For money like a Jew!" He turned and spit on the floor. "We are sons of the Cossacks. You understand? For this, we fight! For this," his eyes narrowing, "we kill."

"The Crimea? You killed Cherkesov because of Crimea?" Scorpion said.

"Crimea is ours."

"When the fuck did I land in the nineteenth century?" Scorpion said, shaking his head. "What the hell is next? Balaklava and the Charge of the Light Brigade?! Did Gorobets say what would happen once Cherkesov was dead?"

"He said Davydenko would be President."

"Davydenko the idiot?"

"Better him than Kozhanovskiy and Iryna Shevchenko, who want to sell us out to the Americans!" Shelayev said hotly.

"So you killed Cherkesov?"

Shelayev looked at him and didn't answer.

"The C-4 in Cherkesov's car," Scorpion said. "How'd you wire it? To the ignition?"

Shelayev shook his head. "Cell phone. I wanted to be sure he was in the Mercedes when it went off. Someone might have started the engine before he got in."

"You were Gorobets's security. It made it easy, didn't it?"

"I did the final security check, so no one would spot it before. I got under the car. It only took maybe twenty seconds." Shelayev shrugged with a faint smile of pride.

"If anyone saw you, you were just doing your job." Scorpion nodded. "Have you heard about the war?"

"I saw the TV yesterday in Chernobyl," Shelayev said sullenly.

"When you planted that C-4, what the hell did you think you were doing?"

"Saving my country," Shelayev said, looking up. "Alyona too."

"The Serb who killed Archduke Franz Ferdinand and started World War One probably didn't mean to start a war either. But he did," Scorpion said grimly. "But why should it bother you? You've already got a lot more blood than Cherkesov's on your hands."

"What?" Shelayev looked startled. "What are you talking—"

"Alyona's friends. Ekaterina and Fedir. Kulyakov killed them because Gorobets was looking for you. If I hadn't got there in time, Alyona would be dead too. And then there's Dennis."

"Who?" He looked wide-eyed at Scorpion.

"My InterInform guide, Denys. Your little Spetsnaz *lavoushka* trap in the apartment in Pripyat killed him. If Ukraine falls to Russia, you'll have done it."

Shelayev stared at him. "Gorobets told me—" he began.

"Can't you get it through your thick skull?" Scorpion snapped. "Gorobets wants you dead. You and Alyona both."

"So you say," Shelayev said, standing up. Before Scorpion could stop him, he snatched a second Spetsnaz ballistic knife from behind a pot on a shelf and pointed it at Scorpion. The force of the knife, if the stories were true, could put the blade through his entire body and out the other side.

"We had a deal," Scorpion said, his eyes on the knife.

"I don't trust you. You're trying to trip me up, you CIA *mudak* bastard. I love my country. My

father was a hero. He fought the Germans in the
Great Patriotic War."

"Before you do something stupid, just one question: Why are you trying so hard to protect the man
who wants you and Alyona dead?"

"It's not true," Shelayev said, shaking his head. "I
did it for my country, but also for Alyona. She was
in the middle. She was desperate."

"I know. Her mother was dying and the authorities threatened to release her brother, Stepan, from
Pavlovka. Do you know who did that?"

Shelayev didn't answer.

"Gorobets," Scorpion said. "But you already
knew that, didn't you?"

Shelayev stared at him, his eyes wide and blue.

"I caused this, didn't I?" he said.

"You lit the match. Gorobets set the explosive."

"I am the traitor," Shelayev said, almost to himself.

"Dmitri, if you are willing to tell the truth we can
stop this."

"And then Kozhanovskiy and the Jews win!" he
snarled.

"And what about Alyona?"

"Alyona was a dream. Besides, after all this radiation . . ." Shelayev gestured vaguely at the house and
the woods. He sat back down at the table but kept
the knife aimed at Scorpion's chest. With his other
hand, he took a long swig of the *horilka*. He wiped
his blond hair out of his eyes.

"Do you know Taras Sherchenko, the poet?" he
asked. He began to recite:

"When I die, bury me
On a grave mound
Amid the wide wide steppe
In my beloved Ukraina . . ."

He looked at Scorpion. "She wants to be an actress. So beautiful," he said.

Shelayev put the knife in his mouth and pressed the release with his thumb. He gagged as the blade shot through the roof of his mouth and brain, the point and part of the blade sticking out of the top of his skull, gushing blood as he toppled to the floor.

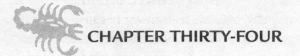

CHAPTER THIRTY-FOUR

Verkhovna Rada
Kyiv, Ukraine

Scorpion drove through the darkness toward the checkpoint at Dytyatky, the road with its patches of snow a ghostly white in the headlights. His cell phone had finally gotten into range and he picked up a BBC news broadcast. The Russians had announced a deadline of midnight, after which Russia "would take whatever steps are necessary, including military action, to ensure the security of ethnic Russians in eastern Ukraine," the cell phone broadcast said.

"In Kiev," the announcer went on, "the meeting between presidential candidate Viktor Kozhanovskiy and acting president Lavro Davydenko has ended without a joint statement or any sign of compromise. Mr. Kozhanovskiy has accused Mr. Davydenko of indifference to the suffering of the Ukrainian people and a callous disregard for the sovereignty of the Ukraine. He again demanded that NATO fulfill its obligations under the Membership Action Plan agreement.

"Mr. Davydenko, speaking through his spokesman, Mr. Oleksandr Gorobets, declared that Mr. Kozhanovskiy has no legitimacy because the crisis was caused by Iryna Shevchenko, Mr. Kozhanovskiy's campaign manager, who is accused of murdering the late Svoboda presidential candidate, Yuriy Cherkesov, whose assassination sparked the crisis. He demanded that Mr. Kozhanovskiy stop protecting her and that she and the accused assassin, a Canadian national named Michael Kilbane, be turned over to the authorities before the Russian deadline.

"In Moscow, the American, British, and French ambassadors have presented a jointly sponsored note to the Russian Foreign Ministry stating that if Russian troops cross the Ukrainian border, NATO will regard it as an act of aggression upon a NATO member country. In London, the prime minister stated in a televised speech to the people of Great Britain that 'all eyes are now turned to the Ukrainian border. We hope and pray that Europe, which knows well the devastation of war, will not see it revisited upon us.'"

At Dytyatky, Scorpion stopped at the checkpoint and stepped into a telephone-booth-like radiation detector. He placed his hands and feet on metal pads. The machine buzzed.

"*Tse ne dobre*," the soldier said, shaking his head. It is not good. "What you are doing in Exclusion Zone?"

"How bad is it?" Scorpion asked.

"You should wash clothes, body. Scrub good," the soldier said, making a fist to indicate strong.

"Very bad?"

"*Tse ne tak uzhe y pohano*," the soldier said. Is not so bad. "Like maybe two X rays. But you wash good, yes?"

"*Tak*," Scorpion said, nodding.

On the road back to Kyiv, he stopped again at the trailer-restaurant in Sukachi. The same woman, Olena, was behind the counter. He had some borscht and *salo*, strips of pork fat on black bread. He told her he needed to shower and change clothes.

"Too much *radioactivnist*?" she said. "What did you do there in *zona*?"

"I am a scientist. We like to get dirty," he said.

"There is no hotel or *banya* bathhouse here," she said. She looked at him. "My late husband. You're almost the same size. Come."

She led him to a house behind the trailer. While he took a shower—ice cold, of course—she laid out a workman's clothes. He put them on and went back to the trailer to pay her. She waved the money away and poured glasses of *horilka* for both of them at the counter.

"They don't fit bad," she said, sizing him up. "May you have better luck with them than my Hryhoriy had, *Tsarstvo yomu nebesne*." God rest his soul.

"He had a bad time?" Scorpion said.

She shrugged. "They were a bad luck family. It started with his grandfather in the Holodomor. He gave his son—Hryhoriy's father—to a Russian woman, a party official. It was to save him. They were starving. This was when the Bolsheviks deliberately starved millions to death. If the Komsomol brigades found you with even a single grain of wheat, they would shoot you. Cannibalism was widespread. Some say four million died, some say seven, some ten." She shook her head. "No one knows. The Bolsheviks said it was part of Stalin's war against the kulaks, but," motioning him closer, "many believe it was to wipe out the Ukrainians. Hryhoriy's father was the only member of his family to survive, but it did no good."

"More bad luck?"

"You could say so. Hryhoriy's father was a partisan in the war, but he was captured by Germans. They took him to Syrets, the concentration camp they make at Babi Yar, where they killed the Jews. When he got out, he weighed thirty-six kilos. But he was only free for not even a year before he was arrested and executed by KGB."

"Why?"

"Who knows?" She shrugged again. "In those days they didn't need a reason. So then comes my husband, my Hryhoriy. All his life he tried to avoid trouble, but it did no good. He was killed in the riots against President Kuchma. He wasn't on any side. They mistook him for someone else. Like I said," she drained her glass, "a hard luck family. You look tired," she said.

Scorpion nodded. The *horilka* was beginning to effect him. Before he knew it, he was back in the house behind the trailer. He fell asleep sprawled on the bed in the dead man's clothes.

In the morning, he drove to Kyiv, where he bought a new set of clothes, overcoat, and fur hat at the Metrograd mall. He thought about calling

Iryna. But first he needed to deal with the video of Shelayev. They were almost out of time. The Russian ultimatum expired at midnight.

At the Internet café on Chokolovsky Avenue he loaded the murky video from the button camera to his laptop. He used Wax, a shareware software video editor, to brighten it so Shelayev was clearly visible. He transferred the video from the laptop to the Internet café's PC and uploaded it to YouTube with a fake new account, putting in *Ukraine* and *Cherkesov* as keywords. It was his fail-safe in case something happened to him or if what he was planning didn't work. He made a DVD of the video and deleted it and all evidence that he had ever been on the café's PC. When he was done, he made the call that would decide everything.

The Mercedes limousine was parked up on the sidewalk in front of the Benetton store on Khreshchatyk Street. Two workers were taping the store's windows. All along Khreshchatyk, crowds rushed past merchants boarding up their windows. In the twenty-four hours Scorpion had been away, Kyiv had been transformed into a city at war. Military checkpoints had been set up at major intersections and at roads leading into and out of the city, and air raid sirens were sounding; practicing for the real thing.

Ukrainian Army bivouacs and tents had sprung up in parks, churning the snow to dark frozen slush. SAM antiaircraft missile launchers were parked in

front of government buildings, many of them surrounded by walls of sandbags. Everywhere, there
were soldiers and a general feeling of fear. People
were leaving town or stocking up on food and
other essentials as if expecting the missiles to hit
any second. It was surreal, Scorpion thought, like a
World War Two movie.

A shaven-headed man stood beside the Mercedes
limousine, an obvious bulge under his leather overcoat. Scorpion recognized him from Villefranche
and the yacht. There was a flicker of acknowledg-
ment in the man's eyes as well. He held the limousine door open for Scorpion, then climbed into the
front.

Akhnetzov was alone in the backseat. Seated on
the side toward the front of the limousine was the
other shaven-headed man, his hand inside his coat,
and Evgeniya, the blond woman from the yacht. As
soon as Scorpion was seated, Akhnetzov indicated
to the driver to start driving. The limousine swung
off the sidewalk and into heavy traffic on Khreshchatyk Street, much of it *militsiyu* and military, the
driver honking his horn to try to get them to move
out of his way.

"Where are we going?" Scorpion asked.

"There is a helipad near the Verkhovna Rada,"
Akhnetzov said. "The road to the airport is completely jammed. Everyone is trying to get out. I have
my plane, a Gulfstream, waiting at Boryspil. Thanks
to you," he growled, "I have to go to Moskva to see
what we can salvage."

Scorpion didn't say anything. He looked at the blond woman, who avoided looking back.

"I do not see the point of this meeting. You failed," Akhnetzov said.

"I was set up," Scorpion said.

"People who fail always have excuses. Our business is done, you and me. Finished," and Akhnetzov made a sideways cutting gesture with his hand.

"We can stop this."

"Don't talk stupidity." He looked at Scorpion in a way that made the shaven-headed man take out his gun.

"I can stop it, damn it."

Akhnetzov regarded him curiously.

"How?"

"With this," Scorpion said, tapping his pocket where he had the flash drive from the button camera.

"Too late. The Russian deadline is midnight. Look at them," gesturing at the people on Khreshchatyk, many carrying plastic bags, rushing from store to store. "They know what is coming."

"I have proof," Scorpion said.

"What proof?" Akhnetzov said. "You have something on Li Qiang?"

"The Chinese were a red herring, what we in the trade call 'black info,'" Scorpion said.

"Still, you made a *govno* mess. I heard somebody found Li Qiang's bodyguard, Yang Hao, in a car with three bullets in him."

"Kyiv's a dangerous city."

"So long as you're around. Why did you want to see me?"

"I know who killed Cherkesov and I can prove it."

"I'm not sure it matters anymore," Akhnetzov said. "Things are moving too fast."

"The Russians have no pretext for war. It rips away their fig leaf."

"Maybe they don't care."

"They're not a monolith. This whole thing is pure SVR. Who are you going to talk to in Moscow?"

"Trust me, they are plenty important. Why?"

"You can bet there are people outside the SVR, people in the FSB and the president's office, who might love an excuse to get out of this mess if they can show they got something for it."

"And tell them what?"

"Cherkesov was killed by a man named Dimitri Shelayev. He was head of security for Gorobets."

Akhnetzov looked sharply at Scorpion.

"The man behind Davydenko?"

"The man who tells Davydenko what to do. Gorobets runs things. The Chorni Povyazky are his private army."

"It may be too late," Akhnetzov said thoughtfully. "What makes you think this will stop the Russians?"

"Because I'm going to put it on TV," Scorpion said. "When we met on the yacht, you told me you own a TV station."

Akhnetzov nodded. "We own Inter. The biggest in Ukraina."

"I want you to put Iryna Shevchenko on in primetime. It'll be a sensation."

"To do what? To say she's not guilty. So what?"

"I have a video of Shelayev confessing he killed Cherkesov on Gorobets's orders. He was in charge of security that night at the stadium. It made it easy for him to plant the bomb. The whole thing was a power struggle inside Svoboda."

For the first time, Akhnetzov looked genuinely interested. "He actually says it? He accuses Gorobets?"

"Better than that. After he admits it, he commits suicide," Scorpion said.

Akhnetzov tapped his finger on his lips. Scorpion watched him work it out. He was reminded again how intelligent Akhnetzov was. He had created a business empire, almost an entire industry, from nothing, from an idea.

"You've got the whole thing, the confession, the suicide, everything on the video?" Akhnetzov asked.

Scorpion nodded. "If we prove this all happened within Svoboda, the Russians have no excuse to intervene."

"No," Akhnetzov said. "It's better than that. It's good television. We'll put it on *Liniya Konfliktu*. It's the top-rated show, primetime." He spoke rapidly to Evgeniya in Ukrainian. She got on her cell phone and made a call. Akhnetzov turned to Scorpion. "I'll have Evgeniya send you a text to let you know when to be at the studio."

The limousine pulled into a park with government buildings and broad expanses of snow. *Militsiyu* guards stopped it and peered inside. The driver said something to them and the guards waved them on.

They drove through the park toward a helipad near a big columned building topped with a dome; the Verkhovna Rada, the parliament building. There were squads of soldiers and two SAM missile batteries parked in front, and a private helicopter was just landing on the helipad. The limousine stopped and the two shaven-headed men jumped out and checked to see that it was clear, then stood by the door as first Scorpion, then Akhnetzov and Evgeniya got out.

The day was gray and cold, the wash from the helicopter blowing against them. From where he stood, Scorpion could see the Puppet Theatre on a snow-covered hill in the distance. The image of Alyona and the bodies hanging in that room beneath the stage flashed in his mind. He hoped it wasn't an omen.

"Here," he said, handing Akhnetzov the flash drive from the button camera. "If what I'm planning doesn't work out, show it to the Russians."

Akhnetzov nodded. As he and the others started toward the helicopter, Scorpion shouted after him.

"If they don't invade, you owe me the rest of the money!"

Without turning around, Akhnetzov waved to acknowledge that he heard and continued toward the helicopter. Scorpion watched them board and take off, heading high over the Dnieper River toward the airport. He took out his cell phone and called Iryna.

"Where are you?" he asked.

"I'm with Viktor—and Slavo," she warned. "We're leaving for the front. It's terrible what's happening."

"Don't go. Meet me. We can stop this."

"You found Shelayev? You have proof?"

"It'll change everything," he said. He heard her talking urgently to Viktor in Ukrainian. She came back on.

"Viktor wants to talk to you," she said.

"Mr. Kilbane?" Kozhanovskiy said. "You found what you were looking for? You can prove we had nothing to do with Cherkesov's death?"

"I have Shelayev's confession on video."

"He says he was acting under Gorobets's orders?"

"It's all Gorobets; all of it."

There was a pause. He heard them talking urgently among themselves in Ukrainian. Kozhanovskiy came back on.

"I don't know what to say," he said, his voice thick with emotion. "This is—" He took a deep breath. "—good news."

"Put Iryna on. We don't have much time," Scorpion said.

Iryna came back. He told her where to meet him.

"One moment," she whispered. He waited until she came back on. She must have gone somewhere to get away from Slavo, he thought. "I'm worried," she said. "I tried to call the clinic about Alyona. No one picked up."

"All right," he said, his teeth clenched.

"Except it's not all right, is it?"

"No."

Scorpion ended the call and got back into the limousine. As they headed toward the center of town, he called the Medikom clinic. The phone rang for a long time. He dialed again. Finally, on the third try, a woman answered. He asked for Dr. Yakovenko. The woman told him the doctor had left on vacation. He asked about a patient, giving her the name they had used to check Alyona into the clinic. The woman told him to wait. After what seemed like a long time, she came back on the line.

"I'm sorry, *pane*," she said. "There's no record of any such patient."

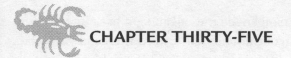 **CHAPTER THIRTY-FIVE**

Shevchenkivskyi
Kyiv, Ukraine

Iryna was waiting for him at a counter at a snack bar in the Central Station. She wore glasses and the curly redheaded wig under her fur Ushanka hat and had ordered coffees and *pampushky* pastries for two. Scorpion had watched her enter the station's main entrance from the McDonald's across the street. It didn't look like she was followed, but he watched for another ten minutes just to make sure.

The TV in the McDonald's was broadcasting news about widespread panic. Tens of thousands were evacuating Kyiv, headed for the countryside. All roads out of the city were packed with cars going one way, military vehicles going the other. In some districts of Kyiv and other cities, there had been looting. Store windows were smashed and supermarket shelves picked clean. Gangs of youths roamed the streets, breaking into houses and taking food and whatever else they could. Gorobets, speaking for Davydenko, declared at a podium that the office of the acting president had declared a state of martial law. "Looters," he said, staring straight at the camera, "will be shot."

Scorpion double-checked one last time, then crossed the street to the station. The main hall was crowded with people, many with families, heavy with luggage and desperate to get out before the war started. He found the snack bar. It was standing room only and thick with cigarette smoke. As he squeezed in beside Iryna, he put his hand on the counter and she gave it a squeeze.

"Why is Slavo still around?" he asked.

"I don't know. I think until you called, Viktor was beginning to question whether I wasn't too much of a liability." She looked around. "Why are we meeting here?" Crowded in at the counter, they could have been any couple trying to get on a train.

"The airport is jammed. Every flight is booked. There's a train leaving for Krakow at 2248 hours. Thanks to a little extra," he said, rubbing his thumb against his fingers in the universal sign for money, "I was able to get two tickets. I want you to come with me."

Her eyes searched his face. "What are you saying?" she asked.

"You know what I'm saying."

"Because of the war?"

"Because after the TV broadcast, we'll have done everything we can." He partly covered his mouth with his hand so only she could hear him. "There are a lot of people who want me dead around here, and after the broadcast, your life won't be worth a plugged nickel either. Not if Gorobets has anything to say about it."

"But Viktor—" she began.

"Maybe he can pull it off. After the broadcast, Davydenko and Gorobets will be on the defensive. But NATO is scared shitless. If there's a way out, they'll take it. The Russians too. They've backed themselves into a corner. Our broadcast will give them the excuse they're looking for. If Gorobets gives them what they want, the Russians will do a deal. Look around you," he said, glancing at the people packing the snack bar. "These people aren't ready to fight a war."

Iryna took a cigarette out of her handbag and lit it. She took a long puff and exhaled thoughtfully.

"What would we do in Krakow?" she said.

"Get on a plane. There are some places I'd like to show you."

She gave a little snort of laughter. "*Gospadi*, all this time I've thought you were the least romantic man I'd ever met." She leaned over and kissed his cheek. "We can't go," she said. "So much depends on us. What about Alyona?"

"You tell me. The clinic said they never heard of her."

"She's gone. Disappeared." Iryna nodded. "I stayed at the clinic all night. In the morning, when I left to meet with Viktor, Alyona was still there. She was in no condition to be moved."

"And now supposedly that doctor, Yakovenko, all

of a sudden, with a war coming, has gone on vacation!"

"After we spoke, I asked Viktor to have someone check it out. All they got was that men came into the clinic sometime after I left and took someone—no one will say who—away. No one saw anything. No one knows anything. The nurse told them if anyone asked her even that, she would swear the patient never existed." She leaned closer. "Shelayev killed Cherkesov? You're certain? You've got proof?"

Scorpion nodded.

"Why?"

"Gorobets lied. He told Shelayev that Cherkesov was planning to give Crimea back to Russia."

"That's crazy. Even Cherkesov—" She stopped herself. "Shelayev admitted on video that Gorobets ordered Cherkesov's death? Will that be enough for the Russians?"

"It'll have to be," Scorpion said, checking his watch. "We better get to the TV station."

Iryna began gathering her things. Before she got up, Scorpion put his hand on her arm.

"About Krakow?" he said.

Iryna stood, pulling her handbag strap over her shoulder. She pressed her body against his. He could feel the entire length of her against him. "I can't leave my country. Not now," she whispered. She took his hand and they went outside.

It had started to snow. Traffic in Vokzalna Square was heavy. They caught a tram heading toward

Prospekt Peremogy. Looking out the tram window at the streets and the falling snow, Scorpion had the most bizarre thought. For no reason he could imagine, he wondered if he would ever see snow again.

The Inter TV station was in a rectangular building in the Shevchenkivskyi district. They walked into the lobby, stamping their feet on a mat to clear the snow. The receptionist's eyes widened when, despite the wig, she recognized Iryna. She gave them directions to the station manager's office on the second floor. Before they got there, Iryna stepped into a women's bathroom and came out wearing the black wig cut the way people were used to seeing her. The change was incredible. She was the Iryna again. Even her walk was different. They knocked and went into the station manager's office.

It seemed he'd been alerted by the receptionist, because he was standing behind his desk, waiting for them. He was a middle-aged man with thick plastic-rimmed glasses.

"*Dobry den*," he said to Iryna. "I am Vladyislav Korobei." He looked at Scorpion. "*Khto vy?*" Who are you?

"*Miy okhoronets*," Iryna jumped in quickly. My bodyguard.

Korobei came around the desk saying something Scorpion couldn't get, but he caught a mention of Pane Akhnetzov. He gestured at the big screen TV on the wall and clicked on the volume with a remote. They listened to the announcer's voice-over while watching a TV spot for Iryna's upcoming appearance. There were images of Iryna, Kozhanovskiy, and Cherkesov, followed by a montage of the rally in the stadium in Dnipropetrovsk and a jumbled video of shooting and people running. The camera froze on the fireball of Cherkesov's car exploding, then cut to a head shot of Iryna, looking drop-dead gorgeous at some function.

Still talking, Korobei led them to an elevator. They went down to a large basement studio where people were busily working. Korobei introduced them around, then to Tetyana, the star of the show, a buxom brunette in a low-cut top who sat on a stool as a cosmeticist applied her makeup. She and Iryna air-kissed cheeks and talked like they were old friends, the two of them preening and eyeing each other like fighting birds. Scorpion studied the layout. There were three cameras pointing at the stage set designed to look like an upper-class living room with a backdrop view of the Saint Sophia Cathedral.

They went into the control room. One of the men—Scorpion assumed it was the director—spoke in Ukrainian to Iryna.

"They want the video," she said, turning to Scorpion, who opened his backpack, fished in the pocket and pulled out the DVD.

The director handed it to one of the men sitting by a monitor with lots of dials, and after a moment it came on. There was Shelayev sitting at the farmhouse table by the light of a lone candle, the image not crystal clear but unmistakably Shelayev.

"How did you find me?" Shelayev said.

"Something Alyona said," he heard himself say, which brought it all back to him, the cold and the terrible isolation of that radioactive place.

Everyone watched the video intently. He glanced over at Iryna. She was as engrossed as the others. She's seeing it for the first time, he reminded himself. There were gasps when he told Shelayev that Alyona had been tortured and Shelayev screamed and banged the table. And a buzz of conversation when Shelayev talked about wiring the C-4 in the Mercedes to a cell phone. The murmurs continued, but there was only stunned silence when Shelayev quoted Sherchenko and stuck the knife in his mouth and killed himself. The video captured him toppling over, the blade sticking out of the top of his skull, then went blank.

"Isus Khrystos!" Jesus Christ, someone said.

There was a long moment, then everyone started talking. The director said something to Iryna. She turned to Scorpion, her eyes glistening.

"He said up till now, he thought like everyone else that we were guilty. He said this changes everything." One of the men said something to the director and he repeated it to Iryna.

"What did he say?" Scorpion asked.

"He said it's not good television, it's great television!" She smiled.

There was an excited buzz on the set. People were whispering to each other. One of the men showed them where he and Iryna would sit and which camera would be on them. Scorpion was surprised to hear that, and as soon as he could, he pulled Iryna aside behind the cameras.

"What the hell's going on? They don't expect me to be on camera, do they?"

"Yes," she said. "They think it's an important part of the story. Tetyana wants to ask you some questions. Is it a problem?"

"I don't go on TV. I don't have my picture taken. Ever. It would destroy what I do," he told her.

"Of course," she said, looking into his eyes. At that moment, the hair rose on the back of his neck. He had the feeling she was falling in love with him. "I'll tell them."

She went over and talked with the director and Tetyana. They spoke for some time before Iryna came back.

"You have to be on. You're the one on the video talking to Shelayev. They've suggested a mask. Is that all right?"

"Not if it shows half my face," Scorpion said.

Iryna had another conference and came back. "You'll wear dark glasses and have the rest of your face covered, plus it will be digitally obscured. Your voice will be electronically disguised. Ilko—"

"Who?"

"The director," she said, indicating the man talking to Tetyana, "he thinks the disguise will make it even better. More believable. Okay?"

Scorpion nodded. He checked his watch. They would be taping in half an hour. Still plenty of time for him and Iryna to catch the Krakow train, although he wasn't sure she would come. Watching her now, the center of attention, the TV cameras getting ready, he wondered if she was ready to give this up for him. *Why would she?* he asked himself. *Why would anyone?*

An assistant led Scorpion to a small room off-stage, where he tried on the dark glasses, a workman's cap, and a wraparound mask and voice device. He looked at himself in the mirror. He looked like a terrorist. If he were a viewer, he thought, he wouldn't believe a word out of his mouth. Then Iryna joined him and studied him critically, tilting her head.

"Ilko's right. It'll make it better," she said.

A female assistant came in and brought them tea, then began to do Iryna's makeup. Scorpion checked his watch again. He was getting antsy. *It's almost over,* he told himself, but his instincts were telling him something was wrong. He heard sounds outside.

"Chto eto?" he asked. What's that?

"They are just getting ready on the set," the assistant said. She checked her watch. "Only five minutes."

Scorpion heard something, people outside the door. He started to reach for the Glock when the door burst open.

Half a dozen SBU team members in full battle gear swarmed into the room, their weapons pointed at Scorpion and Iryna. Even if he reacted, Scorpion realized, there was a good chance that Iryna, if not both of them, would be killed. Two men grabbed him and forced him to the ground. Out of the corner of his eye he could see they had done the same to Iryna and the assistant. His body was patted down and someone kicked him in the ribs. Someone else ripped his Glock out of its holster as his hands were shackled behind him with tight plastic cuffs. Iryna was lying nearby, two SBU men on top of her, one of them with his hand between her legs.

An SBU team officer holding a pistol walked into the room. Even from the floor, with a knee pressing hard on his neck, Scorpion could see who it was—the man's cheek and broken nose still swollen and bruised from where he had kicked him.

Kulyakov.

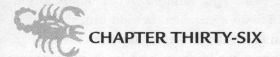 **CHAPTER THIRTY-SIX**

Lukyanivska Prison
Kyiv, Ukraine

The screams echoed off the walls of the cell. Scorpion couldn't tell where they were coming from or even whether they were from a man or a woman. They sounded barely human. They seemed to go on for hours, though he knew it might have only been minutes. It was part of the process, he thought. Time deprivation, sensory deprivation, loss of control of your own body, humiliation, pain. "Reports from subjects have repeatedly confirmed that the anticipation of torture is worse than the torture itself," he remembered Sergeant Falco quoting from the KUBARK book, the CIA's classified manual on torture. Buzz-hair-cutted, fat-faced, massive-shouldered, no-necked Sergeant Falco tapping the desk with a rubber hose. Scorpion had encountered him during his Level C SERE training at Fort Bragg, North Carolina, back when he was in JSOC's First Special Forces Operational Detachment Delta Force. The rules for Level C SERE were that interrogators were allowed to break no more than one major and two minor bones. For five straight days and nights he'd had Sergeant Falco's undivided attention.

Not an easy man to forget, Sergeant Falco.

The screams subsided. For a moment there was nothing. Suddenly, he heard a terrible piercing scream, louder, higher pitched, worse than anything he had heard before. A woman, he thought. Definitely a woman. Then he understood. They wanted him to think it was Iryna.

Maybe it was.

Scorpion was penned naked in a small cage, his hands plastic-cuffed behind him, in a squatting stress position. There was no room to straighten any part of him, and the pain in his knees and back, shoulders and neck, was becoming unbearable. In a little while he would fall against the side of the cage and it would be even more uncomfortable.

The cell the cage was in was concrete and pitch-black and unbelievably cold. When they first brought him into the prison with his hands zip-tied behind him, Kulyakov had watched, smiling, as three SBU *mussory* took turns beating him with rubber truncheons. One of them got too close and Scorpion nearly took his head off with a Brazilian *capoeira*-style heel-kick that laid him out. He head-butted another and started to take the third man out, but Kulyakov had called for help and another three or four beefy guards piled in, swinging truncheons. One of them slammed his truncheon into Scorpion's groin as he was kicking, bringing him down.

His body ached all over from the beating they had given him, angry that he had hurt two of their comrades. But it was worth it, he thought, even as they were hitting him. It was worth it to let them know that they weren't completely in control. The pain was bad though. It was hard to know which was worse, the bruises from the beating, the pain in his joints from the stress position, or the cold.

The cold, he decided. He was shivering violently, approaching hypothermia, which he remembered starts when body temperature drops below 35 Celsius, 95 Fahrenheit. His breathing was becoming shallow. He needed to do his thinking now, he realized, while he still could, before the cold robbed him of his mind too.

"Sooner or later you'll break. Everyone does," he remembered Sergeant Falco saying. It was a contest between interrogator and captive. Between Kulyakov and him. Kulyakov wanted confessions. If he didn't get it from him, he would try to get one from Iryna.

Scorpion tried to calculate if she could resist. How bad would they go on her? Would they sexually abuse her? Probably, he thought. How did he feel about that? He didn't want to think about it, he realized. *Well, you better, because they're going to do it.* If they survived—and realistically, for him at least that was almost an impossibility—would he take her back? Even if he would, would she let him? *You're in a dream world*, he told himself. *It's the cold. It's the cold and the pain and the screams doing the thinking. Not me*, he decided. He would take her back no matter what they did. And even if Iryna didn't break—she would try not to, he knew that about her—Kulyakov also had Alyona. He'd get his confessions.

So what weapons did he have? Kulyakov had two limitations. First, he knew that Kulyakov couldn't afford to let him die. He needed to parade him for the Russians. And second, a confession from Iryna alone wouldn't do. Kulyakov needed a confession from him too. They would likely try to use him and Iryna against each other.

"It's about fear and pain," Sergeant Falco told them in that mock prison camp that was way too real. "At some point, there's only pain. It'll blot out everything. Your wife, your mother, your country, your god. You think it won't, but it will. You need to hold onto one idea. Only one. My job is to get past that. Believe me, I will," Falco said, smashing the rubber hose on the desk with a loud thunk. "Before I'm done with you, the only thing you'll believe in is me."

That would be his one idea. Kulyakov didn't want him to die.

Was someone screaming again or was it in his mind? He wasn't sure and tried to move his head. Cell by icy cell, his brain was beginning to shut down. *The cold doesn't matter*, he told himself.

He remembered once, when he was a boy, Sheikh Zaid sent him out wearing only a *thawb* robe and a knife, to be alone in the desert for three days; part of his education in what it was to be a man of the Mutayr. It was winter and the temperature in the northern desert dropped 100 degrees from daytime to night. He remembered laying on the sand looking up at the stars like ice crystals in the sky. It was bitterly cold and he shivered in the robe, unable to sleep. There was no one, nothing, for as far as the eye could see anywhere. He was hungry and utterly alone. The nearest source of light were the stars.

"How should I deal with the heat and the cold?" he had asked Sheikh Zaid before he set out.

"Be patient," Sheikh Zaid replied. "Remember, Allah is merciful. The pain always ends. Either you die, or if Allah wills, you will see the sun, but either way the pain ends."

He looked up in the darkness of his cell and saw stars. His mind was beginning to blur, he thought. He fought to keep it clear. There were plenty of unanswered questions. What had happened with the war? He had heard no explosions or air raid sirens, so maybe his YouTube video had been seen or Akhnetzov had gotten through. Or maybe the city was under attack right this second and he was buried so deep behind Lukyanivska Prison's thick walls he couldn't hear it.

What had happened to Alyona? And Iryna? Would she give him up? How had the SBU found them at the TV station? He was certain they hadn't been followed. Was it Akhnetzov? Or someone at the station? Or even Kozhanovskiy? Someone had tipped the SBU about the upcoming broadcast. Who was it? Who stood to gain from stopping the video from getting out?

Gorobets? Gabrilov and the SVR? But how could

they have known about the broadcast or where he and Iryna were? Because they knew. Kulyakov had come himself with the SBU team to the TV station because he knew they would be there. But how? It was almost as if there were another agent, an invisible player in the game. But how could that be?

He heard footsteps and the door unlock, and then a blinding light came on. It hurt his eyes and he had to squint to see. It was Kulyakov. This time he came with four big guards. They had learned to take him seriously, he thought with a tiny touch of satisfaction. The battle had been joined.

"So Kilbane aka Peter Reinert aka Scorpion. Ready for a little chat?" Kulyakov said.

Jesus, where'd he get "Scorpion"? he thought in panic. Then he remembered, Akhnetzov knew it. Possibly Boyko too. And Iryna. He'd told her that night in the apartment in Zaporozhye.

No, not Iryna, he told himself. He didn't want to think they'd gotten it so soon from her or what they might have done to her to get it. Still, point for Kulyakov, he acknowledged. Good move and right out of the KUBARK playbook. Show the captive that you know more than he thinks you do and he'll assume you know a lot more. The CIA, the SBU, the FSB, they all played by the same rules.

"*Khuy tebee v rod?*" Scorpion said. With my dick in your mouth? His teeth were chattering like castanets from the cold, and one of the guards snickered. *Hold onto one thought*, he told himself as they took him out of the cage. *Only one. No matter what, he can't afford to let you die.* Straightening his arms and legs was agony, but Scorpion forgot about it when one of the guards smashed him in the small of the back with a rubber truncheon, straightening him up.

Two guards, one on each side, half dragged, half carried him down a long gray corridor lined with steel cell doors. The corridor smelled of urine and disinfectant. As soon as they heard footsteps, prisoners began catcalling from behind the locked doors. Calling out, *"Skazhit im nichoho, brat!"* Don't tell them a thing, brother! And *"Dopomozhit!"* Help! And *"Yob tvoiyu maty, mussor mudaky!"* Fuck your mothers, cop bastards!

The guards hauled him into a large room with a mirror that he assumed was a two-way glass and strapped him into a heavy metal chair bolted to the door. He was able to see implements on a bench and electrical wiring before they strapped his head so he couldn't move it. *It's coming*, he told himself, trying to keep his heart rate down as the adrenaline started pumping. One of the guards attached electrodes to his genitals. Just the clamps alone were painful. He started breathing shallowly and forced himself to breathe more slowly.

Kulyakov came in along with a pudgy blondish man in a guard's uniform, which he wore with the jacket open, a wrinkled shirt hanging out of his trousers. The man had a smile painted on his face like a doll's. Scorpion wondered if he was a mental defective. He walked over to an electronic box connected to the electrodes. He touched it, almost caressed it, with his fingers, then licked his fingers with his tongue. Kulyakov sat in a chair facing Scorpion. Two of the guards left the room. The other two stayed behind Scorpion's chair, ready to grab him if he tried anything.

"The guards have gone to get their guns. You can't get out of this room. Not till I say so," Kulyakov said.

Scorpion didn't say anything.

"I've been looking forward to this." Kulyakov allowed himself a small smile.

"I should've killed you in the Puppet Theatre," Scorpion said.

"Why didn't you?"

"I wanted to question you first. Then Iryna needed help." He tried to shrug, but was unable to move.

"One of your many mistakes," Kulyakov said. "You know why you're here?"

"An unpaid parking ticket?"

"Good." Kulyakov nodded. "You're going to make this fun." He smiled and looked at the guards, who began to laugh. The blondish man grinned and made a strange "uh, uh, uh" sound, showing wide gaps in his teeth. "You're going to be tried and convicted of the assassination of Yuriy Cherkesov and the members of his staff who were in the car when you blew it up. You and your fellow conspirator, Iryna Shevchenko."

"If the verdict's already been decided, why bother with a trial?" Scorpion said.

"Tribunal," Kulyakov corrected. "By the SBU."

"Of course. Less chance of anything resembling the truth sneaking in."

"You see," Kulyakov said, turning his head toward the unseen watchers behind the glass. "This is good. We have a dialogue." He gestured at the blondish man. "We should try out the equipment. Not too much."

There was the briefest electric hum before the pain hit Scorpion like a sledgehammer. His penis felt like it was pulverized and on fire. He gasped in the chair, jerking desperately against the straps. It seemed to go on a long time, getting worse by the second. When it stopped, despite the cold in the room, he was drenched in sweat.

"That was a low setting. We can make it a lot worse," Kulyakov said.

Again, right out of the KUBARK manual, Scorpion thought. Create anticipation of greater pain by telling the subject how much worse you can make it. Begin the obscene intimacy between torturer and subject, where the subject comes to regard the torturer as his ally in a conspiracy to limit the pain.

"So? No clever retort? Are we done with that?" Kulyakov said, putting one leg over the other and leaning forward.

"How'd you find us?" Scorpion asked.

Kulyakov gestured at the blondish man and there was an instant hum of pain. Scorpion felt his back arching and the agony in his loins. A loud groan escaped him. At a sign from Kulyakov, the machine stopped. Scorpion slumped in the chair. He was soaked with sweat.

"You have it backward. I ask the questions," Kulyakov said, glancing at the mirror to make sure his wit was appreciated. "Let's talk about the assassi-nation. Who ordered you to kill Cherkesov? The CIA?"

"We both know I didn't kill Cherkesov," Scor-pion said.

"We expected you to say that," Kulyakov said, signaling to the blondish man.

This time the hum was louder and the pain much worse. He felt as if someone were stabbing his gen-itals with a red-hot knife. He screamed, the tears coming out of his eyes. Abruptly, the pain stopped and he became aware of the faint smell of burning flesh. His own.

"So let's get this over with. For the record, who do you say killed Cherkesov?"

"Dimitri Shelayev killed Cherkesov," Scorpion gasped. "I know it, you know it. By now, lots of people know it."

"You have evidence?"

"You know I do. Shelayev's confession. The video."

"What video?"

"The one at the TV station."

Kulyakov shook his head. "We searched thor-oughly. There is no video."

"People at the station saw it."

"We questioned everyone at the station. They all deny it."

"How can anyone deny seeing something you say doesn't exist? How would you even know to ask for it?" Scorpion asked quietly.

Kulyakov reacted angrily. He reached over and

slapped Scorpion hard in the face, then gestured to the blondish man. There was a louder hum and Scorpion screamed as the worst pain he had ever experienced radiated from his groin to his brain. He heard someone screaming and some part of him realized it was him. The pain seemed to go on and on, getting worse and worse. *He doesn't want you to die*, he told himself. *Sheikh Zaid. Be patient. The pain always ends. He needs a trial. He can't afford to have you die.* But the hum and the pain didn't stop.

Now there was no more thought. Only pain. It went on and on. *Stop it, stop it, please stop it*, he said, not knowing if he said it out loud or in his head. *Stop it. Please stop. For the love of God, stop.*

The pain always ends. He doesn't want you to die.

He didn't remember them dragging him back to his cell. All he knew was that at some point he awoke. He was dimly aware of lying on the freezing concrete floor of the cell. He was naked. His hands were zip-tied behind him as before, a fire between his legs. The pain was an agony that wouldn't stop, but not like when the electricity had been on. He had never experienced anything like that. Not at Fort Bragg, not anywhere.

Nor had he ever been so cold. He was shivering violently, his shivers triggering more pain in his genitals. He could feel himself slipping. A piece of who he was was dying. *But who was he?* He had had so many identities, he was no longer sure. He never told even Iryna who he was. If he thought about it, Kulyakov would find a way to get him to tell. They're going to make me confess, he thought. Not that it mattered. Because he still had one ace in the hole. The video was on YouTube.

Regardless of what was happening to him and Iryna, the Russians and the Americans would see the video and know about Gorobets. Then they would kill him or imprison him or let him go, but the torture would stop. He just had to hang on. *Hold onto that,* he told himself. *All you have to do is hang on and you'll win.* And if he had told Iryna about his real identity, Kulyakov and Gorobets would now know. He didn't think the leak came from Akhnetzov. It wouldn't have been in Akhnetzov's interest to tell them about him. *Don't go there,* his mind told him. *Think about Iryna. She loves you.* Yeah, but she told them. They put the screws to her and she told them about him.

He tried to picture Iryna's face but couldn't. Something was bothering him. He had seen something. A face. He couldn't pin it down. It wasn't Kulyakov. He'd made a mistake not killing him when he had the chance. If he ever got out of here, he thought grimly, if there was one thing he did, it would be to terminate Kulyakov. The cold penetrated his bones. And the terrible pain in his groin. It was getting harder to think, lying on the icy concrete. *One thing. Hang on to one thing. Sheikh Zaid. The pain always ends. Either you die or if Allah wills, you will see the sun, but the pain always ends.*

How long had he been in this hell? he wondered. It had to have been days. Maybe weeks. It was impossible to tell. And what of the war? Had it started? He didn't think so or there would have been bombing or missiles or air raid sirens. Some sign that they were at war. He hadn't slept or eaten in days. The minute he dozed off, guards would rush into his cell and start beating him with their truncheons.

"*Prosnis-s-sh!*" Wake up! the blondish man lisped, slapping him hard across the face, then stepping back so the guards could start pounding at him. As they whacked away, he could hear the blondish man's strange "uh, uh, uh" laugh. Scorpion groaned and spit out some teeth.

There was hardly a single inch of his body that wasn't battered or bruised. They had only given him water twice. Both times it was a filthy-looking brownish liquid in a tin dish that he'd had to lap at like a dog, and when he tasted it, he gagged because someone had pissed in it.

And what of Iryna? Was she still alive? And Alyona? What had happened to her?

It was during the fourth or fifth or sixth interrogation—he had lost count—that they wrung the confession out of him.

"Why did you kill Cherkesov?" Kulyakov demanded. He nodded to the blondish man, who barely had to touch the dial for Scorpion to start screaming. *Let go*, he told himself. *It's time*. But why hadn't they mentioned the YouTube video? It was his lifeline.

"I don't remember," Scorpion muttered.

"You can do better than that," Kulyakov said, putting his hand on Scorpion's shoulder. "Stepan," he said, nodding to the blondish man, and there was a sudden jolt of electrical agony. At first there was only the pain, and then it hit Scorpion. Stepan! He knew now who the blondish man reminded him of. Alyona! He was the crazy brother!

"Wait!" Scorpion cried out. Kulyakov gestured and the current stopped. Scorpion struggled to turn his head to look at the blondish man but couldn't move his head. "What happened to Alyona?" he managed.

"You figured it out, haven't you?" Kulyakov said, bringing his face close to Scorpion's. "Yes, Stepan's her brother. Say hello, *dobry den*, Stepan," he said to the blondish man.

"Uh, uh, uh," Stepan said.

"What happened to Alyona?"

"We let Stepan question his sister. Seemed only right, but Stepan wasn't very nice. He poured kerosene on her and set her on fire. Didn't you, Stepan?"

Stepan didn't answer. Kulyakov looked at Scorpion.

"She's dead," he said.

Scorpion closed his eyes. In his mind he saw the photograph of her at the Black Cat café and felt sick. He'd tried to save her and instead had delivered her to the one thing she feared above all else. He didn't say a word about Iryna. He didn't want to know what they might have done to her. He didn't want to know any of it. The only thing left was YouTube. He had to find out. The only way was at the tribunal.

"Who ordered you to kill Cherkesov? The CIA?" Kulyakov said.

Scorpion nodded, his head hanging down.

"And you now admit that you and Iryna Shevchenko, acting on behalf of Viktor Kozhanovskiy as an agent of the CIA, murdered Yuriy Dmytrovych Cherkesov?"

Scorpion nodded again. "Sure," he said. "I also killed Rasputin, Kennedy, and Martin Luther King," he whispered.

Kulyakov gestured to Stepan, who hit Scorpion with a hum of pain worse than anything they had done to him before. It seemed to go on and on forever. He was screaming, begging, not knowing what he was saying. He felt like he was going insane. The pain overwhelmed everything. It was like someone shoving a red-hot iron up his urethra through his penis and testicles.

"I did it! Stop! *Please!*" he screamed. He couldn't take it anymore. "I did it. I did it," he sobbed.

Then it stopped. Kulyakov grabbed his face, dripping with sweat and snot.

"Don't think you're fooling me," he hissed, flecks of spittle flying. "If you recant later, what you just got will seem like nothing."

Scorpion's head hung down. They'd broken him, he thought. He would've said anything to make it stop. *No*, something inside him said. *It's just retreat.* He remembered Shaefer in Afghanistan arguing with a senior officer and quoting Sun Tzu: "To retreat elusively, outspeed them."

They dragged him back down the corridor to his cell. From somewhere came more screams; someone else being tortured. They threw him back into the cell. Just before they shut the steel door, Kulyakov leaned in.

"You know how they execute people in Lukya-nivska? You think it's picturesque, maybe? They stand you up against a wall at dawn like in the movies? *Ni*," he sneered. "They drag you into a tiled room, the floor sloping down to a hole for the blood. They make you kneel and then they shoot you in the back of the head. *Pah!*" he said, pointing his finger and making a gunshot sound. "Your *sud*," your tribunal, "is tomorrow. Day after, *pah!*" pointing his finger and making the gun sound again. "Your real name, who you work for, will no longer matter. You are no more."

The cell door slammed shut with a metal clang, final as death.

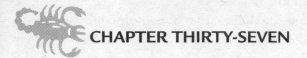 **CHAPTER THIRTY-SEVEN**

Sud
Kyiv, Ukraine

The *sud*, or tribunal, was held in a whitewashed room somewhere in the bowels of the Lukyanivska prison. They had taken him in shackles, escorted by half a dozen guards, down an elevator. Emerging from it, Scorpion had a sense of being deep underground, of moisture and pipes in the empty concrete corridors. He was in too bad shape to think of escape. Walking was painful, his groin aching badly, in addition to the shackles that made him hobble. They had put his clothes back on him, suit, shoes, shirt, no belt or tie. He must've lost a lot of weight in just the few days he had been the prison, he realized, because his clothes hung loosely on him and he had to hold his pants up with his hand.

They sat him in a chair in the middle of the room facing a narrow table. There were two rows of benches behind him. The *mussory* guards who had brought him down took up places by the door and along the wall, truncheons in their hands. He had hoped he might see Iryna, but there was no sign of her. They waited in silence, just him and the *mus-sory*. They don't want this getting out, he thought. That's why they had to do it right away; even in the middle of a war.

The door opened and three men, all with short hair and wearing the dark suits favored by Ukrainian *nomenclatura* officials, came in and took their seats behind the table. The middle *suddya*, or judge, was a thin, hatchet-faced man with short iron-gray hair. He wore a black tie with the yellow Ukrainian cross, suggesting he belonged to the Chorni Povyazky, and glanced down at the sheaf of papers he had brought in with him. A moment later a woman in a suit, carrying a laptop computer, came in and sat at a side desk, apparently to take notes. A technician entered the room and hooked up a video camcorder pointed at Scorpion. As the technician set up the camera, Kulyakov, also wearing a black suit and Chorni Povyazky tie, came in and sat in a chair on the side.

"Nam skazali, vy ne govoryat na Ukrainskom." the hatchet-faced *suddya* said. We have been informed that you do not speak Ukrainian. "So this *sud* will be conducted in Russian. He glanced at the woman taking notes on the laptop. "For the record, this is a *sud* authorized by the Sluzhba Bezpeky Ukrayiny," or SBU, "and the office of the Ukraine President Lavro Davydenko for the purpose of determining the guilt of the prisoner known as Michael Kilbane, also known as Petro Reinert, also the foreign agent Scorpion, in the murder of Yuriy Dmytrovych Cherkesov. The penalty for this crime is death. Let

it be noted that this *sud* has authority to impose this sentence."

He leaned forward and stared at Scorpion as if through a gun sight.

"You understand, prisoner, here is no prosecution, no defense. We ask questions. You answer. We decide. I am told that you will not reveal your real name or nationality. This is correct?"

"What difference does it make what my real name is?" Scorpion asked.

"A man who will not tell you the truth about his name will not say the truth about many things."

"You could take it that a man who will not lie about his name will not lie about other things," Scorpion said.

"But you are known by false names and also the code name Scorpion, *da*?"

"*Da.*"

"Are you an agent of the CIA or some other Western country? MI-6? DGSE? Mossad?" He pronounced "agent" the Russian way, with a hard *g*.

"*Nyet.* I am an independent. I work for different people."

"Like a business?"

"It is a business."

"A good business? You make a lot of money?"

"Sometimes."

"You work for anyone? So long as they pay?"

"Not anyone."

"There are people you won't work for no matter how much they pay?"

"*Eta verna.*" That's right.

"A spy with morals!" The hatchet-faced *suddya* smirked, glancing at his fellow judges, who smirked with him. "But you took this assignment?"

"I took an assignment, *da*."

"*Tak*," the hatchet-faced *suddya* said, rubbing his hands together like a businessman who wants to make a deal. "Who hired you to assassinate presidential candidate Yuriy Cherkesov?"

"*Nikto ne*." No one. "I was hired to prevent his assassination."

The judges looked at each other.

"*Tak vy govorte*," the hatchet-faced *suddya* said. So you say. "You have admitted killing Cherkesov. We have seen the video."

"Did you also see the electrodes attached to my *genitaliy*?"

"That is not relevant. You confessed. That is sufficient here. Who hired you?"

Scorpion shook his head. "I protect my clients. That's the basis of my business."

The hatchet-faced *suddya's* short laugh cracked sharp as a gunshot. "You really think after this you will still have a business?" He glared at Scorpion. "You will be dead, you *mudak* spy!"

"Then I'll be dead," Scorpion said. "If you want, get the electrodes. I won't tell you who hired me."

"Your job was to save Cherkesov?" the hatchet-faced *suddya* said sarcastically, leaning toward Scorpion.

"It was understood that Cherkesov's death might lead to great difficulties with Russia. My client wished to prevent this."

"Not very good at your job, are you?" one of the other judges, a thin man with bloodless lips, put in.

"Not this time," Scorpion said, thinking how close he had come to pulling it off. Just a few more hours and it would have been over. "I was led to believe that a *baklan* punk working for the Kozhanovskiy campaign named Sirhiy Pyatov was the assassin. I managed to stop him."

At this, the judges began to whisper among themselves. The hatchet-faced *suddya* leafed through the papers in front of him, then looked up.

"This Pyatov was one of those killed at the stadium in Dnipropetrovsk?"

Scorpion nodded.

"Did you kill him?"

"Two *militsiyu* did. There was much shooting."

"But you were ready to kill him?"

Scorpion nodded, and the judges looked meaningfully at one another.

"You killed *militsiyu* and *politsiy* at the stadium?"

"Two *militsiyu*. Also several of the Chorni Povyazky, not *politsiy*."

"How many Chorni Povyazky?"

Scorpion thought for a moment. "Five," he said.

The judges looked at each other.

"A total of seven men dead, murdered by you?" the hatchet-faced *suddya* said.

"Not murdered. Killed. They were shooting at Iryna and me."

"Not even counting Cherkesov?"

"I didn't kill Cherkesov. One of the Svoboda security men, Dimitri Shelayev, planted the bomb that killed Cherkesov and his people in the car."

"So you say," the hatchet-faced *suddya* said.

"This is *absurdnyi*!" Kulyakov said, standing up. He pointed at Scorpion. "This man has confessed to the crime. Trying to lay the blame on another, a patriot, in the hour of our country's peril, is obscene!"

"How many times do you change your story, Pane Scorpion? Whenever it suits you?" the hatchet-faced *suddya* said.

"I can prove it," Scorpion said.

The hatchet-faced *suddya* turned to Kulyakov. "Where is this Shelayev? Can we bring him to the *sud*?"

"I know Dimitri Shelayev," Kulyakov said. "We were colleagues, friends. He went missing the night of the attack at the stadium."

"So where is he?" the hatchet-faced *suddya* demanded.

"He was hiding in the Chernobylska Exclusion Zone," Scorpion said.

"So you say," the hatchet-faced *suddya* said once more, staring at Scorpion. "And where is he now?"

"Dead." Scorpion looked down. "He killed himself."

"Not true," Kulyakov said. "We found Shelayev's body. There was evidence of a struggle. He was murdered. This man," pointing at Scorpion, "was the last man to see him alive." He faced Scorpion. "More blood on your hands, *ubeetsa*." Murderer.

"*Tak*," the hatchet-faced *suddya* said, steepling his

fingers and squinting at Scorpion. "You are a dangerous man to be around, aren't you?" He turned to the other judges. "We'll have to execute this *mudak* bastard fifty times over!" He turned back to Scorpion. "You keep saying you have proof."

"Shelayev confessed. It's on video," Scorpion said.

"Where is this video?"

Time to show his cards. "Everywhere. It's on the fucking *yob* Internet. On YouTube," he said.

The judges didn't react. Neither did anyone in the courtroom. Scorpion got a sickening feeling in the pit of his stomach and the pain in his groin started up. Sure, Kulyakov and Gorobets had suppressed the TV video and gotten rid of everyone at the TV station, but how is it that they didn't know about YouTube? What the hell was going on? Somebody had to have spotted it. It was impossible not to. Who the hell could have gotten to Google or forced them to suppress it? Could Gorobets have done that? He looked at Kulyakov. He was smiling. Someday I'll kill you, Scorpion thought, but he couldn't think anymore. The pain in his groin was getting worse. He clenched his fist.

"You see! He makes up stories and says he has proof, but all his witnesses are dead or nonexistent. Where is this video that no one has seen or heard of before?" Kulyakov said. "Cherkesov was sure to win the election. They hired this assassin to eliminate him."

"Then why did I come to Gorobets in Dnipropetrovsk and warn him? You should know," Scorpion said, pointing at Kulyakov. "You were there!"

Kulyakov looked coldly at Scorpion. "To get access to the stadium, to the tunnel where Cherkesov would be coming to his automobile. And to make an alibi for yourself and Iryna." He turned to the judges. "Can you see? He is clever, this one."

One of the other judges leaned over and said something to the hatchet-faced *suddya*.

"We see very well," the *suddya* said. "What about the other criminal?" He looked down at his papers for a moment and back at Scorpion. "Iryna Mikhailivna Shevchenko. What part did she play in this?"

"She had nothing to do with this," Scorpion said.

"Then what was she doing at the stadium with you, in the tunnel?" Kulyakov demanded.

The *suddya* held up his hand to quiet Kulyakov. He turned to Scorpion. "You admit she was at the stadium?" he said.

"Yes," Scorpion replied.

"With you?"

"Yes."

"Why was she there?"

"To make sure we stopped Pyatov. She didn't trust me," Scorpion said.

"*Eta lozh!*" That's a lie! Kulyakov shouted, leaping out of his chair and pointing at Scorpion. "They're in it together! They're thick as bedbugs, those two!"

"*Molchat!*" the hatchet-faced *suddya* said, holding his hand up for silence. "Is prisoner Iryna Shevchenko here?"

"She's outside," Kulyakov said.

"Have her brought in," the *suddya* said.

Kulyakov signaled to one of the guards and a moment later Iryna was led into the room. She wore a gray prison shift, her hair in its pixie cut. She looked pale and very thin. They sat her in a chair a few feet from Scorpion's. As they led her in, his eyes searched hers. She looked frightened, worried, he thought. He tried to smile at her, but he could see she was shocked at his appearance, his gauntness and bruises.

"You are Iryna Mikhailivna Shevchenko?" the hatchet-faced *suddya* asked. She nodded. He looked at his papers for a moment. "You were the campaign manager for Viktor Ivanovych Kozhanovskiy?"

"Yes," she said, her voice so soft they had to strain to hear her.

"Speak up!" one of the other judges, a balding man with a goatee like Lenin's, demanded.

"*Da*, yes," she said louder.

"You know this man?" the hatchet-faced *suddya* said, indicating Scorpion.

"*Da*."

"You were with him at the stadium in Dnipropetrovsk when Yuriy Cherkesov was murdered?"

She looked questioningly at Scorpion.

"Look at me, not him!" the hatchet-faced *suddya* thundered. "You were with him?"

"*Da*."

"To kill Cherkesov?"

"No, to stop Pyatov!" she cried. "We tried to stop it!"

"Even if it meant forcing Ukraina into war with

Russia? Your political ambition was more important than the Motherland!"

"No! My father was Artem Shevchenko, founder of the Rukh, the Independence movement without which we wouldn't even have a country! Ukraina would still be an oblast of Russia! How could I ever go against the Motherland?"

"Lies! You see how she twists things?!" Kulyakov said, leaping to his feet. "What business did the head of the Kozhanovskiy campaign have at a Cherkesov rally? She did it to make sure her lover," pointing at Scorpion "went through with it! They are equally guilty!"

The hatchet-faced *suddya* looked at Iryna.

"You were lovers with this man, this Scorpion?"

Iryna looked desperately at Scorpion.

"I'm sorry," she told him. "They made me." She looked at the hatchet-faced *suddya*. "They did things to me, those *mudaky* bastards! *Gospadi*, do I have to say it?"

"*Molchat!*" Silence! the hatchet-faced *suddya* demanded, slapping the table sharply with his palm.

"She seduced him," Kulyakov said. "Part of his payment for killing Cherkesov. She was his *sooka* whore. Tell them," he said, coming up to her and grabbing her face tightly with his hand. "Admit it!"

"Is it true? You were lovers?" the *suddya* asked, his eyes focused on hers.

She tried to look desperately over at Scorpion, her eyes glistening.

"*Da*," she whispered. "It's true."

"Why do we waste time listening to these lies?" Kulyakov said. "They have admitted they were there together. This man," he pointed at Scorpion, "has admitted killing seven people at the stadium, not even including Cherkesov and the others in the automobile. He was the last one seen with Shelayev, who was also found murdered. Both these criminals have confessed to their crimes! They have shown no evidence of innocence or remorse. What more is needed?"

"I agree," the goateed *suddya* said. "The evidence is overwhelming."

"And I," the hatchet-faced *suddya* said.

The judges began to confer among themselves. They talked and nodded their heads.

Iryna turned toward Scorpion. "I'm sorry. I couldn't hold out," she said.

"Did you tell them about my code name, Scorpion?" he whispered to her.

"*Gospadi!*" she cried, looking away. "Is that what you think of me?"

The three judges passed around a paper. Each of them signed it in turn.

They were going to execute both of them, Scorpion realized. For him it was foregone, but there might still be a chance for Iryna.

"We have concluded—" the hatchet-faced *suddya* began.

"*Podazhdite!*" Scorpion cried out. Wait! "You've got it backward. She didn't seduce me! I seduced her! I killed Cherkesov! It was a Western plot. Iryna," nodding at her, "tried to stop me. I forced her to come with me after the assassination. I did it! She is innocent!"

"*Tak*, you admit you killed Cherkesov?" the hatchet-faced *suddya* said.

"I did it!" he said, looking at Iryna. "She had nothing to do with it."

"Why? What was your reason?"

"I was paid."

"But by whom? Who wanted Cherkesov dead?"

"An international conglomerate who thought Kozhanovskiy would be more sympathetic to their interests. Everyone here knows that Kozhanovskiy wanted to be closer to the West."

"An American company?" the goateed *suddya* put in.

"An international company, but yes, of the West," Scorpion said.

For a moment no one spoke.

"He's lying. He's trying to save her," Kulyakov said, looking at Scorpion.

"That's stupid," Scorpion said. "If as you contend, she brought me into this, if I'm about to die because of her, why would I want to save her? I'd want to see her dead!"

The hatchet-faced *suddya* stared at Scorpion for a long moment. No one in the room said anything. He turned and whispered quickly with the other judges. The goateed judge was disagreeing about something. Suddenly, there was a stir.

Two Black Armbands came into the room, their hands on their gun belt holsters. Someone followed them in, followed by two more Black Armbands.

The hatchet-faced *suddya* was about to object to the interruption when he saw who it was. Scorpion recognized him instantly. Heavyset in a dark suit, bald, horn-rimmed glasses.

Gorobets.

"*Vybachte*," Gorobets said in that same soft voice. "Excuse the interruption."

"The *sud* is honored, Minister," the hatchet-faced *suddya* said.

Gorobets walked over to the bench and, leaning over, spoke with the three judges. Once, he turned to look back first at Scorpion, then at Iryna. He and the judges spoke for another few minutes, then Gorobets turned to leave. He glanced again at Iryna and fixed Scorpion with a long hard look. Then, without a word, Gorobets and his Black Armbands left the room.

"What happened?" Iryna whispered to Scorpion.

"Whatever they planned just changed. You're a hot potato," he whispered back.

The three judges talked among themselves, one and then another glancing over at Scorpion and Iryna. They seemed to have reached a decision. The hatchet-faced *suddya* marked something on the paper and signed it. He turned the paper so the other two judges could initial it, then turned back to Iryna.

"Iryna Mikhailivna Shevchenko. Based on the prisoner known as Scorpion's confession and additional information that has come to the attention of this *sud*, we find there is insufficient evidence to hold you for the assassination of Yuriy Dmytrovych

Cherkesov. You are free to go, but with the understanding that if additional evidence should be found,
you may be charged in the future. You may go."

Iryna came and stood next to Scorpion.

"This is not an open *sud*, Iryna Mikhailivna.
Leave at once!" the hatchet-faced *suddya* demanded.

"What are you going to do with him?" she asked,
indicating Scorpion.

"Take her out!" the *suddya* ordered.

Two guards came and grabbed her.

"*Nyet!* He's doing it for me, you fools! He is innocent!" Iryna cried out, looking at Scorpion as if
to memorize his face as two guards dragged her out
of the room.

The hatchet-faced *suddya* stared coldly at Scorpion.

"Mikhail Kilbane, also known as Peter Reinert, also known as the foreign agent Scorpion, the
sud sentences you to death for the murder of Yuriy
Dmytrovych Cherkesov. Sentence to be carried out
within twenty-four hours. The *sud* is concluded," he
said, picking up his papers.

The three judges stood and filed out of the room.

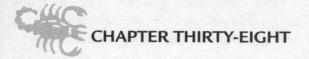 **CHAPTER THIRTY-EIGHT**

Boryspil
Kyiv, Ukraine

He sat shackled on the floor of his cell, waiting for his execution. They had left the light on, and a guard peered in through the peephole. He no longer thought of escape. Even shackled and with his groin aching, he might be able to take a couple of the guards out, but they knew how dangerous he was. They would come with more than enough men to subdue him. In the end he would only hurt a few brutes.

He hadn't thought it would end this way. With so many questions unanswered. What had happened with the war? No one seemed to act as if they were at war, and he hadn't heard any explosions or sirens. Had he managed to stop it or was he buried so deep behind Lukyanivska's thick walls that missiles had hit the city and he hadn't heard them? Had Akhnetzov gotten through to someone in Russia? What had happened with YouTube? Why did everyone act as if no one knew anything about it? How had they managed to track him and Iryna to the TV station? Who had betrayed them?

What of Iryna? He had tried to save her, but it was whatever Gorobets said to the judges that did it. Why would Gorobets want to save her? Was it because she was too much of a hot potato for them? The daughter of Artem Shevchenko, founder of the Rukh, was that it? At least she was safe—for the moment. She cared for him. Maybe even loved him. He'd seen it or something close to it in the last desperate look she had thrown at him when they dragged her from the courtroom. He wished he could see her, touch her.

For a moment he allowed himself the fantasy of the two of them on his sailboat, the *Laawan*, named for the friendly west wind in Arabia, its sails bellied with a fresh breeze somewhere in the Cyclades islands, say the ink-blue waters between Syros and Paros. He pictured how she would look in a bikini, the sun warm on their skin, the blue of the Mediterranean for as far as they could see, the two of them digging into a freshly grilled sea bass hot from the galley, washed down with a good Bâtard-Montrachet grand cru wine.

He'd almost pulled it off, he thought. He cast his mind back over everything that had happened. Where had he screwed it up? What had he missed? How had the SBU known they were at the TV station? Who tipped them? Akhnetzov? The station manager, Korobei? Why? They wanted the show to take place.

He was sure they hadn't been followed from the Central Station. It wasn't the SVR. He'd taken care of Gabrilov, and anyway, he'd gotten past the

SVR's part in this. Unless there was another player in the game. But who? He'd stayed away from the CIA's Kiev Station, and in any case, the Company wanted him to stop this thing. And what about that YouTube video he'd posted? Even if the CIA was involved, they would have wanted it to be seen. It would have either defused the crisis with Russia or proven that the U.S. was in the clear and had had nothing to do with it.

Unless there was another mole inside Kozhanovskiy's office.

Then it hit him.

Slavo.

But how had they tracked Iryna? He was sure she hadn't been followed to the train station. But maybe they didn't need to. If Slavo had gotten hold of her latest cell phone number, they could have tracked her that way with GPS.

He looked up. There were sounds in the corridor. His heart began to beat rapidly. His life was about to end. For a moment his mind flashed on Iryna, then Najla that night in Amsterdam. He thought of Kelly and how she looked, her skin burnished like gold as the sun set over the Sea of Galilee. He was leaving a lot of unfinished business behind. Who doesn't? he thought. Everyone leaves unfinished business behind.

He heard the guards coming closer. It sounded like at least a half-dozen of them. They stopped outside his cell door. His throat was dry. He couldn't swallow. It was hard to breathe.

He remembered a night in the desert when he

was a boy. One of Sheikh Zaid's sons, Malik, by his second wife, Latifah, had died. The boy had fallen and the wound became infected, and by the time they got him to a hospital, it was too late.

They were sitting by a fire in the tent at night during the three days of mourning. Latifah started to cry uncontrollably, and Sheikh Zaid, instead of comforting her, sent her away. When Scorpion looked at him questioningly, Zaid had said: "She does not understand. There is a *hadith* of the Prophet of Allah, *rasul sallahu alayhi wassalam*, peace be upon him, of ibn Umar from his father. The Prophet said: 'The deceased is tortured in his grave for the wailing done over him.'"

"So we should not cry?" Scorpion had asked.

"It makes no difference. But it is better not," Sheikh Zaid said, but Scorpion could see the tears in his eyes.

A key scraped in the lock and the cell door clanged open. He steeled himself. *A bullet in the back of the head and the pain ends. Say nothing. Show them nothing,* he told himself. *Everyone dies.* He took a deep breath and looked at the man who stepped into the cell. The man was looking to the side, his face in shadow, saying something to a guard, and at first Scorpion couldn't be sure who it was. Then he stepped into the light and he could see his face. A well-built man in his sixties in an Armani suit and steel-rimmed glasses, his hair almost completely white. *It's impossible,* Scorpion told himself. He must be hallucinating.

"Scorpion," the man said, and the voice was unmistakable.

Ivanov. Alias Checkmate, director of the Russian FSB Counterintelligence Directorate. Ivanov himself. Looking much as he had the last time Scorpion had seen him in Saint Petersburg. Immediately, it brought it all back. Najla. The Dacha Club on Nevsky Prospekt, and how it ended in the warehouse near the Narvskaya port. Scorpion struggled to his feet, his groin aching.

"Take off his shackles," Ivanov told the guard in Russian, and said to Scorpion in English: "Can you walk?"

"I'm not sure," Scorpion managed.

"Come on," Ivanov said, grabbing his arm to help support him. The guard supported him on the other side. "We don't have much time."

Scorpion tried to walk. Without the shackles, he could do it, but just barely.

"So there was no invasion, no war?" .

"No. Why are you stopping?" Ivanov asked, as Scorpion stopped walking.

"There's something I have to do," he said.

"Not now. We only have a few minutes," Ivanov said. "I don't want this to turn into a nomenclatura administrative shitting contest."

Ivanov and the guard helped him hobble down the corridor toward the locked steel door to the cell block. Screams echoed from behind several of the cell doors.

"Where's Kulyakov?" Scorpion asked, leaning between Ivanov and the guard. There were two plainclothes men with them—he assumed they were FSB—and another prison guard.

"He's not here," Ivanov said, looking at the guard.

"*Pravda,*" the guard said. It is true.

"What about Stepan?" Scorpion asked.

"Who?"

"A crazy blondish man who helps with interrogations."

"*Yego krysha ushla,*" the guard said to Ivanov—his roof is gone—meaning, he's crazy as hell.

Ivanov stopped. He looked at Scorpion.

"We don't have time for this."

"He killed a young woman. She didn't deserve it. Not from him," Scorpion said, pushing them off and hobbling forward on his own.

"I was right," Ivanov frowned. "You're a sentimentalist."

"It'll only take a minute," Scorpion said. "*Gde on?*" he asked the guard. Where is he?

The guard indicated the staircase. They went up two floors, Scorpion wincing at every step, to an office off a corridor. Ivanov opened the door and peered inside. He motioned the guard closer.

"Is that him?" he asked.

The guard nodded.

Stepan was sitting alone at a table. He was staring at a lit candle, where he held a squirming white mouse, its pink eyes bulging, over the flame with a pair of tongs.

"I'll give you one minute," Ivanov said, checking his watch. "Then we leave—with you or without you."

Scorpion went in and closed the door behind him.

* * *

"You saved me. Why?" Scorpion asked. They were sitting in the backseat of a Lada Riva sedan driving along Grushevskogo past government buildings in Mariinsky Park. For Scorpion, the setting was surreal. He felt like any second the view would be revealed as a dream and he would be back in his cell, about to receive a bullet in the head.

"I am superstitious. All Russians are, even the atheists. Especially the atheists." Ivanov smiled. "Here," he said, pouring a shot of vodka from a flask into a shot-sized metal cup. "Stolichnaya Elit, not that Ukrainian piss they drink here. You look like you need it. *Budem sdarovy*," he said.

Scorpion drank and wiped his mouth with the back of his hand. "What's superstition got to do with it?" he asked.

"Twice now you have helped Russia," Ivanov said. "The funny thing is both times you had no intention of doing it. These *idiotsky adventuristov!*" he growled, and Scorpion knew he was speaking of SVR adventurism. "Dragging us into a war with NATO that we have no business in and could not win, and for what? A Ukrainian politician we could buy, sell, or replace a hundred times over? *Chto idiotism!*" What idiocy! "Anyway," he poured another slug of vodka into the metal cup and drank it down, "I had a feeling, a premonition, that someday we might need you again. '*Bog lyubit troitsu*,'" he said, quoting the old Russian proverb that God loves threes. He shrugged. "Call it superstition, or an insurance policy." Scorpion started to laugh but had to stop, wincing because of the pain, and then laughed and winced at that.

"For a man who was within minutes of being a corpse, you are surprisingly jolly. What's the joke?" Ivanov looked at him curiously.

"Superstition. Really?" Scorpion grinned. "I suppose the fact that keeping me alive as a witness to who really killed Cherkesov, and gives you leverage over both the SVR and whoever wins the election in Ukraine, has nothing to do with it."

"I was right," Ivanov said. "I always tell my subordinates one should never underestimate the Americans. Because they often do stupid things doesn't mean all of them are stupid." He shook his head. "If I thought I could trust you and if you weren't such a damned sentimentalist, I would hire you in a second. I'm glad I didn't terminate you that time in Saint Petersburg."

"Makes two of us," Scorpion said. "What happened with the invasion?"

"We did a deal."

"What deal?"

"Davydenko and Kozhanovskiy jointly signed an agreement with the Russian foreign minister that regardless of who wins the election, Ukraina will conclude a treaty guaranteeing Russia a renewed lease on the Russian Black Sea Fleet naval base at Sevastopol, with an easement in Crimea to supply the base for another fifty years. In exchange, Ukraine gets a discount on the prices we charge Europe for oil and gas."

"So the crisis is over?"

"For today."

"You know about Shelayev? That he killed Cherkesov?"

"I have the video. It proved quite useful within our own . . ." He hesitated. ". . . discussions. What will you do now?"

"You mean, am I leaving Ukraine?"

Ivanov smiled. "*Yei bogu*, but it's a pleasure doing business with someone who understands how the game is played."

"You don't want me dead because I give you leverage, but my presence here is a problem."

"Let's just say we have an understanding with Davydenko," Ivanov said. They were driving on a bridge across the Dnieper. Scorpion looked out at the river, white with ice. He had the sense that he would never see it again. A ray of sunlight beamed through a crack in the clouds, making the snow and gold-domed spires look like a fairyland city.

"You mean with Gorobets," Scorpion said.

"*Gospodin* Gorobets is a friend and ally of Russia."

"What if Kozhanovskiy wins the election?"

"He won't."

"How do you know?"

"We've done our own polling. If absolutely necessary, we'll create another crisis, but it won't be necessary."

"Where are we going?"

"Boryspil Airport. You can use your Reinert passport. There won't be any difficulties," Ivanov said, tapping a cigarette on a slim crocodile-skin case.

One of the FSB men leaned over from the front seat and lit it for him.

"I need to see Iryna Shevchenko first. I won't leave without talking to her."

"She's waiting at the airport." Ivanov spoke briefly with the FSB man who had lit his cigarette. The man made a quick call and nodded to Ivanov. "*Da*, yes, she's there."

"Why did Gorobets intervene to let her go? The video?"

"You see how useful you've been?" Ivanov said. "That stupid charge against her was a liability. Anyone would have seen through it. She would have become a martyr—more dangerous in death or prison than she could ever be on her own. It would have given Kozhanovskiy a cause."

"You want me out of Ukraine too, don't you?"

Ivanov took a deep puff and exhaled. Through the window, Scorpion could see industrial sites and rows of apartment buildings. They were on the highway to the airport.

"I have something to tell you. Call it professional courtesy," Ivanov said. He seemed uneasy.

"I'm listening."

"You need to know who betrayed you. Who do you think tipped where you were to the SBU?"

"Kozhanovskiy's aide, Slavo. Even though we kept changing, he got her latest cell phone number and they tracked it."

Ivanov shrugged. "You are talking about a Joe. The real question is, who was running him?"

"The SVR. Gabrilov."

Ivanov shook his head and exhaled smoke. "Gabrilov is back in Moscow."

The fact that Ivanov was here meant that he had ordered it, Scorpion thought. Gabrilov was probably being beaten to a pulp in a Lubyanka cell by the FSB that very minute. The SVR had played with fire, and now the Kremlin was reining them back in. He looked at Ivanov, sitting there so calmly. The Russian was waiting to tell him something, and he wasn't sure he wanted to hear it.

"All right, Checkmate. I know you want to tell me. It's probably why you came to Kyiv. So let's have it. Who set me up?" Scorpion asked.

Ivanov smiled. A tiny sign that he was enjoying their mental chess game and appreciated Scorpion's having figured it out.

"It was the CIA's Kyiv Station. One of yours. Somebody in the Company doesn't like you."

Scorpion didn't say anything. He wanted to tell Ivanov to fuck off, but it made too much sense. Back when he was about to die, he had realized there was another player in the game. He didn't want to believe it, but it had the feel of truth. But why? If the Russkies wanted Davydenko to win, Washington sure as hell didn't. What the hell was going on?

"You could be feeding me black info," Scorpion said.

"If I thought it would work, I would." Ivanov smiled. "But it might bring you back to Moscow. Don't come to Russia, Scorpion. After going to so much trouble to save you, I wouldn't like to have to kill you anyway."

"I wouldn't be too crazy about it myself. What's going to happen to them, to Viktor and Iryna, when Davydenko wins?"

"They'll make noise, and when the noise dies down, they'll be arrested. Not for Cherkesov; something else. Corruption perhaps." Ivanov shrugged. "There's a lot of corruption in this country."

"As opposed to Russia?"

"Or America?" Ivanov grinned, showing his teeth. They both smiled.

"And Russia controls Ukraine?" Scorpion said.

"There are people who believe Ukraine is part of Russia. That someday we'll get it back. I've heard people at the highest levels say such things."

"Still, you opposed the SVR in this."

"I opposed their tactics. Not necessarily their goal." Ivanov glanced out the window at the traffic on the M03 highway and beyond to the buildings and the endless snow-covered plain. "Maybe they would be better off. Look at their history. This is a tragic country."

Scorpion thought about Alyona and Babi Yar and Olena, the woman in the trailer-restaurant, and the millions starving to death in the Holodomor. He thought about Gorobets with his Black Armbands and what was coming.

"Yes, it is tragic," he said, looking up. A highway sign up ahead read: AEROPORT BORYSPIL 6 KM.

They put him in a private airport holding room, empty except for bottles of Svalyava mineral water on a console and a few plastic chairs. The walls and everything in the room was white, even the plastic chairs. There was nothing personal there. It was a place where people waited, their lives elsewhere.

Even before he reached the center of the room, Scorpion spotted two hidden cameras. They were taking no chances, he thought. In addition to the cameras and bugs, they had a half-dozen FSB and SBU plainclothesmen and *militsiyu* stationed outside the door to make sure he got on the plane. He had less than an hour till his Lufthansa flight to Frankfurt.

He asked to go to the men's room. On the way, he pickpocketed a cell phone from one of the SBU plainclothesmen. After asking the guards to wait outside and checking the stalls to make sure they were unoccupied, he called the Dynamo Club and asked for Mogilenko. A rough-sounding man's voice got on the line.

"*Idi na tsuy huesos,*" he was told. Fuck off. "What do you want with Mogilenko?"

"*Ya frantsoos,*" Scorpion told him. I'm the Frenchman.

After a long minute, Mogilenko came on the line.

"*Tu es fou, salaud?* Or should I call you Kilbane? I knew you weren't French," Mogilenko said.

"I need a favor," Scorpion replied in French.

"When I cut off your head and balls, you'll consider it a favor, *fils de pute*. Where are you? No matter how far you go, it won't save you."

"*Écoutez,* don't be stupid. This is business," Scorpion said.

"*Va te faire foutre*," Mogilenko said, telling him to fuck off. Then after a moment, "What do you want?"

"You know Kulyakov? Prokip Kulyakov."

"Maybe. What about him?"

"Be too bad if someone did to him what you were planning to do to me," Scorpion said.

"He has friends."

"So do I. Fifty thousand of them."

"What is this? A joke? A miserable fifty thousand *hryvnia*?"

"Dollars," Scorpion said.

There was a moment of silence.

"It must be admitted, you are *un type inhabituel*." An unusual type. "What you did to my men on the bridge was *exceptionnel*. Kulyakov's SBU. It's a complication."

"How much more complicated?" Scorpion asked.

"Seventy-five."

"A hundred thousand. Half now, half when it's done. In five minutes I'm getting rid of this cell phone. Text me a bank account number."

"Maybe you come back to the club and we discuss it," Mogilenko said.

"One more thing," Scorpion said. "It has to take a long time. A work of art."

"What did he do, this Kulyakov?" Mogilenko asked seriously.

"The same to a woman. Young, beautiful like Marilyn Monroe. You'd have liked her," remembering the photograph of Alyona in the café.

"This changes nothing between us, *salaud*. You still owe me," Mogilenko growled.

"At the end, he needs to be warmed up. Use *l'essence*." Gasoline. "And he has to be still alive when you do it."

"One hundred thousand. Half now, the rest within twenty-four hours of Kulyakov's . . ." He hesitated. ". . . *sortie de grand*." Grand exit. "And Kilbane, on the second payment, don't make me wait."

"*D'accord*," Scorpion said, ending the call.

On the way back to the waiting room, he slipped the cell phone back into the SBU man's pocket. He had just finished transferring the money for Mogilenko with his laptop when Iryna came in.

She looked the way she had when he first met her. She wore a black sheath dress, pearls, the Ferragamo purse, the pixie cut that, if anything, made her more striking, and then there were those stunning lapis lazuli eyes. It was as if she hadn't been touched by prison or anything else that happened. When she saw him, she gave a little cry and ran into his arms. He could feel her trembling as he held her.

"I've been crying since yesterday. I thought you were dead," she sobbed. He let her cry, holding her tight. Finally, she pulled back and looked at him. "I'm a mess. I wanted to look good for you."

"You look damn good. You look as good as anything I've ever seen," he said.

"I thought I'd never see you again. Then they told me you were at the airport. I don't understand." She shook her head. "Not any of it."

"The Russians. I'm their insurance policy. In a

way, it's funny." He half grinned. "Sometimes you need your enemies more than your friends."

Her eyes scanned his face as if there were an answer for everything there, if she could just find it.

"What are you talking about? Insuring them against what?"

"In case Gorobets ever decides to do any original thinking that isn't first preapproved in Moscow."

"The Russians know about Shelayev? Is that why there wasn't an attack?" He watched her wrinkle her brow and figure it out. "I see," she said, fishing in her purse for a cigarette.

"For what it's worth," he shrugged, "you should feel good. We stopped the invasion. Without you, it wouldn't have happened."

She lit the cigarette and exhaled. "But we're losing the election. The latest polls . . . they're going to elect that idiot, Davydenko. Can you imagine?"

"Idiots get elected all the time. Welcome to democracy."

"What do we do now?" she said, and it was like opening a floodgate. He couldn't help himself. He had to ask it.

"If we hadn't been captured, would you have come to Krakow?"

She got up, tossed the cigarette on the floor and stepped on it.

"Damn you," she said. "Don't you understand anything besides yourself? Can't you see what's happening? This isn't America. Once Gorobets takes over, democracy is dead. Ukraine is finished. Viktor is a fool! He's listening more to Slavo than to me these days. If I leave, there's no opposition. Only Gorobets. My father," she choked, "would roll over in his grave. I can't."

She grabbed both his hands tightly. Her eyes burned like blue fire. "Stay here. Stay with me. We'll fight it together."

"I can't," he said. "I'd always be on the run. Too many people want me dead." That was true enough, he thought. Mogilenko and the Syndikat, even with their deal. Gorobets. Kulyakov and the SBU, the SVR, even the CIA. "A whole alphabet wants me dead. Even worse, they would use me against you." He looked into her eyes. "It won't work. Either you get on the plane to Frankfurt with me or we're done. I can't stay."

She leaned back and let go of his hands.

"You work for the CIA, don't you? That's what they could use against you, us, isn't it?"

"No, I told you. I'm independent."

"But you were with the CIA at one time?"

He nodded.

"Of course. It had to be something like that," she said. "Politically, it's impossible. We're impossible."

It's worse than that, Scorpion thought. It was the CIA that betrayed them to Kulyakov.

She put her hand to his cheek. "You look like hell," she said. "So why am I so damned attracted to you?"

"Maybe you just like men who are trouble. It's very Slavic."

She looked at him curiously. "We never fought, did we? Does that mean we don't love each other? Not even enough to fight?"

"I don't know what it means. Right now I feel like I lost a game I didn't know I was playing."

"I'd have walked to Krakow to be with you if I wasn't tied hand and foot to this country," she said, and a shiver went through him. "I'd've crawled," she said softly.

"It would have been worse if the Russians had come in. We saved a lot of lives," he told her.

"Not everyone," she said, and he knew she was thinking of Alyona.

"No, not everyone."

One of the FSB men who had been in the car with him and Ivanov came in.

"*Gospodin* Reinert, the plane is boarding," he said.

Iryna came close to Scorpion. She smelled of cigarettes and Hermès 24 Faubourg, and it took everything he had not to put his hands all over her. The FSB man watched them from the open doorway, the sounds of the terminal flooding in. A boarding call for group two for the Lufthansa flight to Frankfurt came over the loudspeaker.

"What will you do?" she asked.

"Someone tipped the SBU to where we were," Scorpion said.

"Do you know who?"

"Yes, but not why," he said, thinking he was going to find out if it killed him.

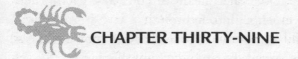

CHAPTER THIRTY-NINE

Tysons Corner
Virginia, U.S.

There were two up, two down, four outside, and two cars mobile. Bob Harris was taking no chances, Scorpion thought. They were to meet at the Tysons Corner mall, just off the Beltway outside Washington, D.C. Not that all the firepower and agents doing surveillance from every angle surprised him. Harris was the CIA's National Clandestine Service deputy director, and their meetings hadn't always been friendly. Scorpion watched from the second floor of the mall as Harris looked around, checking that his men were in position before getting on the escalator.

He hadn't changed much. A touch older, a little sleeker, but still the fair-hair-just-starting-to-gray postgraduate in a Jermyn Street style blue pinstripe suit that screamed Capitol Hill. He watched Harris come toward him, a determined smile painted on his face, like he wanted to sell him a condo.

"Are you wired?" Scorpion asked.

Harris grimaced. "You didn't have to be so skittish," he said. "We could have done this at Langley."

"No, we couldn't," Scorpion said. Not that it made much difference whether Harris was wired. He had to assume that several of the agents had mobile receivers and that anything he said was being recorded.

"Now what? Do we walk or go sit at a California Pizza Kitchen?" Harris letting his snobbery show.

"Don't be a prick. We walk," Scorpion said.

"How are you doing?" Harris asked, glancing sideways at him. "Are you all right?"

"Please don't pretend you give a damn. Lying always gets things off on the wrong foot."

Harris stopped walking and looked at him. "I don't think you realize what's been going on here. The President himself has been involved. He wants to know, are you okay?"

"He's feeling guilty?"

"He said it was the toughest decision he's ever had to make. I think it really got to him."

"Tell him I'm fine." That was true enough. He had spent the last three weeks in Lausanne, Switzerland. The clinique was very private, very discreet; the kind of place where movie stars and dictators went when they didn't want anyone to know where they were. Thanks to Akhnetzov paying him the rest of his fee, he could afford it.

From his room he could see Lake Geneva and the snow-covered Alps in a jagged line across the horizon. During the day he worked with the physical therapist, doing rehab. The doctors said he had been lucky. There were no scars on his genitals, and as the pain receded, he would be sexually active again. He also spent some time with a dentist replacing the teeth that had been knocked out. At night he would walk up the steep rue du Petit-Chêne to the Place St. Francois in the old town, stopping at a bistro for dinner. It was there that he read in the *International Herald Tribune* that Davydenko had won the election in Ukraine.

That night, thinking about Kiev and Iryna, he couldn't get to sleep. Several times, he started to call her, then stopped. Toward the end of the second week he met a French female graduate student studying at the École Polytechnique. She was pretty and funny and approached sex as if it were an equation she was dying to solve, and he was able to prove to himself that sexually, at least, he was still functional.

Harris frowned as a trio of teenage girls walked by. They wore tight jeans and tops and talked nonstop, all three on their cell phones, with eyes only for the shop windows and any boys as they passed the video games store.

"What about the girl? This Iryna Shevchenko?"

"What about her?"

"You had an affair?"

"Christ, you take it to the edge, don't you?" Scorpion said, walking so rapidly Harris had to hurry to keep up.

"Take it easy," Harris said.

"It's none of your damn business!"

"You're wrong," Harris said, his voice cold. "It is

business." He looked around the mall as if scouting a battlefield. "Look, if you promise not to go crazy on me or throw whiskey in my face," referring to the last time he and Scorpion had met, "can we find someplace civilized and get a drink?"

"Someone tipped the SBU about where I was in Kiev. I need to know why."

"I know. But it's a problem," Harris said, trying his most winning smile, the one that got half the female interns in Washington to drop their pants when he was younger. "What do you say? Truce?"

"I won't waste any more whiskey by throwing it in your face," Scorpion said. "But I won't promise not to kill you."

"Close enough," Harris said, and signaled to one of his men. A few minutes later a car pulled up at one of the entrances and drove them out of the parking lot and across the street to the Tysons 2 Mall. They walked into the Ritz Carlton and went into the lobby bar, still busy with the lunch crowd, found an empty table and sat down. Two of Harris's men sat at a table near the doorway. Scorpion didn't bother to check; he was confident Harris had every entrance and exit covered.

"It's like a spooks' convention," Scorpion said, looking around the crowded bar. "Is there anybody left minding the store at Langley?"

"This is the place," Harris agreed as the waitress came over. She was slim and good-looking enough to help justify the price of the drinks. "What'll you have?"

"Belvedere Bloody Mary," Scorpion said, thinking it was too bad you couldn't get Stoli Elit or Nemiroff in the States.

"The same," Harris said.

They waited till the waitress walked away. There was no one near their table. Scorpion wasn't worried about bugs. Harris and the other spooks wouldn't be there if they were being listened to.

"You said there was a problem," he said.

Harris toyed with the triple dish of nibbles the waitress had brought. He looked uncomfortable.

"Look, maybe in some cosmic accounting sense, I—we—owe you. I'll give you that. But frankly, if that's all it was, I wouldn't give a rat's ass about it or you." His eyes were blue and very cold. "It's worse than that. If I tell you anything, I have to break protocol, every rule we have, and then I have to trust you. A Green Badge!" he said, referring to the fact that within CIA facilities, CIA personnel wore blue badges, while contractors and other nonemployees wear green badges. "And even if I could trust you," his eyes narrowed as he looked straight at Scorpion, "what happens next time you go off in the wild blue yonder and get captured by the opposition? Then I not only have to trust that you won't reveal something against someone you don't like, on a matter of the highest national security, but you won't do it under torture! You see my problem?" he finished, just as the waitress returned with their drinks.

Scorpion didn't say anything. He watched the

waitress as she wiggled to another table, wondering whether she had heard Harris's last words about torture. She's probably used to hearing all kinds of bizarre talk around here, he thought.

"You set me up, you son of a bitch," he said, his voice soft, controlled, but intense. "You, Rabinowich, and Shaefer practically sent me an engraved invitation to Ukraine. You begged me to go and then you cut me off and then you sold me out. I was a couple of minutes away from a bullet in my head, so I'm supposed to give a shit about your problem? I'm your problem, Bob old buddy. If you really want to worry about something, I'd worry about me."

Harris nodded grimly. He let his gaze wander around the bar at the gilt-framed paintings and men in expensive suits sitting over drinks.

"You look around and you'd think we live in a civilized world," Harris said, "but that's not true at all, is it? Who pointed you at us? Checkmate?" meaning Ivanov and the FSB.

Scorpion smiled. He took a long sip of the Bloody Mary and put it down on the table.

"I was wondering when you'd bring that up. Did I think he was feeding me black info? The thought occurred, but no, I didn't think so. You know why?"

"You tell me," Harris said.

"Because when I was laying there in that freezing cell, tortured to within an inch of my life, I realized there was another player in the game. Only I had neutralized them all: Kozhanovskiy, the Syndikat, the SBU, Gabrilov and the SVR, the Guoanbu's Second Bureau, Shelayev, the Chorni Povyazky. Christ, I got to everyone but the Boy Scouts. But there was someone else, someone I didn't know about. When Checkmate told me, I knew it was true."

"What made you so sure?"

"The dog that didn't bark."

"What?"

"Sherlock Holmes. As a fail-safe, in case something happened to me, I uploaded the video of Shelayev's confession to YouTube. Guess what? Nobody knew about it. It disappeared. This isn't China. Who on earth could have gotten Google to take it off? Who has that kind of leverage over an American corporation? The minute Checkmate said it, the person I thought of was you." His eyes focused on Harris like a laser.

Harris finished his Bloody Mary. The waitress started toward them, and he waved her off.

"As soon as I heard about Checkmate being in Kyiv, I knew you'd be knocking at my door," Harris said. "You know what the DCIA called it? 'Our moment of truth.' That's what he said. Twenty-plus years in the Company and neither of us had ever faced anything like this." He shook his head. "I met with the President. He's thrilled you're alive, but he's not sure that lets him off the hook. It bothered him. A lot."

"Yeah, I know how tough you guys have it. West Wing chicken sandwiches, Ritz Carlton and all," Scorpion said, looking at the spot on Harris's throat where a single blow would end it. "Cut the bullshit, Bob. Why'd you set me up?"

Harris smiled grimly. "I guess it's time to—what was it the old-timers used to call it—to *'fallen die hose,'* to drop your pants." He leaned forward. "I need your word. What we say now never leaves this table. Never. No matter who, no matter under what circumstances, no matter anything."

Scorpion looked at him sharply. "Or else what?"

Harris glanced at the two men he had stationed by the door. Scorpion followed his glance.

Go to hell, he thought, but didn't say it. If Harris was this serious, it meant that what he was about to say went higher up. If he wasn't lying, it went all the way to the Oval Office. It might also explain why people he had trusted—Rabinowich and Shaefer—had gone along. Also, he didn't need a war with the CIA. "I'll want something in exchange," he said.

"What?" Harris asked.

"I'll tell you when we're done."

Harris exhaled sharply. "God, you're a pain in the ass. You want another?" indicating the drinks.

"You're buying," Scorpion said.

Harris waved the waitress over and gestured for another round. They watched her walk away in her tan Ritz-Carlton-worth-the-money skirt and top. Harris hesitated.

"I have your word?" he began.

"For Chrissake, let's have it," Scorpion said.

"It was a walk-in," Harris said. "Can you believe that? A walk-in! Like having a single dollar bill in your pocket and, as a throwaway, you give it to the clerk and you win the lottery."

"Where was this?"

"Madrid. An all-expenses-paid NATO and wannabes' conference. Tapas and whores. That's not the story."

"What's the story?"

"The father. Let's call him 'Leva.' Leva Nikolaevych. But you need the context. In 1964, Leonid Brezhnev becomes General Secretary of the Central Committee of the Soviet Union. Brezhnev was a Ukrainian of ethnic Russian parents from Dnipropetrovsk oblast. He was a protégé of Nikita Khrushchev, who, although Russian, was himself born near the Ukrainian border. Brezhnev brings with him several key Ukrainians whose loyalties belong to him. Among them is a certain KGB agent, our Leva Nikolaevych. Leva is instrumental during the period when Brezhnev is jockeying for power with Suslov, Kosygin, and others. He gets very close to Brezhnev, who will eventually consolidate all the power in his own hands. Life is good.

"Fast-forward to 1968. In Czechoslovakia, Alexander Dubček launches a wave of reform that came to be known as the 'Prague Spring.' This created a major crisis for the Soviet Union. You have to remember, 1968 was a time of great unrest: the Tet Offensive in Vietnam and the resulting student protests, the assassinations of Martin Luther King and Robert Kennedy, demonstrations and protests all around the world, the riot at the Democratic Convention in Chicago. Within the Russian Politboro there were serious disagreements as to how to deal with Czechoslovakia. They feared a wave of revolt and reform that if unchecked could lead to the breakup of the Warsaw Pact and the Soviet Union. Some argued for a hands-off attitude, others for political and economic pressure, still others wanted a full-scale military invasion to crush the reform.

"The head of the KGB at that time was Yuri Andropov, who was also a member of the Central Committee and had ambitions of his own. He provided intel to the Central Committee that the CIA had instigated the Prague reform, that we were running Dubček and were planning a coup, and that NATO was about to move to support Czechoslovakia and break up the Warsaw Pact."

"Were we?"

Harris shook his head. "The truth was that the U.S. was ass-deep in Vietnam. We had our own problems. The Company had nothing to do with Dubček or the Prague Spring, but Andropov had a majority of the Central Committee convinced they were on the brink of either the dissolution of the Soviet Union or nuclear war and that it was all a CIA plot. He demanded that the Soviet Union crush the Czechs. Preparations were made for a Soviet intervention.

"In August, 1968, Russian tanks led a massive invasion of Czechoslovakia by the Warsaw Pact. The Prague Spring was over. Reforms were ended. KGB agents arrested thousands of reformers, many of whom were killed. Thousands more were imprisoned and tortured. Most were never heard from again. Dubček was hauled to Moscow and forced to sign a protocol that basically restored Soviet-style communism to Czechoslovakia.

"But there was a problem. Something called the 'Kalugin Papers'; internal KGB documents that proved beyond any doubt that the CIA had nothing to do with the Prague Spring, NATO wasn't planning anything, and Andropov had fabricated all his intel. Guess who was Kalugin's superior within the KGB and had the documents?"

"Of course," Scorpion said.

"Leva." Harris nodded, taking a sip of his drink. "Now Andropov had a problem. The Soviet Union had already invaded and was widely condemned in the West. Andropov couldn't afford to have the Central Committee learn he'd deliberately sold them a bill of goods. Kalugin, who was based in Washington, was easy. His body was found a few days later floating in the Potomac River. Leva, on the other hand, was no case officer like Kalugin. He had friends. And he wasn't just Andropov's problem, he was Brezhnev's too. Neither of them could afford to let it get out to any of their competitors in the Politboro or the Central Committee.

"Plus, Leva was Brezhnev's *droog*—his buddy. Brezhnev had bounced Leva's son on his knee how many times? In those days in Russia, you didn't just get rid of somebody. The whole family would disappear into the Gulag and never be heard from again. But Brezhnev didn't want to do that with what was in effect his own godchild. The boy was eight years old and adored his father. So to save the child *and* both their asses, Brezhnev and Andropov did a deal. They sent Leva to the Gulag, to Strafnaja Kolonija 9, a prison camp in Siberia so secret, even most KGB officers didn't know it existed. The mother and the rest of the family disappeared in the Gulag. That was common at the time. But the little boy, Leva's son, they sent him back to Ukraine."

"Jesus," Scorpion said, looking up. "It's Gorobets."

Harris nodded. "Gorobets. Even after Brezhnev and Andropov and the Soviet Union itself were all long gone, the KGB, now the FSB, knew that if Gorobets ever entertained even the slightest anti-Russian thought—and of course, how could he, raised as a pro-Russian patriot?—they would kill his father.

"Except, one fine day, who comes strolling in out of the hot sun on the Calle de Serrano into the American embassy in Madrid? A walk-in. The one-in-a-million you don't plan for because it's impossible, it doesn't happen. That same little boy, all grown up and the most important person in the Svoboda party—if not the whole damn country of Ukraine. And he wants revenge."

"You believed him?"

Harris brushed the thought away as though it were a fly.

"Of course we didn't believe him. You have no idea how long and how hard it was to find out and vet everything I'm telling you. Two years. After that thing in Rome, we had Rabinowich working on it full-time for months."

"What made him turn?"

"That was the part we had to get right. It was quite an odyssey. Brezhnev, who was the leader of the Soviet Union—and after he died, Andropov, who became General Secretary—kept an eye on the boy. They guided him into the KGB, and after Ukrainian independence, the SBU. He was Leva's son, all right. He had no father or mother. The Gorobets you know, the ruthless Gorobets of the Black Armband thugs, is a child of the KGB; they made him.

"The problem was, he was old enough to remember his parents. He still loved them. That hole in him had never been filled. And someone had survived. An aunt. Tetya Oksana, Aunt Oksana."

"What happened two years ago that made him walk into the embassy in Madrid?"

"Somebody gave him something. Someone in the Metro in Kiev pressed it into his hand, and by the time he turned around, they were gone. It was a cross. One of those Ukrainian crosses; you know, with the two crossbars and the extra slanted crossbar where they would've nailed Jesus' feet. I've seen it. A little silver thing about this big," holding his thumb and forefinger about an inch apart. "It was cheap. The kind of thing you could pick up for a buck in a flea market.

"At first, he told us, he almost threw it away. But the way it came to him, and something inside—because they had never told him what had happened to his family—made him keep it. That night he got together with Tetya Oksana—by then she was an old woman living in a retirement home. She told him. He understood that all those years his father had been alive, but someone giving him the cross meant his father was finally dead.

"Mind you, it took us a while to vet what had happened. As best as Rabinowich was able to tease it out, Leva died after all those years in the prison camp, and a fellow prisoner, Pyotr Shunegin, gave it to a Dr. Ghazarian who came to the camp once a month. He in turn smuggled it out and passed it along through a kind of underground Armenian network from city to city in Russia till someone in Kiev—we don't know who—handed it to Gorobets in the Metro along with a message letting him know it was his father's before disappearing into the crowd.

"Tetya Oksana filled in the rest for him. What happened to his family. How they died in the Gulag. How his father had been alive all those years and still kept in prison, long after Brezhnev and Andropov were dead and there was no more Soviet Union—just to make sure Gorobets would always do what they wanted."

"He wanted revenge?"

"Big-time," Harris said. "He was already the head of the SBU and a power in the Svoboda party. He wanted to do something dramatic, but we changed his mind. We convinced him he could hurt them more and be infinitely more valuable where he was and as he was.

"Don't you see what we had? He was the ultimate

AOI," meaning Agent of Influence. "The holy fucking grail of intelligence. Not only could he direct Ukraine, the largest country in Europe, in the direction we set, but he was a direct pipeline into the SBU, the SVR, and right to the very top of the Kremlin itself!" He looked at Scorpion. "Gorobets is the single most important asset, the most important secret, this country has. And you were about to destroy him by exposing him on YouTube and TV! We had no choice."

Scorpion looked around the bar. It was the in-between hour, between postlunch and happy hour, and except for Harris's men by the doorway and one group by the fireplace, they were the last customers.

"Why did Gorobets really save Iryna? Was that you?"

Harris nodded. "After the election, Kozhanovskiy is history. Gorobets will trump up some charge against him—or maybe he won't have to, Christ knows there's more than enough corruption in Ukraine to go around—and put him into prison. We need a viable opposition. Iryna Shevchenko is perfect. Good-looking, idealistic, daughter of a national hero. You couldn't order up better out of central casting. Maybe she goes to prison for a while, but if she didn't exist, we'd have to invent her."

"But if she were to actually try to win an election, you'd see she'd lose?"

Harris threw a credit card down and motioned the waitress over. She came and took the card and the check.

"What do you think?" he asked.

"The asset is more important than the country."

"Exactly." Harris put his hand on Scorpion's arm. Scorpion looked at it, and Harris removed his hand. "For what it's worth, the President said it's the hardest thing he's ever had to do. To knowingly allow an American who is innocent and an absolute hero to be tortured and put to death in order to save a nasty son of a bitch because he's too valuable to lose. He said he had to think long and hard. It challenged his sense of who he really is. He says he still thinks about it."

Scorpion put his drink down.

"Yeah, well you can tell him for me to go—" He stopped. "I don't give a damn what you tell him. So who's running Gorobets? Not Kyiv Station? Too iffy."

Harris nodded. "You're right." The waitress came. He signed the slip and retrieved his credit card. They waited till she left. "I'm sure a smart guy like you can figure it out."

Scorpion snorted. It was in front of him all along and he hadn't seen it.

"Shaefer," he said. Bucharest was close enough, and yet not under the microscope like anything Gorobets did in Kyiv. He realized that was how Akhnetzov had gotten to him in the first place. Shaefer wanted to send in the best agent they could get, to aid and abet Gorobets while forestalling a Russian takeover. They needed someone who could stop a disaster from getting out of control and that might have led to the end of NATO or even war. Scorpion hated to admit it, but if he had been in

Harris's and Shaefer's place, playing for the stakes they were playing for, he might have done the same thing.

"So are we done?" Harris said, pulling his things together to get ready to leave. "Nobody wants to kill anybody? All debts squared? I'm told Akhnetzov paid in full."

"Where's my quid pro quo?" Scorpion said.

Harris folded his arms across his chest.

"What do you want?" he asked.

"Yemen."

"Christ. It's a powder keg. I don't suppose I could ask you not to—" Harris stopped.

"You could ask," Scorpion said.

CHAPTER FORTY

Amran
Yemen

The four young men danced in a line, their old-fashioned muskets slung on their shoulders, waving their curved *jambiya* knives to the beat of the drums. They chanted the words of a tribal melody played by the drummers, an old man with an oud, and a barefoot musician with a meter-long *khallool* flute. Others in the crowd sitting on the floor joined in, a chorus of harsh male voices.

> *"We are the Hashidi*
> *Born of bitterness and hate*
> *We are the nails driven into solid rock*
> *We are the flames of Hell*
> *He who defies us will be burnt."*

There were cheers and the sounds of men banging the butts of their AK-47s and other weapons on the stone floor to show their approval, and shots were fired in the air outside. If the implied threat of the display troubled the bulky man in the military uniform of a Yemeni colonel seated on a pillow next to the full-bearded Sheikh al-Ahmari of the Hashid, he didn't show it. The colonel wore the *shaal* turban of a *sayyid*, a descendent of the Prophet, of the Bakil. The Bakil were deadly rivals of the Hashid tribe, a fact that had been noted by every man in the room. The colonel was also director of the CSO, the Yemeni government's internal security force, and thus doubly powerful.

"It is well, *ahwadi*, my brothers. *Inshallah*," God willing, "we can make a truce between the Hashid and we of the Bakil," Colonel Sayed al-Zuhrahi said. "The current conflict between the tribes and the government is in no one's interest."

"*Inshallah*, but we of the Hashid are secure here in Wadi Qa'a al-Bawn. What is offered?" Sheikh al-Ahmari said. He gestured as a *naadil* came in with a tray of ginger coffee in thimble-sized cups and little *bint al sahn* honey cakes. The *naadil* had dark skin, a bad overbite with rotted, yellowing teeth and strange gray eyes. The *naadil* placed the tray on the floor in front of them, but instead of leaving, squatted beside a group of Hashid tribesmen cradling their AK-47s by the open window, their cheeks bulging with *qat*.

"If the Hashid and the Bakil were to unite, Sana'a would be ours. We could rule Yemen," Colonel al-Zuhrahi said. The alliance he was proposing would end a long-simmering conflict between the two tribes. It would also create the most powerful player in the cockpit of competing factions and lawlessness that Yemen had become.

"We—or al Qaeda? For whom do you speak, *sayyid*, my brother?" Sheikh al-Ahmari said, looking at his advisors seated cross-legged on the floor, who nodded approvingly. He was challenging Colonel al-Zuhrahi to acknowledge that the Bakil tribe, like the Abidah, had been so infiltrated by al Qaeda that the alliance he was proposing would, in effect, hand control of Yemen over to AQAP, al Qaeda in the Arabian Peninsula.

"Truly, what difference, my brothers?" The colonel smiled. "Who would dare oppose us?"

"You will bring the Amerikayeena"—the Americans—"and their drones down upon us," said one of the sheikh's advisors, an older man with a white beard and a vertical scar from an old wound that seemed to split his face into two unmatched halves.

"We do not fear the Amerikayeena," Colonel al-Zuhrahi said.

"We fear nothing. Not the Amerikayeena nor the AQAP either. But the Amerikayeena pay well," making the sign for money. "What do you—or should one say AQAP—offer?" Sheikh al-Ahmari asked.

"We would give the Hashid an exclusive access to all the *qat* trade of Wadi Dar and the highlands. Together with AQAP, we would control all the *qat* trade in Yemen and Somalia."

"*Inshallah*, this is something to be considered," al-Ahmari said, stroking his beard. "But let us drink, my brother," and he picked up one of the cups and offered it to the colonel. As he did so, the gray-eyed *naadil* çame over and whispered something into the colonel's ear. The *naadil* did not serve the colonel as might be expected, but instead walked on out of the room.

Colonel al-Zuhrahi pulled a cell phone out of his pocket and looked at it. *"Wa' alif'a afoo*, a thousand pardons, brother, I have a call I must take," he said, getting up. *It's the president's office*, he mouthed to Sheikh al-Ahmari, pointing at the phone. He walked quickly out of the room, followed by two of his soldiers, both wearing the turban *shaals* of the Bakil.

"What is this *ibn himaar*," son of a donkey, "up to?" Sheikh al-Ahmari said as the colonel left the room, looking at his fellow tribesmen.

Two of the Hashid tribesmen who were near the window unslung their AK-47s and followed the colonel's men out of the room. There was the sound of men running and shouting, and tribesmen standing by the window saw Colonel al-Zuhrahi and his men run out of the building to a waiting Humvee. The *naadil* was with them.

The Humvee started with a roar and soon was twisting through the narrow winding streets of the town, dirt streets without sidewalks designed for donkeys, not cars. They barreled down the road in a cloud of dust toward the Bab al-Kabeer gate in the city wall.

"You're sure of this?" Colonel al-Zuhrahi said to Scorpion, who was still wearing the *shaal* turban of a lowly *naadil* of the Hashid tribe.

"Cyanide. I saw the cook put it in. Was there not a scent of bitter almonds in the coffee?"

"I did smell something," the colonel replied, and nodded.

"Another moment, *sayyid*," Scorpion said, "and that cup of coffee would have been your last."

"The Hashid are all lying *khaneeth* queers," the soldier in the front passenger seat said. "Sooner or later they would have betrayed us."

"Of course," Colonel al-Zuhrahi snapped. "We expected no less. But we will put it out that they have agreed to join the Bakil, just to see who or what crawls out from under the rocks." He turned to Scorpion. "You are not Hashidi. Your Arabic is of the Peninsula," he said, meaning Arabia.

Scorpion nodded. "Of the Mutayr."

"You are of AQAP? Who sent you?"

"You know who sent me, *sayyid*," Scorpion said, his eyes boring into al-Zuhrahi, suggesting it was Qasim bin Jameel, the leader of AQAP. "It was to protect you. If I hadn't risked my life, you would be with the virgins even now."

"So you say," Colonel al-Zuhrahi said.

Scorpion nodded again, his eyes scanning the road ahead. They were approaching the checkpoint. Hashid tribesmen with rifles were in and around a pickup truck parked across the middle of the road as a roadblock. They must have been alerted, Scorpion thought.

"Don't stop," Colonel al-Zuhrahi ordered.

The Humvee raced directly at the pickup. As soon as the Hashid realized it wasn't going to stop, they started shooting at it as it came toward them. At the last second the Humvee swerved around the pickup, bullets pinging off the metal and nicking the bulletproof glass. The Humvee was armored. That hadn't been part of the intel, Scorpion thought, as they raced out of the town and down the road toward Sana'a. The soldier in the passenger seat leaned out the window and fired his M-4 rifle back at the checkpoint to slow them down. Looking back, Scorpion saw the tribesmen jumping into the pickup.

Abruptly, the Humvee slewed to a stop. The soldier with the M-4 jumped out and placed a small IED in the middle of the road. He got back into the Humvee and they drove on. Scorpion looked back as the pickup approached that place in the road. The soldier pressed his cell phone and the IED exploded, sending the pickup flying and in flames. They drove on.

For several minutes no one spoke, then Colonel al-Zuhrahi turned toward Scorpion. "If you indeed saved me, you will be rewarded. But first we'll check you out with Qasim when we get back to Sana'a. If you are not who you say, better for you not to have been born."

Scorpion nodded. He spotted an outcrop of rock ahead and looked around quickly. There was no one following them. The desert stretched empty in every direction to the distant barren hills.

"If you doubt me, *sayyid*, stop the Humvee here," he said, indicating the rocks, his hand slipping unobtrusively down to his calf, where his Glock was holstered. "Those Hashidi dogs know now I am not one of them. Let me out and leave me. I'll be dead within the hour."

"Pull over there," Colonel al-Zuhrahi ordered, gesturing toward the rocks. "We won't wait till Sana'a. Let's find out now."

As the Humvee rolled to a stop, Scorpion whipped out the Glock and fired twice, killing the driver with a shot in the head and the soldier through the back of the front seat. He pointed the gun at Colonel al-Zuhrahi.

"*El' churmuzh!*" he said. Get out! He motioned to the colonel with the gun. Al-Zuhrahi got slowly out of the Humvee. Scorpion followed, shoving him toward the outcropping of rocks to a spot where they were no longer visible from the road.

He looked around once again. There was only desert. He didn't have much time. The Hashidi would be coming any moment now. He fired a bullet into the colonel's knee. Al-Zuhrahi screamed and fell on his side. Scorpion bent over, put the muzzle of the gun against the other knee and fired again. Al-Zuhrahi moaned. Scorpion pulled the colonel's *jambiya* knife from his belt and took it out of its sheath.

"What is this? Who are you?" al-Zuhrahi asked.

"Do you remember the American, McElroy? The one whose skin they undressed?"

"I had nothing to do with it. That was bin Jameel! You know how they are!" al-Zuhrahi said.

"And what you are, *sayyid*."

Al-Zuhrahi looked angrily at Scorpion from where he lay curled on the ground.

"There was no cyanide, was there?" he asked.

"Only paranoia."

"What did I smell?"

"I ground some almonds and put it in the coffee. From so little a thing is a conspiracy made."

"I'm hurt, you son of a donkey," al-Zuhrahi gasped. "What is this about?"

"You're the director of the CSO, aren't you?"

"Why ask if you know?"

"I was in the room just now. I heard you myself, Colonel. So whose side are you on? The government? The Bakil? Al Qaeda? All three? Or maybe just yourself?"

"As is everyone," al-Zuhrahi said. "Why are you doing this?" he groaned.

"There was another American. Peterman. You tracked someone to a meeting with him, didn't you?"

"*Umka sharmota*," al-Zuhrahi growled, cursing Scorpion's mother for a whore.

"Who'd you track?"

"Someone from Jebel Nuqum. I don't know who."

"Who was it?"

"If you are going to kill me, do it. I know nothing," al-Zuhrahi said.

Scorpion kicked his knee. Al-Zuhrahi screamed.

"Who was it?"

"I don't know!"

"Was it someone new?"

"What do you want me to say?"

Scorpion kicked his knee again.

"Was it?"

"Of course someone new," al-Zuhrahi snapped. "Another American. That was of immediate interest."

Ramis, Scorpion thought.

"You had someone put the Trojan horse software on Peterman's laptop. Then after the ambush in Ma'rib failed, you had him killed."

"So you say."

"How did you know Peterman was CIA? His laptop?"

"You'll never know," al-Zuhrahi said grimly. The realization that he was not going to survive had hit him. His expression was set.

"It was your men who killed him, wasn't it?" Scorpion said. "One last thing. What do you know about Scorpion?"

"A *jinn*. A name to frighten children. He doesn't exist."

"You knew Peterman had met with Scorpion?" Scorpion said, kicking al-Zuhrahi's knee again, causing him to gasp in agony.

"We knew it was on his laptop! That's all, *inshallah*!"

"This Scorpion, what does he look like?" Scorpion said, putting the Glock back in his calf holster and taking the prosthesis with the bad teeth out of his mouth. He took out a packet of makeup remover wipes and began removing the dark skin coloring from his face.

"I don't know," al-Zuhrahi said, staring wide-eyed as Scorpion wiped the makeup off. There was no flicker of recognition in his eyes, Scorpion thought excitedly. Al-Zuhrahi didn't know what Scorpion looked like. His identity was safe.

He finished removing the color from his face and hands and put the used wipes and prosthesis in his pocket. Then he moved behind al-Zuhrahi and knelt on his knees. After knocking al-Zuhrahi's *shaal* off, he pulled his head up by his hair, the *jambiya* knife in his other hand. The steel blade gleamed in the sun.

"Wait," al-Zuhrahi said desperately. From his voice, it was clear he knew he was about to die. "Who are you doing this for?"

"Myself," Scorpion said.

"What are you talking about? I've never seen you before."

"I had to be sure of that. But there's something else." Scorpion hesitated. He had never put it into words before. In a way, the fact that he was telling someone who was about to die made being honest imperative. "When someone on your team is lost, even if you didn't know him or even if you couldn't stand him, you can't just let it go. It's why men seek Allah. Because things need to be made right."

"I don't understand."

"No, you wouldn't," Scorpion said, thinking, This is for McElroy. And Peterman. And Alyona. And me, drawing the curved edge of the blade across al-Zuhrahi's throat.

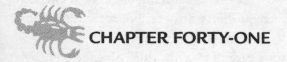 **CHAPTER FORTY-ONE**

Constanta
Romania

The two men approached from opposite directions on the promenade by the Casino, a massive art nouveau building on a promontory overlooking the Black Sea. The promenade was along the seafront with nothing else around, so it was easy to spot if there were any watchers or tails. The two men were alone as they walked toward each other. The wind blew off the choppy waves, sending a chill spray over the deserted seawall. Shaefer wore an overcoat and a black sheepskin hat, Scorpion a Burberry raincoat. For a moment they stood facing each other.

"Are we still friends?" Shaefer said.

"Let's walk," Scorpion said.

They walked side by side around the curve of the promontory, past hotels and palm trees swaying in the wind. It was cold and there were no sailboats out on the water, only the distant silhouette of a freighter on the horizon. In summer, Constanta was a crowded resort town, but in winter the city had the deserted feel of a carnival that had closed.

"They say this is where Jason brought the Golden Fleece," Shaefer said, gesturing vaguely at the seacoast. Scorpion didn't answer. For a time they just walked.

"You took care of al-Zuhrahi?" Shaefer said.

"He was working with al Qaeda. He was responsible for McElroy and Peterman," Scorpion said, pulling his collar up against the chill. "What about this guy, Ramis?"

Shaefer grimaced. "Don't ask. Fucking pickle factory," using one of the insider slang names for the CIA.

Scorpion stopped walking, and Shaefer did too.

"Who's protecting him? Not Harris?"

"Not Harris," Shaefer agreed, and they started walking again. "You heard about Kulyakov?"

"I saw something about a mutilated body found in one of the old Stalin tunnels in the online *Kyiv Post*."

"Whoever it was took their time. They spent two days and nights cutting pieces from him before they burnt him alive. There's a rumor it was a Syndikat hit. SBU was buzzing, then suddenly the case was closed," Shaefer said, glancing sideways at Scorpion. "Must've cost someone a pretty penny."

"Couldn't have happened to anyone more deserving," Scorpion said.

They walked on along the promenade. A young Gypsy woman was sitting on the pavement by the rail overlooking the sea. As they approached, she got up and came toward them.

"*Pleaka!*" Shaefer snapped. Go away! For a moment

she kept coming, then looked at his expression and how big he was and stopped. She watched them walk by, her dark hair blowing in the wind. "Gypsies, beggars, and thieves. That's this whole country. You know the joke? You're traveling on a train in Europe. How do you know when you've reached Romania?"

"How?" Scorpion said, a faint listening-to-a-joke-smile on his lips.

"Keep looking at your watch. When it isn't there, you're in Romania," Shaefer said. "Look," he pointed at a dilapidated blue building with a faded sign. "There's a café. It's crap, but we can get out of this wind."

They went into the café and sat at a table by the window. At that hour there were only two other customers, an old couple who were sitting at a table reading newspapers and not talking to each other. Music came from a radio on the counter; a male singer was singing a bizarre combination of Romanian *doina* and Eurotrash rock. Scorpion looked out the window at the empty promenade and the choppy gray water against the gray sky and wondered if this winter would ever end. The waiter came over.

"You want some brandy?" Shaefer asked.

Scorpion indicated no. "Just a Turkish coffee."

"Doua cafea Turceasca si cozonac," Shaefer ordered. He turned back to Scorpion. "How are you doing?"

"I'm okay," Scorpion said. "It took a while, but I'm all right."

Shaefer leaned toward him. "It was the job. I had no choice. It was either lie to you or blow the mission. For the record, I hated it. Every minute."

"I wasn't too crazy about it myself," Scorpion said.

"I'm sorry," Shaefer said.

The waiter put down the coffee and two brioches on the table.

"How's Iryna?" Scorpion said after the waiter left.

"She's heading the opposition in the Verkhovna Rada. She's making a name for herself. But things are deteriorating. You heard Kozhanovskiy's in Lukyanivska Prison?"

"My old stomping grounds."

"He's been charged with taking bribes. A bit ironic considering he was probably the only politician in the country who wasn't on the take, but there it is."

"Gorobets is consolidating his power," Scorpion said.

Shaefer nodded. "Russia's happy. Washington's happy. Brussels is happy. NATO didn't fall apart, so everybody still has a job. Akhnetzov's happy. Even you. You made money and found out you weren't blown. Everybody wins," he concluded, raising his coffee cup and taking a sip.

"Not everybody," Scorpion said, thinking of Alyona and Ekaterina and Fedir and Dennis and the look on Iryna's face when he boarded the flight to Frankfurt at Boryspil.

"No, not everybody," Shaefer conceded. "What will you do now? Take some time off? Take out that boat you told me about? You deserve it."

Scorpion looked out at the sea, a single ray of sunlight glittering on the water. The last time he'd thought of his ketch it was a fantasy of him with Iryna as he lay in his cell, waiting for a bullet in the head.

"I'd like that," he said. "Why?"

Shaefer leaned close. "The Israelis are dying to talk to you. They said it was urgent."

"What are you, my agent now? Why the hell is everybody coming to you?" Scorpion asked.

Shaefer shook his head. "Not everybody. Rabinowich. The Mossad must've figured he'd know how to reach you." Of course, Scorpion thought, Rabinowich had liaised with the Mossad during the Palestinian operation.

"Do you know what it's about?"

Shaefer shook his head. "Only that Rabinowich said they were desperate. Something big. 'Special Access Flash Critical' level for both the Israelis and the U.S. Not that you need the money." He shrugged. "I heard that after this last one, you were pretty well fixed."

Scorpion stared at his coffee. He put a sugar cube in and stirred, but didn't drink. Special Access was the highest top secret classification, and Flash Critical meant an imminent emergency.

"You know what was the worst?" he said. "Not the torture. The worst was knowing that people I trusted sold me out."

"I know," Shaefer said. "I had to choose: my country or my friend. We were the last two." Scorpion knew he was talking about Forward Operating Base Echo, those last thirty-odd hours when they were pinned down by nonstop Taliban gunfire, the only two left alive of their entire team.

"FOBE?" Scorpion said; a peace offering. It was the job, he thought, wondering if he would have done any differently if he had been in Shaefer's shoes.

"FOBE," Shaefer said and nodded, letting out a breath. He smiled for the first time.

"Ask them to call me a taxi. Okay?" Scorpion said, gesturing at the café owner in the corner.

"Sure," Shaefer said.

He called out something in Romanian to the owner, who took out his cell phone and made a call. The man finished the call and said something to Shaefer.

"Be about ten minutes," Shaefer said. "So about the Flash Critical? You gonna do it?"

"I'll think about it. I barely survived this last one with a penis."

Shaefer grinned. "I hear you."

They talked until the taxi came. Scorpion asked Shaefer to keep an eye on Iryna.

"You liked her?" Shaefer asked.

"Hell of a girl."

The taxi pulled up in front of the café, and the driver came in and looked around.

"Take care," Scorpion said, getting up.

"Keep in touch," Shaefer said.

Scorpion left him sitting there looking like a man who was very much alone, an African-American as out of place in a corner of Romania as anyone could be. Come to think of it, he thought in the taxi on the way to the airport, he didn't know much about Shaefer. He didn't know if he was married, had kids, any of it. The truth was, none of them in this business knew much about each other.

As the taxi drove out of the city to the airport, Scorpion checked out flights from Constanta on his cell phone. Bucharest was the only major city he could fly to; a bare thirty-five minute flight. From Bucharest he could go anywhere. He could go to either Istanbul and on to Tel Aviv, or to Rome and from there to Civitavecchia and back to Sardinia. Go see that sexy Abrielle in Porto Cervo and get reacquainted with his dogs. Or talk to Rabinowich about the Flash Critical. Or go anywhere in the world. He'd had enough of winter. Maybe go someplace sunny, where the girls wore bikinis and drinks came with umbrellas in them. Going to Rome would give him time to decide.

While waiting for his flight at Coanda airport in Bucharest, Scorpion checked the news on his laptop. In Yemen, fighting had been reported between the Hashidis and a force comprised of AQAP allied with elements of the Bakil and Abidah tribes. Meanwhile, in Ukraine, there had been a massive demonstration in Kiev's Independence Square against the new president, Lavro Davydenko, after restrictions were announced following the country's financial rating being downgraded by the IMF.

There had been riots and looting in Kiev and fighting in the streets between those backing Davydenko and supporters of Iryna Shevchenko, who was calling for a vote of no confidence against Davydenko in the Verkhovna Rada. A Jewish synagogue in Donetsk had been torched, and a gang of

Black Armbands killed two Jewish college students in Lviv.

"Everybody wins," Shaefer had said.

In the Horn of Africa, a famine had created a terrible humanitarian crisis. Millions of people were starving. There were images of potbellied children with shrunken limbs and dazed eyes. The Islamist extremist group, Al-Shabab, had banned international food relief efforts in the areas of Somalia they controlled. For some reason, Scorpion couldn't take his eyes off the images of the starving children.

Later that afternoon, he boarded the Alitalia flight to Rome. It was a short flight, just over an hour. By the time he landed at Fiumicino airport, he knew what he was going to do.